THUNDER ON THE MOUNTAIN

WATCHDOG MOUNTAIN DIVISION
BOOK 5

OLIVIA MICHAELS

FALCON IN HAND PUBLISHING LLC

 Formatted with Vellum

This one's for Diamond Dave. Family man, Beatles fan. Love you, Daddy.

ONE

Shane Foti took another drink of what looked like whiskey on the rocks and studied the room reflected in the mirror behind the bar. Cocks and Strippers was jumping tonight, just like any other Saturday after nine. He nodded at the bartender who pointed at his glass and raised his eyebrows with a look that asked *another?* Then Shane went back to sweeping the room. Typical crowd—women dressed for clubbing, guys sizing them up, gauging their chances at taking one home after a dance or two.

The bartender, Jimmy, walked over, but instead of setting another drink in front of Shane told him, "You're cut off, friend."

Finally.

Jimmy did a chin lift over Shane's right shoulder. Shane watched the reflection of a man approaching a table where a lone woman sat nursing a Cosmo. She looked up at the guy's charming smile and visibly relaxed as he presumably introduced himself, then sat down across from her. He pointed at the half-empty Cosmo and the woman smiled and nodded, then lifted the glass and finished off her drink in anticipation of the next one as the guy stood and walked to the bar.

If all went well—and Shane was sure it would—she'd never have the chance to taste it.

Jimmy turned his attention to the man now standing to Shane's left. "What can I get you?"

"A Cosmo and a pint of that." He pointed at the non-alcoholic option on tap at the other end of the bar. Jimmy nodded and started on the Cosmo. As Shane pulled out his phone, he spared a glance at the woman who was still waiting patiently at the table. Then he glared at the bartender's back. Jimmy turned and set the Cosmo down in front of the man, then grabbed a pint glass and started toward the end of the bar. The man watched Jimmy's retreating back as he passed his hand over the top of the Cosmo. Jimmy took his sweet time pouring the beer, pausing to talk to a huge guy with intelligent eyes who'd been watching the whole scene.

As soon as Jimmy returned, beer in hand, Shane downed the last of his drink and slammed the glass on the bar top. "Said I wanted another," he slurred.

Jimmy hoisted the non-alcoholic beer. "Happy to get you one of these, friend."

Shane snorted. "You think I'm in high school?" He pointed at his empty rocks glass. "Another one, *now*."

"I'd like my beer, please," the guy said. His voice was all charm but his eyes had gone as cold as a couple of ice chips.

Jimmy hesitated as he glanced at Shane.

Come on, man, he silently willed.

Then the guy next to him picked up the cocktail glass.

Perfect.

"Can you believe this asshole?" Shane asked, as he

slammed his shoulder against the other man's. Half the Cosmo sloshed over the rim and splashed onto the bar.

"Fuck!" the guy snarled.

Shane held up his hands. "My bad, my bad. I'll buy your woman a new one." Shane turned to Jimmy. "Set 'im up."

Jimmy nodded and grabbed a new glass.

The guy's mood abruptly shifted and he chuckled. "Hey, no need to dirty another glass. Just pour it into this one."

Jimmy shook his head as he mixed the new drink. "That's against the health code."

A very tall waitress appeared as if by magic. "I'll take it over to her," she said.

"No, I got it," The man said. "Don't trouble yourself."

Jimmy was already setting a fresh Cosmo on her tray. "No need."

The man's mood shifted again and his eyes blazed. "I said I've got it." He grabbed for the Cosmo just as the waitress lifted the tray above her head and stepped back in one fluid movement. He turned to pick up the spilled Cosmo but Shane had already picked up the glass with a gloved hand and set it aside.

"What the hell is going on here?" He whipped his head back and forth, not sure where to direct his anger—at Shane, the waitress, or Jimmy.

He realized he was wrong on all counts the moment a huge hand dropped onto his shoulder.

"I think we need to take a walk outside," growled the big man from down the bar.

"Take your hands off me," the guy said as he half-turned. His face paled as he looked up—and up, and up—into Ben's face.

Shane stood and grabbed the guy's other arm as he shared a look with his brother. "Yeah, we all need some fresh air." He set the burner phone on the bar.

Then he and Ben marched the scumbag around the bar toward the back door leading to the alley behind Cocktails and Chicken Strips—the official name of the dive bar, though almost no one ever used it. The tall waitress—better known as Charlie to her friends at Watchdog, where she worked as a bodyguard—was already on her way over to the confused woman to let her know she'd narrowly missed being roofied. She'd also ask her if she wanted to press charges once the cops got there.

The tainted glass and drink, plus the footage on Shane's burner phone of the guy dropping the drug into the Cosmo, would be turned over to Officers Sylvie Hoff and Carla DeVivo along with testimony from Jimmy. The bartender had become suspicious of the guy who only paid in cash, and whose last date was strangely falling-down drunk after a single drink. She'd been rescued by Jimmy, who'd sent her home in a rideshare (she'd called the next day to thank him and confirm that she'd been drugged) but the perp slipped away and the glass had already been rinsed.

After that, Jimmy had called his buddy, Ben. Mountain Division set up a rotating sting every night for a week before the idiot came back. This time, they had him dead to rights and he'd be on his way downtown in ten minutes.

Shane and Ben intended to use that ten minutes to show the son of a bitch the full error of his ways.

By the time Sylvie and Carla pulled up, Bill Ferguson—the name Shane read on the guy's driver's license—looked like he'd fallen down three flights of stairs face-first. He might have been foolish enough to return to the same bar, but he wasn't stupid enough to admit to the true reason for his broken nose and bruised ribs. He didn't have a death wish, after all.

———

BEN AND SHANE sat across from each other at an all-night diner on the outskirts of Longmont. Ben insisted on buying Shane midnight breakfast for his help with Ferguson. The lifelong friends sat in comfortable silence, sipping coffee as they waited for the server to bring their meals. That hadn't been the case when Shane returned to Lyons, Colorado after he left the Navy. Ben was already out of the military and home, renovating the Victorian house that had been practically falling down when they were younger. Their other friends—Elias Hunt, Waylon Ramsey, Gabe O'Neal, and Jon "Bear" Behr—weren't far behind, though it would take Bear a couple more years to come to terms with his ghosts and return to Colorado.

So, Ben and Shane had had time to reconnect one on one before then. Which was not pleasant for Shane, considering the reasons he'd left town at eighteen. Ben was the only person—besides Shane and April—who knew the full truth about their early relationship.

Much to Shane's embarrassment and shame.

Ben wasn't the type to hold a grudge against a friend—unless that friend had knowingly and willfully fucked up. Or so Shane had thought. Ben and Shane had had reason to see each other a few times since high school—once, to help Waylon out of a dark place. Shane had barely been able to look Ben in the eye the whole time, though Ben gave no outward sign of anger or judgment toward his old friend. Shane had assumed he'd put their differences aside only for Waylon's sake. So, he'd avoided Ben after coming home, until one day the big man showed up at his doorstep with a case of the cheap, crappy beer they'd guzzled by the gallon at backwoods bonfires when they were teenagers.

They drank to their military service. To the friend they'd lost to that service. To the memories they'd made back when they were young and naive, believing they were bulletproof. And, they drank to their unbreakable friendship.

Neither man ever brought up April.

Ben set his coffee down and cleared his throat, bringing Shane back to the present. "Thanks again, Shane. I wish I could—"

Shane held his hand up, knowing where Ben was going. "Don't even think about saying you wish you could pay me. I'd do this no matter what. If you so much as tried to give me a dime, I'd refuse."

Ben shook his head. "But it's taking time out of your life when you could be off doing other things."

"Yeah, what life? Not like I'm gonna be hanging out with Elias and Waylon at Cocks and Strippers, even if they weren't married now. Truth is, it never was really my scene."

Ben grunted. "Mine, neither. After tonight, even less."

Shane grinned. "Not even seeing Charlie made it good, huh? I'm surprised she's not here eating with us."

Ben turned a damning shade of red, all the way up to his ears, confirming what all of Ben's friends already suspected—their leader had the hots for Charlene King.

Shane leaned in conspiratorially. "I can put in a good word for you with her. I see her all the time at work and I've only known her for, oh," he pretended to check his watch, "the better part of a decade." He was pretty sure Charlie felt the same way about Ben. Shane had known "King

Charlamagne" since they served together as Swicks, right up until their honorable discharges, so he could read her well. Shane had caught her more than once checking out his friend and there was definitely interest there.

Ben waved him off with a smile as the waitress set their plates down and they tucked into their food.

"Seriously, Moose," Shane pressed. "How long have you two been dancing around each other?"

"What about you and April?" Ben said, taking Shane completely off-guard, enough that he almost choked on his coffee.

"What *about* us?"

"Things haven't been the same since..." Ben trailed off.

"The drive-by on Riversong? I know."

"It's been a year and a half, Shane. The hit wasn't directed at them. Do you know why they circled the wagons after?"

Shane knew what Ben was really asking—did he know why April had gone from finally beginning to accept Shane's advances, to pushing him away. It went beyond her initial snarkiness—which Shane one hundred percent deserved—to not even responding with snark of her own. Whenever everyone got together, she avoided talking to him, and kept her son, Kevin from talking to him as well. That killed—Kevin was an awesome little guy, even if he was a handful.

"I wish I knew, Ben. They acted like the hit was personal, which, sure, who wouldn't? But you'd think they'd relax once they knew it had nothing to do with them."

"You think they're jumpy because of Sonny's past?" Ben asked.

"Always a possibility. Though, Sonny never went into the drug trade like his sister did. But, considering what happened to Brianna and Brian Junior, maybe they're wise to be jumpy."

Brianna and Brian were April's cousins, and they'd run into trouble a couple years back, thanks to their parents' dispensary.

Ben nodded as he chewed on a strip of bacon. "It's bothered me ever since. Where there's smoke, there's fire. The whole family's worried about something, or at least they were."

"Seems like they've gone back to normal," Shane said.

"Not all of them. April's gone cold toward you, Elk."

Shane felt his chest tighten. It would be easy for him to lash out at Ben, tell him to butt the hell out, that it was none of his business. Accuse him of inferring that Shane had done something to fuck up the potential relationship.

Again.

But that was just projection on Shane's part. Ben wasn't accusing him of anything, and he was the last person on earth who deserved Shane's anger.

"I'm asking because maybe I could t-talk to her for you," Ben said, looking down into his coffee mug.

There it was. The slightest stutter gave Ben away—he was remembering the way Shane had treated April. And now he was offering to play peacemaker again. Same old Ben.

"No, brother. I got this. Thanks."

They finished their midnight breakfast in a silence that was anything but comfortable, Shane lost in his thoughts, thinking back to his betrayal.

TWO

THE BUS STATION bench was hard and cold through the back of her thrift-store sundress, and the lights buzzed overhead with a flicker that got on her last frayed nerve. April Taylor crossed and uncrossed her legs as she twisted the strap of her duffel bag around one wrist like a tourniquet.

Shane was late. But he was coming. He had to be.

She glanced at the giant clock above the ticket counter. Twenty minutes before their bus left.

He said he'd meet me here. They were supposed to be on their way to California, kissing this shitty little town goodbye and leaving every bitter memory behind. He was going to defy his family and join the Navy, become a SEAL. She was going to work for one of the tech start-ups and build something amazing, then retire as a multi-millionaire at twenty-five. Shane had told her if that didn't work out, she was gorgeous enough to be an actress or a model.

He'd also told her he loved her. That he'd marry her once they were settled.

That was the plan. *Their* plan.

She blinked hard, eyes burning.

All throughout the graduation ceremony yesterday, April kept telling herself it was the last time she'd see any of those assholes from high school again. Especially Leslie Trent. It wasn't good enough that Leslie and Shane were the king and the queen of Homecoming, and the Snow Ball, and the prom, while April stayed home pretending she didn't care about a stupid dance. Leslie Trent had booted April right out of being valedictorian with that smirky smile and her lies about April cheating on her mid-term exams. Those lies had cost April a full-ride scholarship to Stanford. Leslie Trent had ruined April's life out of jealousy over Shane.

April clenched her jaw. She'd done everything she could to prove her innocence, but the principal stared right through her while she laid out her case, then told April she was lucky she wasn't getting expelled.

She should've known the system would never let a girl like her win. Not when she came from a family of drug dealers and black sheep. Not when everyone in town was just waiting for her to screw up and prove they were right about the Taylors—every last one was a criminal and a loser.

But Shane hadn't cared about any of that.

Had he?

She glanced toward the door again. Ten minutes.

Still no Shane.

April never thought she'd be the girl to catch Shane Foti's eye. Not in a million years.

Shane was the kind of guy who'd been born with a spotlight already shining on him. Rich, handsome, athletic—

destined for prom king before he'd even gotten to high school. The kind of boy who never had to try too hard because the world just... tilted in his direction. Teachers smiled at him. Girls practically melted into their lockers when he walked by. And the guys? They could have been jealous but most of them liked him anyway. Shane Foti had swagger.

Everybody wanted to be his best friend but he'd kept the friends he'd made as a kid. There was Elias, the charming disaster. Waylon, quieter but just as dangerous. Gabe, the golden retriever of the group, all kindness and decency. Badger, who was exactly as obnoxious as his nickname. Sean Volker, who threw a baseball like God's favorite pitcher and whose last name spoke of generations of successful Coloradans. Teachers and old-timers nodded approvingly at everything he and his little sister did.

And then there were the two big guys—Jon Behr, but no one dared call him anything but Bear. And Ben. Sweet, stammering Ben who people whispered about like he was slow, which just showed how little they paid attention. April had shared honors classes with him. Ben always sat in the back, quiet as a shadow. Teachers forgot to call on him half the time. Students barely noticed him at all. But April did. And she knew the truth. Ben wasn't dumb. He was a goddamn genius who just didn't like taking up space or making noise.

Maybe that's why Shane had paid attention to her. If he had a smart, quiet friend like Ben, then he could see beyond the pretty, popular girls always vying for his attention. See *her*—smart, hard-working, determined to make a better life for herself.

They were friends, sure, especially since she was constantly helping him out. However, April never expected

Shane Foti to fall for her. Fall hard enough to share his dreams with her and to take hers seriously. Just not seriously enough to be open about their relationship. She told herself she understood—he was protecting her in his own way, from bullies like Leslie who would openly attack her. From his parents who would never understand or accept her and could not only make life hard for April, but for her whole family if they wanted to.

April looked at the clock again. Five minutes. The speaker overhead crackled to life and announced departures. If Shane didn't hurry, they'd miss the bus and have to wait until tomorrow for the next bus to California. Her parents would read her letter and know where she'd gone. They'd come and get her, and that would be—

The top of a head of dark hair caught her eye.

Shane! Thank God.

April stood up and smoothed out the cotton skirt of her sundress. She bent to pick up her suitcase handle and her backpack. They'd have to sprint to catch the bus but they could do it.

He came around the divider and his familiar face caught her by surprise.

Not Shane's. Ben's.

Ben knew about them? Had Shane told him and he was here to stop them? *Or...* Joy sparked in her heart. Maybe Shane had told all his friends he loved her and they had come to see them off.

She tried to look past Ben. Heaven knew half a dozen guys could get swallowed up in his shadow.

But, no. No other friends following the big guy.

And no Shane.

Ben spotted April. He looked at her sadly.

April shook her head in denial as Ben ambled toward her.

"What happened?" she asked. "Where is he? Is...is he all right?" The sudden, horribly welcome thought that he'd been in a car accident popped into her head. She'd rush to his bedside, stay there without being afraid of getting chased away. She'd rather face that than believe he'd abandoned her like this.

"Sh-Shane's not c-c-oming," Ben said. He was upset enough that the stutter he fought hard to control and hide was on full display.

April's heart broke right there and then. Ice-cold fury filled its place.

"He couldn't even show his face? He couldn't come and tell me himself that he changed his mind? That he didn't care enough..."

Enough about me.

"...Enough about what he wants versus what his parents want to at least come and tell me that I'm on my own?"

Ben shook his head sadly. "It isn't right, what he's d-doing to you."

"To *me*? I don't care about him," she lied. "This is just convenient for us to go together, that's all."

Ben's eyes told her he could see right through her lies. He reached into his pocket and pulled out his wallet and an envelope.

"What are you doing?" She took a step back.

"He sent a note and the money he'd planned on using for both tickets and your first six months' rent. I told him he should turn over his entire bank account to you." Ben pulled a stack of bills from his wallet. "He said he w-was." Ben held out the cash and the envelope.

He didn't even buy the tickets in advance. How long did he know he was going to leave me here?

"I don't want that," April said. "I don't need it. I don't need anything from him. Ever."

"April, just take the money. You can just toss the letter. I w-would."

"No." She crossed her arms, wishing to God she wasn't so stubborn. If she had no job nibbles whatsoever, that money plus hers could keep her afloat for eight or nine months—ten if she stretched her budget until it broke. Without it, she'd better hope someone hired her right away.

Just take it the quiet, practical voice in her head told her. *You've earned it.*

That last thought made her stomach heave. *Earned it. Right.*

"April. California is expensive," Ben said. "Take the money."

She reached out—and curled Ben's fingers closed over the money.

"I don't care if you give it back to him or keep it for yourself, Ben. I'm not taking it."

Ben finally nodded. "All right then."

"I'm going to be fine," April said, smiling harder than she felt.

Ben studied her. "Yes. You will be. You're amazing, April." With that he turned and left.

April watched the bus to California pull away.

I can't go home. I left a letter saying I was leaving.

April went back to the ticket counter and studied the day's bus schedule. She mentally counted up her money to see how far she could get without starving once she got there.

It looks like I'm heading to Las Vegas.

———

IT WAS the middle of the night when the bus finally reached the terminal in Vegas. April was exhausted. She'd had hours to cool down and think about Shane's betrayal. While she wasn't sure she could forgive him, she also knew firsthand what he was up against with his father, the only person Shane ever feared. Daniel Foti ruled his family with a steel grip. Or maybe an iron fist was more accurate. Shane was often bruised and he laughed off his bruises, saying they were from playing sports, or skiing the Alps, or from whatever adventure his family took. April knew better. Daniel Foti had no problem beating Shane whenever he was caught rebelling. Or talking back. Or just breathing the wrong way.

She'd witnessed it once when she'd arrived early for a tutoring session. The man's voice echoed through the cavernous house, shouting Shane's name and calling his own son all sorts of horrible things. But instead of leaving, April had marched on into the house, following Mr. Foti's bellows until she found them in the library. Shane got his height from his father, but not the man's bulk, built through countless hours of boxing. Shane had been backed against a wall, arms up in defense.

As soon as Mr. Foti realized she was there, his demeanor changed. Laughing, he tried to pass off beating his son as just horsing around. April was sickened when Shane agreed with the obviously false story, but she went along with it for his sake. Only later did Shane admit to being beaten all his life. He swore April to secrecy—one of a thousand secrets they kept from the world.

Maybe now that I've left, he'll feel safer meeting me here. He'll have a place to go.

After she got her bags, April pulled out her phone. Coverage was spotty on the bus, but she thought she'd have full coverage now that she was in a city. April had thought about calling Shane for the last two hundred miles. No, the last five hundred if she was being honest with herself. If she wanted people to give her a second chance, then she needed to be ready to give other people second chances, too.

April listened to the phone ring. Would Shane even answer? Would she really tell him where she was, ask him to take a risk and join her?

Shane picked up. Before he even had a chance to say hello, April started in.

"I know you're afraid of what your dad will do, but Shane, you're stronger than him. You have your own dreams, and I believe in you. You can still leave and come with me. I'm in Vegas. You could fly here—"

"Shane will be doing no such thing."

April froze, the blood in her heart turning to ice water.

"Mr. Foti."

"Don't 'Mr. Foti' me, April. My son will not be joining you in Vegas. I'm glad to know he's afraid of me."

April winced. Now she'd just betrayed Shane's biggest secret. He wasn't afraid of his father—Shane was terrified of the monster.

"He shouldn't be afraid of you," April said in her coldest voice. "Bullies like you are weak little cowards."

"Listen here, you little bitch," Daniel Foti snapped back. "I could ruin your family tomorrow if I wanted to. How's that for weak?"

April shivered. Mr. Foti ran the bank where her parents had taken out a loan for the start-up costs and the building housing their coffee shop, Riversong. "What do you mean?"

Mr. Foti gave her a laugh full of spite. "That loan your

idiot father took out? He didn't read the terms closely enough. I can call it in at any time for any reason. I doubt your parents have the cash to cover it. I'm not the weak one, he is."

Mr. Foti went on. "Shane came to his senses and realized what a whore you are. That you only wanted him for his money and that he'd be throwing away his life if he ran away with you. He's been accepted into my alma mater back east and he's going in the fall."

The ice water in April's veins froze solid. College had been her dream and she'd worked so hard for it. All Shane had to do was be born in the right family. And the kicker was, he didn't even want to go.

"He was accepted thanks to me," April seethed. "I'm the one who made sure he didn't flunk any of his math classes."

"You flatter yourself, you arrogant little girl. Go ahead and gamble away that money I gave you to leave town, and then we'll see how proud you are when you're living in the gutter. Maybe it won't bother you though. You came from trash and you will always be trash."

April had stopped listening. "What do you mean *you* gave me money to leave town?"

"The money Shane said he gave you." Then Mr. Foti laughed. "Don't tell me you thought it was from him. The sentiment in the letter was his though—he wants you gone as much as I and his mother do. But that money was from me. Remember that. And remember too, if you ever try to contact him or set foot in Colorado again, I will destroy you and your worthless family. I'll bury them so deep in debt they'll have to take out another loan to buy a stick of gum."

The line went dead.

April shut her eyes and pressed her lips together. Life

was so unfair. She didn't know if she should believe what Mr. Foti said about Shane or not. It hurt to think he didn't love her, but people like her didn't have the luxury to mope over a broken heart. She needed food and a place to stay. She wheeled her luggage away from the station and toward the street. The bright lights of The Strip glowed in the distance. A beam of white light shot straight up into the sky and April wondered if that was Luxor. Well, she was about to find out.

Even in the middle of the night, the street was fairly busy. April raised her hand and waved the minute she saw a yellow cab. She'd never taken a taxi in her life, but she wasn't stupid. She'd watched enough TV shows to know how to hail one.

The cab slowed down and parked alongside the curb. April was relieved to see that the driver was a woman. The trunk popped open and April quickly put her suitcases into it, then slid into the back seat. There was a photo of the driver with her name under it. Bunni.

"Hi there!" April said in the most chipper voice she could muster. "Thank you *so* much for picking me up. Could you take me to...oh, what was the name of the casino? Gosh, I'm so tired, I can't even remember. It's not one of the big ones. It's smaller, still family-owned? Do you know it maybe?"

The cabbie looked at April's reflection in her rearview mirror. "You old enough to set foot in a casino?"

April gave Bunni a small laugh. "I get asked that all the time. I'm twenty-two." She opened her purse and took out a driver's license. It was a real one, not a fake, but it had belonged to a twenty-two-year-old woman who looked a lot like April, and even shared her first name though not her last—April Meyer. Shane had bought it for her. God knew how he'd found it—or possibly talked some woman into faking one—but that's what having money could do for you. It could create an entirely new life just waiting for you to slip into it.

"Here." She tried to hand Bunni her license but the woman waved her off.

"Don't *ever* hand a stranger your ID in this city. You don't know me from Eve. I could grab it, kick you outta the cab, sell it, you'd be screwed."

"Oh." April quickly pulled her hand back and shoved the license into her purse. "Right." She laughed nervously. "I told you I was exhausted."

The cabbie continued looking at her in the rearview. "You ever been here before?"

"Sure, lots of times."

"No you haven't." The cabbie sighed. "What do I do with you?"

April pushed down the urge to tell Bunni to take her to the nearest cheap but decent motel where she could stay the night, then come back tomorrow and buy a ticket straight home.

"You can take me to a smaller casino with hotel rooms."

"How old are you really, girl?"

April sat up straighter and squared her shoulders. "I'm not a girl. I'm a legal adult."

"So eighteen." Bunni sighed again. "If you were younger, I'd take you straight to the cops. They could figure out what to do with you. But I can't because, like you said, you're an *adult*." She said the word sarcastically. Then she squinted. "You're alone. You got some pimp waiting here for you?"

"Oh God no!" April squirmed at the thought.

"He call himself your boyfriend instead? Tell you he's going to take care of you?"

"No!" She immediately thought of the last guy who said he'd take care of her. Shane. *And look how that turned out.* No, I don't have...anyone."

"Anyone? Or anyone *here*?"

April looked down at her hands. Her parents had to be worried sick by now. The note she'd left said California. They didn't even know where she really was.

"Look, kid. Take my advice. Go home, wherever home is. I can tell you've got a good family and they're worried about you."

April looked up quickly. "How?"

Bunni laughed. "Living here, you learn to read faces real quick. What's your name?"

"A-April."

"Go home, April. Look, lemme take you someplace decent. Spend the night. I'll give you my number, you call me tomorrow, I'll bring you back here, you head back home. You got enough money for that?"

"I do." She nodded and sucked in her lower lip. It was the responsible thing to do.

It was also giving up before she'd even started.

There's nothing but more shame, more humiliation back home.

April wondered if Shane had told everyone what a fool she was. How she believed the school's golden boy would throw his life away and run off with the town trash.

"I have enough money...to stay here," April told Bunni. "Now please, take me to a casino with a hotel."

Bunni shook her head. "It's your life, kid. I tried." She lit a cigarette and cracked her window open, then pulled away from the curb. Bunni didn't say a word as the cab crawled through the Vegas streets. April watched out the window as the lights grew brighter. Her stomach tightened in anticipation and fear. Where would Bunni take her? Did she have enough money?

Casinos rose on both sides of the Strip, impossibly big. People lined the sidewalks, everyone laughing and drinking while showgirls in feathers weaved through, stopping only for photographs. April's belly loosened. She could do this.

Bunni kept driving—past all the casinos.

"Where are we going?" April asked in alarm. She turned to look out the rear window at the receding lights as her fear kicked back into high gear.

"You think you can afford to stay at one of the big casinos at a moment's notice?" She laughed. "I'm taking you where you requested."

"Oh, right." April sat back and tried to relax. Were there casinos in the Vegas suburbs?

But they weren't headed for the suburbs. The buildings around them turned older, darker, shabbier.

"Here we are, old downtown Vegas," Bunni said as she slowed in front of a seedy-looking building with a tall, flashing sign reading *The Western Pioneer Casino*. Some of the bulbs were burned out. "Just what you wanted, a small casino with rooms. Hotel's next door and it's decent... enough."

"It's perfect," April said with as much bravery as she could put into her voice. "Thank you."

"The Pioneer's full of locals. Felix should be at the desk tonight. Tell him Bunni sent you."

April tried not to blanch at the dollar amount on the meter. She wouldn't be taking many taxis if they cost *that* much. She reached for her wallet and took out enough cash plus a generous tip just to prove she could.

Bunni took the money, counted it quickly, and handed back the tip. "Nope, keep it, you'll need it. And this." She pressed an old receipt with her name and a phone number written on the back into April's palm, holding her gaze. "Remember to ask for Felix. And call me tomorrow."

"Thanks," April said as she got out and walked to the open trunk to retrieve her bags. Cigarette smoke wafted from the window and Bunni pulled away the moment April set her bags on the sidewalk. She looked up at the doors just as an old guy lurched out and lost his dinner all over the pavement.

I've got this she told herself. Then April squared her shoulders and wheeled her luggage past the man, on a mission to find Felix.

———

APRIL WOKE up the next morning having no idea where she was. The metal bed frame squeaked as she turned over and opened her eyes. Right, she was in a hotel room in Vegas, one that cost her more than she thought it was worth. At this rate, she'd burn through her money twice as fast as she'd predicted. *Damn my pride for not taking Shane's—I mean, Mr. Foti's—money.*

But, she had a plan, one that ironically came from tutoring Shane.

April showered and dressed, then went downstairs for breakfast. At least she'd eat one meal—a breakfast buffet was included in the price of her room. And it was surprisingly good. She noticed familiar faces from the night before. Felix had told her this was more of a local place, confirming what Bunni had said. Everyone looked tired and she wondered how many had been up all night and were simply refueling for another day of gambling.

That won't be me she promised herself as she carried a plate heaped with scrambled eggs, bacon, and toast over to a small table in the corner of the room. *This is only temporary. As soon as I have enough money, I'll head for California like we...I...planned.*

After breakfast, April went outside. Dry Nevada air hit her, shockingly hot already, and it was barely eight o'clock. She'd been hoping for a craps table in the casino, but it was all slots, and electronic poker machines lined up around a bar. The receipt Bunni had given her the night before crackled in her hand as she squeezed it. Standing in what little shade an awning provided, April called the number on the back of the receipt.

"This April?" Bunni's gruff voice answered.

"Yes, it is. I—"

"You wised up and going home?"

"I'd like a ride to the Strip, actually," April answered. "Please."

She heard Bunni swear and told herself it was directed at the traffic. "Fine. Okay. Great. I'll pick you up out front. Warning, I'm going off shift right after."

"No problem," April said. "I'll find my way back after I'm done." She didn't want to be rude and say Bunni wasn't the only cab driver in Vegas. The woman was trying to do April a favor. She just didn't understand.

Bunni had already hung up. April waited about ten minutes before a yellow cab pulled up to the curb. While she waited, April was treated to a parade of people coming into and out of the Western Pioneer.

I'm not staying. I am not staying.

April scooted out to the curb, opened the cab's door, and jumped into the back seat.

"Where to," Bunni asked, her tone sounding like she and April were meeting for the first time.

"Someplace with craps tables," April said. If Bunni wasn't going to say hi, neither would she. She'd also push down the disappointment that went along with it.

"Craps, huh?" Bunni said.

"Yes, please. Thank you."

They were quiet the entire drive to one of the big casinos squatting along the Strip. She pulled up under a wide porte-cochere that could have covered a small house. April tried not to wince—again—at the total on the meter and pulled out enough bills to cover it plus another generous tip.

And again, Bunni took the money but refused the tip.

"Keep it, you'll need it."

"Thanks."

Bunni shook her head and refused to look April in the eye. The service light on top of the cab clicked off as she drove away.

April turned to go inside the massive building. She'd been nervous to the point of nausea the whole ride, but now with the sounds of the slot machines inside, the valets in their neat uniforms parking expensive sports cars, her fear turned into excitement.

I can do this. I'll be driving one of those cars before I know it.

April took a deep breath, squared her shoulders, and marched in, head held high. She found the craps tables and settled in to watch the first few games, her brain already calculating odds.

———

APRIL STEPPED out of the third casino of the day and looked up at the night sky. She'd had no idea it'd gotten so late—there wasn't a single window in any of the casinos, and even if there were, the Strip was so bright it would have looked like daylight. She pulled out her phone and dialed Bunni's number, hoping she was back on shift.

"You're calling late," Bunni answered.

"I'm ready to be picked up, if you're driving."

"You stayed all day at Flamingo?"

April smiled. "No, actually, you can pick me up at Luxor."

"Huh. Made it all the way down the Strip, I see. Did they keep kicking you out for being too young?"

"No they did not," April scoffed. She hugged her new purse to her chest, the pebbly white leather gleaming in the lights under the gigantic Sphinx. The rainbow-colored LV monograms looked like candy sprinkled across the surface.

Bunni scoffed. "I'll be there in five." She hung up.

True to her word, Bunni pulled up five minutes later. April strutted proudly to the cab, watching Bunni's eyes grow bigger.

"Looks like you had some luck," she said as soon as April closed the cab door.

"I did."

"You spend it all on that new purse?"

"It's a Louis Vuitton Murakami," she said, savoring the words as much as she had the champagne they'd handed her when she walked into the boutique at the Forum Shops. "Speedy Thirty."

Bunni gave a low whistle. "That's no knockoff."

"It better not be," April said, running her fingertips over the buttery vachetta leather handles. She had no idea what 'vachetta' meant when the sales associate told her, but it sure felt nice under her fingers. "Considering how much it cost me."

Bunni shook her head, pulling away from the curb. "You win a hand and march straight into Louis Vuitton?"

April grinned. "I didn't march. I... glided." She could still feel the smooth marble floor under her sandals. The air inside the shop had smelled like leather, expensive perfume, and the faintest hint of fine cigars drifting in from the casino. April had only gone into the store on a whim, thinking maybe she could browse for a few minutes before the clerks started clearing their throats and shuffling their feet—a not-so-subtle way of telling her she wasn't welcome.

Instead, the sales associate—Amélie, with perfect eyeliner and a French accent—had offered her champagne without even glancing at her scuffed sandals or the cheap fake gold hoops in her ears. She treated April like royalty, especially when she lifted bag after bag from their displays like they were the crown jewels and presented them to her one by one. For a full hour, April had been someone else entirely—not the town trash but a woman who bought whatever she wanted, no questions asked. She justified buying the bag by telling herself that if she tied up some of her earnings into something that she'd have to return or sell, she wouldn't be tempted to gamble the cash away quickly. Though, with her skill, that might not be a concern.

"You know that purse'll be an investment if the tables turn," Bunni said. "The rooms at the Pioneer don't have safes. You might want to use it as a pillow."

"Oh, that won't be a problem," April said. "I'm only going back there to get the rest of my things. The Luxor is putting me up for the night."

She'd just cashed out, the weight of her winnings a solid, satisfying heft in her new purse, and was weaving her way toward the exit when a man in a black suit stepped smoothly into her path. "Excuse me, Miss."

Oh God, they figured out I'm underage. Would they call the police, or worse—would she disappear into the bowels of the casino, never to be seen again?

Maybe they'll find my bones out in the desert, or at the bottom of Lake Mead.

"Congratulations on your win tonight," he said, his voice as smooth as his silk tie. His eyes flicked to her new purse, then back to her face. "We'd be happy to make sure your evening continues in style. If you don't already have accommodations, the Luxor would like to offer you a complimentary suite."

April had glanced around, certain there must be a mistake, unless 'suite' meant a backroom where they'd teach her a lesson about gambling underage.

"A suite? You mean one *upstairs*?" She pointed up.

"It would be our pleasure." He handed her a small black paper sleeve with the Luxor's golden logo printed on it. "Your room key. If there's anything you need, just ring the front desk and ask for your host, Jim." He bowed his head slightly. "Or call me directly. My card's tucked inside with the suite number on it."

April studied the top of the glossy keycard poking out of the sleeve. It looked real enough. *I'm pretty sure they wouldn't give me a keycard to my prison cell.*

Jim mistook her pause. "If you're staying elsewhere already, we'd be happy to send someone to collect and transfer your bags if you'd like. And," he pulled out a thick, glossy black card with gold lettering embossed across the top reading Luxor Executive Host, "dinner is on us," he said with an easy smile. "Or breakfast. Or both. It doesn't expire." Jim flipped the card over and handed it to her. A handwritten signature was sprawled across the back above the words: $100 *dining credit – Pyramid Café or Tender Steakhouse.*

April blinked. One hundred dollars. That could cover several meals if she played it smart. She'd been planning to eat crackers and a granola bar back at the Pioneer. Her stomach gave a hopeful growl she prayed was covered by the slot machines.

She tucked the card carefully into her purse, right beside her cash. "Thank you," she said. "I won't be needing help with my bags,"—no way was she sending someone over to the Pioneer; that would give her away as a fraud—"but I will be back with them shortly."

Jim gave her a nod of approval. "Call my number before you arrive and I'll make sure a bellhop is waiting for you, Miss..."

She hesitated. "Meyer. April Meyer."

"Miss Meyer. Enjoy your stay." Jim smiled, nodded, then walked away.

And just like that, her new identity was sealed.

Bunni gave her a sidelong glance in the rearview mirror now. "You got a host on your first night in Vegas?"

April grinned. "Guess I made an impression." *Or at least my lucky purse did.*

"Well all right then," Bunni said, sounding impressed herself. "You keep making impressions like that, you might become the queen of the Strip. You could have a future here after all, kid."

"No. Vegas is just temporary."

But April did have a future in Vegas—a much longer one than she had planned.

THREE

YOU ARE THE QUEEN OF YOUR DOMAIN APRIL THOUGHT to herself as she rested her elbows on the counter and looked around Riversong, her family's coffee shop. *And right now, your domain is in desperate need of a new espresso machine, or at least someone who can actually repair the one you've got.*

Bang!

"Dammit!"

April turned and bent sideways to check on her dad. "Was that your noggin hitting something?"

Sonny growled as he rubbed his forehead. "Yes. And if I hit my head one more time, I might finally knock loose the genius fix this damn thing needs."

He scooted out from behind the antique espresso machine, wiping his hands on a threadbare rag. "Pump's on its last legs, boiler's more scale than metal, and I just found a cracked solenoid valve. Honestly, April, if this thing was a horse, I'd have shot it by now."

She winced. "How bad?"

"Worst case? New pump, new boiler, full descale, plus

labor. We're looking at three grand minimum—and that's only if she's worth saving." Sonny fondly patted the espresso machine he'd cursed out only a moment ago. "I don't want to replace her. She's been good to us, and they don't make 'em like this anymore." He considered. "Well, they do, but they start around thirteen grand."

April flinched. She knew a brand-new espresso machine the size and quality of the one they had would be expensive, but thirteen grand? "That's a lotta lattes."

Sonny nodded in agreement. "A lotta-lotta lattes." He stared past the counter at the empty tables during the slowest part of the day on the slowest day of the week, Thursday. Even April's friend Rochelle, who practically lived at Riversong while she was working, was not in her usual spot in the window seat. The late-spring day was just too beautiful to waste sitting inside.

Sonny sighed as he ran a hand through his short, graying hair. "Think we can make it through the weekend with just pour-overs and drip?"

A fresh pit hollowed out in her stomach. "Maybe. But half the town runs on lattes, and if word gets out that River-song can't pull a proper espresso..." She didn't finish the sentence.

Sonny folded his arms and leaned against the counter. "Perfect. Just what we need. A thirteen-thousand-dollar paperweight and our caffeine-deprived regulars taking their business elsewhere."

April offered her dad a tired smile. "We could always put it on display. Call it industrial art. 'Mid-Mod Heart-breaker.'"

"Smartass." But he said it with a grin as he reached out to tousle her hair like he'd done since she was a kid.

"Here's what we'll do," April said. "It's supposed to be

hotter this weekend, so let's get a few cases of seltzer water and use our syrups to make Italian sodas. I'll send out a newsletter and put a sign out front advertising cool, refreshing summer drinks and iced, pour-over coffee."

Sonny's grin turned into a full-fledged smile. "That's my girl. Always thinking." He tapped his temple as he picked up the shop phone's receiver. "I'll order the seltzer, you start on the newsletter."

"Sounds good."

Sonny covered the mouthpiece. "I mean it when I say we couldn't do this without you."

"Thanks," April said as she tried not to wince. Her dad meant it as a compliment, not as a barbed reminder of the years she wasn't around to help. At least not physically around—she'd wired money home as soon as she could, to help pay off the loan. That damned Mr. Foti had also made sure there was a huge penalty for paying it off early—which Sonny had agreed to, figuring he wouldn't ever have the cash to do so anyway—ensuring her family would be at his mercy for years. So she sent several payments a year, always a different amount and from a different city.

When she'd returned home years later—Mr. Foti's threat laughably small now that she was older and sadly wiser—her mom told her Sonny had hired a PI to find April after she started sending the money home. They would have kept looking for her, but he'd eventually told them, 'She's in fucking Billings now. Last time she was in Coeur d'Alene. The time before that, the money came from Reno. She's all over the place. God knows where she's at now. You might as well just give me the money she sends you because that's how much it's gonna cost for me to try and track her down. You could buy a new coffee shop for the same amount you'd pay me to find her. Just let her go. She's obviously doing good enough to send you money and she loves you enough to do it. You're lucky. Trust me. This story has the happiest ending you can hope for. I've seen worse.'

So, her family stopped trying to find her, settling for the money and the yearly Christmas card telling them she loved them, she was doing well, and she was happy. At least the first two were true.

It was all the contact April could bring herself to make. *Worst daughter in the world.*

Now, she did everything she could to make up for those lost years.

April pointed to the door leading to the back while her dad talked to one of their vendors. He nodded, and she headed for the office, leaving the front of the shop in his care. Her younger sister, Hannah, was taking the day off along with their mom, for Hannah's birthday. The two were shopaholics and loved bargain hunting. They were hitting the thrift stores up in Vail, the outlets at Silver Plume, then dinner in Idaho Springs followed by a couple hours soaking in the hot springs (April's gift to her sister) and wouldn't be home until around midnight.

Hannah had texted April earlier, sending her a photo of a pair of used Jimmy Choo shoes with a ridiculously low price. Vail and Aspen both had the most amazing thrift stores thanks to the rich folks who lived there. April had smiled at the photo and remembered when she'd had a closet full of Jimmy Choos and other designer clothing, all bought at retail price. Almost all of it was gone now.

She looked around the scruffy office with its second-hand office chairs and desks, the walls covered with photos of her family, and smiled. There was no place in the world she'd rather be, and she was grateful for it.

April sat down and woke up the computer. She'd have

enough time to draft the newsletter, find some cute photos, and send it out before her son, Kevin, would bike to River-song from school. He was in detention yet again. She was halfway through drafting the newsletter when her cell-phone buzzed on the desk. April groaned as she looked at the name that popped up—Principal Jackass.

"Great. What does he want now?" She blew out a breath before hitting speaker.

"Ms. Taylor, this is Principal Pirogue. I'm calling you about Kevin."

April rolled her eyes. As if his name didn't show on her phone and she had no idea why he'd be calling. It sure wasn't to invite her to meet the wife and go yachting. She set her elbows on the desk, spread her fingers, and pressed her forehead against her fingertips.

"Yes, Principal Pirogue. What is it this time?"

He'd called her countless times to tell her Kevin was daydreaming in class again, or had too many timeouts for talking during quiet time (that was a big one—Kevin used quiet time to practice his stand-up comedy routine, it seemed.) and that he wouldn't have the 'privilege' of recess for another week—which of course only made the problem worse. A kid like Kevin needed to run off his excess energy at least twice a day. Most boys did. So she'd fought to get his recess reinstated.

Principal Jackass sighed. "I'll get right to it. Kevin punched another boy on the playground today."

April bolted upright. "He did what? Wait, are you sure? Kevin's a handful, but he's not a fighter."

Pirogue's voice sounded measured, practiced. "It always comes as a surprise to parents to find out their child has oppositional defiant disorder—"

"Oh, you stop right there, Pirogue. Who's the other kid? Was he bullying my son and he was defending himself?"

"Revealing the identity of the other party would be violating the privacy laws laid out in the student handbook. Which, you would know if you read it."

April closed her eyes. *Lord, grant me the strength not to throttle this jackass in his office after he—*

"I'll need you to come into my office as soon as possible."

April mouthed the predictable words as he said them, a sneer on her face. When she opened her eyes, she saw Sonny standing in the office doorway. She wondered how much he'd heard. Judging by the look in his eye, probably most of it.

She put on a fake, sarcastic smile that seeped into her tone. "Of course, Principal Pirogue. I'll be there right away." She hit disconnect, wishing he'd called on the land-line. "Swear to God, if kids these days knew how satisfying it is to slam down a receiver, they'd toss their smartphones. It's a totally underrated pleasure." April rubbed her temples.

"Do they even use 'em as phones anymore?"

"I have no idea. Kevin will be at least thirty before I let him have one." April swiped her phone off the desk, stood up, and searched around for her purse. "How much did you hear?"

"Enough to call bullshit."

April gave her dad a grateful smile.

"What?" he asked, spreading his arms. "It's like you said —my grandson's a handful, but he ain't violent or a bully. If he took a swing, the other kid deserved it." He watched April pick up her purse and drop her phone into it. "You got any idea who the kid might be?"

"Yes, I do." She gritted her teeth. "HRH Regis Sumner."

"Shoulda guessed that myself. Regis Sumner," he scoffed. Sonny turned sideways to let April pass him in the doorway. He had a big frame and was still in pretty good shape after a career in the military, so she squeaked by and continued marching down the hall to the front of the store. She glanced around at the still-empty tables as she pulled her keys out of her purse.

"You got the seltzer ordered?"

"Yes, ma'am."

"The newsletter's written, just upload the photos off the desktop and hit send."

"Aye-aye."

"Thanks." She reached out to open the front door. "We'll be back after Kevin's out of detention. Maybe about an hour if we're lucky."

"April."

She stopped and turned around. Sonny covered his heart with his hand and tapped it as rapidly as a beating hummingbird's wing. His special sign to his daughters that he loved them forever.

April returned the gesture, hoping she could keep the prickling in her eyes from turning into tears.

———

OF COURSE, principal Jackass had waited to call April until school was almost out—inflicting maximum humiliation as she'd have to walk past a host of moms waiting to pick up their kids. She was suspicious that the rumor mill was already going at full speed, and that was reinforced when she saw the way other moms looked at her right after they stopped whispering to each other. Though not all of them. Diane Andrews, whose daughter Laurie was one of Kevin's friends, gave her a warm smile and a wave. April waved back, then kept her head held high, serene smile on her face as she walked past the others. She'd had years of practicing her poker face, after all.

Her other suspicion—about the bully's identity—was confirmed when she saw Regis' mother standing in the secretary's office.

Leslie Trent Sumner, who had cost April her scholarship. Arms crossed, designer purse dangling from one elbow, she glared daggers at April.

"Your son is a *menace*," she hissed.

So much for that privacy policy, April thought. *I guess it applies to every kid but mine. How shocking.*

"Sorry—"

"You'd better be sorry," Leslie cut her off.

"—but I think you have your son confused with mine."

Leslie tilted her head for a second. "What? No, I don't. Kevin attacked Regis out of sheer jealousy."

"Oh, I doubt that. There is absolutely nothing your son has that would ever make mine jealous."

When she saw Leslie's cruel smile, she knew too late she'd walked straight into a trap.

"Not even a father?"

April felt her eyes widen for the merest second. Before any hurt could show, her poker face clicked back into place. "Really? That's the best you've got? Then again, you always did go for the lowest hanging fruit. *Your* husband, for example."

That struck a nerve. Leslie's eyes narrowed. "What's that supposed to mean?"

Before April could tell her something Leslie probably

already suspected—that some of April's friends had seen him over at Cocks and Strippers with no Leslie in sight—Principal Pirogue poked his head out of his office doorway.

"You're finally here, Ms. Taylor. I've been waiting for you." He gestured for her to enter his office.

Leslie gave her a brittle laugh. "There's a gesture I'm sure you're familiar with, if memory serves," she sniffed. "You've been nothing but trouble your entire life, and it looks like the rotten apple doesn't fall far from the tree. Expect a lawsuit from the Sumners." She turned on her heel and trotted out of the secretary's office.

You bitch! You snotty, stuck-up bitch.

"I'm waiting, Ms. Taylor," Pirogue said, not bothering to hide the impatience in his voice.

April took a deep breath, squared her shoulders, and walked into Pirogue's office like she owned it.

"Take your usual seat," he offered as he rounded his desk.

"Just couldn't resist saying that, could you?"

Pirogue ignored her. He folded his hands on the desk like a judge about to deliver a death sentence. "Kevin's behavior is inexcusable. Frankly, I'd strongly suggest you consider ADHD medication. Perhaps even an antipsychotic, given his..."

April was leaning back in her chair and actively studying the walls of Pirogue's office.

Principal Jackass paused. "What are you doing?"

"I'm looking for your medical degree. Not seeing it. Therefore, you don't get to diagnose my son because he doesn't sit like a zombie for six hours a day."

Color rose up his neck. He adjusted his tie. "I don't need a medical degree to recognize disruptive behavior."

April returned her gaze to the principal. She leaned

forward. "Fun fact. I've talked and listened to the other moms. If Kevin goes on ADHD meds, then guess what? That makes him one of the *eighty-eight percent* of boys in his class already on them. You want compliant little robots, not kids."

Pirogue's jaw tightened. "Kevin's violent, uncontrollable behavior will not be tolerated at my school."

April gaped at Principal Jackass. "His uncontrollable violent behavior? Excuse me, my kid doesn't just throw punches for no reason. He was defending himself."

"Ms. Taylor, Kevin was the one who threw the first punch."

April shook her head in disbelief. "No. He's not the aggressor here. If he punched Regis, it's because that little shi...brat...was picking on him."

"That's not the story I got from the child Kevin assaulted—"

"Stop playing games. You mean *Regis*. And I'm sure Kevin didn't 'assault' him but was defending himself. Granted, he should have used his words like he's been taught to do, so *Regis* must have either been picking on him all week—like usual, may I add—or he said something so horrible, Kevin felt threatened enough to defend himself physically."

"Well, I asked Kevin to explain himself and he refused to discuss his reasons for lashing out—"

"Lashing out? Come *on*."

"—and I can't force him to talk, so this is why I wanted to talk to you first alone before he comes in here after detention." Pirogue cleared his throat like he was preparing for a speech. "Children often act out physically when something is wrong." He tilted his head and adapted a totally fake look of concern that matched his condescending tone. "What's going on at home?"

April folded her arms. "What do you mean what's going on at home?"

"Well, we all know that Riversong was the scene of a criminal act. So, what I'm asking is, is Kevin safe at home with you and your family?"

April closed her eyes and exhaled like she'd been punched. She took a deep breath, composed herself, and opened her eyes.

"Listen. The drive-by shooting was over a year ago and it had nothing to do with Riversong or my family. One of our customers was the target and she just happened to be in our shop. If anyone feels unsafe in Riversong, it would be her, and she doesn't. She's still a regular. We explained to Kevin that he was safe, that nothing was going to happen to him or us, it was just bad luck." April forced herself not to squirm in her seat. She wasn't about to let this asshole see that he'd just given voice to her worst fears. "And my son understood. He's *fine*."

"Bad luck." Pirogue nodded like he'd just caught April in a lie. "How often does bad luck happen around you and your family?"

And there it was. It didn't matter how many years—no, decades—had passed since Sonny Taylor had anything to do with the criminal activities his parents committed with the hippie commune they lived in. It didn't help that Sonny's sister and brother-in-law had gone from being pot dealers to owning a legitimate dispensary, which had been targeted a year before the drive-by at Riversong.

No matter that my cousin is now a famous musician. No matter that my branch of the family owns a legitimate busi-

ness that people love. No matter what we do, to some people we're always going to be the town trash.

"Wow," April stretched the word out. "That sounded almost rehearsed. Do you keep a little folder labeled 'Taylor family talking points' or do you just wing it and hope the condescension sticks?"

Pirogue's thin smile didn't reach his eyes. "Ms. Taylor, it's no secret that children from... fractured homes... tend to act out more. Single parents do the best they can, of course, but a boy Kevin's age really needs a strong male role model."

April said nothing. Not because she didn't have a comeback—she had dozens—but because it hit too close. Kevin already had the best male role model any kid could ask for in her father. Sonny had stepped into the role of grandpa without hesitation. He loved Kevin fiercely, guided him gently, never missed a milestone or an everyday moment, just as he'd done for his daughters and niece.

A traitorous little voice hissed in her mind: *What if it isn't enough? What if nurture can't overcome nature?*

She refused to let Pirogue see any of that. He'd weaponize it in a heartbeat.

April's fingernails bit crescents into her arms as heat shot up her neck. She wanted to launch herself across his desk—but instead she smiled, cold and sharp. "He has an excellent role model. My father is the most respected man I know. He served this country, built a business from nothing, and shows up for his grandson every damn day."

She leaned in, voice low and deliberate. "Funny, I've never once seen you at the park coaching your son's Little League, or even showing up for recess duty here. If you're so concerned about role models, maybe take a closer look at the one the kids see at school—because I wouldn't want Kevin picking up your example."

Pirogue's jaw tightened, his ears flushing red. He straightened the stack of papers in front of him with unnecessary force.

"If Kevin continues to be a problem, Ms. Taylor, he won't be welcomed back in the fall."

"And if his last name were Sumner instead of Taylor, I doubt we'd be having this conversation at all."

"Donors don't influence my decisions," he said, looking affronted.

"Sure they don't." April pushed her chair back, scraping the linoleum. "Fine. He's suspended? I'll save us all some time and go pull him out of detention ten minutes early."

"Ms. Taylor. This is unacceptable behavior."

"I guess it's a family trait, huh?" she called over her shoulder. She stormed down the hall, Principal Jackass behind her flapping like an angry duck and squawking for her to come back, until they reached the detention room.

"If you go in there, I'll consider it trespassing," he threatened.

"It's not trespassing if my kid is in there."

"I'm calling security."

April ignored Pirogue and pushed the door open. The room monitor was sitting behind a teacher's desk. She looked up from a crossword at April, then at Pirogue.

"What's going on?"

April scanned the room. She counted ten kids of various ages. But no Kevin.

"Where's my son?" She directed her question at the monitor.

"Who's your son?"

"Kevin Taylor."

"Oh, Kevin? I heard about the fight earlier and thought he'd been sent straight home."

April froze. "Well, he wasn't. He's supposed to be in detention." She looked back and forth between the monitor and Pirogue. "Where is my son?" April fought the panic building in her stomach and climbing up the back of her throat.

"I—" the monitor looked desperately at the principal as she shook her head. "I haven't seen him."

"What do you mean you haven't seen him? Where. Is. My. Son?" Suddenly, April felt far away. This couldn't be happening. This couldn't be real.

Pirogue's face paled. "Ms. Taylor, I'm sure there's been a misunderstanding. Kevin must be hiding around here somewhere." He laid his hand on April's shoulder.

April jerked away from him. "Don't you *dare* touch me. Where the hell is my son?"

By now the kids in detention were laughing and catcalling, making this living nightmare that much worse. In her head, she chanted, *Don't panic. Don't panic. Don't panic. Panicking won't help Kevin.*

"Miss Davis, please call school security," Pirogue told the monitor. She nodded and reached for the phone on the teacher's desk.

"School security?" April reached into her purse for her phone. "I'm calling the police."

"Listen, we don't need to escalate this, April. I'm sure Kevin is hiding out of fear of punishment. Poor little guy." Pirogue was going for a comforting tone, but to April, it sounded like nails on a chalkboard. Then he had the nerve to reach for April's phone. She spun around, ducked, and dodged past him. She sprinted down the hall with no idea which direction to go. She needed to know where her son was *now*. April turned a corner, unlocked her phone, and dialed 911.

Kevin. My baby. He's gone. What if he found... Oh, God, what if Kevin's been taken?

FOUR

SHANE STOOD AT ONE END OF WATCHDOG SECURITY'S dog training yard, ready to put Pete through his paces. The dog was practically vibrating with excitement—or more likely in anticipation of a treat. Alex Hoff, Watchdog's kennel master, stood at the other end. Pete's gaze never left the peanut-butter-stuffed Kong in Alex's hand. Between Shane and Alex was a doggie obstacle course designed by their boss, Kyle "Pup" McGuire. Kyle hoped to become one of the suppliers of dogs for the U.S military, like the Military Working Dog breeding program based at Lackland AFB.

"Ready, Shane?" Alex called. He gave the Kong a shake and then lowered it so a half dozen floppy-eared puppies could see it, too. The little pack let out squeaks and yips, tripping over each other in their eagerness. They weren't old enough for obstacle work yet, but Alex liked to bring them out when Pete ran the course. Modeling behavior, he called it.

Shane wasn't so sure. Right now, the pups looked more

like a pack of toddlers on a sugar high trying to grab a piñata filled with candy.

"Pretty sure Pete's not impressed with the new recruits," Shane said.

Pete gave a sharp bark as if to agree: these little punks were not ready for his course.

Alex grinned. "Just wait. They watch him, they learn. By the time they're ready to hit the course, half the work's already done."

"Or they learn bad habits, like how to guilt a handler holding a peanut butter Kong into giving them extra treats," Shane said, scratching Pete's ear. The dog leaned into him, a smug look in his eyes that said *I've got you wrapped around my paw, buddy.*

Alex chuckled, then gave a sharp whistle and signaled. Suddenly all-business, Pete launched forward, muscles bunching and stretching in perfect rhythm as he hit the first hurdle. The puppies tumbling around Alex's feet became alert, watching Pete's every move. All but the runt of the litter, whose attention remained riveted on the Kong.

Shane couldn't help it. The sight of Pete nailing the weave poles with military precision filled him with pride. He'd helped raise and train Peetie from when he was no more than a distracted puppy begging for a Kong like this new litter was doing, to the skilled dog he was today. Pete paused along the course, sniffed, then trotted forward a few steps and started digging in the dirt until he found the sock scented with chemicals that simulated a WMD. He barked to signal his find, then stepped back as the two men converged on him. The puppies trailed Alex, hoping for a snack, but the Kong was all for Pete.

"Good boy," Alex praised as he handed the Kong to Pete. The dog was suddenly swarmed by puppies. Alex stepped back a few yards, then commanded the puppies to come to him. To Shane's astonishment, they stopped their begging and dutifully ran back to their trainer. With the notable exception of the runt, who tried to nose in past Peetie's paws to get to the Kong on the ground. Pete simply picked it up and trotted away. The little guy started to follow, but was almost immediately distracted by a butterfly flitting across his path.

Alex shook his head at the puppy. "That one's about to wash out. Benny! Benny, come!" he clapped his hands but Benny kept following the butterfly until it flitted to the roof of the kennel and out of sight.

"Benny!" Shane called. The puppy turned, tilted his head as if to say *Who, me?* But then made a beeline for Shane. He pulled up, just shy of running straight into Shane's legs, and stuck his butt in the air, tail wagging, begging to play.

Shane chuckled as he bent to pet Benny's head. "Good boy. See? He listens. I think he just likes me better than you."

Pete trotted over with his Kong, now licked clean of peanut butter and covered in slobber. He dropped it at Shane's feet and Benny attacked it immediately, followed by his littermates.

"I need to talk to the boss," Shane told Alex. "I'll let you clean that up." He pointed his chin at the slimy Kong.

"Thanks, brother," Alex answered with a bright smile. "You're on kennel KP."

Shane laughed as he and Pete went inside and headed for Kyle's office.

"Hey, boss, got a minute? Whoa, what's wrong?" Shane stopped dead in Kyle's doorway. All thoughts of what he wanted to talk about fled his mind when he saw the look on the Pup's face. Kyle waved him in and pointed at his phone on the desk.

"George, I've got Shane Foti in here with me now. Please repeat what you just told me."

Shane closed the door behind him after Pete scooted in. Kyle could only be talking to George Williams, the sergeant in charge of Lyons' law enforcement. George was not only Alex's father-in-law, he was good friends with just about everyone at Watchdog.

There was a pause at the other end, then George's voice came through the speaker, grim and clipped. "We've issued an all-points bulletin. Kevin Taylor is missing from the elementary school."

Shane felt adrenaline hit his system. April's Kevin? "What the fuck, George?"

"He got into a fight on the playground during an afternoon break and was sent to the principal's office. Principal lectured him, sent him back to class. Apparently, he never showed up. His teacher and then the detention monitor assumed he was sent home. He's been missing for just over two hours." George blew out an angry-sounding breath. "The principal waited until school was almost out to call April, asking her to come in to discuss Kevin's suspension. They talked, then April went to pull Kevin out of detention and he was gone. That was ten minutes ago. School security's combing the building, but I doubt he's there."

Shane fought back his worry, replacing it with anger. "Sounds like he took off after the principal lectured him." *Probably for the tenth time this week* he thought. It was well known among April's friends that Kevin could be a handful and was often in trouble at school. Shane had a slightly different take on it. He remembered well how her whole family was treated when they were growing up. Bile pooled in his stomach along with guilt.

"My thoughts exactly," George said. "He rode his bike to school and he hasn't shown up back at the coffee shop, which is only a ten-minute ride away and where he's supposed to go after school, and he didn't go home. April checked the front and back porch cameras. Kid might have been afraid of getting in trouble and took off. I've got a patrol car cruising the surrounding streets. No sign."

"He *might* have been afraid," Kyle said. "Though the kid is pretty resilient. He's used to being in trouble and it doesn't faze him."

"A suspension, though, is next level," George said. "And with a two-hour head start on a bike, we're expanding the search. Considering he's April's kid, I thought I'd reach out to you guys as well."

Kyle stood up. "All hands on deck here. We'll fan out from Watchdog, head toward Lyons. George, any leads on someone taking him?" He looked at Shane. "We all know their family's had enemies in the past."

Yeah, including my own father. The thought threatened to bring the bile up from Shane's stomach.

"We're looking into that—"

A sudden knock on the door interrupted them. The door opened a crack and Jodie, Watchdog's receptionist peeked in. She had a funny smile on her face as she spotted Shane. "Oh, good, I was coming in to ask Kyle if he knew where you were. You have a visitor waiting for you in reception."

"Tell them to keep waiting. I've got a lost kid to find."

Jodie stepped into the office. "Any chance it's Kevin?"

"Uh, yeah. How'd you know?"

"Because he just showed up in the lobby wanting to talk to you."

"What?" Relief so sudden and so complete washed over Shane, threatening to make his knees buckle.

"He says he needs to talk to you, Shane."

"Kevin's been found," Kyle told George in the meantime. "Apparently, he's standing in my lobby right now."

"I'm right here, Mr. McGuire." Kevin appeared behind Jodie. His eyes went straight to Pete standing beside Shane and a huge smile spread across his face. He dashed past Jodie and went to his knees beside the dog. He started to reach out to pet him, then stopped and looked up at Shane. "Can I pet him, or is he on duty?"

This kid. Sometimes, he was so damn conscientious.

"Well, Pete was just about to go on duty, because Sergeant George called asking for help to find a missing kid. Any idea who that could have been?"

Kevin's eyes went round. "Oops."

"Yeah, oops. Your mom's been worried sick."

"Am I going to get arrested?"

"No, son," George said over the speaker. "But you might be in more trouble than that with your mom. I'm going to call off the search. I'll call April first."

"Leave that to us," Kyle said. "No need to keep anyone out longer than necessary looking for him."

"Thanks, all." George disconnected.

"What's going on, Kevin?" Shane asked.

Kevin stood up and solemnly said, "I need to talk to you, Mr. Foti. Man to man."

Shane couldn't stop his grin. *What a kid.* But, something in Kevin's eyes and in his voice told him this was genuinely serious. "Look, we can't let your mom be scared for another second. I'm going to call her and say that you're here and we'll take you back to her. You can talk to me on the way over to Riversong, or wherever she wants to meet up."

Kevin looked alarmed. "But... It might take longer than that to tell you."

"I'll drive slow. This is as much as I'm going to negotiate with you." He leaned down. "Man to man."

Kevin nodded as he considered the offer. "Okay, that's fair."

More than fair, little man, Shane thought. But instead of rebuking him, he reached out to shake Kevin's hand. The seriousness with which Kevin regarded Shane's hand before shaking it impressed him. He caught a glimpse of the man Kevin would become and that man was a good one. But in the meantime, where was the squirrely boy who couldn't stay quiet or in one place for more than ten seconds before something new and shiny overtook his attention?

This has got to be serious.

Kevin looked up at him, all boy again as he asked. "Can we take Peetie?"

Shane grinned. Kevin adored Peetie as much as Shane did. "Yeah, buddy, we can take Peetie."

Kevin looked relieved. "Good, because I think I'm gonna need him to soften up Mom." Then he considered. "And if that doesn't work, he can always guard me from her."

Shane held back a snort. This kid was killing him.

"Do any of you have her cell phone number?" Shane asked.

"Affirmative," Kyle said. "Arden's got it. I'll text her."

"You don't have to do that, Mr. McGuire, I've got it."

But of course, Kevin had his mom's number even though he didn't have a phone. The adults in the room looked at each other, feeling foolish for not asking him first. Kevin rolled his eyes like *Adults, sheesh.* He gave Shane

April's number. He punched it into his phone. Then he ruffled Kevin's hair and told him to go out to reception where there was a charity box of snacks on the desk.

"Pick something that doesn't have sugar in it." He looked at Jodie. "Put it on my tab."

She grinned and nodded. "You got it."

Shane pointed at Kevin. "And don't even think about leaving reception. I'll be there right after I text your mom." But Kevin was already halfway out the door at the mention of 'snack.'

"Wait up, Kevin," Jodie said. He stopped and came back to her. "Let's go find something to do while we wait." Jodie put her arm around Kevin's shoulders and led him back to the lobby.

Shane held his phone up and told Kyle, "I'll call her and take him home."

"Noted." Kyle said. "While you're at it, tell her I'm hiring Kevin as my new security troubleshooter. What is it with people sneaking onto Watchdog property with bicycles? First it was Ellie, now it's a little kid sneaking past my cameras and alarms."

Shane chuckled. "It's not just any little kid. When he's not distracted, Kevin's a wicked smart little guy. Just like his mother." He turned to leave Kyle's office.

"How are things between you and April these days?"

Shane stopped in his tracks. How could he even begin to answer that question?

"Fine." Shane said flatly. "Let me go call her before she tears the entire state of Colorado apart to find him." He started down the hall toward an empty conference room before Kyle could ask anything else.

Were things fine between them? *Oh hell no.*

He never, *ever* talked to anyone about his feelings for

April. Except for Ben, who knew the whole story. But, Shane was a fool if he thought his boss hadn't noticed a change in their relationship, ever since the drive-by. April had gone from flirting right back at Shane to avoiding him when possible, and when not, doing her best to not engage.

Shane shut the conference room door, hit call, and April answered immediately.

"You bastard. Where is my son?"

Shane flinched from the icy venom in her voice, directed right at him. Then he realized his number came up on her phone as private. This wasn't personal, this was the voice of a mother who would scorch the earth to get her son back.

"April, it's okay. It's Shane. I've got Kevin. He's safe."

She gasped. "Shane? Oh, God, I'm so, so sorry. I didn't know it was you, the number came up private. I thought it was...never mind what I thought. Kevin's okay? Where did you find him?" Her words practically ran together.

"Yes, he's okay. He just—"

Shane almost told April that they didn't even have to go searching, Kevin had shown up at Watchdog's doorstep. But, he decided to hold off until he knew what had inspired —or more like driven—Kevin to come all the way out to Watchdog.

"—took off on his bike after the fight to cool down."

She sighed wearily. "I was worried sick, but I can't say I blame him. I used to do the same thing whenever I fought with Regis' mother in high school." She laughed bitterly. "I guess she's right; the apple doesn't fall far from the tree. Only, she called my son rotten."

Shane frowned, then it clicked. "You mean Leslie? Are you telling me her little brat's been picking on Kevin? And when did she have the nerve to say that bullshit to you?"

"Yeah, Kevin punched Regis today, and of course Pirogue called in Leslie first and told her everything. She shot her shitty little remark at me on my way in to talk to him. Also, she's going to sue us." If April sounded weary before, she sounded downright dead-tired now. "I'll come get Kevin. Where—"

"No need, I'll bring him home." Shane paused. He hadn't been to April's place since he'd returned to Lyons. Bringing Kevin there felt too intrusive, especially since the freeze-out after the drive-by. "Are you at Riversong?"

"Yeah. I'm here." Then quieter, almost to herself, "I'm *always* here."

"Then we'll meet you there," Shane told her. "See you in a few."

"Yeah, see you. Oh, and Shane?"

"Yeah?"

"It really means a lot to me that *you* found him. Thank you."

Her words surprised him and the heaviness in her voice tugged at his heart. Maybe this was a new beginning for them. "April, I'd do anything for you and Kevin. Anything."

But she'd already disconnected, and his words floated out into nothing.

———

TRUE TO HIS WORD, Kevin was still in the reception area. He was sitting across from Jodie at the desk, the two of them engaged in a puzzle. Shane had no idea where Jodie had gotten it, but he wasn't surprised—she was twice as resourceful as some of their bodyguards, and that was saying a lot.

"Looks like you grabbed more than one snack," Shane

said, eying two empty potato chip bags beside the beginnings of the puzzle.

Kevin turned and looked up, but only for a moment before his entire attention zoomed in on Peetie, leashed and standing at attention beside Shane. Kevin's smile threatened to split his face as he jumped up and out of the chair and sprinted toward the dog. Just like in Kyle's office, he pulled up at the last second and looked back up at Shane.

"*Now* is he on duty, or can I still pet him?"

Shane's eyebrow quirked at Kevin's self-restraint. But when it came to Peetie, Kevin wouldn't risk doing anything that might get him banned from playing with the dog.

"You can still pet him. Besides," Shane pointed out Peetie's barely contained wiggling that had started the moment he caught sight of the boy, "I think Peetie would never forgive me if I didn't let you."

"That's because Peetie and me are buddies, isn't that right, Pete?" Kevin said as he dropped to his knees (Shane envied kids whose knees hadn't been banged up by life yet and could stand the impact of a move like that) and vigorously scratched behind Peetie's ears as the dog groaned.

Jodie stood. "The second bag's on me," she said as she picked up both wrappers and tossed them in a wastebasket. "I'm just glad he's okay. You hear that, Kevin?" Kevin ignored her in favor of Peetie, who was now rolled over on his back for a tummy rub.

"Thanks, Jodie," Shane said. "You're the best."

"I try."

"You succeed. Always." Shane smiled at her before looking down at Kevin. "Ready?"

Kevin stood immediately, suddenly serious. "Yeah." He looked at Jodie. "Thanks, Ms. Jodie. I wish I could finish the puzzle with you, but me and Shane have matters to discuss."

Jodie's eyes widened and she quickly swallowed a laugh. "Matters to discuss, huh? Well then, I won't slow you down, Mr. Taylor."

"Can you keep the puzzle like it is though?" he said, right back to being a kid. "Maybe we can finish it later?"

"I'll set it up on the credenza behind me until your next visit," Jodie said solemnly, eyes twinkling. "But, maybe next time you'll let your mom bring you, or at least tell someone where you're going?"

"Yeah, okay." He rolled his eyes, but it was a good-natured gesture.

"Ready?" Shane nudged Kevin.

"Ready."

They headed for Shane's Watchdog SUV. "Hang on," Shane said, stopping. "Where's your bike?"

Kevin looked blank for a moment. "Oh yeah, my bike." Then he tore off around the building.

"Kevin, wait!" Shane and Pete jogged after him. By the time they got around to the other side, he was gone.

"Kevin!"

The boy reappeared out of the woods surrounding the entire Watchdog compound, which included the main building and kennels, a shooting range, two obstacle courses —one for humans and one for canines—a town front façade for training dogs and their humans to find enemies and explosives, and three safehouses. Arden's farm was just up the road, safe behind Watchdog's gates. Everything was on one of the solitary foothills just a few miles east of Lyons, which was in the Front Range foothills proper.

Grinning, Kevin pushed his bike out of the trees and headed toward Shane and Pete. Shane had to laugh—Ellie had appeared the same way, walking her bike out of the woods and into Bear's life as he was fixing up one of the safehouses. She'd put all of them on high alert and Kyle had beefed up the cameras.

Looks like he's going to be dropping some more cheese on cameras for the woods.

Got it!" Kevin shouted needlessly.

"Double-time. Your mom's waiting."

Kevin hopped on the bike and sped past Shane and Pete to the back of the SUV. Shane followed, shaking his head. When he got to the vehicle, he opened the passenger-side door.

"Hop in. I'll get Pete and the bike secured, then we'll be on our way."

Kevin peeked around the side from the back. "Can I help?" he asked eagerly.

At first, Shane thought Kevin might be stalling for time, that maybe the reality of an angry mom waiting for him was sinking in. But the eagerness in the boy's face told him a different story. Kid was absolutely crazy about dogs, Peetie especially.

We've got that in common. His heart constricted even as he smiled at Kevin. "Sure, yeah."

He should have been mine.

Those selfish, forbidden words slipped past his defenses for the thousandth time since he first laid eyes on April's son. Followed immediately by the same old shame and regrets. If he hadn't been such a pussy and stood up to his father. If he hadn't been so selfish and gone off to college like the old tyrant wanted. If he'd tried harder to find her after he rebelled, dropped out, and flew to California to enlist in the Navy with the hopes of becoming a SEAL.

Selfish.

With Shane's help, Kevin lifted his bike into the back of the SUV and secured it. Then, Pete jumped up, and into his cage he went. Kevin made sure Peetie was comfy, had enough toys, and wasn't going to get car sick.

Shane started to open the passenger-side door again and stopped. *Oh, shit, I didn't think. I don't have a kid's car seat. And kids can't ride up front anyway, can they?*

"Sorry, Kev. You've gotta sit in the back."

"Can I... I need to sit in front to talk to you. Man to man."

Oh my God, this kid is killing *me.*

"Alright, alright, but better not let your mom know."

Kevin beamed at Shane and scrambled into the passenger seat. He pulled the seatbelt over his shoulder and Shane helped him adjust it down.

"And don't make me regret this. if I get pulled over, you better scramble back there as fast as you can." He pointed to the back seat.

"Oh, it's okay, George won't arrest you. We're all friends."

Shit, the kid's smarter than I am.

Shane closed the door, went around to the other side, got in and started the engine. "Alright, I'm driving slow and careful, but it's not a long drive, so talk fast. Why did you run away?"

"I didn't run away. I came to you to talk," Kevin replied in a perfectly reasonable tone.

And he's on his way to becoming a lawyer.

"Man to man. Right. So, you got me. What do you want to talk about?"

Kevin hesitated. "Well, today I got into a fight with Regis Sumner."

"Regis Sumner, huh? Between you and me, I'd fight him, too," Shane joked. Out of the corner of his eye, he watched Kevin's body relax into the seat.

"Regis is always a jerk. The teacher doesn't do anything about it, and I hate being a tattletale anyway." He looked at Shane. "Snitches get stitches."

Shane tried not to snort. "Go on."

"I try to ignore him, but it just makes him madder. Today, I couldn't anymore."

"Why not today?"

"Because Regis was saying bad things about my mom, so I defended her."

Why the fuck am I not surprised?

"Okay, well, that's... noble."

Kevin smiled. "See? I knew you'd understand me, Shane."

God, that gutted him in a way that also made his heart swell with a fierce love for this kid.

"It's Shane, now, huh?"

"Well, we *are* talking man to man right now."

"Yeah, good point."

"When we're done, I'll go back to calling you Mr. Foti around the grownups."

Jesus.

"So, what was His Royal Highness Regis Sumner saying about your mom?"

"That's funny. Mom calls him that, too, only she abbreviates it to HRH Regis Sumner."

Just like she did to Leslie in school.

"But not when she thinks I'm listening," Kevin continued. "Just when she's talking to Gramma or Grandpapa. She's trying to teach me to be respectful."

I'm. Dying. Right now. "You think it's respectful to eavesdrop?"

"No, but everybody my age does it. It's how we learn

stuff. That's how Regis heard what his mom said about mine."

"Well, man to man, I'm not surprised to hear that. Les... Ms. Trent Sumner and your mom didn't get along in school. *And that's putting it lightly.* "So, you gotta understand that whatever she says about your mom comes from a place of deep jealousy and doesn't mean shi...squat."

"It's okay, you can say shit, Shane. I can handle it."

Shane's abs were getting a workout just from fighting his laughter. He bit down hard on his lower lip to keep it from coming out. He really was trying to match Kevin's seriousness.

"Regis said he heard her talking to her friends at their book club—"

You mean wino club.

"—and she was talking pretty loud—"

Called it.

"—and she was saying my mom was always trash, as long as she's known her. My whole family is trash."

Shane practically growled, "Don't you dare believe that bull...shit. Because that's all it is. A big, stinking pile of bullshit pouring out of Leslie Trent's mouth."

Kevin snickered. "Gross."

"And I can tell you, it's been coming out of her mouth as long as I've known her, so how about that?"

"Yuck!" Kevin laughed.

"So don't let Regis get to you. He's not worth it."

Kevin's laughter dried up. "I don't. I'm used to him saying *bullshit* like that. It's what he said after that made me punch him. Because it scared me."

Suddenly, Shane didn't feel like laughing, either. "I'm listening." He turned off the main highway into Lyons onto a dirt road that snaked up and around and would give Kevin more time to talk.

"Regis' mom said that after high school, my mom disappeared for years and nobody knew what she was doing, so she was probably a criminal who went to jail. All they know is that she came back pregnant. With me. And that my dad is probably in jail or dead, if she even knows who he is." Kevin's voice wobbled.

Shane's heart broke for the little boy spilling his story. At least he could clear some of that up. The rest... he had no idea. And apparently, Kevin didn't, either.

"Oh, man. Kevin, your mom never went to jail, okay? She's not, nor has she ever been, a criminal. So, don't let that scare you."

But Kevin was already waving Shane off. "I know that. Mom would never break the law. She's different from my great aunt and uncle. But they don't break the law anymore, either. They went legit. But that's not what scared me."

"So, what scared you?"

"Regis said, 'Your mom's so bad, somebody tried to kill her at Riversong. They tried to shoot her to death."

Shane relaxed. He could handle this part. But he wondered why Kevin's family hadn't talked to him about it. It seemed out of character.

"Buddy, what happened was awful, and it put your mom in danger, but it could have been a lot worse. No one was killed. And I know for a fact that no one was trying to kill your mom. Unfortunately, they were after Rochelle. But, we caught the bad guys. Your mom is safe. Everyone's safe." He hesitated, then asked, "Didn't they talk to you about it?"

"Yeah, they did. I know they weren't after Mom now."

"So why are you scared, buddy? The bad guys aren't coming back."

"Regis said she got lucky that time. But the next time, someone would kill her, and he and his mom would laugh and the whole town would be happy that my mom was dead because we're all trash, and that's when I punched him."

That evil little shit.

"I shouldn't say this, but if some guy had said that about my mom, I'd have punched him, too."

Kevin studied him for a moment. "Would you punch Regis for saying it about my mom?"

Shane chuckled. "Naw, I'd never hit a kid no matter what he said. Now, if a grownup said anything about your mom, it might be a different story."

Shit. That probably went too far. I'm outta my league, I don't know what I'm doing here. I'm screwing this up.

"Look, what I'm trying to say is, ignore His Royal Highness Regis. Who cares what he or his mom think? They're both wrong about your whole family. And I promise, no one's after your mom."

"But that's just it, Shane. That's why I'm scared. Someone *is* after my mom."

"No—"

"Yes!" Kevin yelled. "She said so herself!"

FIVE

SHANE PULLED THE SUV OVER AND KILLED THE engine. He needed to talk to Kevin face to face without any distractions.

"I thought you had my attention before, but you've sure got it now, kid. Your mom told you someone's after her?"

"No, she didn't tell me. I was eavesdropping." He looked sheepish. "I told you everybody my age did it."

Shane grinned. "Yeah, you did. I'm not judging you, Kevin. What did you overhear?" Shane asked. "Who was your mom talking to?"

"She was talking to Grandpapa and Gramma and Aunt Hannah. It was the same night the bad guys shot at River-song. We were all staying at Grandpapa and Gramma's house. It's big and has rooms for everybody. They thought I was asleep upstairs, but I couldn't sleep. I started going downstairs for a snack and I heard Gramma yelling. Gramma never yells. So, I stopped on the stairs and listened."

"What was your Gramma yelling about?"

"She was saying, 'Nope, you're not running. We're not

losing you a second time, April. This is not happening again.' Then Grandpapa said, 'Little girl, you are not leaving. You are not taking our grandson. You will stay here and we will face this together. We don't even know for sure yet who did this.' Then Mom said, 'If he's after me, you're not safe as long as I'm here. I'll do anything to keep everyone safe, even if it means Kevin and I have to disappear.'"

By now, Kevin was fighting back tears, but he kept going. "I didn't want to go anywhere. So, I ran upstairs and hid under my bed. That was like a whole year ago and I was just a dumb little kid back then. I didn't think they'd find me."

Shane smiled softly. "There's not a dumb thing about you, Kevin."

Kevin gave him a small smile. "I fell asleep under there, and Mom found me right away the next morning. She thought I was scared of the bad guys, and I didn't want to tell her the truth because I wasn't supposed to be out of bed eavesdropping, and I didn't want to get in trouble. We all stayed at Gramma and Grandpapa's house for a few days, and then one morning, Mom hugged me and cried and told me that the bad guys weren't after us. I was just glad that we weren't leaving. So, I stopped worrying and pretty much forgot about it until Regis said all that." Kevin paused. "I do that a lot. I forget things." He looked at Shane sheepishly. "I get in trouble with my teachers all the time for it."

"Kid, everybody forgets things. Some days, if my head wasn't attached to my neck, I'd leave it behind on my pillow."

That made Kevin laugh. "I don't believe that. You're really cool, Shane. You taught Peetie all sorts of tricks and he loves you. And people trust you to protect them." He sat up straight and squared his shoulders. "That's why I want to hire you."

Shane jerked his head back in surprise. "Hire me? For what?"

"To be Mom's bodyguard. Even though Regis is stupid and a jerk, I think maybe he's right. Someone might come after my mom, or she wouldn't have said all those things."

Dammit. The kid had a point. *If* he was correct about what he'd overheard. Kevin had already been scared, and he could have misunderstood what April said.

But the truth was, Shane didn't know much about April's life after high school. He'd told Kevin that she wasn't a criminal...but he had no proof one way or the other. Except that he *knew* her.

Didn't he?

"So, how much do you charge?" Kevin asked. "I got fifty dollars for my birthday. But I was kind of hoping that you would only charge forty, because there's this video game on Steam for ten bucks and it looks really cool and I wanna get it."

Shane grinned. "Well, Kevin, it costs a little more than forty bucks to hire a bodyguard."

Kevin went from looking hopeful to devastated.

"Hey now, don't be upset. I'm not saying no. Watchdog does take on cases *pro bono*. Do you know what that means?"

"No."

"That means free. Sometimes we protect people for free, Kevin."

His face immediately lit up. "Really? You would watch Mom and protect her for *free*?"

Hell yeah I would, kid. And you, too. Always.

"Yeah, Kevin. I never want to see anything bad happen

to her, or to you, or to anybody else in your family. But, let's not jump to conclusions, all right? You don't know for sure that anyone is after her. I'm going to start up the truck again. Your mom's waiting for us, and I don't want to keep her waiting any longer. She's gonna wonder where we are, and she's been through enough today." Shane started the engine. "One more thing though before you can hire me."

"What's that?"

"I'm going to talk with your mom, privately."

Kevin paled. "I'm not in trouble, am I? Well, I *am* in trouble already because I didn't tell anybody where I was going, but I promise that I'm never gonna do that again. But..." He looked desperate. "Please, Shane, please. I don't wanna be in trouble for eavesdropping and snitching, and—"

"Calm down, calm down. It's going to be all right. I've known your mom a long time. Just let me talk to her about this, alright? I'm telling you right now instead of going behind your back and ratting you out. Not after we've talked man to man."

"So, it's like a code of honor?"

Shane nodded. "Yeah, Kevin, it's like a code of honor." He extended his hand and Kevin shook it solemnly.

Shane had no words for how good, how *right*, that felt. He'd long ago stopped considering himself father material, not after the rat bastard of a father he'd had. It wasn't that Shane thought he would turn into his father and become abusive. He didn't have that in him. He'd never hit a kid, just like he'd told Kevin. No, Shane thought he was too selfish to ever devote his life to someone who needed him so completely. Not after the way he'd let April down.

"Now, how about you take a seat in the back and buckle up. We're about five minutes from Riversong."

Kevin changed seats without a word of protest. Shane pulled back onto the road. They rode the rest of the way in silence, each lost in his thoughts. Shane turned Kevin's words over in his mind. He remembered how the family had circled the wagons right after the drive-by, and who could blame them? Their business had seemingly been targeted, and the Taylors had old enemies. They re-opened once they knew it was safe, and business slowly picked back up until it was like the shooting had never happened.

Except for one thing. April had gone from flirting with Shane to shutting him out.

Shane grimaced as his memories drifted back to a few years ago when he returned to Lyons after his discharge from the Swicks. He'd tried for years to find April, using all the connections he could, but she'd remained hidden. He didn't want to bother the Taylors; Shane—and his father— had done enough to them already.

Shane didn't dare hope that April had come back home, but maybe after all this time her family would tell him where she was, if they even knew. He dressed up that day when he went to their coffee shop, hoping to beg forgiveness if they knew he was partly responsible for her leaving. He'd tried to find her, from the moment he'd recovered from his father's beating the day after graduation, all the way through his first year of college, then after he'd secretly dropped out and enlisted with the Navy. He didn't end up a SEAL, but a SWCC—Special Warfare Combatant-craft Crewman, or Swick—instead, along with Sean, one of his best friends from home. He thought with his new connections, he could track her down, but April Taylor had vanished into thin air.

The only reason he knew she was still alive was, ironically, through his father's bank. Once Shane had the money, he started wiring it to the Taylors—as a big fuck you to his father, and as a way of easing his guilt. Turned out, April was doing the same thing.

So, the day he returned to town, when he walked through the doors of Riversong he was shocked to see April behind the counter. She had her back to him, wiping down the gleaming espresso machine. But Sonny saw him right away. Shane would never forget the look on the man's face. It was the same expression he'd seen on the faces of his enemies in battle.

Sonny knew everything.

"April," Sonny said quietly.

"What, Papa?" She had a warm smile on her face for Sonny, but when she turned and saw Shane, shock overtook her features.

"Shane. You're back in town."

"Got in today," Shane quickly said. "I wanted to...to ask about you." His gaze flicked from April to Sonny and back. "But you're here."

"I'm here. Past three years." April set the towel down on the counter slowly, like she was in a dream. Or, maybe Shane was the one who was dreaming. She looked as beautiful as she did the day they graduated. The same bright, intelligent eyes, the same dark, glossy hair. He wanted to drop to his knees that moment and beg her forgiveness. There was no excuse for abandoning her. He should have fought harder.

"April. I—"

"Mommy!" A little boy, the spitting image of April, burst through the door at the back of the shop and ran toward her as fast as his legs could carry him. April's mom was on his heels, laughing and trying to catch him.

"Kevin, come back to grandma. Mommy's working."

All of April's attention left Shane and went straight to the boy.

Shane's heart split open down the middle.

"How was preschool, sweetie?" April asked as she swept the boy up in her arms.

No, not just a boy. Her son.

He clung to her neck and landed a big kiss on her cheek. "Fun!" She closed her eyes and pressed her cheek against her son's head. When she opened her eyes, her gaze was a silent challenge to Shane to say anything.

He couldn't help it. He scanned her left hand for a wedding ring. Her fingers were bare. Did she take her rings off to work, or was she single? Treasonous hope burned in his chest.

By now, April's mom had spotted Shane. All her humor disappeared. "April, I need you in the back for something."

"I've got the shop, honey," Sonny said flatly, his stare burning a hole through Shane. "Go on back."

April gave Shane one last inscrutable look, hoisted Kevin higher onto her hip, and followed her mother through the doorway without looking back.

"I suggest you leave," Sonny told Shane.

"I understand you don't want me here. You're remembering who I was, all those years ago. I was a scared kid and I did all the wrong things. But I've changed, Mr. Taylor. Just let me prove it to her."

"You broke my little girl's heart, Shane. Made her feel like she wasn't good enough for you and yours. She ran off to Vegas and that's where all her trouble started. She doesn't need you in her life right now. Neither does my grandson."

Shane nodded. "I'll leave now. But that doesn't mean I won't be back. I'm going to prove myself, sir, to her. I hope to prove myself to you one day, too, but if I never do, I don't care. She's the one who matters."

Shane turned to leave.

"Shane."

His heart thumped at the sound of his name coming from April's lips. He turned back around.

She stood in the doorway. "You gonna leave without even ordering something?"

Sonny looked at her like she was crazy. "April—"

"Papa, I can't believe you're turning away a paying customer. What's wrong with you? We got a mortgage to pay."

Bam. With that reminder, she might as well have gut punched Shane. If anyone else in the world had said that, he would have walked away. But that's how April was—strong, no-nonsense, proud. It was what made him fall in love with her in high school—she never let anyone push her around, not even the school's golden boy. She never failed to put him in his place when he deserved it. She won his trust that way, and she would always have it.

April walked past her father to the counter. "What can I get you?"

Shane walked toward her, holding her gaze, almost afraid that if he looked away, she'd disappear. She didn't look away, either.

He reached the counter. "Large coffee, black. Hot as you can make it. One sugar."

"Here or to go?"

"Here."

Sonny swore under his breath.

April nodded once. She rang him up, then turned to pour his coffee. They both caught sight of her little sister

Hannah and her cousin Brianna peeking at them from the doorway.

"Here you go." April set Shane's coffee on the counter. Steam rose from the white mug. "Try not to hurt yourself," she said pointedly.

Shane grinned back. "I'll take full responsibility if I get burned."

"Oh my God, did you *hear* that?" Hannah stage-whispered to Brianna.

April's head snapped to the side and she shooed them away. They disappeared in a cloud of whispers and giggles. She rolled her eyes at him and for a moment, they were both back in high school, getting spied on by two annoying little girls as April tutored Shane in math. Thank God they never caught them when they were doing more than that.

They snapped back into the present the moment they realized they were remembering the same thing.

"Thanks." Shane dipped his head and pulled a bill from his pocket. He stuffed it into the tip jar.

April's eyes went wide. She reached into the jar, pulled it back out, and slapped the hundred on the counter.

"I'm not taking that."

"What? I'm just tipping you in advance. I plan on coming in here every day." He planted his finger on the middle of the bill and pushed it across the counter. Then he picked up the coffee mug and carried it to the nearest empty table.

April watched him, shaking her head, until the next customer walked in the door.

True to his word, Shane returned to Riversong every day. His order was always the same and she always asked what he wanted anyway, claiming she never remembered. As the tension eased between April and Shane, Shane started flirting with her and she flirted back in the sexy, snarky way that drove him insane. After a few weeks, Sonny eased up on the death rays he shot Shane's way.

Just when he thought they might have their second chance, the drive-by happened and April changed. Even though she was back at Riversong every day, she closed herself off inside.

Shane glanced at the boy through the rearview mirror. He was quietly looking out the window. Kevin was almost never this still, and not for this long.

"Are you sure you want to hire *me* for a bodyguard?" Shane teased.

"Yup."

"Maybe your mom should have a say in who's guarding her. She might want someone else."

Kevin turned away from the window, caught Shane's eye in the rearview, and smiled. "No, she likes you."

"You think so?"

"I know so. Whenever we're going to see you, she always makes sure to fix her hair extra nice."

"Oh really?"

"Yup." Kevin nodded with all the confidence in the world.

Shane grinned and shook his head as he pushed down any stirring hope. He went back to focusing on what Kevin overheard, trying to piece it together. Shane knew April had been thriving out on her own years ago. Then something happened that sent her back home to Lyons. Something bad? Something she was afraid had caught up with her?

They pulled into Riversong's parking lot. Shane was determined to find out what had April spooked enough to want to take Kevin and run again, leaving behind everyone else she cared about.

SIX

APRIL SQUEEZED THE BRIDGE OF HER NOSE AS SHE
watched Riversong's parking lot through the front windows,
waiting for Shane to bring her son back to her. She replayed
the last hour in her head. The way Pirogue had tried to
handle her with kid gloves, right up until she got the call
telling her that Kevin was safe. Then, he went right back to
insinuating that she was a bad mother, and worse—that
Kevin was a bad kid.

"He's still suspended three days for fighting," Pirogue
had said.

April wasn't about to stand for that.

"Since this is a Thursday, how about two of those
suspension days are Saturday and Sunday? I'll keep him
home tomorrow, but I'm not letting him get three days
behind in school and flunk his finals."

"April, that's not how this is going to work. You're lucky
it's not for the rest of the school year, to be honest."

She'd stopped, turned, and squared her shoulders. "You
know what? I should sue the school for losing my kid. Kevin

was still under your care. He could have been kidnapped. He could have gotten hit by a car. Anything could have happened, and you know it."

"Fine," Pirogue had sputtered, his face turning red. "He can come back on Monday. I don't want to see him—or you, or your lawyer—until then."

April had smiled. "The feeling's mutual."

It wasn't until she'd driven away that the tears started. Not for Pirogue—he wasn't worth the salt in her tears. She was crying because of how afraid she'd been when she looked in that detention room and Kevin wasn't there.

This could have been so much worse. This could have been the end of my world.

The familiar whisper crept in. *It's only a matter of time.*

She'd had to pull over, hands shaking too hard to drive safely. The memories hit like a physical blow, dragging her back to a frantic packing session and a desperate escape from Vegas. She felt the same fear, the same irresistible desire to run until she found safety again—not just for herself, but for her entire family.

But that's why this time was different. This time, she was with her family who loved her, she owned a business that mattered, lived a life worth protecting. And of course, Kevin had all of that now, too. She remembered the night she argued with her parents and her sister about leaving and felt their love all over again. And then the guilty relief when they realized April wasn't the one in danger. *Even now, I'm still safe*, she reminded herself.

This time, I'm not running.

She only prayed that was the right decision, one that wouldn't ultimately hurt the ones she loved.

Through the front windows, she saw Shane's SUV

pulling into the lot, snapping her back to the present. Her heart did that same fluttery dance it had done since high school—Shane Foti still had the power to unravel her with just a smile through a windshield.

Sonny appeared beside her, his big frame radiating protective energy. "You okay?"

"I'm okay." April watched Shane park and then turn to say something to Kevin in the back seat. "Can you—"

"I already texted your mom and Hannah. Told them Kevin's safe and they don't need to cut their trip short after all." His normally booming voice quieted. "Unless you need them home?"

April's throat tightened with gratitude. "No. Let them enjoy their day." She made the quick hummingbird gesture over her heart that told her Papa she loved him, and headed out the front door.

The back passenger door opened and Kevin unfolded from the seat—lanky legs, backpack strap over his shoulder, that careful set to his mouth that meant he knew he was in trouble. But his eyes were bright, almost...relieved?

Mom-scan first, always. No blood. No bruises. No obvious missing limbs. *Check, check, check.*

"Hey, baby," she said, one palm settling at the back of his head as she did her second inventory—ten fingers, ten toes, pupils even, breathing steady.

"I didn't run away," Kevin announced before she could say another word. "I was on a mission."

"A mission?" April's gaze flicked to Shane getting out of the driver's side, all controlled movement and watchful eyes as he headed to the back of the SUV.

"Mr. Foti will explain," Kevin added.

"O...kay," she managed—more air than word. She

smoothed Kevin's hair, and he tolerated it like a soldier under inspection, then made a dash for the back of the SUV, undoubtedly to help Shane with Pete. The kid was crazy for the dog. April followed, her heart squeezing at the sight of Kevin helping Shane with Pete. Her son looked happy, and so did Shane. He glanced up at her with a smile and a shrug that said *This kid. What can you do?*

If I were a better mom, I'd ground Kevin this minute and not let him near Pete. But, she couldn't find it in her heart to do it. They looked so...natural together.

If only things had been different.

She threw that thought back into the locked box of things she wouldn't let herself think about.

"Thank you for bringing him back," she said, forcing her voice to stay steady. "I know you're busy and I don't want to keep you—"

"Actually, April, we need to talk."

Kevin froze mid-pet, flicking a nervous look at Shane.

"It's okay, buddy," Shane said gently. His gaze returned to April. "Kevin and I had a talk."

April's pulse skipped. "What kind of talk?"

"Man to man."

A startled laugh escaped her. "He's a third-grader."

"He's also scared."

April's stomach dropped through the asphalt. The world tilted. April's hands went cold, her mind immediately jumping to the worst possibilities. *Why go to Shane and not to me—or to his Grandpapa?* Guilt punched hard and mean.

"Oh God, did something else happen?" Her voice came out wrong, barely there.

"Mom," Kevin said in an annoyed voice that was more defensive than disrespectful. "I'm fine."

Shane's fingers brushed her arm, a familiar touch from long ago that still sent shivers through her. "He is. Let's just go inside and talk, okay?"

His gentleness threatened to undo her. This wasn't Shane the Bad Boy with his cocky swagger. She knew how to handle that Shane, not this careful one who was treating her like she might break if he said or did the wrong thing.

She wasn't sure if she liked the change in attitude or hated it.

The bell chimed as they entered Riversong, the familiar scents of coffee and cinnamon wrapping around them like a hug.

Sonny looked up from the register, his quick scan of Kevin shifting from worry to relief.

"Sonny, can you cover for a bit?" April asked. They always used first names in the coffee shop in front of customers. "We need a minute in the back."

Sonny's gaze moved between his grandson and Shane, still guarded but not openly hostile. Progress at a glacier's pace.

"It's fine, Sonny," April reassured him.

Sonny nodded curtly and returned his attention to Kevin. "You hungry?"

Kevin nodded. "Can I have a black-and-white cookie?"

"You'll have a sandwich," April answered for Sonny.

Shane looked solemnly at Kevin. "And do me a favor? Keep Pete company while your mom and I talk."

Kevin's face lit up. Pete duty was serious business. "Yes, sir."

"And don't give Pete half of your sandwich," April added.

Kevin rolled his eyes. April rolled hers right back. Shane chuckled, the sound warm and familiar.

"Back office," she told him. "Follow me."

The air in the back office was different—less cinnamon, more roasted beans and old wood. April left the door propped open a crack and turned to face Shane, her heart hammering against her ribs.

If Kevin needed a 'man-to-man' talk, why not with his grandfather? Why not Gabe, or Ben, or any of the good men who would drop everything to stand between her son and harm? The answer stung hotly behind her eyes.

Because I taught him I can carry anything. Maybe he thought he had to carry me.

"Before you say anything," she blurted, edges fraying now that she was safely out of sight, "if Kevin needed to talk to a man about something. If some adult—" Bile rose. "If something happened and he didn't want to tell me, I can take it. I won't make it about me. I just need to know."

"No." Shane shook his head firmly. "Nothing like that." He reached out and gently gripped her upper arm. His touch calmed her at once, just like it used to. "No one else hurt him. The only person who attacked Kevin was HRH Regis, that little shit."

Relief flooded her so fast it made her dizzy. She couldn't help the giggle that slipped out. "HRH. You remembered my nickname for Leslie."

Shane chuckled. "How could I forget? It was too perfect." He paused. "I remember everything you said, April. Everything you did." His gaze went soft and warm, the look that used to signal he was about to lean across their homework and kiss her. Her lips parted reflexively. She bit the lower one as soon as she realized what they were doing, but it was too late. Shane's gaze darted to her mouth and his eyes smoldered. April felt her legs turn to jelly again but for completely different reasons.

Shane seemed to catch himself. He let go of her arm and grew serious again. "You have an amazing kid there. He loves you," Shane said simply. "He's worried about you."

That didn't compute. She was the one who did the worrying. She looked down and realized she was clutching a Sharpie. When had she picked it up?

"Worried about me why? I'm fine." She tried for a convincing smile. "Well, except I need to come up with a few grand to fix the espresso machine."

Shane saw right through it. "April, stop. I know you. You're not fine." His voice gentled. "I need you to trust me, if only for today."

April closed her eyes and pinched the bridge of her nose. Do I even have a choice? No, she didn't. Not if Kevin was scared. A kid his age should never have to worry about his mom; it was her job to worry about him.

She nodded. "Okay. What did you guys talk about?"

"He asked if he could hire me as a bodyguard for you."

"A bodyguard for me?" April's voice pitched higher.

The corner of Shane's mouth tilted up, not quite a smile. "Said he had fifty bucks and was hoping I only cost forty because there's a ten-dollar game on Steam he wants."

A laugh burst out of her before she could stop it. "Yeah, that sounds like my boy."

Shane wasn't smiling now. His hand flexed against his thigh, then stilled. "I told him money wasn't the question. Sometimes Watchdog takes cases pro bono. But I also told him I'd talk to you first."

"Oh, I get it. We're 'discussing' this to put him at ease."

But Shane wasn't sharing her amusement. "No, we're discussing this for real."

"Are you serious? Shane, you don't have to—"

"April." His voice cut through her protest, gentle but

firm. "Kevin told me about the fight with Regis. About what that little bastard said."

Her mouth tightened. "Let me guess. More poison from Leslie."

"Most of it was the usual trash talk about you and your family. But then Regis said something that hit Kevin different." Shane's jaw ticked like the words physically hurt. "He said people were glad the drive-by happened because you had it coming. And that next time, you won't be so lucky."

April's fingers curled around the back of her chair, gripping it like an anchor that would keep her from drifting away.

"I told him the truth as I know it," Shane continued, his voice steady and sure. "The shots weren't about you. Nobody died. We found the people responsible. It was handled."

April felt herself breathing again.

"But that wasn't the part that scared him," Shane said quietly. "He heard you talking to your folks that night after the shooting. He was supposed to be asleep, but you know how kids are. He heard you say if someone was after you, you'd take him and disappear to keep everyone safe."

The words hit like a physical blow. April stared at the floor, breathing once, twice.

"He put it away in his head because you told him later the bad guys weren't after you," Shane said. "But when Regis mentioned 'next time,' it brought it all back."

Her chest ached. All this time, she'd thought Kevin had moved past the drive-by. Instead, he'd been carrying this fear, this knowledge, protecting her from his own terror.

"Here's what I didn't tell him," Shane continued, his voice dropping lower, "because it isn't mine to say. I don't know what happened to you after high school. I don't know if that night pulled up old ghosts or if there's new trouble."

His hands were deliberately open, nonthreatening. Showing her he wasn't here to interrogate her.

"So I'm asking," he said quietly. "Did Kevin misinterpret a family argument, or are you in danger, April?"

SEVEN

April drew in a deep breath. "Not...*immediate* danger."

She watched Shane's expression shift from concern to frustration, and she couldn't blame him. "Look, I'm not trying to be vague, but this is difficult to talk about."

"April, that neither clears anything up or makes me feel better." He reached for her hand. She was struck by how different it felt from when they were in high school. Not as soft—his calluses spoke of a life of hard work and military training. The thought flickered through her mind that if Daniel Foti had gotten his way, Shane's hands would still be soft, probably manicured, and he'd be sporting a pot belly from sitting behind a desk all day. She almost laughed at the ridiculous image. Shane was top-to-bottom still the fittest, handsomest man she'd ever seen.

"You can tell me anything," he said softly, stroking his thumb across the back of her hand. "Who did you think was shooting at you?"

She bit her bottom lip as she inhaled hard through her nose. This was a conversation she never wanted to have with Shane. It was the reason why she'd pulled away after the drive-by.

"I thought it was my ex."

And there it was—Shane stiffened, his pupils dilated. She watched his Adam's apple bob. She took it for jealousy until he said, "I won't let him near you or Kevin, I swear."

She should have known he'd go straight to protectiveness. That made everything more difficult.

April took her hand out of his. "I won't let you get in trouble, not over this."

"April—"

She held her hand up in a 'stop' gesture. "Like I said, I'm in no immediate danger. Neither is Kevin, trust me. We may never be."

I hope.

"How can you say that when you thought he was trying to kill you?"

"Let me start from the beginning, from the day after graduation." The words came out rougher than she intended. "The day you..."

Shane's jaw clenched, his eyes filling with an emotion that stripped her bare. "Go ahead and say it. The day I abandoned you."

She tried to smile. "Water under the bridge." At least she could say the words lightly, even if they felt like stones weighing down her heart.

"Not for me. I looked for you, April."

"You did?" She hated how hopeful she sounded, like that eighteen-year-old girl calling him from Vegas.

"For years." Shane shook his head. "But that's not what matters right now. Tell me what happened."

April gripped the back of the chair harder. Anchor, anchor.

"I never made it to California. I stopped in Las Vegas. It was supposed to be temporary." April gave a short, humorless laugh. "Remember how your parents hired me as your tutor because you were flunking math?"

The corner of his mouth twitched. "Of course. Hard to forget." April felt her cheeks flush. Most of those lessons had ended in groping sessions.

"Remember how I taught you statistics?"

This time, Shane beamed. "Yup. Statistics didn't click with me until you laid out the dice and showed me how the odds shifted with every roll. Card counting, too. You didn't have my attention until you taught me how to win at poker."

"And craps." She shook her head, remembering. "You finally sat up straight, like I'd cracked the code to the universe."

"You did. For the first time in my life, everything made sense." His smile turned faint, bittersweet. She tried not to let it cut her.

"Well, when I got to Vegas, turns out those skills paid better than tutoring. I lived off the tables for years. I didn't always count cards or win big—it attracted heat. I was careful, and worked out a rotating strategy that kept me from getting kicked out of too many places."

Shane tilted his head. "But when you got there, you were—"

"Underage, yeah. Remember that fake ID you gave me?" Guilt flashed across his face like lightning. "Came in handier than either of us planned. By twenty, I'd built a little nest egg left over from what I sent back home. Always from a different location and at random times of the year. I hoped to make up for leaving, and to let my family know I was safe and successful." She carefully gauged Shane's reaction, looking for his tell, confirming what she had suspected the minute she'd come home and looked over the accounting.

And there it was. That tick in his jaw. Now she knew for sure and her heart squeezed.

She went on smoothly, without pausing. "I had my own place, a nice one. My friend Bunni—" Her throat tightened on the name, "kept me out of trouble, made sure I didn't piss off the wrong people."

Shane's eyes softened, but he didn't interrupt.

"And I was treated with respect." She squeezed the back of the chair harder. Anchor, anchor. April's throat felt raw. "At twenty-four, one of the casino hosts at Aria said I'd caught someone's eye and sent me to the new high-stakes Ivey Room. They renamed it Table One a few years ago." She smirked. "Ironic that I met Vince there, considering Ivey and his partner were caught edge-sorting at baccarat. Cheating."

"Your ex?"

April nodded. "Vince Romano. I thought I was being rewarded complimentary drinks and a chance at playing high-stakes poker. Turns out, I was being hunted."

She could still smell that room after passing through the gold-and-glass doors—supple leather, a hint of polished wood, the faint bite of top-shelf bourbon poured neat into crystal. No smoke. No annoying slots. Just the quiet call and response of dealers and players, and the slide and click of high-value chips getting stacked into neat towers on the tables.

Shane's intense gaze stayed steady on hers.

"He didn't approach right away. He was already sitting at the low bar tucked against the wall, talking with the bartender like I wasn't even the reason he was there. He ignored me as I slammed the bourbon to calm my nerves and sat down at a table."

April felt her heart tick up, the old excitement of sitting down at the tables returning like she'd never left. "I was way out of my league. My buy-in was fifty thousand dollars. One guy was in for a million. The first player opens it up to two K in three hundred/six hundred with five hundred antes. I placed my first bet—eight thousand dollars. I had the button —the best position—and made a successful steal when the BB and SB both folded. So I won the biggest pot I'd ever won. If I walked away at that moment"—she grinned wide as she rolled her eyes skyward—"I would have been set for the rest of the year. But I stayed and played for three hours. I still came away with my money doubled, feeling like the luckiest woman in the world." Her smile faded as her lips twisted bitterly. "Shows what I knew."

Shane's hands curled into loose fists against his thighs, then deliberately flattened again.

"I stashed my earnings in my lucky purse and turned to leave. That's when he finally crossed the room. He congratulated me on my win like he already knew the exact amount I'd walked away with. 'Not everyone does their homework before they sit down at a table,' he said. He made it sound like a compliment, but it was bait."

April closed her eyes, hearing Vince's voice. When she opened them, Shane was watching her like he wanted to tear time itself apart.

"He asked if I'd ever thought of consulting. Not in a serious job-offer way, more like he was planting a seed. 'A brain like yours shouldn't waste its luck at the tables. People pay for that edge, bella.' He'd said it casually, but I remembered it later when security really did recruit me to spot card counters and frauds. I knew he had to be behind it somehow."

And now comes the hard part.

"He asked me out on the spot and I turned him down. He pursued me for over a year before I agreed to date him. Bought me expensive gifts, which I declined at first, until he figured me out. He knew I could buy myself whatever I wanted so gifts didn't work. What I wanted—needed—was respect and protection. So, he showed it to me. Wore me down little by little. I was dumb enough to think persistence meant love, that control was protection."

Her voice cracked. "He only ever knew me as April Meyer. Thank God, because after we got engaged and I moved in with him, the mask slipped. He became...short-tempered." She tried not to flinch, remembering the first time Vince hit her, what a shock it had been. "And it turns out he just wanted to use me. He wasn't just playing tables —he was running scams. Fake chips, past-posting. He figured that if we were married, he could control me. I wouldn't turn him in. He miscalculated that one."

Shane's throat worked. He looked away for a second, then back—like he needed the pause to keep from breaking something.

April wrapped her arms around herself as she told Shane about her last day in Vegas.

———

I DON'T KNOW *how much time I have.* April rushed around the house, looking at all the things she'd accumulated in the years since she'd left Lyons, deciding what would stay and what she'd take. She'd bought most of it over the past three years. Well, bought or had it bought for her in what she realized much too late amounted to bribery.

Jewelry is valuable and transports easily, but what about the coins? Will TSA confiscate them? She felt another wave of nausea, placed her hand over her belly, and darted to the bathroom, making it just in time. Wiping her mouth, she looked at herself in the mirror over the double sinks—pale, clammy skin, dark circles under her eyes, colorless lips, constant nausea, all of which she'd attributed to stress. She looked haunted, like a zombie.

Fitting, since I've been sleepwalking through my relationship. God, she'd been a fool. And now... She placed her hand over her belly for the thousandth time since taking the pregnancy test. *But now I know the truth. All of the truth.*

I have got to get out of here.

April splashed some cold water on her face and eyed multiple tubes of lipstick in fancy golden cylinders. She pulled out a basket from underneath the sinks and swept them into it along with the sable makeup brushes and bottles of perfume, wincing as the glass clinked, hoping she didn't just break anything. She could resell them online for good money if she had to.

I'm thinking like I did when I first got to Vegas. Gaging the value of everything and how I can squeeze out every last penny. She'd gotten soft the past few years, too comfortable. Vulnerable. Weak.

"I don't even know where I'm going," she told her reflection, realizing even as she said the words it was a straight-up lie. She was going to the one place she didn't ever want to see again.

"Home."

But saying the word didn't hurt like it had since she'd left Lyons. Instead, it coated her insides like warm honey.

Her mom was there, a woman who'd shown her nothing but love. Her little sister, who'd always looked up to her. Same with her cousin, who might as well have been her sister. And her Papa, the model of a loving, protective man. The opposite of the bastard she'd married.

"I'm going home," she whispered to her reflection. She cupped her belly. "We're going home."

Three hours later, she stood in the foyer with four large suitcases and a stack of boxes to be mailed. She shrugged her lucky Louis Vuitton bag higher onto her shoulder and scrolled through her contacts until she found the one she trusted the most and hit call.

Bunni answered on the first ring. "I saw the news."

April's stomach tightened. Word had gotten out quickly, which was no surprise. But, she was hoping her old friend would still be there for her.

"So, whatcha need from me, kid?"

April smiled with relief. Bunni understood. "I need a ride. I'm leaving town."

"Fucking finally," Bunni sighed. "But why not drive yourself?"

"The car is in his name, and it can be traced. He might even accuse me of stealing it."

"Ah, yeah, gotcha."

"I've got everything packed and ready. Could you come—"

"Uh-uh, no," Bunni interrupted her. "We're not doing it that way. I'm not coming direct to you. Too many eyes. Here's what you do." Bunni gave April instructions that made her sigh with relief. She wasn't thinking straight, so Bunni had her back.

An hour later, April relaxed in the back seat of Bunni's cab. She'd picked her up at the bus station after April had mailed her boxes at the post office, driven to the station, and parked her ex-fiancé's car on the street nearby. Then, she went inside and bought a one-way ticket to Los Angeles, using her credit card. She went back outside to the curb. When Bunni pulled up and parked, her eyes went straight to the white Louis Vuitton slung over April's shoulder. The rainbow LVs flashed in the sunlight, and her brows shot up.

"Still got your lucky bag," Bunni said as April slid into the back seat.

April smiled faintly and rested her hand on the smooth leather handle. "I don't know if you can still call it lucky, considering how everything turned out. But I love it as much as the day I bought it. My first splurge. And I never had to pawn it."

Bunni nodded as she pulled away from the curb and pointed the taxi at the airport. "What time's your flight?"

"I haven't bought the ticket yet. I'll buy one and pay in cash when I get there." She knew paying cash would probably flag her for an extra security screening, but that was a risk she'd have to take. Her April Meyer identity had held up, especially after she renewed 'her' driver's license and got a Nevada one. Once she got home, she'd slip back into her April Taylor identity. She was sure her mother had held onto her birth certificate.

"I'm glad you're getting out, but I'm gonna miss you, kid."

April felt her heart breaking. She'd never see Bunni again, since returning to Vegas would practically be a death wish. "I should tell you, my real name is—"

"Stop right there. What'd I tell you about Vegas?"

"Not to trust anyone." April laughed sadly. "I guess I never learn. But you're the only one I trust, Bunni. My name is April Taylor."

The cab pulled up to the curb at Departures. Bunni popped the trunk while April snagged an abandoned baggage cart for free—*my lucky purse must be working* she thought ironically. The women loaded the bags onto the cart then faced each other. April blinked back tears.

"Don't say it because you're gonna make me cry and I don't do tears." Bunni held up her hand. "Just be happy."

April lunged forward anyway and hugged her old friend. "I'll never forget you."

"Better not."

"I feel like I'm going home a failure, Bunni."

Bunni pulled back from their hug just enough to glance at the purse again. A slow grin tugged at her lips.

"Remember how you felt walking out of that store the day you bought this thing? Shoulders back, like you were the queen of the whole damn Strip?"

April's throat tightened. "Yeah."

"Hold on to that feeling all the way home. And for the rest of your life, kid."

———

"APRIL—" Shane's voice came out rough, guttural, bringing her back to the present. He reached for her but she held up her hand. If Shane touched her now she just might shatter, proving him right—that she was fragile after all.

"So, the day he got arrested, I packed my bags and ran. Same day I realized I was pregnant with a baby he never wanted." She suppressed another shiver, hearing Vince's threatening voice that morning when she'd excitedly told him her period was late. He'd told her to 'do something about it.' That was when she really knew she needed to leave.

"I came home. I told my family everything. They kept quiet and I went back to being April Taylor." She smiled softly. "Sort of a do-it-yourself witness protection program. I worked with the detectives, helped build the case, Vince went to prison, and they kept my true identity a secret. As far as I know, he still thinks I'm April Meyer."

She swallowed hard. "But I know him. He's very charismatic and he knows how to make deals. He always knew a guy who knew a guy who could get things done. When the drive-by happened, we all panicked. We thought it might be him, that he'd found me and was seeking revenge. That he'd sent some goons to shoot up Riversong." Her lips twisted bitterly. "I felt equal parts horrified for Rochelle and guilty relief when I knew it wasn't Vince."

Shane's hands flexed, his chest rising with a long, deep breath.

"So that's it," April said quietly. "That's what Kevin overheard."

Shane was quiet for a long moment, processing. "When is Vince supposed to get out?"

April gave Shane a tentative smile. This was where she could reassure him. "He's been out on parole just over a year. He got out right before the shooting, so you can understand why I was afraid. But, he hasn't shown up here in all this time. Really, with each day that passes, the less I think he's coming for me."

"Except for today, right?"

April closed her eyes. Busted. "Except for today."

"When you answered my call, you thought I was him."

She nodded. "I...did."

When she opened her eyes, she expected Shane to look angry. Instead, his eyes were full of sympathy.

"Baby," he whispered. "I don't know how you've carried this fear for so long without breaking."

"I have my family." She shrugged. "They're the best. They talk me down, as you know now. And I have—"

You.

"—a whole lotta friends who would protect us."

"Friends." Some of the light left Shane's eyes when he said the word.

April grabbed his hand. "Good friends."

He glanced away for a moment. "Let me help you with that worry." He pulled out his phone and typed quickly.

"What are you doing?"

"Sending Vince Romano's name to Kyle now. We'll keep an eye on him, make sure he's behaving himself."

"Shane, you don't have to—"

"Yeah, I do." He looked up from his phone, and the intensity in his eyes made her breath catch. "Kevin asked me to protect you. But even if he hadn't..." His voice dropped lower. "I'd do anything for you, April. Anything."

The words hung between them, heavy with old pain and new possibility.

"This is ridiculous," April said, but there was no real heat in it. "I'm probably just being paranoid. What would you even do—park yourself at a corner table all day?"

Shane's eyes lit with humor and something warmer. "Twist my arm."

Despite everything, April found herself smiling. "You're serious."

"Dead serious. Kyle can run background, track his movements, see what he's up to. If he's behaving himself and staying put, we'll know. If he starts heading this way, we'll know that, too." Shane leaned back slightly. "You don't have to look over your shoulder anymore, April. Let us do that for you."

April studied his face—the quiet confidence, the way he made it sound so simple and reasonable. Not like she was asking for the moon, just basic peace of mind. And after the day she'd had, how could she say no to that?

"Thank you."

"It's the least I can do." He grinned. "Now, about the bodyguard gig."

"Of course you don't have to."

"Mom?" Kevin's voice came from the crack in the door. April and Shane moved apart quickly.

"Hey, I thought you were up front watching Pete," April said, her voice pitched just a little too high.

"He has to go potty so I'm taking him out the back." April opened the door to see Pete wagging his tail beside Kevin, looking way happier than her son. "You need a body-guard and Shane said he would."

"I said I'd discuss it with your mom," Shane corrected.

"Please, Mom. I don't want you to get hurt."

April blew out a breath. "I'm not going to get hurt, honey."

Kevin switched his stare to Shane. "Then if Mom's not going to hire you, teach me how to be a bodyguard. Please." He was near tears.

Shit. If I tell him no, I'll find him hiding under the bed again. I'm not going to let my stubbornness get in the way of my kid's happiness.

She looked at Shane, whose expression told her he was out of his league. Funny to see such a tough guy look so helpless in the face of a third grader.

"For Kevin's sake," she said quietly. "A trial period?"

Shane nodded, though something in his expression suggested it was for his sake, too.

Kevin's grin could have powered half of Lyons. He dug into his pocket and pulled out a crumpled fifty-dollar bill and tried to give it to Shane.

"For your retainer," he said solemnly. "You can keep the whole thing."

Shane looked down at the money, then back at Kevin. With one smooth motion, he folded Kevin's palm and wrapped the boy's fingers around the bill.

"Pro bono, remember? But I appreciate the vote of confidence."

As Kevin beamed and launched into questions about bodyguard protocol, April felt something she hadn't experienced in years: the dangerous, terrifying sensation of inviting Shane back into her life.

Shane caught her eye over Kevin's head, and his small smile promised everything she was afraid to hope for.

Don't get used to this, she warned herself. *Remember how he ran out on you when you needed him the most.*

"Better take Pete outside before he starts doing the pee-pee dance," April warned.

"Okay, Mom." He threw himself at her and hugged her around the waist, almost knocking her over. "Thanks." Then he dashed out the door with Pete more than happy to run at his side.

Kevin came back a minute later and they all walked back into the main shop together. Kevin ran up to Sonny and launched into a complex negotiation that involved giving Pete the other half of his sandwich. It sounded like an elaborate international trade agreement.

"April." Shane's voice was soft beside her. "Whatever

happens next, you're not handling this alone. You won't ever have to run again. I promise."

Looking into his eyes, April tried to believe him.

EIGHT

SHANE DROVE BACK TO WATCHDOG WITH HIS HANDS steady on the wheel and his mind spinning like a slot machine.

That bastard.

The thoughts kept cycling through. He felt a wave of something that felt too much like jealousy and not enough like the detached protectiveness he wanted it to be. Oh hell —there was no way he could be detached when it came to April. Or Kevin. That little boy had found his way into Shane's heart years ago. But his jealousy surged—some other man had touched April, held her, made promises to her. Made her believe in love again after Shane had destroyed that for her the first time.

Then he'd tried to use her. He'd given her a son he wanted no part of. He'd hurt her deeply.

Shane's knuckles went white on the steering wheel. *Vincent Romano.* The name had burned itself into his brain, right next to a mental list of everything he wanted to do to the son of a bitch if he ever showed his face in Colorado.

Focus, Elk. She's safe. He's been on parole for a year and hasn't made a move.

Shane parked in front of the kennels and killed the engine. The building was quiet when he and Pete walked in. Jodie had already gone home for the day, but Kyle's office light was on. Shane headed straight for it.

"Boss?" Shane knocked on the doorframe.

"Come on in," Kyle said as he looked up from his computer. Camo, Kyle's half-gold, half-black Lab stood and wagged his tail. Flint was already there, sitting across from Kyle with his laptop. He worked in Watchdog's IT department officially. Unofficially, he could hack into almost anything. He'd been trained by a woman named Elissa who ran Watchdog HQ in Los Angeles and was a legend.

Shane nodded at Flint who gave him a chin lift before going back to his laptop. Shane settled into the other chair across from Kyle's desk, organizing his thoughts. This was about April's safety, not about Shane's tangled-up feelings. Pete laid himself down beside Camo. The two were old friends.

"So who is this Vincent Romano you want us to check out?" Kyle asked. "What's his connection to us?"

"He's April's ex-fiancé. Kevin's father."

Flint's typing stopped. He looked up with raised eyebrows that matched Kyle's.

"No shit?" Kyle asked.

"He's the reason Kevin played hooky and came here earlier." Shane rubbed the back of his neck. "He'd overheard April talking about going on the run if someone found her. Romano was arrested for casino fraud almost ten years ago. Fake chips, past-posting. April had been living under a fake identity in Vegas—she was using the name April Meyer. She left the day he was arrested. Same day she found out she was pregnant. She testified against him, and when the drive-by happened, the family thought he might have found her."

Flint was typing again, faster now. "So as far as he knows, his ex is April Meyer, not April Taylor?"

"Right. The question is whether he's been looking for April Meyer and coming up empty, or if he's figured out who she really is, then what are the chances he might come looking for her."

After several minutes, Flint's screen filled with data. "Here we go. Vincent Romano, age forty-two. Sentenced for fraud, oh, and wiring money across state lines. That got him a few extra years. Released from Nevada State Prison a year ago for good behavior, on parole for three years. He's been checking in regularly with his parole officer in Vegas. Last known employment..." Flint squinted. "Dishwasher at a restaurant just off the Strip. Lives in a better apartment than I'd expect." More typing, then, "No travel outside Nevada that I can see."

Shane felt some of the tension leave his shoulders. "So he's staying put."

"For now, looks like. But if this guy was smart enough to run a long-term casino fraud operation, he's smart enough to eventually connect April Meyer to April Taylor. Especially if he's motivated."

Kyle leaned forward. "Talking to April, what do you think the threat level is here, Shane? Do we need to move April and Kevin to a safe house?"

Shane shook his head. "No immediate danger. April's been worried about it, got spooked by the drive-by at River-song, but she's not in crisis mode. This is more about giving her peace of mind. And Kevin..." Shane couldn't help smiling. "Kid offered me fifty bucks to be his mom's bodyguard."

Kyle chuckled. "Smart kid." He turned his attention to Flint. "Keep monitoring Romano's parole status. We'll go on high alert if he misses a check-in, changes his address, or makes any moves toward Colorado. And run deeper background—who he was working with, who might have reason to help him find April."

"Done." Flint's fingers flew across the keyboard. "I'm setting up automated monitoring. I'll get alerts if anything changes."

"Thanks, Brother," Shane said.

Flint closed his laptop. "No need. If this were somebody after Harper, I'd feel the same." He stood up. "Speaking of, she's waiting for me in town. We're having dinner with one of her old colleagues from the lab. I think Harp's wanting to find her someone."

Kyle chuckled. "If it's who I think it is, she's got her work cut out for her."

Flint grinned. "You said it, not me. Sweet lady though, just quiet and more than a little nerdy." As Flint reached for the doorknob, Shane stood to leave as well.

"Hold up, Shane," Kyle said.

After Flint left, Kyle fixed Shane with a stare. "This is personal for you."

Shane met his boss's eyes with a steady gaze. "Yeah. But I'm not going to let that cloud my judgment."

"Good. Because if this Romano asshole decides to cause trouble, we'll handle it professionally. No vigilantes this time. You're representing my company."

Shane bristled but tried not to show it. "Understood."

"That said, April and Kevin—the whole Taylor clan—is family. So we'll do whatever it takes in the end."

His tension eased. "Understood, Brother."

Kyle nodded, then his expression shifted to amusement. "So, you're April's bodyguard now?"

"Kevin thinks so. April and I are...humoring him."

"Uh-huh." Kyle's grin was knowing. "And how exactly are you planning to humor him?"

"I was going to discuss it with you tomorrow morning, let you get home to Arden."

"She's got a late patient up to the ranch." Kyle's wife, Arden, ran a therapeutic program out of their ranch for kids with PTSD, autism, or ADHD, using therapy animals. "I've got time right now."

Shane sat back down. "I talked it over with April and I was thinking—with your permission—I could bring Kevin up here tomorrow. Teach him 'bodyguard skills' and show him how we train the dogs."

Kyle's smile widened as he warmed to his favorite subject—the canine training program at the heart of Watchdog Security. "Affirmative. Bring them here. Kevin can see how Watchdog operates, help Alex with the puppies. Kid will eat it up."

"Thanks." Shane took out his phone and brought up April's number. He texted:

> Tell Kevin it's all set up. Can you two come to Watchdog around 9 tomorrow?

April's response came almost immediately.

> He's already getting his 'gear' ready. See you then. Thank you, and thank Kyle for me!

"She says thank you and they'll be here at nine," Shane told Kyle.

"Perfect. And Shane?" Kyle's expression went serious

again. "If Romano starts moving, you know we've got April's back."

"I know, Brother."

Shane left Kyle's office feeling better than he had since Kevin walked into the lobby. Professional distance was exactly what this situation needed.

Now he just had to convince himself that the warmth spreading through his chest at the thought of seeing April again in the morning was purely professional, too.

———

AT QUARTER TO NINE, Shane was in the training yard with Alex and the puppies when he heard the distinctive sound of April's laugh coming from inside. His pulse kicked up a notch, which was ridiculous. This was about Kevin's training. Nothing more.

Kevin burst through the door like he'd been shot from a cannon, April following at a more reasonable pace. The kid was dressed in what looked like his interpretation of tactical gear—tan cargo pants, a black t-shirt, and a baseball cap turned backwards.

"Shane! I'm ready for training!" Kevin announced, then spotted the puppies and nearly vibrated out of his shoes. "Are those the puppies you were telling me about last night?"

"Easy there, soldier," Shane said with a grin. "Rule number one of being around working dogs—calm energy."

Kevin immediately tried to compose himself, standing straighter and lowering his voice. "Yes, sir. Can I help train them now?"

Shane watched April grin at her son, looking both surprised and proud. He caught April's eye and felt that same electric awareness they had in high school. She was wearing jeans and a green tee that brought out her eyes, her hair pulled back in a ponytail that made her look younger. Beautiful. *His.*

Not yours, jackass. Focus.

"You better believe you're gonna help. These pups need to socialize with different people, and we could use an extra pair of hands."

Alex looked up from where he was setting up individual elevated platforms for the puppies. "Absolutely. But first rule of dog training—the dogs have to respect you before they'll follow you."

Kevin's eyes widened. "I don't have to yell at them if they do something wrong, do I?"

"No way," Shane said. "Training puppies is all about getting them to love learning. We do that with praise and treats, like this." He squeezed the clicker in his hand and Elton gave him his full attention. "Good boy." Shane immediately gave him a treat. "See? That's how you gain trust."

Kevin nodded solemnly. "Like a leader."

"Exactly like a leader."

Shane watched as Alex showed Kevin how to approach the puppies, how to let them sniff his hand first, how to give a command, wait for a response, then work the clicker and reward a puppy for good behavior. The kid was a natural—patient and gentle, reading the dogs' body language instinctively.

Alex started with the most promising pup while the other puppies watched from their platforms. Well, at least two of them did. Benny hopped down from his platform the minute a swallowtail butterfly flitted overhead and started his chase.

"Hey, little guy, come back here!" Kevin chased after

Benny and swooped him up, laughing. He clutched the dog closer and let Benny cover his cheek with kisses. As he carried him back to the platform, he asked the puppy, "What's your name?" He set Benny down on his platform.

"That's Benny," Alex said with a sigh. "He's...easily distracted. I think he's going to wash out of the program."

Kevin looked shocked. "Wash out? What happens to him then?"

"He'll find a good home," Alex assured him. "Not every dog is cut out for protection or service work. Benny might be happier as someone's pet."

Kevin's face scrunched up with concern. He looked at Benny, who had abandoned the platform and was now rolling on his back in a patch of sunshine, completely oblivious to the training happening around him.

"Maybe he just learns different," Kevin said quietly. "Maybe he's not distracted. Maybe he's just...thinking about different stuff."

Shane felt something squeeze in his chest. The kid was defending the underdog. Of course he was.

"You might be right," Shane said. "Why don't you work with Benny while Alex runs the other pups through their exercises? See if you can get him to pay attention to you."

Kevin's face lit up. He settled cross-legged on the ground near Benny and started talking to him in a low, patient voice. Within minutes, the puppy was focused on Kevin like he was the most interesting thing in the world.

"I'll be damned," Alex muttered.

Shane glanced over at April, who was watching her son with a mixture of pride and something that looked like sadness.

"Kevin was right," he told Alex. "Benny just needs a different approach to keep his attention."

"He's really good at reading the dogs," Alex said.

"He's good at reading people, too."

"I can believe it."

Shane felt eyes on him. April had switched her attention from her son to the two men. She crossed her arms and gripped her elbows. She'd overheard them and her expression was unreadable. Shane nodded at Alex and moved to stand beside April.

"Kevin's good with the underdog," Shane told her quietly.

"Always has been." April's voice was soft. "He helped out Laurie Andrews when she was going through that horrible trial."

Shane and his brothers had protected the sweet little girl as she'd testified against her abuser. "Yeah, I remember. Laurie told us that she'd lost some friends in her class, but Kevin started sitting next to her at lunch and played with her on the playground."

"Well, at least when he wasn't in recess detention." April rolled her eyes. "They're still good friends."

"I'm not at all surprised he'd do that for her."

April nodded, her hands squeezing her elbows. "He knows what it feels like to be different. To not fit the mold."

Shane gave a small nod, eyes still on Kevin and the pup. "And instead of lashing out, he sympathizes and helps."

"Eh, sometimes he lashes out. He's a kid after all." April shifted her weight.

"Well, I've seen him help more than harm. Kid didn't get that kind of heart by accident."

April's cheeks pinkened up. "I hope you're right," she said under her breath. Then she couldn't help herself. "Diane still asks about you sometimes."

"Asks about me?"

"Yeah. If...you're single."

Shane stiffened. "Answer's still the same, April. Her daughter's a sweet girl, Diane's a nice lady, and I have zero romantic interest in her."

They stood together watching Kevin coax Benny through a simple sit-and-stay exercise. The puppy was actually listening, his tail wagging but his attention firmly on the boy.

"Shane?" April turned to face him, and he caught a whiff of her perfume—something light and clean that made him want to step closer. "Thank you. For this. For...everything. I know Kevin hiring you as a bodyguard is probably the most ridiculous thing you've ever heard, but—"

"It's not ridiculous at all." Shane's voice came out rougher than he intended. "Not if it makes him feel safer. Not if it makes *you* feel safer."

The pink in April's cheeks darkened. "So, did you know bodyguards eat and drink free at Riversong?"

"Do they?" Shane's eyebrow rose as he grinned.

"Yeah, new policy starting at lunchtime today."

"Is that an invitation?"

"Mom! Shane! I got Benny to sit on command! Watch!" Kevin waved at them and they turned their attention back to the boy. He gave the command and for once, Benny actually listened *and* obeyed.

"Great job, sweetie!" April clapped and started toward her son. Shane couldn't help but admire the way her hips swayed. Just before she reached Kevin, April looked over her shoulder. With an almost carefree smile, she asked, "How does noon sound?"

"Perfect," Shane answered. He brushed April's shoulder before heading back to Alex.

Absolutely perfect.

NINE

As she watched Kevin work with Benny, April let out a breath she hadn't realized she was holding. Kevin had taught Benny to sit and to heel and the dog never once got distracted. He led Benny back to the other puppies and got him to stay on his platform for a record amount of time. Both Alex and Shane praised him like he was the newest dog trainer at Watchdog.

Her son—her daydreaming, wild-hearted boy—stood beside Shane like he belonged there. His whole body leaned forward, trying to will that silly puppy into greatness.

"Yeah, I think Benny might just avoid washing out after all," Alex said. "What do you think, Shane?"

"This is the first day he's shown real promise," Shane concurred. "I say we keep him on, give him another chance. You were absolutely right about Benny, Kevin."

Kevin looked at Shane with a huge smile on his face and his eyes full of pride.

April felt that pride, sharp and hot behind her breastbone.

Shane and Alex weren't just giving Benny another

chance. They had agreed with Kevin. Shown him respect. Men who wore competence like a second skin. Men who were respected themselves, who walked into a room like they owned it.

Shane had just told her son he was right. Not that he was some cocky little upstart who 'could use a little humility,' as that jackass Principal Pirogue once said. Shane thought he was a boy who could read a person like musicians could read sheet music. A boy who could tell when someone felt scared, or small, or was pretending to be big. Who could sniff out injustice and bullshit the way military dogs sniffed out bombs.

And sometimes, yeah—Kevin spoke up. Called it what it was.

Which made him a 'problem.'

Not at home. Never at home.

At school. At church. With people who only knew the stories about the Taylors and didn't much care to rewrite them.

Her hands tightened around her elbows.

Kevin wasn't missing anything because he didn't have a father. He wasn't broken or unmoored. He had other male role models to teach him about honor and loyalty or whatever else the people who judged Kevin all assumed a woman couldn't provide.

He had Sonny. Her dad had been there since the day she came home, shaken but stubborn as hell. Her mom, Hannah, Brianna—they'd all wrapped Kevin in love so thick, he glowed with it.

But still.

Still, something about the way Kevin looked at Shane now made April's throat go tight. He'd found a new pillar, strong and steady, someone who saw the same spark April did. Someone who didn't flinch when Kevin asked hard questions or called out unfairness in that small but clear voice of his.

Shane didn't shrink from that intensity. He matched it. Respected it. For the first time in a long time, someone outside her family saw her boy and didn't either yell or just smile and say, "He's a handful."

Shane said *He's right.*

And that scares me more than anything.

Because if she let herself believe Kevin needed someone else to respect him that much? Then she might have to admit that she still did, too.

"Let's break for lunch," Alex said as he glanced at his watch.

Shane raised his eyebrows at April—*Are we still on?* She nodded before realizing they'd reverted to the silent communication they'd used in high school. One look, and she knew exactly what he was thinking.

"Come on, Kevin. We need to get back to Riversong."

"Aw! Benny was just warming up. Can I come back later?"

"We'll see." April caught Alex's eye.

"I'm holding a class for the Boulder police K9 squad this afternoon, but you're welcome back if Shane's got nothing else going on."

"Fine with me," Shane said.

"Alex, would you like to come to lunch with us?" April asked. "It's on the house."

Alex grinned. "Next time. I gotta prep for class. But thanks."

Kevin tugged on April's hem. "Can Shane...Mr. Foti come with us?"

"Already in the plan, kid," she told him.

"Yes!" He clenched his fist and pumped the air. "Shane! I'll help you kennel the puppies then we're going to lunch. It's on me."

Even as she felt a tinge of worry—one she refused to think about straight on—April cracked up. Shane just winked at her.

"In that case, I'll have both a sandwich and a black-and-white cookie," Shane said. As they led the pups into the kennel, Shane rested his hand on Kevin's shoulder. April was struck once again by how natural it looked.

———

WHEN THEY GOT TO RIVERSONG, Rochelle was in her usual window seat. Open laptop plastered with stickers from her favorite romance authors, reading glasses perched low as she tapped at the keys. Another translation job, no doubt. April knew Rochelle's rhythm when she was deep into her work—rapid typing, scattered notebooks covered in notes, second or third coffee cooling untouched beside her elbow. She didn't look up right away when they came in, even when Kevin dashed from the door to his grandma and aunt Hannah, who had come in once they got home from their trip.

It wasn't that April was trying to hide the fact she was about to have lunch with Shane. If she'd wanted to do that, Riversong would've been the last place she'd bring him. But, she hoped Rochelle wouldn't make a big deal about it. Honestly, other than Ellie, Rochelle was the least likely among their friends to make a fuss. Thank God Wren wasn't in today. April adored her, but she had a flair for the dramatic. Though Wren came nowhere near Stephanie's league. April tried not to cringe, thinking about what

Stephanie might say or do. She swore her matchmaking days were over after Frankie and Waylon, but no one believed her.

April greeted her sister and her mom with hugs. She couldn't help but notice the shop was quieter than normal and wondered how many customers had turned and walked out because the espresso machine was on the fritz. She wasn't about to ask, not in front of Shane.

April went around the counter to grab their sandwiches from the cooler. She asked Shane what he wanted.

"That roast beef on rye looks good, thanks." He reached for his wallet as he stood in front of the cash register.

"Shane's lunch is on the house today," April quietly told her mom. She gave April a side-eye, then smiled at Shane.

"She's the boss. Your money's no good here today," she told him.

April watched Shane's expression turn uneasy. Money was never an easy topic for him, especially when it came to her family, not after what his father pulled. But he had no reason to feel ashamed, at least not in April's eyes—not if what she suspected he'd done for her family through the years was true. She actually felt a little bad for him at that moment.

Shane shifted to the side and that's when April saw that Rochelle had come to the counter. She was looking right at her.

Shit.

April flushed as she smiled and waved at her friend. Rochelle smiled and waved back, her smile quiet but knowing.

Great. I hope she didn't overhear me buying Shane's lunch.

"Hey," Shane said, surprised as he turned and spotted Rochelle. "Didn't see you there."

"Hi, Shane. Don't let me interrupt your lunch." Her eyes flicked to Shane, then back to April, mischief softening into warmth.

Busted.

"I just wanted to tell you, April," she said, tucking her pen behind her ear, "Ellie wants to have us all up this weekend to see Star. Can you make it?"

April hesitated. She could already picture it: Ellie, Wren, Frankie, Arden, Stephanie, Gina—all of them gathered close, drinking wine, swapping stories, and watching April out of the corners of their eyes, waiting to see what she'd say about Shane.

She wanted to hide, to keep pretending that he meant nothing to her. And at the same time, she wanted just one day in her life where she wasn't hiding anything, especially from the women who had become her friends over the past couple of years. Still, April hesitated.

"Go ahead, honey," April's mom, Miriam said. "You and your father held down the fort while Hannah and I had our little getaway." She turned to her husband. "That goes for you, too. Take a day off, my love." That was met with a wave-off, and she rolled her eyes.

"Yeah, okay," April heard herself say. Her voice came out lighter than she felt. "Of course I'll be there. I haven't met Star yet. Too busy here."

Rochelle's smile widened, gentle and satisfied. "Great! I'll let Ellie know. She'll be so happy to see you." She gave Shane a smile and nod, but before she drifted back to her perch in the window, she added, "Oh, I almost forgot! Bear's mom is going to be there."

April almost dropped the bottle of soda she'd just

grabbed. When she was in town, Ellie's mother-in-law ran in the same social circles as Shane's mother. They attended the same galas, fundraisers, and New Year's Eve balls.

"That should be interesting," Rochelle went on, not noticing April's discomfort.

"Yeah, should be." She gave Rochelle a strained smile, but her friend had already turned away.

April plated up the food and Shane picked up his and Kevin's plates before she could protest. Heart thudding, she took her seat beside Shane. She took a tiny bite of her sandwich, suddenly too aware of how close Shane's knee was to hers beneath the table.

"If you want," Shane started, "Kevin can come back up to Watchdog tomorrow for more training while you're visiting Ellie. That way, your dad can have a day off and your mom and Hannah can focus on working."

Kevin's eyes lit like twin fireworks. "Mom, can I?"

I could say no to Shane, she reminded herself. She could build walls, keep distance, protect herself like she had all these years.

But sitting here, with Kevin glowing and looking so hopeful, Rochelle watching, and Shane's calm, steady presence across the table, April knew she had no choice.

"That's...very generous of you."

Shane cocked an eyebrow. "That doesn't sound quite like a yes."

"*Please*, Mom. I *promise* I'll be good." Kevin sat up as straight as he could in his chair. "Benny needs me."

It didn't escape April that Kevin's focus had shifted from protecting her to watching over the scrappy little puppy. *That could only be a good thing, right?*

"All right, if you pinkie swear you'll listen to Shane and Alex and Kyle and anyone else who's training dogs."

Kevin's hand was up, pinkie extended before she could finish. April hooked her little finger around his and they swore on it.

"Shane, I have another idea how to help Benny." Kevin launched into yet another elaborate scheme to get the puppy to learn new tricks.

April barely touched her food. She let herself just... watch. Kevin was still buzzing from the morning at Watchdog, words tumbling over themselves as he explained his ideas. Every time she looked at Shane—his easy smile as Kevin spoke, the steadiness in his eyes—her chest tightened.

Her heart ached with pride as she remembered the morning. Kevin had lit up in a way she hadn't seen in months, maybe since the drive-by. He'd stood taller, shoulders squared, voice steady as he'd worked with Benny. He'd been bold and bright and brilliant, and Shane had been right there, listening like everything Kevin said mattered.

But her pride in her boy had teeth that threatened to sink into her heart. Kevin was eating up all the attention. He was puffing himself up at the table, recounting one more time how he was the only one to get through to Benny. *Him.* His grin was turning smug, his voice too self-assured, and for a heartbeat April's stomach twisted.

She caught the echo of Kevin's arrogant father, and it made her skin prickle.

He's acting a little too much like Vince.

Except Kevin's joy was sweet, pure, nothing egotistical or selfish in it.

Right?

"Kev, sweetie, don't brag," she said gently. "Benny listened to you because you were kind to him. That's the important part."

Kevin shrugged, unfazed, and reached for another potato chip beside his sandwich.

Shane gave her a small smile across the table, one that said he understood, maybe more than she wanted him to. And that was the problem, wasn't it? A part of her wanted to let Shane into their lives, especially after yesterday and today.

He left me.

Abandoned her at the bus station with all her hopes and dreams packed in a thrift-store suitcase. The rational part of her knew he'd grown, changed, that he'd matured into a responsible man. Knew she was older now too, wiser, strong enough to walk away if she had to. But the voice in her head whispered cruelly.

You're doing it again, April. Falling for the bad boy who'll break you.

She took a sip of her soda, as if that could wash the thought away.

It wasn't only about April's heart anymore. If Shane ever walked away from Kevin, she didn't think she could ever forgive him.

Or myself, for letting Shane into our lives and breaking my son's heart, too.

———

THE NEXT DAY, Saturday, sunlight spilled like honey across the hills, warming the road that climbed toward Watchdog Security. It was the kind of May morning that made Colorado feel like heaven—blue sky stretching forever, wildflowers just peeking over tufts of new grass.

Kevin had been practically vibrating on the way up to Watchdog that morning—baseball cap slightly askew, lunch packed like he was heading off to boot camp. She loved the change in him—excited, carefree. And best of all, fearless. He'd dropped right off to sleep the night before, tuckered out from his day. She'd been checking on him in the middle of the night ever since she discovered he was afraid for her. He'd been restless, but last night when she peeked in, he was smiling in his sleep.

"Benny's gonna be the best dog ever, Mom!"

April grinned at him in the rearview mirror. "I'm sure he will."

"You want him to be, right?"

"Of course."

"I have a proposal."

"Uh-oh." She tried to hide her smile and failed miserably. She knew what was coming.

"All the other dogs in service training live with families so they can acc...accli...."

"Acclimate?"

Kevin beamed. "Yeah, that's the word Shane used. Acclimate to being around people all the time. Right now, Alex, I mean, Mr. Hoff, is caring for all the Jets. That's what the litter is called. Each litter has a name to keep track of them."

April laughed softly. "I get it. Benny and the Jets."

The musical reference flew right over her son's head and he was too invested in his proposal to ask about it. "Mr. Hoff and his wife already have trained dogs at home, but no kids. And service dogs need to get used to kids, just in case they get assigned to one."

"Mmm-hmm." Yup, she knew *exactly* where this was going.

Kevin's shoulders sagged for a moment—he knew that tone and it didn't bode well. So he spoke faster, as if rushing the words out would help his case. "So, for Benny to be the best service dog ever, he needs to be around a kid."

"I see."

"And just think how great it would be if he was around a kid he trusted, who understands him."

"That would be something." April turned onto the stretch of road that snaked up a hill to the Watchdog guard house and front gate, still marveling at how her son had managed to bypass all the cameras.

"And Alex...Mr. Hoff, said it would be alright with him if it was okay with you."

"What would be?"

"*Mom*." Kevin frowned. "You know what I'm getting at."

This time, April laughed. "Yes, I do. You want us to foster Benny."

"Mr. Hoff said it wouldn't be full-time, just a couple days here and there. So, can we?"

"That depends. What is this proposal?" She slowed down as she approached the gate. The guard saw her coming and slid his window open.

"I'll take full responsibility for Benny. I'll feed him, and take him for walks, and train him, and he can sleep in my bed. I'll even pay for his dog food. I'm good for it since Shane's working pro bono."

April stopped at the window and showed the guard her pass. He wished her a good morning and opened the gate. "You're forgetting the biggest responsibility."

"Right. I'll give him tummy rubs and make sure he knows he's loved."

Oh my God. That went straight to her heart. How could she ever think Kevin was anything like Vince?

"Okay, that *is* the most important thing. But I was thinking of something not so...fun."

"Oh, you mean the poop? I'll scoop it all up, I promise."

"Pinkie promise?" She watched Kevin's entire face light up in the mirror.

"Does that mean yes?"

"Only if it's totally all right with Mr. Hoff."

"Yes!" Kevin stretched his arm toward the front seat, pinkie extended.

April could see the kennel parking lot up ahead—and Shane casually leaning against a pillar waiting for them outside. Cargo pants, t-shirt stretched tightly over his sculpted chest and muscled arms, mirrored sunglasses, and that old familiar sexy-cocky smile from high school.

April let Kevin's arm hang in the air. "One more thing though. And it's another biggie."

"What?" Kevin huffed.

Shane took off his shades and April met his gaze evenly as she tried not to let her tummy fill with warmth. "Just remember, he won't stay with us forever. When the time comes, you need to be ready to let him go."

Kevin's hand didn't waver. "I know, Mom. I'll be ready."

April parked the car as Shane pushed off from the pillar to meet them. She half-turned and stuck out her pinkie to hook Kevin's when he pulled his hand away.

"What?"

"I just thought. Benny's easy to love. You've gotta be ready to let him go, too."

April smiled softly. "Don't worry about me. I have plenty more experience letting go than you do." Her smile brightened. "And besides, we'll still have each other, right?"

"Right. Thanks, Mom."

They hooked pinkies.

Shane opened her door.

"Good morning," Shane said in the sexiest, early-morning gravelly growl as he extended his hand for her to take. She hesitated.

Come on. I can handle this.

April gripped his hand, trying to resist the shiver his touch sent down her arm. There was something about his firm, sure grip that drove her wild. She stepped out of the car, uncomfortably close to him. She wished he'd kept those sunglasses on because the look in his eyes was positively sinful.

In the meantime, Kevin had unfastened himself from his booster seat in the back and climbed out. "Shane! I'm going to ask Alex about keeping Benny."

The look in Shane's eye disappeared like it had never been there as he turned his head. "Keep or foster? Remember, there's a difference."

"I know. He's gonna have a big, important job to do one day. Mom and I already talked about being ready to let him go."

Shane glanced at her, making her cheeks redden. "And you're fine with it?"

"I am. No choice, really."

He cleared his throat as he gestured for them to go inside. Kevin ran ahead.

"I can bring Kevin back to your place after the party, no problem," he said casually, like he wasn't offering to walk straight into the most private corner of her life. "Save you some driving time."

No problem. Right. Except for the part where letting Shane Foti onto her property felt like handing over the last unguarded piece of herself.

But when he looked at her like that—like the fate of the

world hung on her answer—she'd never been able to say no. Ironically, Kevin had the same expression—the one he saved for when he *really* wanted something.

Like a bodyguard for his mother.

"Sure, why not?" She gave Shane a tight-lipped smile and started toward the kennel entrance.

"Or, I could drive him up to their cabin and we could do a handoff."

No way!

"No, it's fine. My house is fine."

Shane caught up with her. "I get the sense it isn't."

She kept walking.

He brushed her arm. "April, hang on."

"Kevin's inside. I'm sure he's getting into trouble already."

"Jodie's in today. They're probably already working on a puzzle." He moved in front of April, blocking her way. "Tell me what's wrong," he demanded, concern filling his eyes.

"What's wrong?" She shook her head. How could she even begin to explain?

April's little house sat along the St. Vrain, built before automobiles and still stubbornly standing through every flood and winter the mountains could throw at it. The white paint was fading to cream, and one corner of the deck still bore the scar of the pine that had fallen during the last big storm. You could roll a marble down the hallway where the floor had settled unevenly over the years—it creaked and groaned during every storm—and she absolutely adored it.

She'd bought it during a market crash for a price that made her father shake his head in admiration, and now it was worth four times that. Sonny still called it her fortress and refused to let her refinance a single board to pay for anything at Riversong. *You earned this one outright, kid. Don't tie it to the business.*

She loved him for that, even as it broke her heart.

And now Shane would see her house if she said yes.

"Shane, the first time I ever drove up to your parents' place, do you know what I thought? I thought I'd made a wrong turn and ended up at a ski resort."

"April—"

"Your mother bragged to me about how your seaside cottage was twice as big as 'this little log cabin out in the woods.' Like it was something Abraham Lincoln grew up in."

"That's impossible. Lincoln grew up in Illinois."

"Shane!" April put her hands on her hips. "Now is not the time to tease me." She frowned at the curve of his lips and the dimples she knew would pop out if she gave it a second.

"Babe, I fail to see what my mother's stuck-up, overblown bragging from years ago has to do with me dropping Kevin off at your place."

She sighed. "I don't live in a 'little' log cabin in the woods. I can only imagine what my house would look like through your eyes."

Shane shrugged. "You think the size of your house matters to me at all? I can guarantee it's beautiful because it's full of love. That makes a shack outshine a castle." He looked away.

"Shane, I'm sorry, I didn't mean to bring anything unpleasant up." April shook her head. "You're trying to do something nice for me, and I'm acting ungrateful."

He looked at her. "You're not, I promise. Your whole family has suffered thanks to mine." He started forward and this time, April grabbed his arm.

"So did you. I remember. You aren't anything like them. You turned into a better man than they could have hoped for. Better than they deserve."

Shane's expression softened. "Thanks. Just so you know, you put every woman in this town to shame." He winked at her and just like that, he was back to being the sexy-cocky boy she remembered.

But all grown up, filling out his shirt like a dream.

She grinned and shook her head. "Whatever. Fine, yes, please, come over tonight after the party."

"That's what I wanted to hear." He held her gaze just a beat too long. "Go home, take some time for yourself, get ready for the party. Have fun and relax for once." He jutted his chin toward the entrance. "I've got him."

TEN

APRIL ROLLED DOWN HER WINDOW, LETTING THE AIR whip through her hair, and tried to breathe past the knot in her chest as she braced herself for the visit.

Stop worrying. Rochelle probably didn't say a word.

Probably.

Even if she didn't, there was Claudia to think about.

Stop it. This isn't about you. It's about seeing an adorable new baby.

April turned onto the last stretch of newly paved road leading up to Bear and Ellie's cabin. Light-green aspen leaves trembled like butterfly wings against the backdrop of darker evergreens, as April pulled onto the wide parking apron and parked beside Wren's new Subaru. She counted cars. It looked like she was the last to arrive. That was her fault. After she dropped off Kevin, she quickly shopped for a gift, then stopped by Riversong one more time just to check in. Hannah and her mom practically picked up brooms to shoo April back out of the shop. At least her dad had gotten the espresso machine to work again, though it was making some truly concerning sounds.

April patted her lucky purse on the seat beside her. It mostly lived in a dust bag in her closet now, but at times like these, she took it down off its high shelf and carried it like a talisman. If Claudia was at the party, she could get a good look at it, see that it was real.

April slung the bag over her shoulder, grabbed Ellie's gift and a pie and started down the short path through the aspen grove, once she cleared it, the view hit her like it always did: a sweep of lake against the backdrop of a cliff covered in pines, the water catching sunlight in broken diamonds. Just ahead of her, the cabin's porch railing was wrapped with string lights, and she could just make out the sound of laughter drifting through the open windows.

The girl squad was already having a blast.

April smoothed her hair, and tried not to think about Shane. Or the fact that, right this minute, he and Kevin were probably knee-deep in puppies and dog slobber, both looking way too happy.

You're allowed to have a day off, she reminded herself as she clutched the gift she'd brought for Ellie. *A few hours where you're just April Taylor, friend, unofficial auntie, human—not mom on red alert.*

The screen door banged open before she even hit the steps. "Come on in." Wren beckoned her. She took the pie and gave April a one-armed hug.

"Sorry, I'm running late."

"This makes up for it." Wren lifted the pie, then turned and started for the kitchen island, already loaded with dessert, snacks, and bottles of wine and lemonade. "April's here!" She called out needlessly. The cabin's front room was full of women. Ellie sat on the couch, holding a swaddled bundle. A Bluetooth speaker tucked near the fireplace played soft music in the background—mostly mellow folk and acoustic ballads. April waved at the room, noting that the only older woman there was Stephanie—no sign of Claudia. Maybe she wasn't coming after all. April set her gift beside a pile of others at Ellie's feet.

"I'm so glad you could make it," Ellie said. "Sorry I'm not standing to greet you."

"Totally understandable. Now, let me see the guest of honor." April knelt so she could peek into the blankets. The tiniest face—sleepy, milk-drunk, perfect—blinked up at her.

"Star," April whispered. "She's beautiful."

"She knows," Ellie said. "Bear can't stop telling her."

Laughter echoed through the cabin, warm and familiar, and April felt something in her chest loosen for the first time all week. Wren appeared at her side with a glass of wine. April accepted it gratefully and took an empty chair. She expected Wren to sit in the empty spot beside Ellie, but she grabbed another chair. Movement caught April's eye in the hallway beside the kitchen. A well-dressed woman who looked like she was in her early sixties crossed the room and sat beside Ellie.

Claudia Behr.

April took a swig of wine as her pulse kicked up. Claudia looked radiant—glowing with the quiet pride of a grandmother—as she leaned in to coo at the baby.

"What did I miss?" she asked.

"My friend April Taylor just got here," Ellie told her. Claudia's eyebrows rose slightly as she looked around and found April. "Nice to meet you, April," she said, blatantly studying her.

"Same, Ms. Behr. Congratulations." April was proud that her voice didn't tremble under the other woman's scrutiny. She imagined Claudia was evaluating her clothing, imagining what she'd tell Yvonne Foti at the next charity fundraiser.

April turned to Frankie, who sat in a recliner nearby—barefoot, radiant, and beaming. Her dark curls framed her face like sunlight caught in motion. She looked healthy and alive, one hand absently smoothing the soft curve of her belly.

"So, how soon do we throw a baby shower for you?" April asked.

Frankie grinned, eyes sparkling. "Oh, I can wait a while. I finally have my appetite back. I could eat half the food on that table." She laughed, light and unselfconscious. "Second trimester is heaven. I feel like myself again—just with a built-in bowling ball." She patted her bump affectionately.

"You're glowing," Wren said. "Seriously. Whatever you're doing, keep doing it."

Frankie wiggled her toes with mock drama. "Thanks, but I'm just waiting for these feet to swell like my mom's did. I'll have to borrow Waylon's boots. The minute I have this baby, I'm getting back into shape and we're going on an adventure—me, him, and the kiddo."

Claudia leaned forward, visibly intrigued. "Where will you go first?"

Frankie's face lit up. "I've got a list. There's this beautiful WWOOF farm in Greece—lemon grove, olive orchard, sheep wandering between the trees. They take whole families. I want our baby's first passport to smell like sunshine and wild mountain thyme."

Claudia smiled, genuinely charmed. "Greece is one of our favorite places. Glenn and I spent a month on Naxos years ago. You'll love the light there—it's unlike anywhere else on earth."

"That sounds perfect," Frankie said, clearly delighted. "Maybe I'll message you before we go, get some travel tips."

"Please do," Claudia replied warmly. "And if you ever need a contact for local farms, I know a few families."

"Wow, thanks!"

"My pleasure."

April caught Ellie's grin; clearly, Frankie was winning over the most formidable mothers-in-law of their circle.

"Are you having a boy or a girl?" April asked.

"Yes," Frankie said, eyes glinting with humor at their confusion. "I told the doctor not to tell me. I don't really care, so long as they're healthy. Waylon's dying to know, but that's his problem," she laughed. "Honestly, he doesn't care either way—just wants everything to go smoothly."

The room quieted for a beat, affection softening the air. Everyone knew what she'd survived to get here. Frankie's doctors were monitoring her pregnancy closely, but so far, so good.

"I bet you can't wait to travel," Wren said.

"I can't," Frankie admitted. "But for the first time in years, I also don't need to. It's nice knowing I have a home that'll always be here." She looked around the cabin, taking in the women who'd become her family. "I'm going to miss the hell out of all of you, though. That's the only drawback."

Star chose that moment to fuss. "I think that means she's going to miss her Aunt Frank," Ellie said as she rocked her gently. "Or, she might be hungry. Or...anything. I'm still learning. I can't believe they let me leave the hospital with her." Ellie looked lovingly down at Star. "I have no idea what I'm doing."

Claudia touched her daughter-in-law's arm. "I didn't either, when I came home with her father," she said, gently stroking Star's cheek. The baby stirred, smacked her lips, and fell back asleep. "I wish I hadn't been so nervous, that I'd enjoyed those first months more, because everything turned out fine." She smiled at Ellie. "Thank you for letting me be here now, so that I can have a second chance at enjoying this." She covered her heart. "I promise that I will do everything I can to help you, so you can enjoy your time with Star. You're such a wonderful mother."

Ellie sniffled. "Thank you," she managed.

April glanced around to see there wasn't a dry eye in the room—including hers. She remembered the early days of her new life with baby Kevin, how scared she was, even with all the help from her mom. She was glad that Ellie had Claudia.

As the conversation faded into a lull, the opening chords of Fleetwood Mac's "Landslide" drifted through the room. Frankie's eyes misted immediately. "Oh no," she murmured, laughing a little. "This one always gets me." She was met with gentle laughter and head nods, and as if on cue, every woman in the room started singing along with Stevie Nicks about fearing change, time bringing boldness, and children getting older.

The song finished. Stephanie shifted in her seat, crossing one ankle over the other with the grace of someone who still taught yoga to twenty-somethings and made them sweat. She tilted her head and smiled. "I met her once. Stevie Nicks. I was hiking around Red Rocks after leading Yoga on the Rocks that morning. Two-thousand people stretched out on yoga mats on the bleachers. Quite a sight. Anyway, I was coming around a boulder and there she was, sitting on a rock, eyes closed, communing with nature. I stopped in my tracks and she opened her eyes and looked straight at me. I apologized for bothering her, and she thanked me for the yoga class earlier. She got a kick out of us having the same name."

"She has a lot of relatives in Colorado," Claudia said. "She comes back every couple of years and visits the Rocks."

Stephanie nodded. "You know," Stephanie said, swirling her wine, "when that song first came out, I thought it was about getting old. About time slipping away."

April leaned back in her chair. Everyone watched Stephanie with open affection.

Stephanie went on, her voice strong and sure. "But the older I got, the more I realized it's about standing in the center of your life as everything seems to fall apart and surviving the landslides happening all around you—and maybe letting them change you without breaking you."

She unfolded her legs and stood, slowly, still graceful. "I remember thinking as a girl that the teenagers next door were so old. Then I was a teenager, and I was surprised at how young and awkward I felt, like a baby deer on roller skates."

Laughter rippled from a few of the women nearby.

"In my twenties, I thought my parents were ancient. Responsible. Wise. Then I hit their age and realized I still didn't know what the hell I was doing. I still didn't feel old. Now I'm older than my granny when she passed and I feel younger than I thought I would when I got to my seventies, despite the aches and pains." Stephanie tapped her forehead. "Up here? Still young." She pressed a hand to her chest. "And in here? Still wide open." Stephanie smiled, mischievous. "Still wild enough at seventy-six to spontaneously kiss my doctor and talk him into being my boyfriend."

April snorted into her wine.

"The truth is, 'old' just keeps moving the goalposts. It stays ahead of you—if you're lucky. I hope I never catch up to it."

"I don't think you ever will," Ellie said softly.

"Damn right I won't." Stephanie walked toward the kitchen island. "I'm hitting the desserts. All this wisdom burns calories."

Laughter broke the quiet spell, but the feeling lingered in April—a kind of tender awe that made her feel seen. How many times had her world crashed down around her? She stood up and turned for the door.

"Are you leaving?" Ellie asked, looking concerned.

"No, I just need some air for a minute."

"Good," Wren said as she sliced the pie April brought. "Because we haven't grilled you yet on your date with Shane."

April's head turned so fast she was surprised her neck didn't break. Before she could speak, Rochelle jumped in.

"I never said April was on a date, just that she ate lunch with Shane at Riversong."

Wren put her hand on her hip. "Exactly. A date."

Nope, nope, nope. As Rochelle said," April turned her stare on Rochelle, whose cheeks pinkened up, "it was not a date. I was just thanking him for—"

Do not tell them your son thinks your life is in danger. Not right now.

"—showing Kevin the new puppies at Watchdog. You know how Kevin is with Pete and the other dogs."

"And how he is with Shane," Wren just couldn't help but add. "It's so sweet."

April loved Wren to death, but right now, all she wanted to do was strangle her friend. It wasn't Wren's fault though. Wren didn't grow up in Colorado; she didn't know all the history. Rochelle didn't, either. They meant well, but with Claudia here, their timing couldn't have been worse.

"Save me a piece of pie," April said as she grabbed the doorknob and escaped outside. She set her wine down and gripped the railing around the porch like the house was about to take off into the air and took deep breaths. She was sorely tempted to do an Irish goodbye and sneak off to her car, but she'd left her purse inside.

The mountain air had cooled down from the afternoon, soft and pine scented. She leaned on the porch railing until she got her breathing under control. She sipped her wine slowly, watching bees hover around bright flowers in Ellie's garden. Her nerves had mostly settled—until the screen door creaked open behind her.

Claudia stepped out and joined her at the rail with a quiet sigh. "Beautiful out here," she said.

"Hard to beat," April replied, careful to keep her tone neutral.

For a moment, they stood in silence. Claudia's manicured nails clicked lightly against her wine glass. "I'm glad I had the chance to meet the woman who has Yvonne Foti so upset."

April nearly dropped her glass. "I..." An apology was on the tip of her tongue, even though Yvonne didn't deserve one.

Claudia glanced over, lips twitching. "Everyone assumes we're great friends because she confides in me. We're not. Yvonne just likes to hear her own voice and I'm a good listener."

April straightened. "I—wow. That's—" She cleared her throat.

Claudia gave a soft, dry laugh. "Surprising?" Claudia turned toward her then, glass cradled lightly in her hands.

"Let me be very clear. I've never liked the Fotis. They are the sort of people who say 'bless your heart' while they poison your tea."

April snorted. "You've got that right."

Claudia gave her a quick grin before continuing. "Yvonne wasn't always that way, but she married a man who enjoys power a little too much. And Yvonne echoes him sometimes." She shook her head. "Cruelty in pearls is still cruelty."

April's mouth had gone dry. "So Yvonne's upset at me because..."

"Because Shane won't talk to Daniel. Shane's been trying to convince her to leave," Claudia said quietly. "Has been for a while. He doesn't bring up his father directly—not anymore—but he makes it clear that he won't come home, won't even set foot in the same room until she walks away from that man."

"What do I have to do with any of that?"

"Yvonne says you're the reason he's digging in. Shane adores you." Claudia said it like it was fact, not a guess.

April's spine went rigid. She shook her head. "He doesn't."

"He does, April. Yvonne doesn't approve. Shane told her he won't introduce Yvonne to any future grandchildren if she doesn't change her attitude."

April set her glass down carefully before she dropped it. She stared out into the trees without seeing them, heart hammering. It was one thing to have Shane flirt with her—he could flirt with any woman and not mean anything by it—but to know that she was still causing problems with his family?

He won't introduce Yvonne to any future grandchildren. He's standing up to his father. Because of me.

"It doesn't matter what she thinks of me. I'm no threat to her. And especially his father."

Claudia's tone softened. "I disagree. Frankly, from what I've seen, I think you're very much a threat. You're exactly what Shane needs—someone who doesn't play games and doesn't back down. Someone with a spine."

That got a bitter laugh from April. "If that had been true, I wouldn't have left Lyons."

"Oh, sweetheart." Claudia's voice was gentle, but it held steel. "I don't know the whole story. But I've watched Shane navigate the kind of childhood that leaves scars. You gave him hope once. And if I'm not mistaken, you might be doing it again."

April's heart leapt, the traitor.

"And I can see that he gives you hope, too," Claudia said.

And maybe a reason to stop running.

"Give him a chance. No, give *yourself* a chance." Claudia clinked her glass softly against April's. "We should have lunch sometime," she said with a smile before she slipped back inside, leaving April staring out into the deep forest.

———

THE PORCH LIGHT flicked on as April pulled into the drive, the laughter from Ellie's cabin still clinging to her like warmth from a fire. Her little white house glowed against the dark like it was glad she'd come home. For once, she saw it the way her dad always said she should—not as something small she had to apologize for, but her little fortress. The crooked porch rail just looked lived-in tonight, not lacking.

For once, she didn't feel like she was racing home to put

out another metaphorical fire. She'd checked in on Riversong. The espresso machine had held it together until
closing time. Kevin was excited to tell her about his day.

The night air smelled strongly of pine sap and willows
from the river as she walked from the car to her front door.
She kicked off her shoes, hung her cardigan on the hook
beside the door, and caught her reflection in the window:
hair a little wild, cheeks still flushed from laughter, a small
smudge of strawberry pie on her wrist. She looked...happy.

That realization startled her enough to make her laugh
out loud.

*Not bad, Taylor. You survived an afternoon with
Claudia Behr.*

She made her way to her bedroom, replaying the afternoon. Frankie's glow. Wren's easy humor. Ellie looking radiant, cradling Star, while Claudia—still crazy to think she's
Bear's mother—was now a potential ally. It had thrown her
off balance in the best way. Maybe she didn't have to keep
proving she was more than the girl who ran.

Maybe I already have.

Of course, the girls had noticed her and Claudia's
absence. April figured that Arden—who had grown up here
—clued Wren and Rochelle in on the old dynamics while
they were outside. No one mentioned Shane, though
Wren's wink and Rochelle's knowing grin had both been
light-hearted, they left April blushing anyway. They looked
the way women do when they already know the truth
you're still pretending not to know.

She opened the bedroom window a crack to let in some
fresh air. Her room still smelled sweetly of the vanilla crème
candle she'd lit that morning. Outside, the river murmured
low and steady like a wise old friend. She emptied her lucky
purse onto the bed. The old Louis Vuitton pattern still

gleamed under the lamp as she transferred her things—lipstick, receipts, keys, wallet, breath mints—into her everyday purse. She slid the purse into its dust bag and placed it high on the closet shelf where it belonged—relic and reminder both.

April's phone buzzed. Her pulse did a traitorous skip when she saw Shane's name.

> Ten-minute warning. Pizza inbound from R66.

APRIL GRINNED. Pizza from Route 66, which they'd loved in high school, especially the wings. Had he picked it for nostalgia—or just convenience since it was close by? She typed back a simple *Got it,* but her fingers hesitated over the screen a moment longer than necessary before sending it. Did her message sound short? How did she want to sound?

What did she want?

April sat on the edge of the bed, phone in her lap. She couldn't stop thinking about the look on Shane's face when he'd told Kevin he was right. The way his voice had softened around her son's name. The way her pulse had tripped like it used to when he smiled at her whenever she showed up for his math lessons—different from the ones he gave her at school, where people would see and judge.

He's not that boy anymore.

And she wasn't the girl who'd waited at a bus station, hope mixed with worry that he'd stood her up. Her chest ached now with the same nervous hope.

The way Shane talked to Kevin with genuine respect,

how he never made promises he couldn't keep. Kevin glowed around him. That used to scare her, the thought of her son latching on to someone who once walked away.

He adores you.

Enough to stand against his parents' disapproval.

And, there was the matter of Riversong, and what she'd discovered when she'd taken over the bookkeeping once she came home.

The ache in her chest eased.

She returned to the front room in time to see headlights sweep across the yard. Gravel crunched under heavy tires and she recognized that engine anywhere—the deep, steady rumble of a Watchdog SUV settling into her drive.

April smiled before she could stop herself. She could hear Kevin's eager, non-stop chatter and hoped he hadn't driven Shane crazy. Pete's bark followed a few seconds later, muffled but eager.

"Right on time," she whispered, brushing a hand through her hair as she headed for the door.

ELEVEN

Twilight laid a soft blue over the river as Shane eased the Watchdog SUV into April's gravel drive and parked behind her. The porch light gave off a soft, golden glow and to Shane it felt steady, warm, a quiet welcome that settled in his chest.

Pete gave one energetic woof from the kennel and thumped his tail. Then he sighed back into that patient, alert calm he'd perfected since the pup years. In the back seat, Kevin had not stopped talking since Riversong.

"And then Benny held the 'stay' for like—okay, maybe not a minute but close—and Alex said the police dogs are coming next week and if we foster him he needs kid time and—"

"We'll see what Mr. Hoff says," Shane said, still smiling. This version of Kevin—lit up, motor-mouthed, buoyant—was a far cry from the solemn kid who'd asked him to be his mom's bodyguard.

He should always feel so carefree. Safe. Proud.

Steam curled from the pizza box beside Shane, fogging

the passenger window. Shane grabbed the box along with two paper sacks sitting on top. One order of hot wings for him, one teriyaki-flavored for April, with a side of ranch because once upon a time she'd dip each piece and declare, *Everything tastes better with ranch.* Shane chuckled to himself. He used to give her hell for it, just to hear her laugh.

After all these years I still know her favorite flavors. God help me.

Outside the SUV, the river took over the soundscape—low and steady winding between the trees. Kevin was already unbuckling when Shane opened the back door. "I'll get Pete," he said, half whisper, half battle brief, and then corrected himself because he was still a kid but trying to be twenty. "I mean, I can get him, if you want."

"Go on, little man. Slow and easy." Shane cracked the hatch and Kevin dropped into his best handler voice, opening the kennel door carefully like they'd practiced. Pete hopped down gracefully, nose tipping into the breeze. He smelled the pizza, sneezed, and looked personally offended. Shane scratched the ruff between his ears. "Not yours, buddy."

Kevin looked up hopeful. "But if he's good, can he have my pizza bones?"

"Pizza bones? What's that?"

Kevin scoffed like Shane was an idiot. "My leftover crusts."

Shane chuckled. "Pizza bones. I like that."

The porch was swept clean, wind chimes tinkling from the eaves. Someone had replaced a deck board; Shane noticed the new grain against the older planks. A planter box skirted the steps—mint and some lemony-smelling herb —cutting through the smell of the water and the trees.

April's house felt like a favorite pair of jeans—comfortable and broken-in. Unpretentious.

Kevin beat Shane to the door and then remembered himself, hovering, waiting. Shane shifted the pizza and let the sacks slide toward his torso. Before he could knock, the door opened and April was there, silhouetted in the frame.

The night went still.

Hair down, the day's curls loosened into soft waves. A soft-looking sweater that his hands suddenly ached to touch. No makeup, just clean skin and a glow in her cheeks that didn't come from rouge.

"Hey," she said, and it landed warmer than a hello. The scent of lilac soap drifted off her skin.

"Ma'am," Shane heard himself say, because apparently he forgot how to be a normal human when she looked at him like that. He tipped the pizza toward her. "Your ten-minute warning is up."

She grinned. "Come on in."

Kevin had already wedged past her with Pete on his heels, narrating as he crossed the front room. "We brought Route 66 pizza. I didn't have to tell him what to order or anything, Mom. He just knew."

April glanced at the bags, then back at Shane. "What *did* you order?"

He set everything on the entry table to free up his hands and pulled a box out of one of the white paper sacks so she could see the label. TERIYAKI. "Ranch is in the bag."

She didn't say anything for a second, just bit the corner of her lip in a way that drove Shane just as crazy today as it did when they were eighteen.

"Everything tastes better with ranch," she said, and Shane almost said *There it is* like he'd been waiting years to hear that line again.

Because I have.

April shook her head, a soft laugh escaping like she hadn't meant to let it out. "You remembered. Everything."

"Never forget a critical detail," he said lightly, because if he said *I remember everything about you* that would be... a lot. "I got the hot wings for me." He picked up the other bag. "As I recall, you're a heat wimp," he teased. "I promise no cross-contamination will occur on my watch."

"Get inside before the food gets cold," she said, stepping back to let him in.

The vanilla scent from a newly-lit candle on the mantel lingered under the smell of pizza. A plaid throw blanket covered the back of the couch. Floating shelves of books—mostly romances if Shane had to guess—lined the wall beside a window. Another wall was covered with framed photos of April's family and friends. A jar of wildflowers Shane recognized from the riverbanks outside sat beside the candle, a couple of wilting dandelions giving away who had picked them. An ordinary room, but so warm and welcoming, unlike the perfect, sterile rooms full of museum-grade art that Shane grew up in, fearing that if he broke anything or left so much as a smudge on the white marble, his father would beat him within an inch of his life.

"My house isn't much, but it's spotless," she said quietly beside him. He realized he'd been looking around.

"It's nice."

"Mmm-hmm."

"April, I mean it. It's so comfortable. So you."

"Kitchen's this way," she said, brushing past him as she started across the room. The whisper of her sweater sleeve against his forearm felt electric. Her smile reached her eyes, bright in a way they hadn't been before. Shane felt like he'd knocked down some invisible wall.

Kevin had already staged the kitchen table, sliding plates, coasters, and glasses into formation like he was setting out gear.

"Good job, kiddo," April said as she studied the table, looking impressed. She ruffled his hair and he immediately ducked.

"Pete, down," Kevin commanded. Pete folded himself onto the braided rug with a put-upon sigh that said he'd been left out of the wing selection and would be filing a complaint.

Shane set the food down. He cracked open the box holding the teriyaki wings first so the steam wouldn't make the skin soggy. April grabbed a container of grated parmesan from the fridge. She turned and saw the open box and the ranch waiting and her mouth softened again, a tiny, involuntary thing.

It felt like being trusted with a fragile object.

It's just dinner, he told his racing pulse as he handed her a plate. It thudded *Liar* in reply.

They set up around the table—Pete within food-drop distance of Kevin on Shane's right, April to his left. The whisper of a breeze floated in through a window over the sink. Outside, the river kept talking. Shane's nerves settled—not the jumpy, hungry energy of a date, but steady, peaceful.

I could get used to this.

"Okay," he said, lifting the pizza lid as if it were the lid of a treasure chest. Cheese-and-oregano-scented steam rose. "One half-pepperoni, one half-everything. Hot wings, teriyaki wings, and an unreasonable number of napkins."

April reached for the teriyaki wings, then paused, gaze flicking up to Shane's. "Thank you," she said. There was a lot packed into those two words.

"Anytime," Shane said, and meant it. Pete thumped his tail in agreement. Kevin dug into his slice of everything pizza like a starved wolf. In between bites, his chatter filled the kitchen like jazz music—uneven, bright, alive. "So if Benny passes his next obedience test, he gets to start tracking classes, and Mr. Hoff said that if we help foster him, we'd be, like, part of his pack. Not just babysitters."

April arched an eyebrow, her eyes dancing with amusement. "Part of his pack, huh? That sounds like a big commitment. You still up for it?"

Kevin nodded hard, sauce on his cheek. "I can do it. I already started a plan." He tugged a little spiral notebook from his back pocket and flipped it open. The pages were full of messy sketches and schedules. Shane leaned closer, pretending to study it like a field report. "Solid start, soldier." He met April's gaze. "Are *you* still up for it?"

She set aside a wing. "I talked to Mr. Hoff on my way home from Ellie's. We'll start with weekends. See how Benny does once school's out." Her tone was practical but warm. "He'd have to be at Riversong quite a bit, which Alex said is good for his conditioning, but I'm thinking with me working so much, keeping Benny full-time isn't fair to anyone."

"I can help with transport," Shane offered. "Pick him up, drop him off for training days. Pete doesn't mind carpool duty." Pete's tail thumped under the table, like he approved the plan.

April smiled—small, genuine. "We'll work something out."

They dove back into their meal—glasses clinking, Kevin dumping extra parmesan onto his slice until he had a mini ski slope, April happily dipping her wings into her sauce.

Shane smiled softly at the sound of early field crickets sang through the open window.

Kevin looked up suddenly. "Hey, Shane, whatcha thinking about?"

"I'm listening to the crickets outside. In another month when the snowy tree crickets start to sing, we'll know what the temperature is."

"What?" Kevin asked.

"You don't know about that? What you do is count the chirps for thirteen seconds and add forty, and that's the temperature."

"No way. That's so cool." Kevin turned to April. "Did you know that, Mom?"

April's lips twitched as if she were re-living the same memory as Shane. The night he took her for a walk under the full moon, showing off his knowledge of the woods until he realized that what she wanted was to get him alone and away from the house for a makeout session.

"I sure do," she said. "Shane taught me years ago, when we were teenagers." She looked at him through her lashes. "He has all sorts of skills once you get him out into the wilderness."

This woman is killing me.

"Cool! Can you teach me some survival stuff in the wilderness?"

"Depends," Shane said, hiding his grin behind a napkin. "You want Ranger skills or basic 'don't-get-eaten' skills?"

"Both!" Kevin shot upright in his chair. "All of it!"

Shane leaned back, thinking it through. "Weather's supposed to be perfect tomorrow. We could take Pete up to Eldorado Canyon, hike a bit. Good place to burn off some energy before school."

At the name, old images tugged at him—rocky trails

winding through wildflowers, sandstone cliffs turned golden in the sunlight. He and his brothers-from-other-mothers had learned half their boyhood courage up there playing soldier, tracking, daring each other to climb higher, run faster, laugh louder. He could still hear Elias's voice echoing off the canyon walls, calling *Last one up buys sodas!*

April's eyes softened, catching whatever memory crossed his face. Then she gave Kevin The Mom look—half amusement, half warning. "I have to open Riversong in the morning and you haven't touched your homework."

"But Mom, it's the last week of school. It doesn't matter."

"Nope, we had a deal. And, I had to twist Principal Pirogue's arm to give you time served with the suspension. I'm not having you go back to school without your home-work. Do you know how bad that would look?"

Kevin shrugged. "I don't care. They all hate me anyway."

April cringed. "They don't *hate* you."

"Yeah, they do, Mom." Kevin looked to Shane for backup. "Whenever something goes missing in the class-room, I get blamed. If a whole group of us is laughing too loud in the hallway, I'm the only one who gets time out. No one else does. No one else ever gets in trouble."

"That's not true, Kevin." April's tone indicated other-wise. She'd gone from relaxed and happy to defeated in a matter of minutes. Shane's heart went out to her. At the same time, he wasn't sure what to do. He didn't want to override her. Kevin wasn't his son.

As much as he feels like my son.

"You know it's true, Mom."

April put her napkin down beside her plate. "We've talked about how important it is to get good grades. It doesn't matter what they think. You aren't doing homework for them, but for you."

"Your mom's right, Bud. Doing your homework builds discipline. Discipline is the foundation of success."

Kevin shifted his attention to Shane. "Did they teach you that in Ranger school?"

"SWCC school, not Ranger," Shane said, smiling softly. "And it was a lesson I already knew." He just didn't want to tell Kevin how his father was the first to beat that lesson into him. "I learned it from my brothers growing up, when we'd play soldier in the mountains."

"You mean your friends? All the guys?"

"Yup. My brothers. Some people are family by blood. Others are family here." Shane covered his heart, "and they are just as important, if not more so."

Kevin nodded solemnly.

"So, maybe if you get your homework done in the morning like you promised your mom, we could all go hiking tomorrow afternoon." He raised his eyes to April. "But only if it's all right with you."

"Afternoon then," she conceded, pointing her fork at Kevin. "You set yourself up at a table where I can see you and finish your homework by noon, we'll go. But it's all up to you."

"Yes, ma'am." Kevin saluted.

Shane hid a smile. Their conversation tightened something pleasant in his chest.

They finished dinner slowly, Kevin now talking about the animals he hoped to see on the trails, April laughing easier than he'd heard in weeks. When she stood to clear plates, Shane reached for one too, brushing her fingers. He wanted to tell her how good this felt, how right. But Kevin was right there.

"Honey, why don't you go brush your teeth and get ready for bed? We need to be at Riversong by seven because I want to make sure the espresso machine's going to behave itself. "And knowing you, it'll take a while to fall asleep." She ruffled his hair.

Kevin nodded. "Yeah, okay. Hey, Peetie. Heel, boy."

Pete stood up and they both took off at a dead run down the hall to the bathroom.

"Slow down, you'll slip on the wood...floor...oh never mind." April laughed lightly as she rolled her eyes and shook her head.

"He's a good kid, April."

"Yeah. He is." The love in her eyes was genuine, but shadowed by something Shane couldn't read.

"Let me help with the dishes. Then I'll give you an update on Vegas after he's in bed."

April shook her head lightly as if clearing it and turned to him. "Thank you again."

He shrugged. "It's just a couple of dishes." He started toward the sink but she laid her hand on his arm. Her gentle touch stopped him as effectively as a tank.

"You know it's more than that." She took the dish out of his hand and brushed past him to the sink. He watched her walk, drawn to the sway of her hips and had to clench his jaw as heat coursed through him. If he wasn't careful, he'd end up bending her over the counter, his hand fisted in her hair, kissing the side of her neck, which used to drive her insane. Now he needed to know if it was still true. He stepped around the table as she turned on the sink until he was standing directly behind her.

"At least let me dry," he said as he craned his neck around to the side of her head, his lips inches from her ear.

The smell of her lilac soap filled his senses. April grinned and...*was that a shiver?*

Shane reached past her, brushing her arm, and picked up a dishtowel. She rinsed the first dish and he took it out of her hand, then wiped it dry and set it on the counter. They worked together in silence, the crickets outside serenading them.

They fell into an easy rhythm—April washing, Shane drying, their bodies close enough that every movement felt deliberate. The back of her hand brushed his forearm as she passed him a plate. His shoulder grazed hers when he reached for the dish rack. Each touch sent little sparks racing under Shane's skin.

"You know," April said quietly, not looking at him, "I used to imagine this sometimes. In Vegas, when things got bad. I'd picture doing something normal, like washing dishes," she laughed, the sound brittle at the edges, "only it was with someone who gave a damn."

Shane set down the plate he'd been drying. "April—"

"I'm done brushing my teeth!" Kevin's voice rang out from down the hall, followed by the thunder of running feet.

They stepped apart like teenagers caught necking. Shane clutched the dish towel like it was a tactical shield. April turned off the water, cheeks flushed pink. They looked at each other and grinned.

Kevin skidded into the kitchen in his Incredible Hulk pajamas. Pete trotted behind him, looking amused.

"That's great, sweetie," April said, her voice slightly breathless. "Do you need me to tuck you in?"

"No." Kevin looked at Shane. "When I was a little kid, I used to get tucked in. I just came out here to say good night."

April nodded, amused. "At least tell me you aren't too old now for a goodnight hug?"

Kevin tilted his head side to side and rolled his eyes. He hugged his mom, and then surprised Shane with a fierce hug. "Good night, bud. See you in the morning."

"Yeah, see ya. Mom, can I read for a little bit before lights out?"

April glanced at the clock. "Twenty minutes. Then it's lights out for real, mister."

"Yes, ma'am!" Kevin saluted—surprisingly sharp for an eight-year-old—and took off down the hall again. Pete followed at a more dignified pace, pausing at the hallway entrance to look back at Shane as if to say, *I've got first watch.*

TWELVE

WITH KEVIN OFF TO BED, THE KITCHEN FELL QUIET again. April turned back to the sink, but there were no more dishes. She dried her hands on a towel, movements careful and deliberate. "Funny, he was a little kid just last night when I tucked him in."

"Time flies," Shane joked.

"That it does." She set the towel out to dry on the counter. "Also, that was sweet of you," she said. "The hug."

"Kid's easy to love."

April's eyes widened for a moment, then she nodded and moved to the coffee maker. "Want some? Or I have tea. Or—God, I sound like I'm stalling, don't I?"

Shane smiled. "Little bit. But I'll take coffee if you're making some."

"I'm *always* making some." She opened a cupboard and took down one of Riversong's roasts. "You're in the hands of a professional." She shook the bag at him before pouring coffee beans into a grinder. Shane fought the impulse to ask about the state of the espresso machine. He didn't want to stress her out when she was already nervous.

Coffee brewed and poured into handmade mugs, they migrated to the living room. April curled into one corner of the couch, tucking her feet under her. Shane sat on the other end, angled toward her, one arm draped across the back. They sat close enough to talk quietly, far enough to be respectable.

For now.

Down, boy. You don't want to take advantage of her, and Kevin's just down the hall.

"So," April said, hands wrapped around her mug. "What's the verdict? Am I safe from my ex-husband for the foreseeable future?"

Shane appreciated that she could just ask it straight. "Flint's got him on full monitoring. Vince is still in Vegas. He checked in with his parole officer yesterday, like clock-work. Working that dishwasher job, going to his apartment, not making waves."

"That's good." April's shoulders relaxed a fraction. "I mean, I figured. But you know how it is. I feel like since we're watching him, he's suddenly going to find me. It's irrational."

Shane grinned. "It's not like you to be irrational, unless you're talking irrational numbers."

"Ha! You still remember some math I taught you, huh?"

"Despite my best efforts to forget."

"Ah." Some of the glow went out of her eyes. It took Shane a moment to speculate why.

Does she think I tried to forget her? "April—"

If he'd found me, he wouldn't be subtle about it."

"You knew him pretty well."

"I thought I did." She took a sip of coffee, eyes distant. "Turns out I didn't know him at all. Just the version he wanted me to see."

Shane's jaw tightened. "If he ever does show up here—"

"I know. You'll handle it." April looked at him then, really looked at him. "You've gotten good at that. Handling things."

"It's my job."

She shifted and looked deep into her coffee mug. "Is that all this is? A job?"

The question hung between them, weighed down by their history.

"No," Shane said quietly. "You know it's not."

April's fingers tightened around her mug. "Shane—"

"Remember that night after I failed the calc test?" he said suddenly, shifting gears before the conversation went somewhere they weren't ready for. "You made me redo every problem while you sat there eating those terrible gas station nachos. *With* ranch."

Her laugh surprised them both. "Those were *not* terrible. They were a delicacy."

"The cheese was radioactive-orange and came from a machine that probably hadn't been cleaned since the Reagan administration."

"You're just mad because I wouldn't share."

"I wasn't going to eat those things. I had standards." Shane grinned.

"Hey, when you're living on a tight budget, you learn to appreciate the finer things. Like questionable gas station cheese sauce." April kicked his thigh lightly with her socked foot.

Shane caught her foot before she could pull it back. He pressed his thumb gently against her arch. April's breath hitched.

"I missed this," he said. "Just... talking to you. Being near you."

"Me too," she whispered.

They sat like that for a moment, Shane massaging her arch, the house quiet around them except for the distant sound of Kevin reading out loud to Pete and the crickets outside singing their springtime song.

"How's the espresso machine holding up?" Shane asked, because he needed to say something that wasn't *I want to kiss you* or *I never stopped thinking about you* or any of the other desperately true things crowding his throat.

April's expression flickered—something careful sliding into place. "It's fine. Just temperamental."

"April."

"What?"

"You're a terrible liar. Always have been." Shane leaned forward slightly. "What's really going on with it?"

She sighed, setting her mug on a side table. "It's dying. Like, really dying. We can probably limp it through another month, maybe two if we're lucky and sacrifice the right combination of kitchen appliances to the appliance gods."

"And then?"

"And then I refinance my house against my father's wishes to replace it and hope nothing else breaks for the next six months." She said it matter-of-factly, not even the ghost of self-pity in her voice. "We'll make it work. We always do."

Shane felt the old rage uncurl in the pit of his stomach. Damn his father. He wanted to offer to buy her a new machine right there. Wanted to fix it, solve it, throw money at the problem until it went away.

Not to mention pummeling my old man.

But he knew April well enough to know that offering her money would be the fastest way to shut her down completely.

"Can I take a look at it?" he asked instead. "I'm pretty handy with machines. Might be able to buy you some more time."

April snorted. "No way. You'd have to fight my father first. That thing's his baby and he doesn't want anyone touching his baby." Her eyes went straight to her foot still resting in Shane's hand and her cheeks turned bright red. "Um, besides, if you electrocuted yourself, I'm not telling Kyle that his best guy got taken out by an oversized coffee maker."

Shane smiled. Another thing that never changed about April—she'd always been quick to make a joke to deflect. "So how was the party?"

April groaned and covered her face with her hands. "Wren is the worst. I love her, but she's relentless."

"About what?"

April peeked at him between her fingers. "Rochelle told everyone that we were on a date at lunch."

"She's not wrong."

April dropped her hands. "About what?"

"About it being a date. Kinda felt like one to me. Just like tonight." He stroked her foot.

"Shane Foti, are you saying we're on date number two and you didn't even ask me first?"

"Hey, you invited me to lunch first." He was grinning now, couldn't help it. "I just brought pizza, that's all. And... date number two, did you say? Is that an admission that lunch was date number one?"

"Oh my God." But she was smiling too, that real smile that made her whole face light up. "You're impossible."

"I prefer 'determined.'"

April shook her head, but the smile didn't fade. "Claudia was there today."

Shane went still. His mom's friend? "Bear's mom? How'd that go?" He dreaded the answer.

"Better than I expected, actually." April pulled her feet back, tucking them under her again. "She pulled me aside. Told me some things."

"Like what?"

April met his eyes as her expression turned serious. "Like how you've been trying to get your mom to leave your dad. How you told her you won't introduce her to any future grandchildren unless she changes her attitude." She paused.

Shane's jaw tightened. "I didn't know she was telling people that."

"Shane." April's voice went soft. "She said you're standing up to your parents. Because of me."

"Because it's the right thing to do. Because my father is —" He stopped, jaw working. "Because they don't get to control my life anymore. And they sure as hell don't get to disrespect you. *Never* again."

April was quiet for a long moment. Shane noticed that Kevin was no longer reading. He was probably fast asleep. Then April said, "There's something else I need to tell you."

"Yeah?"

"When I came home from Vegas, Riversong's book-keeping was a mess. God love my parents—math is not their strong suit."

"Which is why my father was able to take advantage of them with the terms of the loan." Shane couldn't help himself.

April smiled wryly. "Be that as it may, I figured something out when I took over the bookkeeping for Riversong."

Shane's stomach dropped. He knew where this was going.

"While I was in Vegas, I sent money home. Always from a different location because I was afraid they'd talk me into coming home."

"And you couldn't risk it because of my father's threats."

April ducked her head. "Yes. And, well, I won't sugarcoat it—I didn't want my folks to know where I was because I was ashamed of how I made my money."

"That's my fault. You should have been at some start-up in California and a multimillionaire by now."

April held up her hand. "Don't even." Her sardonic smile returned. "Besides, compared to what tech bros do these days, counting cards in Vegas is way more honest work."

Shane chuckled. "True."

"It became apparent to me that my parents were actually ahead of where I expected them to be financially. I went back over those old records and I found something very interesting," April continued, watching his face. "Someone *else* had been sending them money, for years. My parents thought it was all from me. But it wasn't, was it?"

Heat crawled up Shane's neck. He let go of her foot. "No. April—"

"It was you." She wasn't asking.

Shane sighed. "My father—what he did—threatening you, holding that loan over your family's head—" His hands curled into fists on his thighs. "I couldn't fix it all. Couldn't make him change the terms or drop that bullshit early payment penalty. But I could still do something. So I did."

"Shane." April's voice broke slightly. "Do you know how much money that was? How many years—"

"I don't care." He looked at her then, and he knew all of his emotions were written across his face. "I would have sent twice as much if I could have. But I was afraid your dad would figure out it was me never accept my money again. So I sent what I could."

April's eyes were bright with unshed tears. "Why?"

"You know why."

"I need to hear you say it."

Because I loved you.

I still do.

He'd never felt more certain of anything in his life. He loved April, loved her son, wanted to make a life with her. With them.

He also didn't deserve that honor, that privilege.

Shane took a breath. "Because my father hurt you and I couldn't stand it. Because even when you were gone, even when I thought I'd never see you again, I needed to do something to make it right."

April nodded slowly. "Because you wanted to make it right."

"I also didn't abandon you at the bus station. My father...prevented me from going."

Pain flashed across April's face. "I can imagine how. He beat the shit out of you, didn't he?"

Shane only nodded.

"At the time, I was so angry at you, at your whole family. It took me a while, but I realized what he must have done to you. Or maybe I talked myself into believing that what we'd had was real."

"It was."

"Was." She pulled her foot out of his grip and stood abruptly. "You should probably go. It's late, Kevin's got homework in the morning."

"April, wait."

Pete appeared from Kevin's doorway, stretching elaborately before padding toward them.

"See? Even Pete's ready to go. Let me walk you out."

"April, wait—"

"Thank you for dinner," she said, hand on the doorknob. "For spending time with Kevin."

She he was already opening the door, Pete slipping through ahead of her. The cool night air hit Shane's face and he sucked in a breath. He may not deserve her, but he couldn't just leave like this, couldn't run away like a coward even though every instinct was screaming at him to bolt.

April grabbed a cardigan from the hook by the door and followed him onto the porch. The boards creaked under their feet. Pete wandered down to the grass, sniffing around with professional interest.

Shane's hand closed around April's wrist. She was backlit by the porch light, her face half in shadow, hair moving slightly in the breeze. Beautiful. God, she was so beautiful it hurt to look at her.

"Don't run away," he said.

She looked surprised. "Running from what? I'm not running."

"Yes, you are. You've been doing it since we were eighteen. Since that bus station." His fingers tightened on her wrist. "I tried to find you. You were always—April, you were always—"

"Thank you." Her voice came out fierce and tender at once. "Thank you for the loan payments. Thank you for standing up to your parents. Thank you for being patient with Kevin, for seeing him the way he deserves to be seen. Thank you for—"

Something in Shane's chest cracked wide open.

April didn't finish the sentence. Couldn't, because Shane had stepped closer. His free hand cupped the back of her neck and every good intention he'd ever had of leaving her alone went up in smoke.

Shane bent his head and kissed her.

The world narrowed to the soft sound she made against his mouth, the way her fingers tightened in his hair, the taste of coffee and something sweeter. Empty years dissolved like smoke. He was seventeen again, stealing kisses in his truck on dark back roads, terrified and exhilarated and so in love he could barely breathe.

Except this was better. Because they weren't kids anymore. Because she was kissing him back like she'd been waiting for this just as long as he had. Because her body fit against his like coming home.

Shane cupped her face in his hands, tilting her head to deepen the kiss. April made a small, desperate sound that went straight to his gut. His thumbs stroked her cheekbones, learning the architecture of her face all over again. She'd changed—of course she had—but the essential April-ness of her was the same. The way she kissed like she meant it, like she was all in.

He'd forgotten how good this felt. No—he hadn't forgotten. He'd just convinced himself over the years that memory was exaggerating, that nothing could actually feel this right.

He was wrong.

April's hands slid under his jacket, fingers splaying across his back through his shirt. Shane groaned and kissed her harder, backing her up until she bumped against the porch post. She laughed against his mouth—breathless and joyful—and that sound did something to him. Made him want to protect it, bottle it up, make sure she never stopped making sounds like that.

"Shane," she breathed, and his name in her voice sounded like a prayer.

He kissed down her jaw to that spot just below her ear that used to drive her crazy. Still did, apparently, judging by the way she gasped and arched into him.

"Waited so long," he murmured against her skin. "So damn long—"

"Mom?"

They sprang apart like they'd been electrocuted.

Kevin stood in the doorway behind the screen. His face was scrunched up with worry, eyes red-rimmed like he'd been crying, or was about to.

April dropped to a crouch. "Hey, sweetie, what's wrong? Did you have a nightmare?" She opened the screen and reached for Kevin.

"Yeah, what's wrong, bud?"

Kevin wiped his eyes. "Shane? I was thinking about the crickets."

"Okay, what about them?" Shane realized he'd gone to his knees beside April. When did that happen?

"If you have to add forty to the chirps, what happens when the temperature is less than forty degrees?"

Oh boy. "Then...you don't hear them because they're gone, buddy."

"Oh," Kevin whispered. Kevin's single syllable landed like a gut punch. "That's what I thought."

Instant regret. *Why did I tell him about the crickets?*

"Honey," April started. "What's this really about?"

Kevin ignored her. "Are you leaving?" Kevin looked at Shane. "You're supposed to be Mom's bodyguard."

"I am—"

"But you hardly spent any time with her today. You spent it with me. What if something happened? It would be my fault."

Shane and April looked at each other in horror.

"I'm okay, sweetie," April said. She stood up and they went inside. She ushered Kevin to the couch and they sat down on either side of him. Pete plopped his head on Kevin's knee. "Nothing's going to happen to me, or to you."

Kevin turned his gaze on Shane. "Can you stay over? Please?" he pleaded.

Shane watched April's expression go straight to mortified.

"Sweetie, nothing's going to happen tonight, just like it hasn't happened any other night." She looked desperately at Shane. "He doesn't even have pajamas, and it's not like he can wear mine."

"Buddy," Shane tried again. "Do you think I'd leave your mom helpless? I've assessed the risks and everything points to you guys being safe tonight."

But by now, Kevin had worked himself up so much he was inconsolable. Tears rolled down his cheeks.

April put her arm around him and pulled him close. "You're just tired," she said in a soothing voice. "You've had a busy, exciting day and some stressful days before that. Why don't I tuck you in?" She glanced at Shane. "We could both tuck you in. Pete could stand guard until you fall asleep—"

"Mom, *please*. Let Shane stay. Let Peetie stay," he sobbed.

Shane raised his eyes to April. "I could stay on the couch. It's plenty comfortable."

April's face went through a complex series of movements that did not look promising. Finally, she closed her eyes and blew out a breath.

"This will not become a regular thing, understand?"

Shane wasn't sure if she was talking to Kevin or to him. Or both.

Maybe to herself as well.

Kevin nodded as one last sob escaped him. He threw his arms around her. She hugged him tightly, eyes still closed. When she opened them, she fixed Shane with an apologetic look. He smiled back softly and mouthed the words, *It'll be alright.*

"Now, let me tuck you in, sweetheart, and I'll get Shane a pillow." April stood and went down the hall with her arm still around Kevin. Pete trotted behind, casting one last look over his shoulder at Shane who could only grin at his buddy. April returned a few minutes later with a pillow and tossed it to him. When he caught it, he could smell her lilac soap and her soft scent all over it.

This is gonna be torture.

"You don't have to stay all night," she whispered, still looking mortified. "You could leave after we're sure he's asleep and come back early tomorrow. If he gets up and sees you're gone, I'll tell him you're out getting donuts."

Shane cocked his head. "Is this a ploy to get donuts for breakfast?"

April snorted as her body relaxed. "Maybe."

Shane chuckled. He reached out his arm in invitation and April sat beside him. "I was serious about spending the night."

April sighed. "If you do, you can sleep in my bed."

"Really?" he teased.

Her eyes about popped out of her head. "I mean, I won't be in it. With you. At the same time."

"That's too bad."

She narrowed her eyes. But not for long, when he reached up and stroked her cheek.

"Can you give us another chance?" Shane heard himself say. "We aren't the same people we were."

April was quiet for a long moment, her body warm beside him. Shane could feel his pulse in his throat, waiting.

Then April shifted, leaning into him until her head rested on his shoulder. The simple gesture hit him harder than any kiss. Trust. She was offering him trust.

"I'm scared," she whispered against his shoulder. "Not of you. Of this. Of wanting something this much."

Shane's arm came around her, careful and sure. "I know."

"What if—" She stopped, trying to find the right words. "What if we try this and it doesn't work? Kevin's already attached to you. Hell, I'm already..."

She didn't finish, but Shane heard everything she didn't say.

"Then we figure it out," he said quietly. "Together. Like adults. But April?" He tilted his head until his cheek rested against her hair. "I'm not abandoning you. Not this time. Even if you decide you don't want me, I'm still going to be here for Kevin. Still going to show up. Everything's different now."

April lifted her head to look at him. Her eyes were bright in the warm light from the lamp as she searched his face for something. Whatever she found there must have been enough, because she leaned in and kissed him.

Not like before on the porch—not desperate or hungry or eighteen years overdue. This was softer. Sweeter. A question and an answer all at once. Her lips were warm against his, offering possibility. Shane's hand came up to cup her jaw, his thumb stroking her cheekbone as he kissed her back gently with all the patience he'd learned, all the hope he'd been afraid to feel.

She ended the kiss but stayed close enough that he could feel her breath against his lips.

"I'm already thinking about it," she whispered.

Shane's chest tightened. He wanted to pull her back, kiss her again, tell her all the things he'd kept locked up for so long. But April was already standing, putting distance between them even as her gaze stayed on his.

She made it to the hallway before she paused and looked back.

"Ask me again after the hike tomorrow."

Then she was gone, disappearing down the dark hallway toward her room. A door clicked softly shut.

Shane sat there on her couch, holding her pillow that smelled like lilac and home. Through the window, he could see stars scattered across the Colorado sky and hear the river murmur its gentle song.

Ask me again after the hike tomorrow.

Not *no.*

Not *I need to think about it.*

Tomorrow.

Shane pressed the pillow to his face and grinned like an idiot into the soft cotton.

He didn't need to be in Vegas to know he'd just won the jackpot.

And this time, he'd do everything in his power not to squander it.

THIRTEEN

APRIL WOKE SLOWLY, SURFACING THROUGH LAYERS OF sleep like rising through warm water.

Pre-dawn light filtered through her bedroom curtains, turning everything soft and blue. Her sheets were twisted around her legs, the pillow warm against her cheek. Outside, the river flowed, the morning air punctuated by the dawn chorus of birdsong. She felt... good. Rested. Safe.

Then memories of the night before crashed in like a wave.

Shane kissed me.

Shane stayed over.

He wants another chance and I told him to ask me again after the hike.

April waited for the panic to hit—the old voice that showed up around dawn in Vegas, whispering that she'd made a mistake, that she was fooling herself, that her luck would turn because nothing good ever lasted. She braced for the familiar clench of regret in her stomach.

It didn't come.

Instead, there was just... peace.

Hope, even.

I've forgotten how good hope feels.

April sat up, pushing tangled curls out of her face. Through the window, she could see the night sky through the trees brightening toward dawn, stars fading like they were making room for something new.

She slipped out of bed and padded down the hall to Kevin's room. The door was cracked open—she never closed it all the way, not since she found him hiding under the bed. Kevin was sprawled across his mattress, one arm flung over his head, mouth slightly open. That boneless, absolute surrender to sleep that only kids could manage.

April's chest squeezed. Kevin looked so peaceful. No nightmares. No fear. Just her boy, sleeping sound.

Is this what it could be like? she thought, leaning against the doorframe. *Shane here, Kevin sleeping sound, everyone safe? No more looking over my shoulder?*

Then she realized Pete was not in Kevin's room.

April pulled Kevin's door almost closed and headed for the living room.

In the pale blue light, she could see that the couch was empty. The pillow she'd loaned Shane sat on top of the neatly folded blanket, corners aligned with military precision. The side table was clear. Both their mugs from last night sat in the drying rack on the kitchen counter, exactly where she would have put them.

He left.

The thought landed like a stone.

Unless he took Pete for a walk.

April moved to the window, pulled back the curtain, and looked out at the driveway. No Shane. No Pete. No SUV.

That sinking feeling opened up in her stomach—disappointment and a sense of inevitability tangled together in a knot she couldn't untie.

Of course he left. You didn't exactly make it easy to stay. You told him to wait for an answer until after the hike.

Not only that, she remembered thinking he'd only sent money because he felt guilty. She was ready to see him out after that. She didn't need pity. She needed...

Never mind what she needed.

That kiss. That's exactly what I needed.

A ball of heat formed in her belly at the memory of Shane's hand tangled in her hair. It had been so long.

April pressed her forehead against the cool glass.

She turned toward the kitchen, needing to do something with her hands that wasn't obscene, and that's when she saw it.

A note. White paper, neatly torn from a notebook, sitting on the counter right in front of the coffee maker.

Her heart kicked hard against her ribs as she crossed the room and picked it up.

Shane's handwriting—neat, precise, the letters strong and sure.

Didn't want to text and wake you, Sweetness. Taking Pete for a run and grabbing some gear. Back by 6:30 with donuts. -S

APRIL READ IT TWICE. Then a third time. She covered her mouth and realized she was smiling.

Relief flooded through her, warm and sweet.

Oh.

She was self-aware enough to know what that hollow feeling meant when she thought he'd left, and this warmth now that she knew he was coming back.

Oh, I'm in trouble.

April set the note down carefully and reached for the coffee beans in the purple bag, the special reserve a local roaster made just for her family as a thank you. What went better with donuts than fresh coffee? She measured, poured, hit the button. The grinder's familiar *whir* filled the kitchen as the sky outside brightened from grey to pale gold.

She was carrying a mug of coffee to the couch when Kevin's door banged open.

"Mom?" His voice carried that edge of panic from last night. "Mom, where's Pete? Where's Shane?"

April turned, mug still in hand, just as Kevin skidded into the kitchen in his rumpled Hulk pajamas, hair sticking up in six directions, face pale with worry.

"Honey, it's okay—"

The sound of tires on gravel cut her off.

Through the window, they watched Shane's SUV pull into the drive.

"He spent the night," April said, unable to keep the smile out of her voice. "He's back with donuts, sweetie."

Kevin looked up at her, eyes bright. "He spent the night," he echoed. Then he ran to open the front door.

And watching Shane's SUV door open, watching Pete bound out and Shane follow him to the door with a colorful bakery box in his hands and that sexy, cocky smile on his face as he spotted her in the window, she realized she'd been waiting years for this moment.

———

SHANE OFFERED to drive them to Riversong so that they could leave straight from the coffee shop for the hike. April sat in the passenger seat holding the box of donuts from a new shop—Do's and Donuts—on her lap while Kevin sat in back chattering about the upcoming hike.

April snuck a glance at Shane. His hands were relaxed on the wheel, one elbow propped against the door, that small smile playing at his mouth while Kevin explained his theory about why Pete was the smartest dog at Watchdog.

"And another thing," Kevin continued, "Pete knew exactly where the donuts were even though they were in a box. That's, like, advanced smell detection."

"That's just Sunday morning training, bud," Shane said, eyes crinkling. "Pete knows the difference between week-days and weekends. Weekends mean donuts."

April shook her head, unable to fight her own smile. Shane answered all of Kevin's questions patiently and with humor, a look of contentment on his face.

It all felt so easy.

So what was this strange tightness in her chest?

Shane turned onto Main Street and Riversong came into view—the painted sign her dad had made, the flower boxes April and Hannah had planted earlier in the spring, the big windows that let morning light flood the whole shop.

Shane pulled into the small parking lot in front of the building.

April's stomach clenched. Her father's truck was already there.

"He's here early," she said, trying to keep her voice light.

Shane cut the engine and looked at her. "You okay?"

Oh, just fine. I'm nervous about what this looks like. The three of us showing up together. You and me and Kevin, like we're...

Like they were a family.

"Yeah, I just—" She glanced back at Kevin, who was already unbuckling. "I wasn't expecting him to be here yet. Usually I open alone on Sundays."

Shane's hand found hers, squeezed once. "If it's gonna be a problem, Pete and I can pick you guys up later."

April gazed through the window and caught movement as her dad moved back and forth behind the counter.

"No." She smiled at Shane. "There won't be a problem at all."

Kevin bounded out of the SUV before April could over-think it further. "Come on! I wanna tell Grandpapa the news!" He ran around to the back to do his customary job of letting Pete out.

Shane came around to open April's door. Always the gentleman. He grabbed the donuts and she took his offered hand—warm, callused, steady—and let him pull her out.

Together, they walked toward the entrance.

Sonny was at the prep counter, measuring out beans for the first batch of coffee. He looked up when Kevin opened the door, his weathered face breaking into a smile.

"There's my favorite grandson—" He stopped mid-sentence, taking in the whole picture. Kevin, Pete, Shane, April. All together. At seven-thirty in the morning.

April felt her cheeks heat.

"Morning, Mr. Taylor," Shane said evenly.

"Shane." Sonny's tone was carefully neutral, but his eyes —sharp and assessing—flicked between Shane and April like he was adding up a math problem he didn't quite like the answer to.

Kevin, oblivious to any tension, launched himself at his grandfather. "Grandpapa! Guess what?"

"What's that, kiddo?"

"Shane spent the night with us!"

Oh God. April thought 'the news' Kevin wanted to share was about the hike today.

The temperature in the room dropped in proportion to how high Sonny's eyebrows climbed toward his hairline. His gaze locked on Shane with the kind of scrutiny that had made April's high school boyfriends—the one or two her father had actually met—never take her out again.

"On the couch," April blurted, her voice coming out higher than intended. "He slept on the couch. Shane was a perfect gentleman and—"

"I made him," Kevin added helpfully. "Because he's Mom's bodyguard and I was scared he'd leave and something bad would happen."

Sonny's intense expression was replaced by amusement. He crossed his arms, still looking at Shane.

"The couch, huh?"

"Yes, sir." Shane met his gaze steadily. "I gave Kevin my word I'd keep watch."

Sonny studied Shane for another long moment. Then his mouth twitched. "Well. I suppose that's all right then." He ruffled Kevin's hair. "Your mom treating her bodyguard okay?"

"She made him coffee this morning!" Kevin reported. "The good stuff in the purple bag."

April wanted to sink through the floor.

Sonny chuckled, the tension breaking like a snapped rubber band. "That's how you know you're in good standing around here, Shane. The good coffee in the purple bag's reserved for family."

The word hung in the air—*family*—and April watched Shane's throat work as he swallowed.

"I brought donuts," Shane said finally, holding up the box like a peace offering.

"Then you're forgiven for giving me a heart attack." Sonny gestured to the small table near the back. "Come on. Let's see what you got."

April turned on the sound system, queued up the coffee shop channel, and the first song that came on randomly was "Falling in Love at a Coffee Shop" because of course it did. They settled around the table—coffee steaming in mismatched mugs, Kevin already elbow-deep in the donut box, Pete lying at Shane's feet with his chin on his paws. April sat between her father and Shane, hyperaware of both of them, feeling like she was seventeen again and trying to hide a secret in plain sight.

"So," Sonny said, wrapping both hands around his mug. "You gonna sit around here all day and stare at my daughter while she works?"

"No, Grandpapa. We're going on a hike," Kevin said through a mouthful of donut, his lips white with powdered sugar. "But I've gotta finish my homework first."

"A hike, huh?" Sonny's gaze hadn't shifted from Shane's.

"Yes, sir," Shane said as he dipped a piece of chocolate cake donut into his coffee. "Eldorado Canyon. Kevin was asking about learning some wilderness skills."

Sonny nodded slowly. "And you're going too, April?" He continued to stare at Shane.

"Yup." She popped the 'P.' "If I can keep up. It's been a while since I went on a hike, but it'll be a great way to work off this donut."

Shane's eyes traveled over her—just a flicker, but enough to make her skin warm. "You look perfect."

Sonny cleared his throat loudly.

"I mean—you're dressed appropriately. For hiking." Shane took a long drink of coffee.

Kevin, mercifully, was too busy picking out another donut to notice the adults being weird.

"Kevin, honey, why don't you go get set up in the office?" April said. "The sooner you start, the sooner you're done."

"Okay!" Kevin grabbed one more donut and headed for the back, Pete trailing him like a furry shadow hoping for a bite of donut.

Once he was gone, Shane turned to Sonny. "Sir, I wanted to ask your permission for something."

Sonny's eyebrows rose. "Go on."

"April mentioned that the espresso machine was still acting up. I called a friend of mine this morning—Ben Massey. He's a blacksmith, does a lot of custom metalwork."

"I know him."

"Yeah, of course." Shane ducked his head, which April found amusing. He might be grown up, but her father had a way of sending him right back to high school. "I told him about the situation and he said he might be able to machine some parts, buy you some more time before you have to replace the whole unit."

April's heart did something complicated in her chest. Shane was trying to help without making it about money or charity, just... problem-solving.

Sonny was quiet for a moment. "Ben Massey's a good man. Made a heat exchanger for my elderly neighbor last winter, wouldn't take a dime." Sonny nodded slowly. "If Ben thinks he can help, I'd be grateful. When's he coming by?"

"I can call him now. Said he could be here around eight-thirty, if that works for you."

"It works." Sonny stood and collected empty mugs. "I appreciate you thinking of us, Shane."

The *us* landed differently than *family* had, turning Shane back into an outsider. April winced just a little bit inside on Shane's behalf. He'd looked so happy, so pleased when her father made the family comment.

———

BEN ARRIVED at eight-thirty on the dot. April heard his truck before she saw it—the distinctive rumble-purr of an engine that had been maintained with the kind of care Ben brought to everything he touched. April went to the entrance to unlock the door.

He filled the doorframe because the man was built like a mountain like his friend Bear, and April felt the years fall away. She was eighteen again, watching Ben lumber toward her in that bus station, carrying money she wouldn't take and an apology that wasn't his to make.

"Hey, April," Ben said, his voice that same low rumble she remembered. Even though they increasingly moved in the same circles, Ben stayed quiet and often left early.

"Hi, Ben." She gave him her brightest, most welcoming smile. "Thanks for coming on short notice."

"No problem." His eyes shown with gentle kindness. "Heard you've got an espresso machine giving you trouble."

"Giving us hell is more like it," Sonny shouted from behind the counter. True to form, it had started acting up again. "But if anyone can sweet-talk it into behaving, it's probably you."

April led Ben toward the temperamental machine.

"She's an old beauty, isn't she?" Ben asked as he ran a hand over the silver machine.

Sonny beamed. "She sure is. I don't want to replace her if I can avoid it. She's part of Riversong's image."

Shane joined them, and April watched the easy way he and Ben moved around each other—the shorthand of old friends, the comfortable silence of men who'd been through hell together. They started taking a panel off the machine, discussing pressure valves and plumbing and heating elements in a language April only half understood.

She busied herself with opening prep—checking the till, filling the cream pitchers, restocking the pastry case when the local bakery made its delivery, thinking she might have to stop in and say hello at the new donut place and get some in here because they were incredible. She checked in on Kevin who sat bent over his homework, actually focusing for once.

And every few minutes, she found herself watching Shane.

The way his hands moved, confident and sure. The way he listened when Ben explained something, nodding, asking smart questions. The way he laughed at something Sonny said, his whole face transforming when he was included.

This was Shane in his element—solving problems, helping people, being useful. No flash, no performance. Just quiet competence and genuine care.

April's throat went tight.

Around nine-fifteen, Ben straightened and pulled a small notebook from his pocket. "I need to grab some measurements, check what I've got in my workshop. Give me about twenty minutes."

"Thanks again," Sonny said.

Shane glanced at his watch, then toward the office. "Kevin! Want to help me take Pete for a quick stroll?"

Kevin appeared in the doorway, pencil still in hand. "Can I?" He looked at April.

"How's your homework coming."

"Good. I just have math left."

"Then you can go."

Kevin smiled and vanished to get Pete, and Shane caught April's eye. Something passed between them—a look that said *we'll talk later* and *I'm here* and a dozen other things she didn't have words for.

Then he was gone, Pete and Kevin at his heels, and the back door swung shut behind them.

April and Sonny were alone.

I should get back to prep work. Check inventory. Do literally anything other than stand here with my father while my thoughts tangle themselves into knots.

But Sonny was watching her with that expression—the one that said he saw right through every defense she'd ever built.

"Does Kevin know it's his father Shane's protecting you from?"

She flinched. "No. All he knows is that his bio-father didn't want to be a dad and that he's missed out on one hell of a good kid."

"When's the last time he asked about his father?"

April's hands clutched a dishtowel. "It's been a while. Not since..." she trailed off. *Not since he'd started idolizing Shane*, she realized.

Through the window, they watched Shane and Kevin rounding the building to the front of Riversong, Pete trotting proudly at the end of his leash. Shane was speaking, probably teaching Kevin something—how to read dog body language, maybe, or some other small lesson in paying attention.

Kevin was eating it up, hanging on Shane's every word.

"He's good with Kevin," Sonny said quietly.

"Yeah," April said, her voice coming out rough. "He is."

"Kevin adores him."

"I know."

"You're scared." It wasn't a question.

April tried to swallow past the sudden thickness in her throat as she tried to find words to address the old fear that had gone into hiding deep in her chest when Shane kissed her the night before.

"Of course I'm scared." She bit her lip as her deepest fear rose to the surface—the real reason she'd pushed Shane away ever since Kevin started to idolize him. "I'm afraid to take the chance that he'll walk away. Again." She wiped her eyes. "Look at them, Papa. Kevin's already so attached. And Shane—"

"What about Shane?"

"He isn't Kevin's real father. I can't afford to believe he'll always love Kevin like his own."

The silence that followed filled the shop like cold lead.

When April finally looked at her father, his face had gone tight with something that looked like deep disappointment.

"April," he said, and his voice carried a weight she rarely heard. "How can you say that?"

She blinked, thrown by his tone. "I just meant—"

"We took your cousins in whenever my sister and her lousy husband got picked up for possession and intent to sell." Sonny's jaw worked. "Brianna ended up staying with us for years. She grew up right next to you and your sister. She's not my daughter, but do you think I love her any less for that? Any less than I love you and Hannah?"

April's stomach dropped. "Papa, that's not what I—"

"Even her brother, for all his problems, I still love him as I would my own son." Sonny turned to face her fully.

"There is no difference in my heart. For you to even think that is the biggest insult you could ever lay on me."

"I didn't mean—" April's voice cracked. "It's different. They're still blood. They're still your sister's kids—"

"No." Sonny's voice was firm. "There *is* no difference, April. Love isn't about biology. It's about showing up. It's about choosing, every single day, to be there." He gestured toward the window. "And it's the biggest insult you could ever lay on Shane."

Tears slid unhindered down April's cheeks.

"I had my opinions about him a long time ago," Sonny continued, his voice softening slightly. "When he broke your heart. But he was a boy then and didn't know his ass from a hole in the ground." He paused. "I wasn't sure he'd changed when he walked through that door a few years back. But I've been watching him. He's a different man now. A good man, April. If you can't see that, you're cheating yourself out of love."

Through the window, Shane, Kevin, and Pete turned to come back in from their walk. Shane was carrying a flat stone, demonstrating the right wrist motion that would send it skipping across a lake. He handed it to Kevin who practiced the same motion.

"And you're cheating Kevin out of it, too," Sonny said quietly.

The words hit like a punch to her sternum.

April watched Shane ruffle Kevin's hair when he finally got the throw right. Watched her son beam up at him like Shane had just handed him the moon. Watched Pete dance around Kevin's feet, tail wagging.

Love isn't about biology. It's about showing up.

Shane had shown up. He'd shown up at Riversong when he'd returned to town. When he heard the report of shots fired. When Kevin needed a bodyguard. He'd shown up on her porch with her favorite wings and ranch dressing. He'd shown up this morning with donuts and a plan to help her dying espresso machine. And he radiated a quiet steadiness that said *I'm here, I'm staying, you can count on me.*

He's been showing up for years, she realized. Sending those anonymous loan payments. To think she'd thought last night that he'd only sent them out of misguided guilt.

No—he'd sent them because he still loved her.

And yet, he'd kept his distance when she got scared after the drive-by. Respecting her boundaries while making it clear that the door was open whenever she was ready. April pressed her fingers to her mouth, trying to hold back the sob that wanted to escape.

"He loves that boy and he loves you," Sonny said. "Anyone with eyes can see it. Question is, are you brave enough to love him back?"

The front door opened and Kevin burst through, Pete wiggling past and bounding ahead. "Mom! Shane taught me how to skip a stone! It's all in the wrist!"

Shane followed more slowly, brushing dirt off his cargos. His eyes found April's immediately, reading something in her expression that made him still.

"You okay?" he asked.

April nodded, not trusting her voice.

Ben returned minutes later, notebook in hand. "Good news," he said to Sonny. "I've got most of what I need and what I don't have will be shipped overnight on Monday. I can have parts ready by Wednesday, Thursday at the latest."

"What's it going to cost me?" Sonny asked.

Ben named a figure that was absurdly reasonable, and when Sonny tried to argue, Ben just shook his head. "Shane's family. That makes you family. Family rate."

Shane's ears went red to the tips.

April decided the next moment she got him alone she'd kiss the hell out of him.

Ten o'clock rolled around and the morning rush started. April worked the counter with her dad, making drinks and ringing up orders, while Shane sat at a corner table with Kevin, helping him finish the last of his homework. They looked like they were having fun.

"I thought you hated math," April called over during a lull.

Shane looked up, grinning. "Nah. Math's easy now. I had the best tutor in Colorado."

"You did not."

"Scout's honor."

"You were never a scout."

"Details." His eyes were dancing. "Besides, this isn't math. It's spelling. Which I'm very good at."

"Oh really? Spell antiestablishmentarianism."

Shane's grin faltered. "That's a trick question."

Kevin cracked up, and April found herself laughing too.

At noon, Miriam came in to take over for April.

"Are you sure you guys are okay with the store today?" April asked her parents. Hannah had decided to take the day off, and it felt weird to leave them.

"We're fine, sweetie," her mom said. Sonny shooed her out the door with a thermos of hot chocolate and a container of scones for the hike and a meaningful look at April that said *don't waste this.*

Shane loaded Kevin and Pete into the SUV while April stood in the parking lot, looking back at Riversong—at this place she'd helped her family build. Outside of time spent with Kevin, she'd poured every spare drop of her life into it since coming home.

But maybe, just maybe, she didn't have to do that anymore.

Sonny caught her watching them through the window. He set down a mug, covered his heart, and made the hummingbird flutter. *I love you forever.*

He immediately followed it up with another shooing motion. Laughing, April sent him a hummingbird right back.

"Ready?" Shane asked, opening her door.

April looked at him—really looked at him. At the man he'd become. At the way he waited, patient and sure, for her answer.

Ask me again after the hike, she'd said.

She already knew what her answer would be.

"Yeah," she said, climbing in. "I'm ready."

FOURTEEN

The weather at Eldorado Canyon was perfect for a hike. The Colorado sky arched overhead in a flawless blue dome. The sky was streaked with fair-weather cumulus —white and soft as fleece, drifting lazy and harmless. Those were fair-weather clouds, but Shane knew how fast they could build into something dangerous. Give them time and heat, and they'd muscle up into thunderheads before the day was done.

He sniffed the air out of habit. The breeze carried the clean scent of snowmelt and pine sap, the promise of the coming summer sharpening everything it touched.

"Whatcha looking at, Shane?" Kevin asked, eternally curious.

"I'm checking the weather using the clouds. See those puffy ones with flat bottoms?" Shane said, pointing skyward. "Cumulus. Fair weather—for now. If they start piling high like towers, that's when you keep your rain gear close."

"Do you think that's going to happen soon?" April asked. She crossed her arms and gripped her elbows.

Shane shaded his eyes, studying the horizon the way some men read faces. The breeze moved steady from the west, dry and cool against his skin, carrying no hint of moisture.

"No haze, no humidity," he said. "We're good. Those clouds will stay well-behaved until tonight and we'll be gone well before then."

April's shoulders eased. "So we won't get caught in a storm?"

"Not if we're back out by four. It's still making its way over the mountains. We may hear some thunder though." He glanced back at her, mouth curving. "But I always pack for a storm anyway. Weather in these mountains can turn faster than gossip about my mother." He winked at April.

That earned him a small laugh—the kind he'd missed for years. The sound warmed his chest like sunlight.

Kevin ran ahead with Pete on the retractable leash, giving Shane a chance to just be with April. The look on her face made his chest tighten—something between curiosity and trust, like she was remembering who he used to be and measuring it against who he'd become.

"What?" he asked, mouth quirking.

"Nothing." But she didn't look away. "I just never realized you knew so much. About everything."

"Not everything." He stepped closer, lowering his voice so Kevin wouldn't hear. "Still figuring out some things."

Her cheeks flushed pink, and Shane knew she was thinking about last night. About that kiss on the porch, about waking up to find his note, about the question he'd promised to ask again.

"Like what?" she asked, barely above a whisper.

Like how to convince you I'm not going anywhere. Like

how to be what Kevin needs. Like how to love you the way you deserve.

"Like whether you still dip *everything* in ranch dressing," he said instead, keeping it light even though his pulse was hammering. "Or if that was just a phase."

April laughed so hard she bent over. There it was—that real laugh he'd been chasing since he walked back into her life.

"Still do. Some things never change."

"Good to know." Shane held her gaze a beat longer than necessary. "Some things shouldn't."

Kevin raced back, breaking the moment. "Are we going or what? Pete's ready!"

April turned away first, but not before Shane caught the small smile playing at her lips.

———

THEY FOLLOWED the trail into the canyon, the sandstone walls rising sheer on either side, streaked with gold and rust. South Boulder Creek ran beside them, swollen with snowmelt, tumbling over boulders the size of cars. Pete trotted as far ahead as his retractable leash would allow, nose down, tail wagging like a metronome.

Kevin darted from one side of the path to the other, stopping to pick up smooth stones. "Can we skip these later?"

"Absolutely," Shane said. "But first, a lesson." He stopped and crouched beside the creek. "See how it's clear here, but down there it's a little murky?" Shane pointed to where the current curled around a bend. "That's the outflow. Water warms as it slows, picks up silt. The cold, clean stuff's the inflow."

Kevin squinted. "So if we got turned around, we could follow the cold one upstream to find the source?"

"Exactly." Shane smiled. "You're already thinking like a tracker."

Kevin touched the surface, yelped at the chill, then laughed. "That's awesome."

They moved along the creek, and April crouched beside them to get a closer look at the water. Her shoulder brushed Shane's, and the contact sent electricity straight through him. He was suddenly, acutely aware of everything—the warmth of her skin through her shirt, the faint scent of her lilac soap, the way her hair fell forward as she leaned in.

"It really is colder here," she murmured, trailing her fingers through the current.

Shane watched her hand, remembered those same fingers tangled in his hair last night. Had to clear his throat before he could speak. "Physics. Cold water's denser, moves slower."

"Show-off." But she was smiling.

April shifted her weight, the rocks under her feet unsteady, and Shane's hand shot out instinctively—catching her waist, steadying her. His palm spread against the curve of her hip, and for a heartbeat neither of them moved.

Her eyes lifted to his. Close enough that he could count the gold flecks in her hazel irises, close enough to see her pupils dilate slightly.

"Careful," he said, voice rougher than intended. "These rocks can be slippery."

"Right. Slippery." But she didn't pull away immediately. Her hand had landed on his forearm for balance, fingers curling slightly against his skin.

Kevin splashed further upstream, oblivious, playing with Pete along the bank.

Shane's thumb moved, stroking once along April's hipbone through her jeans. He watched her breath catch, watched color bloom across her cheekbones.

"Shane," she whispered.

"Yeah?"

"We should probably—" She tilted her head toward Kevin.

"Yeah." But Shane didn't move. Couldn't seem to make himself let go of her.

Finally, April squeezed his arm once—a silent *thank you* or *wait until later* or maybe if God was smiling down from heaven today *I feel it too*—and stepped back onto solid ground.

Shane's hand fell away slowly, reluctantly, still feeling the phantom warmth of her against his palm.

Kevin called out something about finding a perfect skipping stone, and the moment dissolved. But when Shane glanced at April, she was touching the spot on her hip where his hand had been, and the look she gave him promised they'd finish this conversation.

Just not with an eight-year-old present.

When they reached Kevin, the kid's grin was bright enough to make Shane's throat tighten a little. He remembered being that age—skinny and scrappy, running these same woods with Bear and Waylon, Elias always a step behind with a notebook full of 'official mission logs.' They'd made spears out of mop handles, fought imaginary bad guys, camped by the creek until their parents dragged them home.

He remembered the sound of Waylon's laugh echoing through the canyon. Gabe trying to light a fire with wet pinecones. Ben explaining how moss grew thicker on the north side of trees—and Bear immediately arguing it depended on moisture, not direction.

Shane smiled faintly. They hadn't known a damn thing, but they learned by doing.

That was where he'd fallen in love with the wild—with the rhythm of moving through terrain, reading the wind, finding quiet in the noise. That was where the idea of becoming a SEAL had taken hold, before he knew the difference between dream and cost.

He didn't tell Kevin any of that, of course. The kid didn't need the weight of ghosts.

April grinned as she watched him. "I take it you were this kind of kid, too."

"Worse," Shane admitted. "The whole gang of us, we all thought we were soldiers and SEALs. Used to sneak out here, play recon. Got in trouble more times than I can count. We called ourselves Mountain Division, all the way back then."

April's eyes softened. "And look at you now."

He shrugged. "Guess the training stuck."

They started walking again.

"I remember," April said quietly.

Shane looked at her, surprised. "Remember?"

"In high school. You and your friends were kind of legendary." Her mouth curved. "The Mountain Division crew, always in trouble for something. I remember sophomore year when you guys 'borrowed' the principal's golf cart for a 'tactical maneuver.'"

Shane laughed despite himself. "In our defense, we returned it."

"With pine cones stuffed in the exhaust and a hand-drawn 'captured enemy vehicle' sign duct-taped to the windshield." April shook her head, but she was grinning. "Principal Hoffman was not amused."

"Worth it though." Shane's chest warmed at the memory, at the fact that April had been paying attention even back then. "You noticed us all the way back then?"

Something flickered across her face. "Dude, I said *legendary*, didn't I? But I mostly paid attention to you."

The admission hung in the air between them, weighted with all the things they'd never said to each other when they were teenagers. When April was the smart girl from the wrong family and Shane was the golden boy who wasn't supposed to look twice at her.

"I didn't know that," Shane said softly.

"That was kind of the point." April's smile turned bittersweet. "You were busy being popular. I was busy trying to prove I was more than my last name."

"April—"

"It's okay." She touched his arm briefly. "We were kids. We didn't know anything."

"I knew enough to tell my parents to hire you as my tutor." Shane caught her hand before she could pull it away. "Best decision I ever made."

"Really? Because I'm pretty sure you failed that calc test on purpose so you'd have an excuse to see me."

Shane's ears went hot. "That is absolutely not—" He stopped at her knowing look. "Okay, maybe a little bit."

April laughed, and the sound chased away the ghosts of who they used to be, leaving only who they were now.

Two people who'd found their way back to each other despite everything.

"Come on," she said, tugging him forward. "Kevin's getting ahead of us again."

She didn't let go of his hand right away, and Shane counted that as a victory.

As they climbed, the trail narrowed, twisting through a boulder field where the sun hit hard and the air shimmered. Shane ran his hand along the nearest slab of sandstone. "Touch both sides," he told Kevin.

Kevin obeyed, palms flat on the rock. "This side's warm. That one's cool."

"Exactly. South side keeps the heat. North side stays shaded. The rock remembers the sun longer than we do."

April brushed her fingers across the same surface, eyes thoughtful. "You make it sound poetic."

Shane smiled. "Guess geology's got a romantic streak."

April held his gaze for a beat too long, something playful dancing in her expression. "Since when did Shane Foti get poetic?"

Shane stepped closer, voice dropping low enough that only she could hear. "Since I started trying to impress you again."

Her breath caught. "Is it working?"

"You tell me." He was close enough now to see the pulse jumping in her throat, close enough that if Kevin wasn't twenty feet away, Shane would've kissed her right there against the sun-warmed stone.

"Maybe." April's voice came out slightly breathless. "A little."

"Just a little?" Shane raised an eyebrow.

"Don't push your luck, Foti."

"Shane! Mom! Look at this!" Kevin's voice carried across the clearing, shattering the moment.

April stepped back, but not before Shane saw the smile she was trying to hide. The one that said he was definitely making progress.

They moved higher, where a light breeze funneled through the canyon. Shane lifted a finger to test the air. "Moisture's dropping. Wind's steady. Perfect conditions."

Kevin copied him, grinning. "I can't tell a thing."

"You will," Shane said. "Takes practice. Easiest way to start is listen."

They crossed a clearing. The sun dipped behind the ponderosas, and the air cooled instantly. The forest went still—birds gone quiet, the hum of insects fading.

Kevin noticed first. "It got quiet."

Shane nodded. "When the woods hold their breath, something's shifting. Sometimes it's a hawk. Sometimes it's weather. Sometimes—" he gave a small shrug "—it's just the world listening back."

He didn't say what memory came with that silence: the heavy quiet after gunfire stopped, the smell of cordite and seawater, the body on the deck that used to be Sean.

For a moment, Shane could see it so clearly: water streaming off his gear; Charlie trying her best to revive him; the rescue boat speeding down the river with the SEAL team they'd pulled out.

Camo standing guard beside Sean's body, refusing to move. That dog had set off a chain of events that brought him to today.

The ache rose sharp and sudden, but Shane breathed through it, the way he always did.

Except this time, he wasn't alone with it.

April touched his arm—gentle, grounding. Shane looked down at her fingers resting against his sleeve, then up at her face. She was watching him with those eyes that had always seen through his armor to the mess underneath.

"You okay?" she asked softly.

No.

Yes.

I don't know anymore.

"Yeah." His voice came out ragged. "Just... remembering."

April didn't ask what. Didn't push. She just stood there with her hand on his arm, warm and steady and real, pulling him back from the dark place his mind wanted to go.

Shane covered her hand with his own, threading their fingers together for a moment. "Thank you."

"For what?"

"For not making me explain."

Understanding flickered across her face. "You don't have to explain everything, Shane. Not to me."

She sees me. Not the golden boy.

And she accepts me, scars and all.

He squeezed her hand once, grateful for her in ways he couldn't express in words.

Kevin's voice called out from up ahead, telling them to catch up.

April squeezed back, then slowly let go. But the comfort of that touch stayed with Shane, warming him from the inside out as they continued up the trail.

The boy didn't notice the change in the adults. He was too busy trying to find another perfect skipping stone.

"Shane," Kevin called. "How many times can you get one to skip?"

"Depends on the throw," Shane said, voice steady again. "And the water. Flat and calm's your best bet."

Kevin wound up and flung a stone into the woods.

Shane grinned. "Good arm."

Kevin looked back, pleased. "You think so?"

"I know so."

The kid's smile widened, and Shane felt something

unclench in his chest. He wasn't a father, wasn't even sure what he was supposed to be to this boy—but maybe this was enough. Teaching him how to listen. How to see. How to find direction when the sky went stormy.

The forest quieted then, as if on cue. Even the birds went still.

Kevin's head snapped up. "Why'd everything stop?"

Shane lowered his voice. "When the woods hold their breath like that, it means change. Could have been the stone you threw. Could be a hawk overhead. Could be weather shifting. Always pay attention to silence—it tells you things noise can't."

April tilted her head, listening, too.

After a moment, the birds resumed their chatter, and the tension eased. "Guess it's clear for now," she said.

"Guess so." Shane reached to squeeze her hand lightly before letting go.

They reached a clearing where the trail widened into a ledge above the canyon. Sunlight poured through the gap, turning the red stone gold.

Shane reached for April's hand, lacing their fingers together. Not a quick squeeze this time but something more deliberate. More permanent.

April's breath caught as his thumb stroked across her knuckles—slow, deliberate, intimate. The touch conveyed everything they couldn't say out loud with Kevin ten feet ahead of them.

I'm here.

I'm not leaving.

Give me a chance and I'll spend the rest of my life proving you can trust me.

April's fingers tightened around his, answering in the same silent language.

I'm scared.

But I want this.

I want you.

They stood like that for a long moment, hands clasped, the canyon spreading out below them in shades of gold and rust. The clouds moved overhead, casting shadows that danced across the cliffs. Pete's bark and Kevin's laugh echoed off the stone walls.

Finally, reluctantly, Shane let go. But the phantom warmth of her hand in his stayed with him, a promise of what was coming.

"Hey, Kevin, c'mere. You hear that?" He pointed toward the mountains where thunder rolled, faint and far away.

Kevin tilted his head. "The storm's coming?"

"Eventually. Count the seconds between flash and sound—divide by five. That's your distance in miles. Works for weather or artillery." He caught himself, softened his tone. "Or, you know, fireworks."

Kevin counted on his fingers, face scrunching with focus. "About twenty-five miles?"

"Not bad," Shane said. "We'll keep an eye on the clouds and the wind but we should have time for a snack break before we head back." Shane dropped his pack and pulled out a blanket and the thermos and container of scones Sonny had packed for them.

"Mission refuel," he said.

Kevin cheered. Pete flopped down immediately, tail thumping.

They sat together, passing around scones, steam curling from the hot chocolate. April leaned back on her hands, her face glowing. Shane handed her a bottle of water. "Gotta stay hydrated."

"You really think of everything."

"Occupational hazard," Shane said, taking out a bottle for himself. "Preparedness beats panic any day."

Kevin took a sip of hot chocolate. "Best ever."

"It's your Grandpapa's secret recipe," April said. "Even I don't know what all's in it."

Shane stretched his legs, looking out over the canyon where the creek flashed silver far below. "He's a good man," he said quietly. "You take after him."

April's gaze met his, tender and wary all at once. "You think so?"

"I know so."

For a while, they sat in easy silence. The clouds drifted slower now, their shadows sliding across the cliffs. Kevin finished his scone and hot chocolate, curled up beside Pete, and within minutes both were asleep—boy and dog tangled together, the picture of trust.

Shane felt the quiet settle deep. The kind that reminded him of waiting on a calm sea before the next mission. Not empty but full—of memories, of possibilities.

Kevin and Pete had been asleep for maybe ten minutes, curled together in that boneless way kids and dogs managed so easily. The canyon was quiet except for the distant rush of water and the lazy hum of insects in the afternoon heat.

April shifted closer to Shane on the blanket, close enough that their shoulders touched. She leaned her head against his shoulder with a small sigh—tired and content and trusting in a way that made Shane's throat tight.

His arm came around her automatically, pulling her closer. She fit against his side like she'd been designed for that exact spot, her weight warm and solid and real.

They sat like that, watching the clouds build and shift, the shadows moving across the canyon floor far below.

Shane could feel the steady rise and fall of April's breathing, could smell the faint scent of her lilac shampoo mixing with sun-warmed skin and sweet ponderosa pine.

This was what he'd been missing. Not just April, though God knew he'd missed her every day since he was eighteen. But this—the quiet intimacy of just being. No performance, no pretense. Just two people who'd found their way back to each other, sitting together while the world turned around them.

"Shane?" April's voice was soft, careful.

"Yeah?"

"When you ask me again..." She paused, and Shane felt his heart kick against his ribs. "I think you'll like my answer."

He turned his head, looking down at her. "You think so, huh?"

She met his look with a sexy smile that heated him through and through. "Maybe I know so."

Shane pressed a kiss to her temple—tender and promising, not the desperate heat of the porch kiss but something deeper. Something that said *I'll take care of this. I'll take care of you. I'll take care of us.*

Our family.

April's hand came up to rest against his chest, palm flat over his heart. He wondered if she could feel how hard it was beating, if she knew what this moment meant to him.

"Ask me anyway," she whispered. "I want to hear you say it."

Shane's arm tightened around her. "Okay."

They stayed like that a moment longer, savoring the quiet, the certainty, the weight of the question he was about to ask and the answer she'd already given. Thunder rumbled far off, deep and patient, rolling through the canyon like an echo from another life. Shane looked out over the sandstone cliffs, the sun catching the clouds just right, and knew he'd remember this moment all his life: the smell of rain on warm rock, the sound of the river far below, the woman beside him.

Then Kevin stirred, and they eased apart—but not before sharing one more look that said everything they needed to say.

Soon.

Yes.

Finally.

"Shane..." Her voice was barely above a whisper.

He caught her hand, held it gently. "I can wait," he said. "But not forever."

She smiled then—small, certain. "You won't have to."

Shane's breath left him in a rush. He cupped her face in his hands, thumbs stroking her cheekbones the way he had on the porch last night. But instead of kissing her mouth, he pulled her close and pressed his lips to her forehead again— soft, reverent, sealing a promise.

Everything. It meant everything.

"We should probably head back soon," April murmured against his shoulder, but she didn't move.

"Probably." Shane didn't move either.

Kevin made a small sound in his sleep, shifting closer to Pete. The dog's tail thumped once against the blanket.

April smiled against Shane's shirt. "We're going to have to be careful around him. At least until we figure out how to tell him."

"Tell him what?" Shane asked. "That his mom's body-guard is hopelessly in love with her?"

April pulled back just enough to look up at him, eyes bright. "Is that what you are?"

"Your bodyguard? Of course I am. Kevin retained me."

April tried not to laugh even as she narrowed her eyes at him.

"Or do you mean hopelessly in love?" Shane's mouth curved. "Yeah, Sweetness. That's exactly what I am."

This time when she kissed him, it was soft and sweet and full of promises of her own. Kevin stirred again, and they broke apart, both grinning like they had as teenagers who'd just gotten away with making out.

"Come on," Shane said, reluctantly standing and offering her his hand. "Let's get you two home before that storm decides to show up early."

April took his hand and let him pull her to her feet. Neither let go right away, even though Kevin was sitting up and rubbing his eyes.

FIFTEEN

THE FIRST FAT RAINDROPS HIT THE WINDSHIELD JUST as Shane pulled onto the highway.

"Uh-oh," Kevin said from the back seat, twisting to look at the sky through the rear window. "Shane, I think the storm's coming faster than you thought."

April glanced at the darkening clouds rolling over the mountains, their earlier puffy innocence gone mean and heavy. Thunder rumbled—closer now, no longer a distant promise but an immediate threat.

"Yeah, bud, I see it. Just goes to show, you can be prepared, but mother nature can still outmaneuver you." Shane's hands were steady on the wheel, but his eyes flicked to the rearview mirror, then to April. "My place is about ten minutes from here. We can wait it out there, have some dinner, wait until it passes."

April's stomach did a little flip. Shane's place. She'd never seen where he lived, never been invited into that part of his world. The thought made her pulse kick up for reasons that had nothing to do with the weather.

"Okay," she heard herself say.

The rain started in earnest as they turned off the main road—big, heavy drops that splattered against the glass and turned the world outside into a watercolor blur. Lightning split the sky, close enough to make April jump.

"One Mississippi, two Mississippi, three Mississippi—" Kevin counted from the backseat, his voice rising with excitement rather than fear.

Thunder cracked overhead like a whip.

"Three miles!" Kevin crowed. "It's getting closer!"

Pete whined softly from the back.

"It's okay, boy," Kevin soothed. "We're almost there, right Shane?"

"Right there." Shane pointed ahead where April could just make out the dark shape of a cabin through the downpour. "Hang on."

He came to the end of the driveway, which was at the base of a rock outcropping. A flight of wooden stairs led to the cabin about ten to fifteen feet above. Rain hammered the roof of the SUV, so loud April had to raise her voice to be heard.

"On three, we run for it!"

"I'll get Pete!" Kevin was already unbuckling.

"Hang on, you two," Shane said, laughing. "Stay here. Let me get Pete out first, then we'll make a run for it." He handed April a collapsible umbrella.

"Don't *you* need this?" But Shane was already out the door and into the storm. A moment later, the back of the SUV opened and Shane let Pete out.

"Okay, one—two—THREE!"

April and Kevin's doors flew open and they entered the deluge, which seemed to be coming in sideways now. April shrieked as cold rain hit her skin, soaking through her shirt in seconds. She grabbed Kevin and held the umbrella over their heads as all of them raced up the steps to the covered porch. Lightning flashed again, turning everything stark white for a heartbeat.

Shane got the door open and they tumbled inside, laughing and dripping and breathless. Pete shook himself immediately, spraying water everywhere, which made Kevin dissolve into giggles. He decided to shake himself just like the dog.

"Kevin! Sorry about the floor," April told Shane, but he was already halfway through the great room and saying something about grabbing towels from somewhere. "Hang on, let me help at least."

But April found herself looking around instead, taking in Shane's space for the first time.

The cabin was beautiful. Not showy, not trying too hard —just clean lines and warm wood and a kind of masculine comfort that fit Shane perfectly. Log walls glowed honey-gold in the soft light. Floor-to-ceiling windows looked out on forest, rain streaming down the glass in sheets. A massive stone fireplace dominated one wall, cold now but clearly well-used. Its mantel was lined with photos.

The furniture was simple but quality—a big brown leather couch that looked butter-soft, draped with sheepskin throws. More throws scattered on the floor over what had to be radiant heat, because even soaked to the skin, April could feel warmth rising from the polished wood beneath her feet. Woven rugs—Afghan, maybe, from his time overseas?— added splashes of deep red and navy on the bare floors.

Everything had a place. Nothing cluttered or messy. Neat as a pin, the way Shane had always kept his locker, his truck, his life.

It was so perfectly *him* that April felt her throat go tight.

"So." Shane appeared beside her with an armful of

towels, watching her face with an expression she couldn't quite read. Hopeful? Nervous? "What do you think?"

April turned to look at him—really look at him, standing in his own home, offering her a towel and waiting for her verdict.

"It's perfect," she said, and meant it. "Very you."

His smile could have powered half of Colorado. "Yeah?"

"Yeah." She took the towel, resisting the urge to step closer, to touch him, to say something ridiculous like *I could be happy here* when they'd barely started whatever this was between them. "It's really nice, Shane."

Kevin was already exploring, Pete trotting at his heels and shaking off water every few steps. "Whoa! Shane, you've got a huge TV! And is that a—Mom, he's got a whole shelf of books about wilderness survival!"

"Don't touch anything," April called, but there was no heat in it. Kevin was too excited, and honestly, so was she. "Actually, grab any book you want...if that's okay with you?" she asked Shane, but he was already chuckling.

"Absolutely. I love that you're comfortable enough to offer up my library." Shane handed her another towel. "You're not too wet, but the house is a little chilly. I can turn up the heat, or..." He hesitated, then pulled a flannel shirt from a hook by the door. Navy blue plaid, soft from washing. "You could wear this. If you want."

April took it, fingers brushing his. The flannel was warm and when she held it up she caught the scent—laundry detergent and something underneath that was pure Shane. Clean and masculine and a little bit woodsy, like he'd been standing too close to the fireplace, or maybe the scent just lived in his clothes now.

She wanted to bury her face in it.

Instead, she smiled. "Thanks. I'll just—" She gestured vaguely toward what she assumed was a bathroom.

"Down the hall, first door on the left."

The bathroom was as neat as the rest of the house. White subway tile, dark fixtures, a shower that looked big enough for two—

Stop it.

April shrugged out of her damp shirt and pulled on Shane's flannel, rolling the sleeves up her forearms. It smelled even better when she was wearing it, surrounding her in that scent that made her want to do extremely inappropriate things. If only her son wasn't twenty feet away in the next room.

She caught her reflection in the mirror—cheeks flushed, eyes bright, drowning in Shane's clothes—and had to take a breath.

Get it together.

When she came back out, Shane had a fire going. Or rather, he was in the process of building one while Kevin watched from a careful distance, firing questions faster than Shane could stack kindling.

"Why do you start with the small stuff?"

"Because it catches faster. Big logs need heat to get going."

"What if you don't have matches?"

"Then you use a ferro rod. I'll teach you sometime."

"Can you teach me now?"

Shane glanced up, caught April watching, and smiled. "Maybe after dinner, bud. Your mom's probably starving."

April was starving, but not for food. She was hungry for this—the easy way Shane talked to Kevin, the patience in his voice, the way he took her son's endless curiosity seriously instead of brushing him off. The way Kevin looked at Shane like he hung the moon.

The way Shane looked at Kevin like the feeling was mutual.

This could be my life, April thought, and the realization hit her with unexpected force. *This could be us. Every Sunday, every day. Coming home to this. To him.*

The thought should have terrified her. Instead, it felt like walking out of a casino with her lucky purse full of cash.

Shane struck a match and the kindling caught, flames licking upward. Kevin leaned in, fascinated, and Shane's hand came out automatically to keep him at a safe distance —protective without thinking about it.

April's chest went tight.

This should have been my life all along.

The thought slipped in uninvited, bringing with it a complicated tangle of emotions she didn't want to examine too closely. She could have had this years ago if things had been different. If Shane's father hadn't been a bastard. If Shane had been brave enough to stand up to him then instead of later. If she'd continued on to California instead of Vegas.

She could have been this happy all along.

Except—

April's gaze landed on Kevin, his face lit by firelight as Shane explained the physics of combustion, and something in her chest twisted. If she'd gone to California with Shane, she wouldn't have Kevin. She'd have different children— Shane's children—in some alternate universe where they'd stayed together and built a life.

But not this child. Not her wild-hearted, brilliant, sometimes difficult, perfect boy.

The dissonance sat heavy in her stomach. She couldn't regret the path that brought her Kevin, but by God, she could grieve the years she'd lost with Shane. The life they could have had if the world had been kinder.

If they'd both been braver.

Stop it, she told herself firmly. *You're here now. That's what matters.*

Shane looked up again, caught her watching, and raised an eyebrow. "You good?"

April pushed off the doorframe. "Yeah. Just hoping your kitchen is as well-stocked as the rest of this place and isn't full of protein powder or old MREs," she teased.

"Oh ye of little faith." Shane stood, brushing his hands on his jeans. "I've got everything you need."

I'm starting to believe that, April thought, but didn't say it out loud.

The kitchen was open to the great room, divided only by a long island topped with butcher block. April opened the fridge and blinked. Vegetables. Actual fresh vegetables, not just beer and leftover takeout. Cheese, milk, eggs. A drawer full of deli meat and another with various cuts of fresh meat wrapped in butcher paper.

"You really do cook," she said, impressed.

Shane came up behind her—close enough that she could feel his warmth. When he reached past her for the butter, his arm brushed hers and sent electricity straight through the flannel.

"Learned from Elias and Waylon when they were running out of the firehouse," he said, his voice low and close to her ear. "Can't live on MREs and protein bars forever."

April's fingers tightened on the refrigerator door. "Good to know."

"I was thinking chili. There's ground beef, chili powder, garlic—" Shane pulled open the freezer. "And I've got tamales from this little place on the edge of town. Best in Colorado."

"Kevin loves tamales."

"I love tamales!" Kevin shouted from in front of the fire.

"Ears like a bat, that one." April laughed.

"Then it's decided." Shane pulled out the package and set it on the counter, then looked at her—really looked at her, in his kitchen, wearing his shirt. His eyes went a little hazy for a moment and his gaze skimmed up and down her body in a way that made her skin tingle and lady bits clench. "You cook, I'll help?"

"Deal." The word came out a little rough and she cleared her throat.

Shane turned on a radio and they fell into an easy rhythm—April browning the meat while Shane chopped onions, their hips bumping as they moved around each other. The fire crackled in the background. Rain lashed the windows and thunder boomed. Kevin set the table under Shane's patient direction, learning where the plates and silverware lived.

It felt like they'd done this a thousand times before instead of this being the first.

April caught Shane's eye as she reached for the cumin, and the look he gave her was so full of want and hope and careful restraint that her breath caught.

He leaned in close, his lips just brushing her ear.

"Careful," he murmured, his breath hot and close. "You keep looking at me like that and I'm going to forget we have an audience."

April glanced at Kevin, who was trying to fold napkins into some kind of elaborate shape.

"Noted," she breathed. "But for the record, you're looking at me the same way."

"Can't help it." Shane's voice dropped lower. "You're in my kitchen. Wearing my shirt. Cooking dinner with our kid setting the table." He shook his head. "I've imagined this more times than I can count."

Our kid.

The words hit her square in the chest. Not *your kid* or *Kevin. Our kid.*

Like Shane had already claimed him. Claimed both of them.

She waited for him to correct himself. He didn't.

April turned back to the stove before the emotion could show on her face. "Chili's almost done. Just needed a little more cumin."

"Good." Shane's hand found the small of her back—just a brief touch, a promise. "I'm starving."

So was April.

But not for chili.

SIXTEEN

THEY ATE ON THE FLOOR AROUND SHANE'S COFFEE table in front of the fire, bowls of chili-and-cheese-smothered tamales, more warm tamales wrapped in corn husks waiting on a plate on the table. The fire crackled and popped, throwing dancing shadows across the walls. Outside, the storm had settled into a steady drumming rain, no longer violent but persistent—the kind that made April grateful to be inside, warm and dry and well-fed.

"This is so good," Kevin mumbled around a mouthful of tamale. "Mom, can we sell these at Riversong?"

"I'll talk to the owner," Shane said before April could answer. "See if they'd be interested in a wholesale arrangement."

April looked at him over her beer. "You don't have to do that."

"I know." Shane's smile was easy. "But why wouldn't I? Good food, good business. Everybody wins."

Kevin was already on to the next thing, his brain going in a million directions at once the way it always did when he was happy and comfortable. "Shane, how many stones did you skip when you were my age?"

"Honestly? I lost count. I was terrible at it until Waylon showed me the trick with the wrist."

Kevin grinned. "The one you showed me."

"Yup. And picking the right stone. You want it flat and smooth, about the size of your palm." Shane demonstrated with his hand. "Too big and it sinks. Too small and it doesn't have enough momentum."

"Can we practice tomorrow?"

Shane glanced at April. "You've got school tomorrow, bud. But maybe after, if your mom says it's okay."

Kevin turned those big hopeful eyes on her. "Mom? Please?"

April felt her heart squeeze.

This could be every Sunday. Every weekend. Every ordinary Tuesday if we want it to be.

"We'll see," she said, which was mom-code for probably yes but I'm not committing yet.

Kevin grinned like he'd won the lottery. "Can we do this every Sunday? Come hiking and then have dinner at Shane's and practice skipping stones?"

The question landed heavy in the warm room. April's chest went tight.

Shane set down his beer, his expression careful. "Again, that's up to your mom, bud."

Kevin looked between them, picking up on something in the adult silence he couldn't quite name. "But we could, right? If Mom said yes? It's okay with you?"

"Yeah," Shane said quietly, his eyes on April. "If your mom said yes, we could do this every Sunday. Every day, if she wanted."

April took a long sip of beer to hide the fact that her

hands were shaking slightly. The weight of the moment pressed down on her—Kevin's hope, Shane's barely contained want, her own terrified longing for exactly this.

"Let's just focus on today," she said finally. "Today was pretty perfect."

Kevin seemed satisfied with that answer, or maybe he was just too full and warm to push. He settled back against the couch, Pete immediately arranging himself as a pillow. Within minutes, Kevin's eyes were drooping.

"I'm not tired," he mumbled, even as his head lolled against Pete's side.

"Of course not," April said, amused. "You're wide awake."

"Mmm-hmm." His eyes closed. "Just... resting my eyes..."

Shane caught April's gaze over Kevin's head, and smiled. They sat in comfortable silence, watching the fire, listening to Kevin's breathing even out into sleep. Pete's tail thumped once against the floor, but the dog didn't move otherwise—content to be Kevin's pillow for as long as needed.

"He's out," Shane said softly after a few more minutes.

April nodded. "He had a big day."

"I'll get him." Shane scooped Kevin up slowly, carefully, and stood. Her son barely stirred, just made a small sound and curled into Shane's chest. Pete stood, ready to accompany Kevin anywhere

April followed them down the hall with a blanket, her throat tight at the sight of Shane carrying her sleeping child like he'd done it a hundred times before.

Like he planned to do it a hundred times more.

The guest room was beside the main bathroom. Shane shouldered the door open and April got her first look at the space—a double bed with a navy quilt, simple wooden furniture, a lamp on the nightstand already turned to its lowest setting.

He laid Kevin down gently, and together they pulled off his shoes and tucked the blanket around him. Kevin mumbled something that might have been "love you" or might have been nothing at all, then rolled onto his side.

April smoothed his hair back from his forehead, the way she'd done since he was a baby.

"He really loves you," she whispered.

Shane was still watching Kevin sleep, his expression so tender it made April's chest ache.

They stood there a moment longer, side by side in the doorway, watching Kevin sleep in Shane's guest room like it was where he belonged.

Finally, Shane eased the door mostly closed—not latched, just cracked enough to hear if Kevin called out. Pete settled on the floor outside the door, assuming guard duty without being asked.

"Good boy," Shane murmured, scratching behind Pete's ears.

They walked back to the living room together. The fire had burned down to embers, casting a softer glow. The storm outside had gentled further to a good soaking rain, the thunder gone. Shane picked up her beer can and offered it to her.

"Thanks." April took it, settling back onto the couch. Shane sat beside her—close but not crowding, waiting for her to make the first move.

She curled into his side like it was inevitable, like gravity pulling her there. His arm came around her shoulders, warm and solid.

"So," Shane said after a moment. "Today."

"Today," April agreed.

"Kevin had fun."

"He did. He hasn't been that happy in..." She trailed off, not wanting to finish the sentence. *Since before the drive-by. Since before he started having nightmares. Since before he hired you to be my bodyguard.*

"You had fun, too," Shane said.

"I did." April took a sip of beer. "This was... this was a good day."

"The best," Shane said quietly.

They sat like that for a while, not talking, just existing together in the warm quiet. April could feel Shane's heartbeat where her head rested against his pec, steady and sure. The flannel she wore smelled like him. Everything in this cabin smelled like him, felt like him—solid and safe and real.

I could get used to this, April thought. *I could get used to him.*

"So," Shane said eventually, his voice careful. "About that question I asked on the mountain."

April's pulse kicked up. "You mean the one about giving you another chance?" she asked, stalling.

"That's the one." His arm tightened slightly around her. "You said you'd answer after the hike."

"I did say that." April set down her empty beer, buying herself a moment. This was it—the moment where she either jumped or backed away from the edge. "Shane—"

"Before you answer," he interrupted gently, "I need to say something."

April tilted her head to look at him. His expression was serious, vulnerable in a way that made her chest ache.

"I know you're scared," Shane said. "I know you have every reason to be. I hurt you once, badly. My father threatened your family. You spent years building a life without me, raising Kevin on your own, proving you didn't need a man." He took a breath. "But, April, I'm not asking you to need me. I'm asking you to want me. To choose this. Choose us."

"What if it doesn't work?" The same words from the night before came out quieter than she intended. "What if we try this and it falls apart? What if—"

"What if it *does* work?" Shane countered. "What if we're happy? What if Kevin gets to grow up with two parents who love him instead of just one? What if we figure it out together instead of you carrying everything alone?"

"But what if you realize Kevin's too much?" April's voice cracked. "What if the reality of a kid who asks a million questions and gets in trouble at school and—"

"April." Shane shifted to face her fully, his hands coming up to frame her face. "Kevin's not too much. That kid is brilliant and brave and kind, and if you think for one second I don't see that, you haven't been paying attention." His thumbs stroked her cheekbones. "I love him. I love him like a son already. That's not going to change."

"Your family—"

"Doesn't get a vote anymore." Shane's voice was firm. "I told my mother—I won't introduce her to any future grand-children unless she changes how she treats you. My father?" His jaw tightened. "He doesn't exist to me. Not anymore. Not after what he did to you. To us."

April felt tears prick her eyes. "What if I'm not enough? What if—"

"Stop." Shane's voice was soft but commanding. "April Taylor, you are more than enough. You've always been more than enough. The only question is whether you're brave enough to believe it."

His mouth found hers then—soft and questioning at

first, then deeper when she opened for him. April's hands fisted in his shirt, pulling him closer, trying to pour years of longing into one kiss.

When they finally broke apart, both breathing hard, Shane rested his forehead against hers.

"So?" he whispered. "What's your answer?"

"Yes." The word came out choked. "Yes, I want this. I want you. I'm terrified but I—yes."

Shane's smile could have lit the whole Front Range. He kissed her again, harder this time. His hands moved to her waist, pulling her closer. April shifted, starting to climb into his lap, but she felt all the fear and guilt she'd been holding onto for so long, surface. That old instinct to stay in control, to protect herself, to not give too much, threatened to overwhelm her, to come between them.

Shane felt it—of course he did. He pulled back, studying her face in the firelight.

"What's wrong?"

"Nothing." But even as she said it, April knew it was a lie.

"April." Shane's hands gentled on her hips. "Talk to me."

She tried to smile, to deflect. "I'm fine. I just—"

"You're holding back." It wasn't an accusation, just an observation. "Why?"

"I'm not—" April stopped, swallowed hard. Because he was right. Even now, even after saying yes, part of her was still braced for impact. Still waiting for the other shoe to drop.

Shane was watching her with those eyes that saw too much, his expression patient and concerned and so damn tender it made her want to cry.

"I don't know how to do this," she finally admitted. "I don't know how to just... let go."

"Why not?"

"Because—" April's voice cracked. "Because bad things happen when I let my guard down. Because I make mistakes and people I love get hurt and—"

"And you've been trying to make up for it ever since," Shane finished quietly. "Haven't you?"

April looked away, but Shane's fingers gently turned her face back to his.

"April, you don't have to keep punishing yourself for leaving home. For what happened in Vegas. For any of it."

"You don't understand—"

"Then help me understand." Shane's thumb stroked her jaw. "Because from where I'm sitting, all I see is a woman who's been carrying the weight of the world on her shoulders for so long she doesn't know how to put it down."

April's breath hitched. God, he saw right through her. Right down to the core of everything she'd been trying to ignore.

"I hurt them," she whispered. "My parents, Hannah, everyone. When I left, when I disappeared for all those years—I hurt them. And I'm still trying to make up for it."

"By running yourself ragged at Riversong? By never taking a day off? By refusing to let yourself be happy?" Shane shook his head. "Baby, that's not atonement. That's punishment. And you don't deserve to be punished."

"Yes, I do—"

"No." Shane's voice was firm. "You don't. You made choices you thought were right at the time. You survived. You came home. You brought them Kevin." His hands tightened on her hips. "Your family has forgiven you. Hell, I bet if you asked your dad, he'd say there was never anything to forgive in the first place."

April's eyes stung. Because Shane was right—she'd apologized a thousand times and her parents had told her to stop. They'd never blamed her. They'd just been grateful she was home.

But April had never forgiven herself.

"I don't know if I deserve to be happy," she whispered.

"Why not?"

"Because—" The tears spilled over then, hot tracks down her cheeks. "Because I did so many dumb things. Brought so much pain to everyone I love."

"You don't think Kevin is a mistake, do you?"

April's head snapped up, fury flooding through her. "Of course not. He's the best thing that ever happened to me. I'd crawl over broken glass through hell and back for my son. I'd go through it all again—every humiliation, every beating, every terrifying night when I wasn't sure if I'd see the morning. All of it to make sure I still had Kevin."

"Then what are you trying to atone for?" Shane asked gently. "Coming home? Asking your family for help? Having the courage to rebuild your life?"

"The pain I caused them. The worry. The—" April's voice broke. "I've been trying to make up for it. Helping with the shop, being there for everyone, going without so they can have extra—"

"But you deserve—"

"Don't tell me what I do and don't deserve." April pulled back, wrapping her arms around herself. "I already know."

Shane was quiet for a long moment, watching her. Then he said, very softly, "You *don't* know, April. You don't have the first clue. You can't drag your past around with you forever. You came back here to get away from it, but you brought all the fear, all the pain, all the undeserved guilt, right back with you." He leaned forward. "Let it go."

"I can't." April squeezed her eyes shut.

"Why—"

"I don't know how!" The words burst out of her, raw and desperate. A tear slid down her cheek and she opened her eyes. "I don't know how to stop feeling like I owe everyone everything. Like being happy would be taking something away from someone else."

Shane studied her, his expression shifting from concern to understanding. "I get it now," he said quietly. "April, you being happy wouldn't take anything away from the people who love you. They don't want to see you sad. They don't want to punish you for anything. They've forgiven you—hell, they never blamed you in the first place."

"But—"

Shane held up his hand. "Even though I'm sure you've given them hundreds of apologies by now."

Damn him for being right. She'd apologized until they'd told her to stop. So she'd converted all that energy into action—helping at Riversong, running errands, taking care of Kevin, never letting herself just... be happy.

Because she didn't feel like she deserved it.

"There is so much going on in your head right now," Shane said softly, reaching for her. "Let me in."

April started to lean toward him, then froze. Old instinct, old fear. She turned her face away—no, she flinched.

Flinched.

Like she was expecting him to hit her denying him anything.

The silence that followed was deafening.

When April finally looked back at Shane, his face had gone pale. Not angry—devastated.

"April," he breathed. "Did you think I was going to—"

He couldn't even finish the sentence. "Baby, I would never—"

"I know." The words rushed out. "I know you wouldn't. That's not—I didn't mean—" She was shaking now, horrified at herself, at the automatic response her body had learned from Vince all those years ago.

Shane hadn't moved. Hadn't reached for her. He'd laid his hands carefully flat on his thighs, giving her space.

"It kills me to see you in so much pain," he said quietly.

April stared at him, not believing what she was hearing. Not anger. Not accusations. Just... grief. For her.

"You thought I was going to slap you for denying me something. For telling me no." Shane's voice was rough with emotion. "You're one of the strongest people I know, April. And the thought of you keeping yourself under lock and key out of fear—fear of being hit by someone who supposedly cares about you—" He shook his head. "That kills me."

"Shane—"

"I just want you to be happy." He said it so simply, like it was the most obvious thing in the world. "That's all I've ever wanted. Even when you weren't mine to want it for."

April's heart cracked open then. She looked at this man who'd seen her at her worst, who knew all her mistakes, who'd watched her flinch away from him and hadn't gotten angry. Who just wanted her to be happy.

"There is no doubt in my mind that you could hold up the entire sky by yourself if you had to," Shane said. "But I'm here to tell you—you don't have to do it anymore. Not because you can't, but because you shouldn't have to. Not all alone. Not as long as I'm in your life." He finally, carefully, reached for her hand. "I'm not here to tell you you're weak. I'm here to help you be strong."

A sob broke free from April's throat. Shane pulled her

close, and she went—collapsing into him, letting him hold her while she finally, finally let herself feel all of it—including the desperate hope that maybe she didn't have to carry everything alone anymore.

"I've got you," Shane murmured into her hair. "I've got you, baby. I'm not going anywhere."

"It's okay to let go," he whispered in April's ear. "I know how you are, April. I know how you carry the weight of the world—of your family, or your business, of the whole world—on your shoulders. You think no one can help you carry it, but I can. I can, April. I'm not the scared, cowed boy I was. I'm a man who's never forgotten you. Who's wanted you for so damn long. Who would do anything for you. Let me have it, April."

"Have what?"

"Have everything you're carrying right now. All your responsibility. All your fear. All your anger. Give it to me. Give it to me, and all I'm gonna give back to you is my strength. My—"

"Don't say it, Shane."

"Don't say what? That I love you?"

"No."

SEVENTEEN

No.

Shane felt her body stiffen under his hands. Stiffen—then go lax.

"Too bad. You're gonna hear it from me over and over. I love you, April. I never stopped loving you. All those nights I worried about where you were. The nights I burned for you, longing to feel you under me, to fill you with my cock and feel you pulse around it as I gave you orgasm after orgasm. To feel you let go and thrash, to know you were powerless—willingly powerless under me—because you trusted me. Trusted that I'd have your back. That I'd catch you and hold you safe in my arms. Always. Always, April." He drew in a ragged breath. "So let me have it all, *now.*"

April turned in his arms, her chest heaving, heart pounding. Her face was a mask of intense emotion. Was it anger? Lust? Maybe both.

"Give it to me. All of it. I'm done asking, April. I'm demanding."

"Shane," she breathed. Then her lips crashed against

his, her body pressed against his chest as he pulled her in tightly. She tasted as good as he remembered—no, years of pent-up desire made her taste better. Better than his memories, better than his filthiest dreams of her.

"That's right, baby," he growled against her mouth. "Let me have you. Let me carry you."

"I hated you, Shane. Hated you for what you did."

"Good. I deserved it. Give me your rage."

April nipped at his lips. She gripped his back, then dug her nails in. Shane gasped at the pleasurable pain of it as his endorphins kicked in. She needed to let herself go and know she was still safe, still loved. But he realized he also needed her anger—her fury—to make things right in his head.

"Tell me what you need, April," he growled.

"Not you," she said before she plunged her tongue into his mouth, making him groan. He ran his hands down her back to her ass and lifted her. She wrapped her legs around his waist and pressed herself against his hard cock. She ground against him while making the sexiest sounds he'd ever heard.

"You sure about that, baby? You sure you don't need me?"

"Shut up and carry me to bed."

Shane didn't need to be told twice.

He stood in one smooth motion and April's legs locked around his waist, her arms wrapped tightly around his shoulders. She was lighter than he expected—or maybe his adrenaline made everything feel weightless. Her mouth found his again, hungry and demanding, and Shane had to tear himself away long enough to see where the hell he was going.

Down the hall. Past the guest room where Kevin slept.

Past Pete, who lifted his head but didn't budge from his post.

Shane's bedroom door was at the end of the hall, standing open like an invitation. Dark inside except for the faint glow from the bedside cut glass lamp reflecting off the walls.

April's fingers tangled in his hair, pulling just hard enough to make him groan. Her hips rolled against him and Shane's vision went hazy for a second. He'd imagined this—God, he'd imagined this so many times over the years—but reality was burning him alive in the best possible way.

"Shane," she breathed against his mouth. "Please—"

"I've got you." His voice came out rough, barely controlled. "I've got you, baby."

He carried her across the threshold and closed the door behind them. His bed—king-sized, navy sheets, the same military corners he'd been making since boot camp—waited in the soft light.

Shane set April down on the edge of the mattress, but she didn't let go. She pulled him down with her, until both of them tumbled onto the bed in a tangle of limbs and desperate hands.

"Wait," Shane managed, bracing himself above her. "April, wait—"

She looked up at him, eyes dark and dilated, lips swollen from kissing. Her hair spread across his bed like a deep, dark river. God, she belonged there. She'd *always* belonged there.

"What?" Her voice was breathy, impatient. "Don't you dare change your mind—"

"Not changing my mind." Shane cupped her face, forcing himself to slow down when every instinct screamed at him to take, claim, possess. "Just need to see you. Need to know you're really here. That this is real."

April's expression softened. Her hand came up to cover his, turning her face to press a kiss to his palm.

"I'm here," she whispered. "I'm really here, Shane. And I'm not going anywhere."

Something in his chest cracked wide open at that—at the promise in her voice, the certainty. April Taylor, who'd spent years running, who'd built walls so high even she couldn't see over them sometimes, was choosing to stay.

Was choosing *him*.

Shane bent his head, kissed her slowly, taking his time. Tasting her. Memorizing every sound she made, every place his touch made her shiver.

"I love you," he said against her mouth. "Always have. Always will."

"I love you, too." April's fingers found the hem of his shirt, started pulling it up. "Now stop talking and show me."

Shane's laugh was low and rough. "Yes, ma'am."

He reached back, grabbed his shirt, and pulled it over his head in one smooth motion. April's hands were immediately on his chest, her touch burning him everywhere her fingers landed.

So sexy how she was wearing his flannel—but it needed to go. He'd been a fool to put that shirt on her. It wrecked him in a way he hadn't prepared for—just like the sight of her in his space had locked something into place in him that wasn't ever going to unlock.

Shane's hands went to the buttons, but April batted them away.

"I've got it," she said with an impish grin. She sat up slightly, holding his gaze as she slowly undid each button.

One. Two. Three. Taking her time. Driving him absolutely insane.

When the flannel finally fell open, Shane's breath stopped. She was perfect. Every curve, every line, every inch of skin he'd been dreaming about.

"You're staring," April said, but there was no self-consciousness in her voice. Just heat.

"Yeah." Shane's voice was barely above a growl. "I am."

"I've gotten a little...curvier since high school."

"Thank you, God. Curvy is good." He bent and landed a kiss on her breastbone. "Curvy is so damn hot." His next kiss landed on her soft, rounded belly. If she'd let him, he'd fall asleep with his head on her belly.

He pulled back and pushed the flannel off her shoulders, and April let it fall away, let Shane toss it on the floor. Her bra quickly followed it, then Shane was gazing at the most beautiful breasts, letting the sigh of her feed his hunger. April let herself be vulnerable.

"Thank you," he whispered.

"For what?"

"For trusting me. For letting me in." Shane's hands skimmed down her sides, gentle despite the desperate need clawing at him. "For giving me everything you've been carrying. I promise I'll take care of it. Take care of you."

April pulled him down to her, wrapped herself around him again like she'd never let go.

"I know you will," she breathed. "Now love me, Shane. Please."

And Shane did. He ran his fingers over her nipples, softly, slowly, to build the fire inside her as hot as it would go.

"Yes," she purred as she arched into his hands, wanting more.

The single word spoken so boldly hit him like a shot of pure oxygen. He stopped moving for a second because he didn't trust his hands not to rush. The thunder had faded to a distant grumble; rain threaded the windows in soft, twisty lines, a steady patter on Shane's roof. The embers shifted and crackled, sending up sparks.

"That's my sweetness," he said, voice low. He smoothed his thumbs over her nipples again, then moved up to her cheekbones and stroked them, the way he'd done on the porch the night before. He angled his head and kissed her gently, banking his heat along with hers. His cock was achingly hard, straining against his boxer briefs and cargos, and he was in danger of coming before he'd even taken it out of his pants.

April's fingers curled into his waistband and tugged. An impatient sound caught in the back of her throat.

He eased back only far enough to look her over. He loved the way the golden light washed across her skin, how it turned her eyes molten. "You ready?"

"Oh yes." She glanced toward the bedroom door, voice dipping. "Should we lock it?"

"Pete's on duty. If Kevin wakes, we'll have plenty of warning."

Her smile went warm and wicked at the edges. "So we have a sentry and rain for cover."

"And time."

"Then lose the pants, Shane."

He started to laugh and covered his mouth. Just what he needed to do—wake Kevin with loud laughter. That sent April into a fit of giggles. She bit down on her arm, trying not to laugh. When they'd both stopped, he took her face in his hands and kissed her. He set the pace, let her catch it and change it at will. Her mouth was delicious, that old

sweetness of hers he remembered so well coming through—
then she gave him a teasing swipe of her tongue that made
him groan into her and lose a notch of control.

"God, sweetness," he breathed against her lips. "I love it
when you're feisty."

She nipped him, then soothed the nip with her tongue,
making him groan and press his cock against her. She
already knew every button he had and it looked like she
intended to press each one in turn.

Then she pulled back again. "It's been a while," she
admitted, embarrassment and humor in her eyes. "Like...
ages."

"Same." The truth cost him nothing with her. "Been a
damn minute." He slid one hand into her hair, the other
down to the small of her back where he'd been touching her
all evening and pretending it was nothing. "We'll take it
slow."

Her gaze flicked over his face, as her impish smile
returned. "We don't have to take it *that* slow."

He laughed—helpless—and kissed her again because he
couldn't resist. Then he swept her up into his arms and
eased her onto the pillows. He came down over her,
propped himself on his forearms so he wasn't giving her all
his weight, and lost himself for a while: the rhythm of her
mouth, the little catch she made when he angled his hips
just so, the way her knees parted to cradle his sides. The
world narrowed to the warm bedside lamp glow and the
hush of rain and her soft skin under his palms.

When he finally trailed his lips down her jaw and along
the notch of her throat, April tipped her head to give him
the line of it like an offering. Her pulse fluttered under his
mouth. He took his time there, open-mouthed kisses that
tasted like salt and rain, gave her his tongue and teeth when

she asked for more with a breathy "yes, please." He slid a hand along her ribcage—her skin warm and silken and his now—and felt her breath stutter.

"Still good?" he murmured, checking because he would never stop checking.

"Better than good," she said, voice roughened. "Don't stop."

He didn't. He palmed the curve of her breast, thumb circling until she arched. Her nipple tightened against his touch, and he felt his control fray. He bent, mouth replacing his hand, and the sound she made—half surprise, half gratitude—went straight through him. He traced the edge of her with his tongue, then closed gently around her and sucked, shallow at first, then deeper when her fingers grabbed a fistful of his hair. He gave her the same patience he'd use coaxing a terrified hiker off a ledge: steady pressure, clear intention, all the time in the world. She responded with a roll of her hips that had him biting back a curse into her skin.

"*Shane*," she said on a gasp.

He moved to her other breast, giving it the same careful attention, drawing out more of those sounds that were making him dizzy. April's body was a landscape he'd never tire of exploring, all hills and valleys and secret places that begged to be discovered. He could feel her heart racing under his lips, her breaths coming faster.

Her hands weren't idle; they mapped his shoulders, his back, his arms, as if she were relearning him, too. Each touch was a spark, igniting high school memories of stolen moments in the back of his truck, lazy afternoons by the river, and fumbling, hurried makeout sessions when his parents weren't home.

He trailed kisses down her sternum, over her soft belly,

feeling her muscles jump under his lips. Her fingers were in his hair, guiding him, urging him on. He hooked his thumbs into the waistband of her pants, looking up at her for permission. She nodded, lifting her hips to help him. He slid them down along with her panties, taking his time, revealing her inch by inch.

God, she was beautiful. All curves and softness, all his. He pressed a kiss to her hipbone, feeling her shiver. He could smell her arousal, sweet and musky, and it made his mouth water. He wanted to taste her, to make her scream his name. But he also wanted to draw this out, to make it last forever.

"Shane, please," she begged.

He spread her legs and gazed at her sweet, wet pussy, remembering how much she loved this. He bent and ran his tongue along her folds and she pressed herself against him. He listened to her muffled moans and licked her harder and faster. His tongue circled her swelling clit and he lapped up her sweetness. Shane slowly slid a finger inside her, then added another. He crooked them until he found the little nub inside and stroked while he licked her clit.

That sent her straight into her first orgasm of the night. She bucked against his mouth, her velvet walls clenching and unclenching around his fingers.

He slowed his movements, only stopping when he knew she had finished and was about to become too sensitive to his touch.

But not for long.

Shane worked his way back up her body, now relaxed. Her eyes were closed, one arm flung over her head and the other—

Oh, mercy. The other one was rolling and squeezing her nipple.

This was new, and incredibly hot.

"You like touching yourself?"

"Yes. It's all I've had for a while now." She lazily opened her eyes and gave him a smoldering gaze. "Do you have a problem with that?"

"No way, sweetness. You touching yourself is so fucking hot. I could watch you all night."

"I hope you'll do more than watch," she teased. She lifted her other arm and brought her hand down between her legs. Her fingers moved in circles. Apparently, she didn't get as sensitive as she used to, or her recovery time was a lot faster.

It didn't matter which to Shane. He reached for the side table drawer and—

Realized it had been so long, he didn't have any condoms.

April's eyes widened, apparently realizing his dilemma. Then she giggled, "Ooops."

"Dammit, April, I should have... Dammit."

"It's all right. It's actually reassuring that you don't have a fresh box of condoms in your bedroom." She looked down, the barest hint of embarrassment on her face. "I know you like to hang out at Cocks and Strippers with the guys."

Shane snorted. "Yeah, no. Last time I was there, it was to stop a predator. And, I've never taken a woman home from there." He rubbed the back of his neck. "I haven't taken a woman home since I came home."

Her eyebrows knitted and she looked confused. "Since you came home?" Her eyes widened. "Oh. You mean, from the Navy?"

"That's what I'm saying."

"Really?"

"Truly. Not as long as I've been back in Lyons. As for

Cocks and Strippers, the most I've done is hang out with my brothers and do some line dancing. Never took a woman home, never went home with one."

"Shane," she whispered, dead serious. "Are you saying I'm about to...take your virginity again?"

It took him a moment, then he was burying his face in the mattress, trying his best not to howl with laughter and wake Kevin at possibly the worst time. April wasn't doing much better, judging by the fact that she'd rolled over and her body was convulsing.

Their laughter subsided after what felt like an hour.

"We are never going to grow up, are we?" she asked.

"At least not in bed," Shane answered.

"Wow, so that means you're never going to have condoms."

Shane fought not to laugh again. Just because I couldn't get a hold of one the first three times we wanted to do it—"

"Did you honestly just call sex 'doing it'?"

He shrugged. "Never growing up. And I did have condoms when we finally did it."

April snorted. "To think I gave my virginity to you."

"Maybe since we were both virgins, we didn't lose our virginity, we just swapped virginities?"

"That's not how that works."

"No?"

"No."

Shane took a nice, deep breath. "So."

"If you're asking if I'm on birth control, the answer is yes. And, I had my annual two months ago, and I'm clean as a whistle."

"Me too."

"So."

"So."

"I guess we're going bareback, sailor."

Oh my God, I love this uninhibited woman.

"Guess we are." Shane stood long enough to shove his cargos and boxer briefs down his legs, the he kicked them aside.

His cock wholeheartedly agreed with this plan. He immediately hardened to steel, even before April reached for it.

And when she did, he almost went off at her barest touch. He threw his head back and hissed.

"Oh my," she said, her voice heavy with desire. She squeezed the base of his shaft and ran her hand up his cock, gently squeezing out a generous drop of precome. She bent down and licked it off and Shane thought he might pass out from the pleasure.

"Oh, you're wicked."

"Mm-hmm." She laid herself back down on the pillows —looking both innocent and wanton at the same time. "What are you going to do about it?"

"This." Shane moved lightning fast. He was on top looking down on her, positioning his cock, teasing her with the tip.

"Please, sailor," she purred.

That was all the encouragement he needed. He pushed into her and knew joy.

"April," he groaned. "Sweetness."

She wrapped her legs around him, encouraging him to go deeper. Then they found their rhythm. They may have been older, but making love to April now was a million times better than when they were younger. She felt so impossibly good. She had no inhibitions, no fear, no nervousness. He wasn't afraid of accidentally hurting her.

She wanted him. All of him.

And he gave himself to her—slow, fast, soft, hard. She begged him to give her everything until he felt the pressure building to a peak, then the long, slow uncoiling as he came hot and fast and hard inside her.

He collapsed beside her. They took each other into their arms and fell asleep satisfied.

EIGHTEEN

Shane woke to pale morning light filtering through his bedroom window and reached for April. His hand met empty sheets. For a heartbeat, panic sliced through him—sharp and irrational and so familiar it hurt.

She left. She woke up, regretted it, grabbed Kevin and—

Stop.

Shane forced himself to breathe, to think. April didn't have a car here. She couldn't have left. Wouldn't have left.

Unless she called someone to pick them up. Unless she—

For fuck's sake, stop it, Elk. Use your brain. Besides, Pete would have let you know if they'd left.

Shane sat up, scrubbing his hands over his face. The cabin was quiet except for the tick of the clock on his nightstand and the chirping of birds outside. No sounds of movement from the rest of the house.

He got dressed, pulled on his jeans and a t-shirt, and padded barefoot down the hall. Pete lifted his head from his post outside Kevin's door, tail thumping once against the floor before settling back down. *Good dog. Still on watch.*

The living room came into view and Shane stopped.

She wasn't gone. She'd just moved to the couch. April was wrapped in one of the sheepskin throws, her hair spilling over the armrest, wearing his flannel from last night. God, she looked so beautiful. Everything he ever wanted.

As if sensing him, April's eyes fluttered open. For a moment she looked disoriented, then her gaze focused on him and a slow smile curved her lips.

"Morning," she said, her voice still rough with sleep.

"Morning." Shane crossed to the couch, then knelt beside her. "You okay?"

"Yeah." April pushed herself up until she was sitting. The blanket pooled around her waist and Shane wondered if his flannel was the only thing she wore. His cock took notice of his thoughts and twitched. "I just... I didn't want Kevin to wake up and see me coming out of your bedroom with you. I feel like we should ease him into this."

Shane grinned. "So you snuck out to the couch in the middle of the night."

"Around four-thirty, actually." April's smile turned sheepish.

"We really haven't changed much since high school, have we?" Shane settled onto the couch beside her. "Still sneaking around, still worried about getting caught."

"Still short on condoms." She laughed. "The difference is now I'm worried about my kid catching us instead of your parents." April leaned into him, her head finding his shoulder.

"Speaking of—" Shane's arm came around her automatically. "When are we telling him? About us?"

"I think after his class trip next weekend. They always have an end-of-the-year camping trip." April tilted her head to look up at him. "That gives us a few days to figure out how to phrase it. It's all happening so fast, though honestly, I think Kevin will be thrilled. And..."

"And?"

Her cheeks flushed slightly. "And it means we'll have some alone time while he's gone. You know. If you wanted."

Shane's pulse kicked up at the promise in her voice. "If I wanted? Sweetness, I've been wanting this for years. Another few days won't kill me." He bent his head, brushed a kiss against her temple. "Yeah. I definitely want."

April's hand found his chest, palm flat over his heart. "Good. Because I've got some ideas about how we could spend that weekend."

"Oh yeah?"

"Mmm-hmm." She was smiling now, that old, secret smile that made Shane want to carry her right back to his bedroom and show her exactly how much he wanted her. "But first, we should probably wake Kevin. School day."

"Responsible parenting," Shane agreed, not moving.

"Setting a good example."

"Being mature adults."

April laughed, soft and warm. "We're terrible at this."

"The worst." Shane kissed her properly this time—slow and thorough and full of promises for later. When he finally pulled back, April's eyes were dark and her breathing had gone unsteady.

"Okay," she said breathlessly. "Now I really need to wake Kevin before I forget why I'm on this couch instead of in your bed."

Shane grinned. "You want coffee?"

"Please." April stood, stretching, and Shane had to force himself not to stare at the way his flannel rode up her bare thighs. "And Shane?"

"Yeah?"

"Thank you. For last night. For... everything."

The vulnerability in her voice made Shane's chest ache. He stood, cupped her face in his hands. "You don't have to thank me for loving you, April. That's just what I do. What I'm always going to do."

She kissed him again—quick and sweet—then headed down the hall to wake Kevin. Shane watched her go, still half-convinced this was a dream he'd wake up from.

But the coffee maker was real. The sound of April's voice gently rousing Kevin was real. The way Pete padded over to bump against Shane's leg, looking for breakfast, was real.

This was his life now. April in his bed. Kevin in his guest room. The three of them—four, counting Pete— figuring out how to be a family.

Shane had fought bad guys in worse conditions than he could count, and won. Had survived things that should have killed him. Had lost brothers and bled and kept going.

But this—standing in his kitchen making coffee while the woman he loved got her son ready for school—this felt like the biggest victory of his life.

———

SHANE DROPPED them at April's house twenty minutes later.

"You're still gonna keep an eye on Mom today, right? Kevin asked. "I can't do it if I'm in school."

Shane glanced at April, who was trying not to laugh.

"Yeah, bud. I've always got my eye on her." He winked at April, who was now pressing her knuckles against her lips, shoulders shaking. "I've gotta go home and change and shower, but you'll see me at Riversong after school."

"Cool." Then Kevin stuck out his hand for Shane to shake. "Thanks for holding up your end of the bargain."

Shane shook his hand. "Well, we had a deal, man to man."

Kevin nodded. "Man to man." He headed for the bathroom to shower.

Shane waited until Kevin closed the door behind him before pulling April close for one more kiss.

"That kid is *killing* me," she said against his mouth. "You don't have to show up if you're busy—"

"Count on it." Shane tucked a strand of hair behind her ear. "I've got some things to take care of this morning, but I'll stop by Riversong before Kevin gets there after school, take you guys out to dinner later if that's okay."

"More than okay." April's smile was soft and tinged with worry. "Be careful, whatever you're doing."

Shane thought about what he was planning—the conversation he needed to have, the leverage he'd need—and nodded. "Always am."

He waited until she was inside before pulling away and making the phone call. It picked up right away.

"Shane. What's up, brother?"

"Hey, brother. I need a favor."

"Name it."

Shane told his brother what he needed.

"Can you do it this morning? It's time-sensitive."

"For you? Absolutely. I'll call you when I've got something."

"Thanks." Shane disconnected and took a breath.

Should have done this years ago.

HOURS LATER, Shane stood in the parking lot of Lyons Community Bank, straightening his tie. He'd gone home, showered, put on the suit he kept for special occasions that required a certain kind of armor. Because that's what this was—going into battle. Just a different kind than he was used to.

His phone buzzed. Shane read the message from Flint.

> Package delivered. Everything you need.
> Good hunting.

Shane pocketed the phone and headed for the entrance.

The bank was busy—early-afternoon rush, people on lunch breaks depositing checks and making withdrawals. Shane moved through the lobby like he owned it. He'd grown up here. How many times had his mother dragged him to this building as a kid, showing him off like a prize? *This is my son, Shane. He's going to be just like his father someday.*

God, he hoped not. He'd never inflict that on Kevin. Or any other child he and April would have. Armed with that thought, Shane went inside.

One of the tellers—probably new, didn't recognize him —started to speak, but Shane was already past her, heading for the executive corner office. His father's name gleamed on the brass plate on the door: Daniel Foti, President.

Shane didn't knock. He threw the door open and stepped inside. He had a moment to look at his father— really look at him. He'd gotten older, softer. He wasn't the towering, muscled bully from Shane's childhood anymore.

It took me too long to realize it.

And even if he were, Shane wouldn't back down. Not this time. Not ever again.

Daniel looked up from his desk, momentary surprise

flickering across his face before settling into cold displeasure. "Shane. I wasn't aware we had an appointment."

"We don't." Shane closed the door behind him and sat in one of the leather chairs facing the desk. "This won't take long."

"I'm busy—"

"Then I'll get right to the point." Shane leaned back, forcing himself to appear relaxed even though every muscle was coiled tight. "You're going to call Sonny Taylor today and change the terms of his loan. Remove the prepayment penalty. Lower the interest rate to what it should have been in the first place and credit the excess into his account, which will probably pay it off. Make it right."

Daniel's face went carefully blank. "I have no idea what you're talking about."

Shane's voice was conversational, almost pleasant. "Sure you do. The loan you gave the Taylors to start Riversong. The one you deliberately lied about when you wanted April to tutor me, dangling it in front of her parents like a too-good-to-be-true prize. It was, wasn't it? You've been using it to control them ever since."

Daniel sneered. "I don't know what you're talking about."

"You structured it to trap them if necessary, then sprung the trap after you found out April and I were together. Though, I think that was the plan all along. I've always suspected that you've been cheating all sorts of people through the years."

"That's absurd—"

"Is it?" Shane pulled out his phone, opened the file Flint had sent. "Because I've got documentation that says otherwise. Dates, terms, internal memos. Funny how the Taylors' interest rate is two points higher than anyone else's with similar credit. Funny how that prepayment penalty just happens to make refinancing impossible."

Daniel's jaw tightened. "Careful, son. You're treading on dangerous ground."

"Don't call me son." Shane's voice went cold. "You lost that right the first time you ever beat me. You had no hope of ever getting it back when you beat me bad enough to send me to the hospital for wanting to leave with April. When you made Mom lie about why I was there. When you threatened April and her family. When you made it your mission to punish them all these years because I fell in love with someone you and Mom didn't approve of."

Daniel shifted tactics, leaning back in his chair with a smile that didn't reach his eyes. "Speaking of your mother, she's devastated, you know. Absolutely heartbroken that you've cut her out of your life. She's become a laughingstock among her friends—the mother whose son won't even take her calls while they all have grandchildren they can see whenever they want. Do you have any idea how that feels? How you're destroying her?"

The words hit exactly where they were meant to— straight to the guilt Shane had been carrying for months. He looked away as he remembered his mother's face at Christmas, the way she'd looked at him with such hope before he'd walked away.

But then he thought about April flinching away from him on the couch. About Kevin asking if Shane would stay because he was terrified something would happen to his mother. About Sonny's face when Shane had promised to protect his daughter.

"That's on you," Shane said quietly. "Not me. Mom has choices. She can leave you. She can choose to respect the woman I love. She can choose her son over her husband's ego and she knows my brothers and I would protect her from you with everything we have." He met his father's eyes. "But she hasn't taken up my offer and I can't force her to. And unless she does, unless she's willing to stand up to you and treat April with basic human decency, then yeah—she's not part of my life."

"You're putting her in an impossible position—"

"No. You are." Shane's voice sharpened. "You're the one who's forcing her to choose. You're the one who's made this family toxic. I'm just refusing to participate anymore."

Daniel's face darkened. "This is about that girl. That trashy wh—"

"Finish that sentence and I walk out of here right now and send everything I've got to the authorities and to the media." Shane's voice was deadly calm. "Try me."

Daniel's mouth snapped shut.

"April Taylor has more integrity in her little finger than you've had in your entire miserable life," Shane continued. "And her family? The Taylors have built something real in this town. Something that matters. They show up for people. They care. They don't use their position to hurt anyone who threatens their ego."

"How dare you—"

"How dare I?" Shane laughed, but there was no humor in it. "You want to talk about daring? Let's talk about how you've been running this bank, Dad. Let's talk about the pattern of predatory loans you've issued. Funny how they all seem to target families you have personal grudges against."

"That's slander—"

"It's documented fact." Shane held up his phone again. "Watchdog's been looking into the bank's practices all morning. We've found fifteen loans with similar structures to the

Taylors' and we're not even done looking. Fifteen families you've trapped in impossible situations because you wanted to punish them for something."

Daniel's face had gone pale. "You don't know what you're talking about."

"No? I've got dates. Dollar amounts. Internal emails. And that's just the lending practices." Shane's smile was sharp. "Should we talk about the property on Canyon Road? The one you foreclosed on last year? Interesting how the appraisal came in two hundred thousand under market value. Even more interesting how your shell company bought it three months later for a hundred grand less than that."

"You can't prove—"

"I can prove all of it. LLC registration documents, property records, bank transactions." Shane leaned forward. "You've been using this bank as your personal piggy bank, Dad. Self-dealing, conflicts of interest you never disclosed to the board, collusion with appraisers—take your pick. Any one of these things is enough to interest the FDIC and state banking regulators. All of them together? That's federal prison."

Heavy silence filled the room. Daniel's hands gripped his armrests, knuckles white.

"What do you want, you son of a bitch?" His voice was strangled.

"Don't insult Mom like that."

"How much to shut you up, fucker?"

"I already told you. Call Sonny Taylor and tell him there has been a bank error in his favor and their loan is now paid up. And while you're at it, you're going to review every predatory loan on your books and make them right."

"That's—that's impossible—"

"Then I guess you're going to prison." Shane stood. "Your choice, Dad. Make it quick."

Daniel stared at him for a long moment, something ugly moving behind his eyes. Shane could see him calculating, trying to find an angle, a way to turn this around.

But there wasn't one. They both knew it.

"Fine," Daniel bit out. "I'll call Taylor. Change the terms."

"And the other loans."

"Yes. Fine. The other loans, too."

"And no more of this bullshit going forward."

"Fine," Daniel gritted out.

"Good." Shane turned for the door, then paused. "And Dad? If you come after April or her family again—if you so much as look at them wrong—I won't give you a warning next time. I'll just send the files."

He left without waiting for a response, walking back through the lobby with his head high. The sun hit his face as he stepped outside, and Shane took a deep breath of mountain air.

One obstacle down.

———

APRIL'S CALL came an hour later, while Shane was back at Watchdog.

"Shane?" She sounded breathless. "Daniel Foti just contacted us about the loan."

Shane straightened in his chair. "Yeah?"

"He says there was some sort of bank error. He's changing the terms. Lowering the interest rate. Taking off the prepayment penalty." April's voice cracked. "Which doesn't even matter because once that all goes through the loan's already paid off with the interest we overpaid on. Did you hear me? *It's paid off.*"

"That's good." Shane's chest felt tight. "That's really good, April."

"That thing you mentioned this morning that you had to take care of. Did you—" She stopped. "Shane, what did you do?"

"Just had a conversation with my father. Made some things clear."

"What kind of things?"

Shane thought about the files sitting on his laptop, the monitoring software Flint had installed, the trap they'd set that would spring the moment Daniel stepped out of line again, and probably before that.

"The kind that makes sure he never comes after you or your family again," Shane said. "The kind that means you're safe. That Sonny and Miriam and your sister are safe. That Kevin's safe."

April was quiet for a moment. Then, softly, "Thank you." She sniffled.

"I keep telling you, you don't have to thank me—"

"Yes, I *do*. Shane, you have no idea what this means. What you've done for us." Her voice was thick with emotion. "I love you. God, I love you so much."

Shane's throat went tight. "I love you too, Sweetness. Always have. Always will."

They talked for a few more minutes—April filling him in on her father's shock, on Miriam's tears of relief, on the celebration they were planning at Riversong for all their friends and loyal customers. Shane listened, smiling, picturing April's face as she spoke.

When they finally hung up, Shane sat at his desk and opened his laptop. Flint's monitoring software was already running, tracking every transaction that went through Lyons Community Bank. Every loan modification. Every property deal. Every suspicious transfer.

Shane leaned back in his chair, satisfied but not finished. His father still needed to see justice—and he would. His father would mess up eventually—men like him always did. And when he slipped up, when he got greedy and vindictive again, or when the red flags rose as he changed the loans, the feds would catch him. Shane would be happy to send an "anonymous" tip. But first, let the old man sweat it and fix the things he broke.

April was safe. The Taylors were free. That was enough.

For now.

NINETEEN

April smoothed down the skirt of her sundress for the third time in as many minutes and told herself to stop fidgeting. It was just a third-grade moving-up ceremony. Not even a real graduation. Nothing to be nervous about.

Except Shane was meeting her here. And Leslie would be here. And those two facts together made her palms sweat.

"You look beautiful, Sweetness."

April turned to find Shane walking toward her across the elementary school parking lot, and her heart did that annoying flutter thing it had been doing for weeks now. He was in jeans and a dark blue button-down that made his eyes look deep and dark and mysterious, and he was looking at her like she was the only person in the world.

"You didn't have to come," she said, even though she was ridiculously happy he had. "I know this is kind of silly. They do one of these ceremonies every grade."

Shane stopped in front of her, close enough that she could smell his cologne and the delicious scent of his skin underneath. "Are you kidding? I wouldn't miss this for the world."

"Spoken like a man who's never sat through one," April joked, to cover her nervousness.

He tilted his head, studying her face. "You okay?"

Busted. Of course he sees through me.

"Nope, I'm great," April said, deflecting. "Principal Pirogue hasn't bothered Kevin since I threatened to sue, Leslie's lawsuit threat was all bluster. Kevin's been thriving. Spending all that time with you has been good for him."

"And the fact that he's stopped asking me to spend the night?" Shane asked quietly. "You convinced him you're okay if I'm not there?"

April felt heat creep up her neck. They'd had to have a very careful conversation with Kevin about how grown-ups needed privacy sometimes, and how April was perfectly safe in her own house, and how Shane couldn't spend *every* night because he had work and his own house and Pete to take care of. Kevin had finally, reluctantly, agreed.

What Kevin didn't know was that Shane would be spending the night at April's house while Kevin was on his class camping trip, starting tonight.

Still sneaking around like teenagers, but it works.

"He's more secure now," April said. "He knows you're not going anywhere."

Shane's hand found hers, warm and steady. "Damn right I'm not."

They walked into the school together, and April tried not to notice the way conversations paused when people saw them. Tried not to care that Leslie frikkin Trent Sumner was standing near the entrance with a cluster of other mothers, her eyes narrowing when she spotted April, then immediately going wide with disbelief when a moment later she clocked Shane.

Okay, she did care. It felt fucking fabulous to see the jealousy absolutely radiating from Leslie.

The classroom had been decorated with streamers and a hand-painted banner that read "Congratulations Third-Graders!" Desks were pushed off to the sides of the room, folding chairs were set up at the back facing the whiteboard at the front, and April led Shane to seats near the middle.

"This seems like a lot of production for third grade," Shane murmured as they sat.

April bit back a smile. "They do this every year, all the way through fifth grade."

"Do they get participation diplomas for aging?"

"Hush." But she was grinning now, relaxing despite herself. "It's sweet. The kids love it." She got her phone ready for pictures so she could show her family later.

The ceremony started with Principal Pirogue welcoming everyone and making a bullshit speech about growth and learning that was mercifully short, then he headed for the next classroom, probably to say the same thing. Then the third-grade teachers called students up one by one to receive certificates and say a few words about their favorite part of the school year.

When it was Kevin's turn, he bounded onto the stage with the kind of confidence that made April's throat tight. Despite all the crap this school gave him, he was grinning at the crowd like he owned it. April held up her phone to record his speech.

"My favorite part of third grade was all the times I actually got to go to recess," Kevin said into the microphone. His classmates burst into laughter and the teachers squirmed, uncomfortable smiles on their faces.

Serves you right.

Then Kevin's eyes found Shane in the audience, and his grin widened. "And my favorite part of this whole year was meeting my friend Shane."

April felt Shane go still beside her.

Kevin kept going, oblivious to the way several heads turned to look at them. "Shane taught me that it's okay to be scared sometimes, but being brave means doing hard things anyway. Also, he has the coolest dog ever."

Laughter rippled through the crowd again. Shane's hand tightened around April's.

After the ceremony, the whole school gathered in the cafeteria for lemonade and cookies. Kevin dragged Shane over to a cluster of his classmates.

"This is my friend Shane," Kevin announced proudly. "He was in the Navy. He was an S-W-C-C," Kevin spelled. "That's Special Warfare Combatant-craft Crewmen. They're the ones the SEALs call when they're in trouble."

One of the boys—April recognized him as Oliver, the class brain—looked up at Shane with wide eyes. "Really? What kind of boats?"

Shane crouched down to the kids' level, and April watched him patiently explain riverine operations in terms eight-year-olds could understand. He was so good with them. Patient. Kind. Not talking down, but not overwhelming them either.

Her heart did that flutter thing again. Worse this time.

"Well, isn't this cozy."

April didn't have to turn around to know who was speaking. Leslie's voice had that particular edge it always got when she was about to say something catty.

"Hello, Leslie," April said evenly as she turned to face her.

Leslie was in white capri pants and a coral blouse that probably cost more than April made in a week. Her son Regis stood beside her looking miserable, his eyes darting toward Kevin and Shane with something that looked like longing. Despite Regis being and utter brat and a bully, April did feel sorry for the little boy.

"I see you brought your *friend*," Leslie said, her gaze sliding to Shane. "Shane Foti. My, my. I'm surprised to see him with you. But then again, some people move on and up in the world." Her smile was razor-sharp. "And some people lower their standards and date trash."

The words landed like a slap. April felt her face heat, but before she could respond, one of the other mothers— Melissa Chen, whose daughter was in Kevin's class— stepped closer.

"That's uncalled for, Leslie," Melissa said quietly.

Leslie's smile didn't waver. "I'm just saying what everyone's thinking. April runs off to Vegas, comes back with a kid and no husband, and now she's got her hooks in Shane? Please. We all know how this ends."

"Actually," Melissa said, her voice still calm but with steel underneath, "we all know that April is a wonderful mother who runs a successful business with her family. And Shane Foti is a decorated veteran who works for the most respected security company in the state. So maybe keep your opinions to yourself."

Leslie's face went red. She opened her mouth, closed it, then grabbed Regis's arm. "Come on. We're leaving."

As April watched her go, she felt her chest grow warm with gratitude spreading through her chest. "Thank you," she said to Melissa.

Melissa waved it off. "Leslie's been unbearable since her husband started spending more time 'at work'," she punctuated the words with air quotes, "than at home. Don't let her get to you." She smiled. "Besides, anyone can see that man is crazy about you."

April glanced over at Shane, still surrounded by grade-schoolers, patiently answering questions about Pete and boats and what it was like to jump out of helicopters. He caught her looking and winked, and yeah. Melissa might have a point.

An hour later, they were standing in the school parking lot watching kids board the bus for the annual end-of-year camping trip. Kevin had his backpack and sleeping bag, and he was practically vibrating with excitement.

But when he got to the bus steps, instead of getting on he turned back and ran over to Shane.

"You're in charge while I'm gone," Kevin said, very seriously. "Take care of my mom."

Shane crouched down, equally serious. "I will. Man to man, you have my word."

Kevin nodded, satisfied. Then he bit his lip. "And Shane? Can you stay with her again? Like, at our house? So she's safe?"

"Kevin—" April started.

"Please?" Kevin looked between them, and April could see the worry in his eyes. The fear that had been there since the day he'd begged Shane to be her bodyguard, the fear that something bad might happen if he wasn't there to watch. "I'll feel better knowing you're not alone, Mom."

April's throat went tight. Shane looked at her, silently asking permission to speak. She nodded.

"If your mom says it's okay," Shane said carefully.

April only barely succeeded in keeping a straight face.

"Okay," she said softly. "Just while you're gone."

Kevin's face split into a grin. He hugged them both—

hard, fierce hugs that squeezed April's heart—and then ran for the bus.

They stood there watching as he climbed aboard, claimed a window seat, and waved frantically. April and Shane waved back.

The bus pulled away, and they stood there in a sea of parents until it disappeared around the corner.

April felt a laugh bubble up in her chest. She tried to hold it in. Failed.

"What?" Shane asked, looking at her with amusement.

"If he only knew we were planning on our own sleep-over anyway," April said, and then she was laughing for real, the kind of laugh that came from relief and joy and the sheer absurdity of their situation.

Shane started laughing too. His hand found hers and threaded their fingers together. "He probably does know. That kid's a tactical genius."

"He really is," April agreed, still grinning like an idiot, even as a tiny thread of worry wound through her stomach. She never wanted Kevin to be like his bio-dad—manipulative to the core. But she dismissed the thought. *Not my sweet boy.*

They stood there in the emptying parking lot, hands linked, both of them grinning and feeling slightly guilty about being so happy Kevin was gone for the weekend.

But mostly just happy.

Shane tugged her closer, and April went willingly, letting him wrap his arms around her waist.

"So," he said, his voice low and warm against her ear. "Your place or mine?"

"Yours," April said immediately. "Pete's there. And your shower is bigger."

Shane laughed into her hair. "I like the way you think, Sweetness."

They walked to their cars together, and April couldn't stop smiling. Riversong's loan was paid off, which freed up money for a new espresso machine—if she could convince Sonny to part with his cantankerous baby. Kevin was safe and happy. Shane was here and staying. And for the first time in longer than she could remember, everything felt... right.

TWENTY

You could tell the day wanted to be perfect from the way the sun came in like a friendly stray cat—pushing through the curtains, laying itself across the foot of her bed, warm and insistent. The window was cracked for the breeze, and the willow by the river made a soft *shhhh* sound that felt like summer telling secrets to the water.

April lay there for a minute just letting herself grin at the ceiling. They'd spent the first night at Shane's place, and last night back at her house. She honestly didn't know which she liked better—though there was that shower at his place—or if it even mattered.

She had this now. She had Shane. Not *maybe*, not *don't-jinx-it*. She had Shane in the bone-deep, coffee-scented, this-is-my-life way that made her want to hum while she brushed her teeth.

Down the hall, Pete's nails clicked softly on the hardwood. A second later he appeared in the bedroom doorway, head cocked, tail wagging, like a gentleman butler asking if the lady was awake yet. He wore his expectant face—the one that translated to: *We said hike today; your words, not mine.*

"Good morning, Pete." She flopped a hand in invitation, and he padded over, resting his chin on the edge of the mattress to accept his ritual forehead kiss. "Tell your dad I'm—"

"Already on it," Shane's voice came from beyond the door, easy and warm. A pan clinked, the coffee maker hissed. "Sourdough French toast and bacon. Not burned."

"You say that like you're surprised, but I know what a good cook you are." She rolled onto her side, smiling into the pillow because she couldn't stop. Kevin was still at camp, which meant no one was waiting for breakfast or a ride or help with algebra. She'd fallen asleep with Shane's hand splayed over her stomach, waking now and then just to press her mouth to his shoulder because she could.

Pete's ears pricked toward the bedroom door. He gave April one last patient look—*I gotta go back on breakfast duty*—and left to supervise.

April stretched like a cat and slid out of bed. Shane's t-shirt hit mid-thigh. She stopped by the mirror, then laughed at herself. This was how teenage girls looked at themselves after kissing a boy behind the bleachers. Except she was a grown, full-bodied woman who owned a business, had a kid, and was building a future on purpose this time. Still, the giddiness felt earned.

"Don't come out yet," Shane called.

Her eyebrows went up. "Bossy much?"

"Don't come out yet," he repeated, laughing, "*please.*"

She laughed. She went into the bathroom, washed her face, brushed her teeth, finger-combed her curly, tangled hair, and swiped on cherry-flavored chapstick because kisses. She stuck her head out the door.

"Is it safe yet?" she asked.

"Okay," he called. "Come look."

She padded down the hallway in bare feet, rounded the corner, and stopped. He'd set the table with his ridiculous attention to detail—folded tea towels as napkins, the little vase she never remembered to use now filled with wild-flowers he must've picked by the river, syrup warmed in her one good pitcher because cold syrup was a crime against pancakes. And at the center the French toast, golden and obscene, covered in powdered sugar like new snow.

"Is this a seduction?" she asked, amused and feeling a little melty at the edges.

"That depends." He came around the table with a plate and a grin that landed low in her belly. "Is it working?"

She waited until he set the plate down, then hooked two fingers in his belt loops and tugged him until his hips almost met hers. He smelled like coffee and clean cotton and a hint of sawdust from the shelves he'd hung for her last night.

"You had me at warm syrup," she whispered, then kissed him just to savor the way he always kissed back—full, patient, like there was never a rush with her.

He cupped her jaw, thumb brushing her cheek the way she loved it, then tipped his forehead to hers. "Eat first. Then shower. Then hike with Petey. Then I take care of that loose board on your porch. *Then* you can decide whether the rest of the seduction succeeds."

"Or," she said as she dipped her finger into the syrup. She stuck it into her mouth and sucked, savoring the way Shane's eyes went hazy with lust. She pulled it out with a light *pop*. "We could... reorder the itinerary."

He chuckled. "You trying to kill my productivity?"

"Your productivity is very productive." She dipped her finger again, then swiped the sticky syrup across his bottom lip. She licked it off, and his hands tightened reflexively on her hips. "Also, Pete told me he's fine with a late start."

Pete, in obvious betrayal, thumped his tail and whined.

"Okay," Shane said. "But we're eating first. Shame to let all this food get cold."

April rolled her eyes. "If you insist."

The French toast was ridiculous. The conversation was light and silly—Kevin's plans for Benny once he got back, a hike they wanted to do, whether Benny should be allowed on the couch.

"Alex said he's already been on the couch," Shane admitted.

"I knew it."

He reached for her hand between bites like he always did, thumb riding across her knuckles.

And when the plates were pushed back and the syrup pitcher licked clean, when Pete had been released from his sentinel duties with a promise of a hike later, April took hold of Shane's T-shirt and tugged.

"Okay," she said, smiling up at him with the pure, fizzy joy of saying exactly what she wanted. "Now I vote rearranging the itinerary."

He set his hands at her waist. "Yes, ma'am."

He kissed her lazily at first, like the morning sun—slow, steady warmth. The kitchen smelled like cinnamon sugar and maple, his scent layered over it. The solid weight of his chest, the steady anchor of his hands. He walked her backward, deepening the kiss until she hit the hallway wall with a soft bump.

"You're trouble," she accused.

"The good kind," he murmured, mouth at her jaw, his smile against her skin.

She couldn't disagree. He tasted like coffee and sugar

and everything sweet. Her blood went molten. She wanted to be playful about it because their moods had risen like sunlight—bright, uncomplicated—but the wanting was also immediate and low and sure.

She nipped his lower lip. He made a sound that melted her knees. "Bedroom?" he asked.

"Mmm-mm." She slid her hands to the hem of his T-shirt. "Too far."

His laugh was pure delight. "Sofa? Floor? Against this very cooperative wall?"

She flattened her palm over his heart. "I love how you think."

"Say it again," he said, soft.

She did, because it never got old. "I love you."

He stilled, then kissed her like the words lived in his mouth too. "I love you, April."

She was happy, dizzy with it. Not careful or wondering or braced. Just *happy*.

"Wall," she decided, because there was a wicked little thrill in being a grown woman in her own home making out in the hallway at ten in the morning. "And then bed, because I like sprawling."

"Copy that." His hands slid under her shirt and closed around the backs of her thighs, lifting. She went up with a surprised laugh and wrapped around him, trusting him the way her body had learned to trust him—without argument. He bracketed her against the wall, careful, his forearms taking his weight, the press of his cock right where she wanted it.

He kissed her mouth, the corner of her smile, down the line of her throat. "Tell me what you want," he said into her skin.

"You," she said simply, shocking herself with how easy it

was to say the things she used to tuck into a box in her mind. "I want to play. I want... fast and slow. I want to feel you being happy because I'm happy."

He groaned like she'd granted a secret wish. "Fast and slow is my specialty."

"I've noticed," she said primly, and then ruined it with a breathy, "please."

He chuckled as he set her down gently and peeled her shirt off in one long, worshipful motion. She stood in the bright band of the hallway window, unselfconscious in a way she hadn't been in years. The way he looked at her helped—no hunger without reverence, no taking without offering. His gaze said, *you are safe, you are wanted, this is ours.*

She reached for his waistband. "Now you," she said, like a cheerful tyrant, and tugged him out of his t-shirt and sweatpants. The sight of all that rangy muscle, that smooth scar under his ribs she'd kissed a dozen times, sent another fizz through her. "Hello, Sailor."

"Good morning, Taylor." He dipped his head, mouth at her collarbone. "Reminder that I'm terrible at patience around you."

"Lucky me."

He eased her shorts down, encouraging her to step out. She did, laughing when her foot got caught and he steadied her with gentle hands. She leaned into the wall while he went to his knees.

"Oh," she said, brightly, a totally giddy, "we're doing this first?"

He tipped his head back, eyes gone playful and hot. "Always happy to put my mouth where my promises are."

"Smooth," she said as she rolled her eyes. But her breath

hitched when he kissed the inside of her knee, then higher. There was nothing shy or apologetic in her this time—no one was home, no one needed her in the next room, nothing could reach this narrow hallway but sunshine and a pleased dog sleeping in the other room on Kevin's bed. She threaded her fingers into his hair and let herself feel everything.

He was unhurried today, which should have been illegal. Slow kisses up her inner thigh that stalled right at where her hip met her torso, his hands anchoring her, his breath teasing where she was already slick for him. He looked up once, checking—always checking—and whatever he saw in her face made him smile at the corner of his mouth in that satisfied way that felt like a secret code only she knew.

Then he put his mouth on her and the world narrowed to a bright, electric line of pleasure.

"Shane," she said, astonished and greedy in the same heartbeat. Her head bumped the wall and she didn't care. He knew her body now, knew how she chased her orgasm and then wanted it to stall so it would feel more intense when it finally crashed over her. He gave her exactly that— firm and sweet, then lighter, then a slow pressure that unwound her spine. He slid a finger inside her and she swore softly because he took that as permission to press his palm against her clit until the world went bright white around the edges.

She laughed once—pure joy, unfiltered, because happy sex was so much better than anything she remembered. He looked up at the sound, still moving his mouth, eyes laughing with her like, *yeah, right?* and then she couldn't laugh because he crooked his finger and she broke open with a gasp.

He held her through her orgasm, steady and greedy for every last tremor, then pressed one last maddening kiss on her folds that made her shiver and swat at his shoulder. "Mean," she accused breathlessly.

"Precise," he countered as he ran his tongue up her body in one long line to her lips where he kissed her slowly, letting her taste herself on his mouth. "And thorough."

Her legs wobbled. "Bed," she said again, because sprawling had been promised and she would not be denied.

They made it to the bedroom with only minor detours—the first because she had to push him onto the couch and climb onto him like a woman who knew exactly what she wanted (she did), and the second because Pete stuck his nose around the door and then, with impeccable timing, turned and wandered away as if to say, *I'm going to check the perimeter, you two continue with your important business, you weirdos.*

Both naked on the bed, she straddled Shane's hips and braced her hands on his chest. The sheer look of him—hands behind his head, biceps carving shadows, chest rising and falling under her palms—did wicked things to her. She leaned forward and kissed a scar under his ribs, then more kisses lower, delighted when his breath quickened.

"You don't have to do—" he began, the gentleman even now.

"I *want* to," she said, and took his hard cock into her mouth.

"Oh fuck," he said in that hoarse whisper that made her feel like a magician. She set an easy rhythm, playful, teasing, loving the way he watched her like the sun had just come up twice. His hand slid into her hair—not to guide or grip—just to touch. When she hollowed her cheeks and wrapped her fist at the base of his cock, his hips twitched and he laughed helplessly. "You are," he managed, "a menace."

"Thank you," she said primly again, then did something with her tongue she'd learned he liked—a nice, slow swirl. He groaned and bucked.

She stopped before he got too close because she was not wasting this incredible hard-on, thank you very much, and crawled up his body to kiss him. His hands came to her hips, careful, reverent. He looked up at her, always careful to make sure she was ready.

She answered by taking his cock in her hand and guiding him. The first slow slide made both of them gasp. She sank down until they fit, deep and perfect, her hands flattening on his chest for balance and because she loved feeling his heart kick under her palms.

"Hey," he said softly, wonder-smile pulling at his mouth. "You with me?"

"Completely." She rocked once and watched his eyes go heavy. "I like this view."

"Likewise," he said, sounding wrecked in the best way. He traced up her sides, over her ribs, thumbs skimming the bottom curve of her breasts, sending tingling shivers through her entire body. "Go how you want, Sweetness."

So she did. She set a pace that matched the morning—sun shining over the ridge, soft breeze in the willows, coffee steam curling in the air, warm, sweet syrup. When she leaned forward he angled up to meet her. When she rolled her hips he swore against her throat. When she took his hands and pinned them to the mattress, playful and bossy, he laughed into her mouth and let her, his own body loose with trust.

She found the perfect angle and rode hard, chasing her orgasm, making small sounds that would have embarrassed her before. Not now. Not with this man who looked at her like her joy was his life's work. He tipped one hand free and slid it between them, fingers finding her clit like he'd studied a map of her body. The double sensation—his cock inside, his fingers outside—made her orgasm hit so fast she had to moan through it, forehead dropping to his, the two of them holding still while the world tilted for them both.

"I've got you," he murmured, anchored and adoring. "Take another one."

She did, and everything went bright again—edges dissolving, body pulsing around him as she came again with a surprised, delighted sound she didn't even try to swallow.

He followed, the sounds he made rough as he gripped her hips to keep her pressed against him. She felt the rhythm of his coming inside her, each wave matched to the steady pulse at his throat where her mouth had landed.

They went still together. She lay draped over him, both of them breathing like they'd outrun a storm and found a porch roof to huddle under.

"Hi," he said after a while, voice like raw silk.

"Hi," she echoed against his neck, smiling.

He smoothed a hand down her spine, palm slow, content. "So," he said, "the seduction..."

"Five stars," she said promptly into his skin. "Warm syrup was a strong opener. Exceptional follow-through. Would recommend to a friend."

"Please don't recommend to a friend," he said, in mock-horror, and she laughed until he rolled her carefully onto her back and kissed the laughter right out of her mouth.

She hooked her leg over his hip and tucked into his side, still smiling against his chest.

Through the window: the river, the willows, a magpie giving loud opinions about the morning.

"Pete's going to demand his hike soon," Shane warned her.

"Pete can have a hike." April traced idle shapes over the scar she loved. "After a nap."

"In broad daylight?" He turned his head, fake scandalized.

She tickled his chest. "Who are we kidding, Sailor? We're going to cat nap for sixteen minutes and then eat leftovers standing in front of the fridge."

"And then hike."

"And *then*," she said, because she loved this part—planning a day that belonged to them alone—"we're stopping at Riversong for a cold brew and one of Hannah's lemon bars. And tonight I'm making fajitas and you're chopping the peppers because you take the seeds out with surgical precision and it's hot to watch."

He huffed a laugh into her hair. "I love your brain."

"I love your hands," she said, shameless. Then, softer, because the happy had an underlayer that was tender as newly-healed skin, "I love this. All of it. You here. Me not... afraid anymore."

He went still, caught by surprise. His palm slid up to her jaw, tilting her face so he could kiss her slow and sure. "I'm here," he said simply. No oath needed; it was in the way he warmed the syrup, in the vase of fresh wildflowers, in the way he looked at her with love in his eyes.

"I know."

"Good." He nuzzled her temple. "But I'm going to keep proving it anyway."

"Please do," she said, feeling light again. "I'm a woman of numbers and I need all the theorems proved."

"Oh, God, not math." He laughed into her hair. The room was full of warm sunshine, making them lazy, their bodies heavy and sweet. She closed her eyes and listened to the river's soft song, Pete's contented dog-snore down the hall, the soft beat of Shane's heart under her ear.

Sixteen minutes, she thought, *and then out for lemon bars.*

Maybe twenty. She could savor her life for a morning.

TWENTY-ONE

THE CAMP BUS PULLED INTO THE ELEMENTARY SCHOOL
parking lot at four-thirty on Sunday afternoon, right on
schedule. Shane leaned against the side of his truck,
watching April pace beside him. She'd been doing that for
the last ten minutes—three steps left, three steps right,
checking her phone, twisting her hands together.

"He's fine," Shane said for the third time. "They would
have called if anything was wrong."

"I know." April didn't stop pacing. "I just missed him. I
missed him so much and I also loved having the house to
ourselves and now I feel guilty about it. Is that weird?"

Shane caught her hand as she passed, pulling her close.
"Not weird. You're allowed to miss your kid *and* enjoy adult
time. That's called being human."

The bus doors opened with a hydraulic hiss, and kids
started pouring out like ants from a kicked hill. Kevin
appeared at the top of the steps, his backpack hanging off
one shoulder, hair sticking up in every direction.

"Mom! Shane!" Kevin waved both arms over his head

like he was directing aircraft. Several other parents turned to look, and Shane felt April tense slightly against his side. They hadn't exactly announced their relationship to the world yet, but that was about to change, once they talked to Kevin.

Kevin hit the ground running, literally, and crashed into April hard enough to make her stumble. Shane steadied them both, one hand on April's back.

"Guess what! Guess what!" Kevin was bouncing. "I remembered everything Shane taught me on our hike and I beat Regis at the orienteering competition!"

"That's wonderful, baby." April hugged him tightly, breathing in the smell of campfire smoke and kid sweat. "I'm so proud of you."

"He got *so* lost!" Kevin pulled back, grinning. "Like, totally lost. And I found the last checkpoint first! The counselor said I was the best young navigator he'd ever seen!"

Shane grabbed Kevin's duffel bag from where he'd dropped it. "Good job, bud. Sounds like you had fun."

"It was awesome! My flag football team won. Oliver was on the other team, and he hates flag football because he's not very good so when he fell, I helped him back up. And at archery I got the most bullseyes, and at the campfire quiz I knew all the answers—" Kevin was walking backwards toward the truck, still talking at full speed. "And when we did the relay race my team won because I was the fastest and I had to help Oliver back up again, and—"

Shane caught April's expression shift. Just slightly. Just enough that he noticed the way her smile went from genuine to fixed.

They loaded into the truck—Kevin in the back seat beside Pete, who he hugged while still talking—and headed toward April's house. Shane drove while April half-turned to look at her son, asking questions about the food and his cabin and whether he'd gotten any sleep at all. He barely answered them and continued bragging.

"Oh, and the spelling bee!" Kevin leaned forward against his seatbelt. "We had this camp spelling bee thing and I *almost* won that but Oliver came in first because he always does, and that's cool. But Regis got knocked out in the *first* round." He laughed. "He was so mad his face turned red!"

"Kevin." April's voice had an edge now. "That's enough." She turned back around and faced the windshield.

Kevin didn't catch it. "But Mom, it was so funny! He couldn't even spell 'necessary' and that's like, super easy—"

"I said that's *enough*."

This time Kevin heard it. He sat back, his grin fading slightly. "I'm just saying what happened."

"You're gloating." April kept her eyes forward. "We don't gloat when we win and we really don't gloat when someone else loses."

Shane glanced in the rearview mirror. Kevin looked confused and a little hurt.

"I'm not gloating," Kevin said. "I'm not competitive. I'm just always the best at everything."

Shane felt April go rigid in the passenger seat.

April whirled around to face her son. "Is *that* your attitude?"

Kevin shrugged. "Not attitude. It's the truth. I beat Regis at orienteering, and at archery, and at the quiz, and—"

He wasn't reading his momma's cues as she raked her fingers into her hair on either side of her head, her face scrunching into a pained frown.

"That's enough. I didn't raise you to be arrogant."

"Mom! I'm not! It's just the truth."

Shane pulled into April's driveway and put the truck in park, but neither April nor Kevin noticed. They were locked in their own standoff.

April pointed toward the house. "Just go to your room. You're so good at spelling? Great, I want you to write 'I am humble' a hundred times in one of your notebooks."

"Mom! That's not fair!" Kevin stomped his foot as his voice rose to a shriek on the last word. Pete lowered his head, then curled into a ball.

April lowered her voice to a dangerous tone. "Go now before you're in real trouble." She pointed toward the house again.

Shane saw it coming, saw Kevin's face crumple and then harden, saw the eight-year-old boy make the worst possible choice—

"I hate you!" Kevin yelled.

April's face went blank. Perfectly, terrifyingly blank.

"Join the club," she said quietly. "It's hardly exclusive."

Kevin slammed his foot against the floor of the truck again, then threw his door open and pulled his backpack and duffel bag out. He dragged his feet walking to the front door. April was already out of the truck and on the porch unlocking it for him by the time he got there. Kevin disappeared inside without looking back.

Shane followed them inside, Pete trotting at his side for once, instead of Kevin's. April stood in the front room, arms wrapped around herself. Down the hall, Kevin's bedroom door slammed hard enough to rattle the pictures on the wall.

April waited for the sound to fade before pinching the

bridge of her nose in a futile effort to keep the tears from falling.

"It doesn't matter whether I left Vegas or not. It doesn't matter that they never met each other," she whispered. "He sounds just like his father."

The first tear fell.

Shane moved toward her, slowly and carefully, like approaching a wounded animal. "April—"

"Don't." She held up a hand. "Just... don't tell me I'm overreacting."

"I wasn't going to."

She looked at him then, and the pain in her eyes hit him like a fist. "I love my boy so much. No matter what. But I hate seeing that man inside him. What if I can't change Kevin? What if it's in him already, that cruelty? And he grows up to be a real bastard and hurt everyone around him and it's all my fault that I couldn't counter it?"

Shane kept his voice steady, though fury at Vince Romano was a hot coal in his chest. "April, that's not gonna happen. Kevin's not cruel. He's a good kid. But when he's angry it comes out in cruel ways sometimes. He's hardly the first kid who's ever yelled 'I hate you' to his momma. Doesn't excuse it, not at all. Totally unacceptable. But it doesn't mean he's a bad seed or whatever."

"So what am I supposed to do?" April's voice broke. " I try reasoning with him, he doesn't listen because he's off in a daydream. I try to punish him, he lashes out. Thing is, he's not wrong about being the best at everything." She laughed bitterly. "But I hate seeing that arrogance about it."

Shane guided her toward the couch, and she let him. They sat, and he angled himself to face her.

"Is it arrogance?" he asked carefully. "'Cause I don't see

it. I see a kid who's confident. He doesn't lord his skills over the other kids."

"No, but he will. He will if I don't change it."

"April, I've never once seen Kevin win at something and be an ass about it. He just told us that at camp he helped Oliver twice. He helped Regis when he got lost—Regis, the kid who's been tormenting him all year. I watched him clap for other kids when they did their speeches at the graduation. I've—"

"Are you saying I don't know my own kid?"

"I'm not saying that at all." Shane reached for her hand, and after a moment, she let him take it. "Actually, what I'm saying is that you don't know yourself."

April reared back, a look of total confusion on her face. "I don't know myself? What's that supposed to mean?"

"You don't see how you're projecting Vince onto your son when they are two completely different people. Kevin is smart and good at sports, yeah. Hell, good at everything he puts his mind to, and he knows it. That's not arrogance. It's confidence. He's just stating fact, not being a dick about it."

"Not yet. That's what I keep telling you. I'm not projecting anything. It's going to turn into arrogance if he keeps doing it. If I don't fix it."

"That's another place where you don't know yourself."

"What? What don't I know about myself?" She threw her arms up, exasperated. "That I can't fix it?"

Shane waited until she was looking at him again. Really looking.

"That there's nothing to fix because you are an amazing mother. I'll repeat—there is nothing to fix because you. Are. Amazing." Shane paused, his mouth tilting into a smile despite the weight of the moment. "You. You're amazing, April Taylor. Amazing."

He took her face in his hands, thumbs brushing away the tears on her cheeks.

"And I love you."

The words hung in the air between them. Shane had said them before, whispered them in the dark, breathed them against her skin. But never like this. Never in the middle of the day in her living room with her son down the hall and fear written all over her face.

April's breath caught. "Shane—"

"I love you," he said again. "I loved you when we were seventeen and I love you now. And I love Kevin. That kid? He's not Vince. He never will be. Because he has you in his blood and in his life."

"But what if—"

"No." Shane's voice was gentle but firm. "No what-ifs. Kevin is a good kid going through a rough patch. He's dealing with a lot—bullying, he's afraid for his mom, probably scared about a hundred other things he can't even name yet. So yeah, he's going to mess up. He's going to say things he doesn't mean. But that doesn't make him cruel. That makes him eight."

April closed her eyes, leaning into his touch. "I'm so scared."

"I know."

"What if I'm not enough? What if no matter what I do—"

"You are enough. You've always been enough." Shane kissed her forehead. "And you're not doing this alone anymore. Not if you don't want to be. I love that kiddo. So much."

She opened her eyes, searching his face. "You really love him?" Her voice came out in a rough whisper.

"Yeah, Sweetness. I really do."

April let out a shaky breath and nodded. Then she pulled back slightly. "I should go talk to him."

"You sure? You could give it a few minutes. Let you both cool down."

"No." April wiped her face. "I don't want him sitting in there thinking I actually believe he's a bad kid. Or that I—" Her voice wobbled. "That I don't love him."

"He'd never in a million years believe that, April. You've shown him time and again how much you love him."

April's chest hitched. She leaned forward into Shane's arms.

"I love you. So much," she said against his neck.

She stood, and Shane stood with her. April walked down the hall and knocked softly on Kevin's door.

"Kevin? Can I come in?"

Silence.

"Baby, please."

After a long moment: "Okay."

April opened the door. Shane stayed in the hallway, giving them space but close enough to hear.

Kevin was sitting on his bed, knees pulled up to his chest. His face was red and blotchy from crying.

"I'm sorry I said I hated you," Kevin said immediately. "I don't hate you. I love you, Mom. So much."

April crossed the room and sat beside him, pulling him into her arms. "I know, baby. I know you didn't mean it."

"Are you mad at me?"

"I'm not mad. I just..." April smoothed his hair back. "I want you to be proud of what you accomplish, Kevin. I really do. But I also want you to be kind. To be humble. To remember that other people have feelings, too."

"I know." Kevin's voice was muffled against her shoulder. "I didn't mean to sound like I was better than everyone. I was just excited about camp."

"I know you were. And I'm proud of you for doing so well." April pulled back to look at him. "And I'm really proud of you for helping Oliver. And really, *really* proud of you for helping Regis when he was lost."

Kevin brightened a little. "He was so scared. I told him it was okay, that the counselors would find us if we stayed put. And then I found the trail marker."

"That was very brave and very kind."

Kevin chewed his lip. "Mom? Can I tell you something?"

"Always."

"I'm glad you and Shane are together."

April went still. Shane tensed in the hallway.

"What makes you think Shane and I are together?"

Kevin gave her a look that was pure exasperation. "Mom. Come on. He spent the night while I was gone. He's here all the time. You smile different when he's around. And also, you kissed him."

"You saw that?"

"I see a lot of things." Kevin rolled his eyes. "Grownups think kids are so dumb." He tilted his head. "Are you mad I noticed?"

April let out a surprised laugh. "No, baby. I'm not mad."

"Good." Kevin paused, then added in a rush, "Because I've been trying to get you two together since forever and I'm really glad it finally worked."

The world seemed to tilt sideways. Shane felt it from the hallway—the moment April's fear kicked back in.

Oh, shit, kid. That was the worst possible thing you could have said just now.

"What do you mean, it finally worked?"

"I mean..." Kevin looked suddenly uncertain. "I kind of... planned it? A little?"

"Planned it how?"

"Like the night we went hiking and he was gonna leave. I kinda pretended to freak out."

April's face went stark white. "You faked that tantrum?"

Kevin was talking faster now. "I just thought if you guys spent more time together you'd realize you love each other and then we could be a family."

April stood up slowly. "You manipulated us?"

"No! I just—" Kevin scrambled off the bed. "You're happy! You love Shane! He loves you!"

"That's not the point, Kevin. You can't trick people into relationships. That's not okay."

"But you *are* happy! Aren't you?"

Shane felt at a total loss. He was so far out of his depth.

But if I'm going to be a good father to this boy and a good husband to this woman, I can't stand here like a coward. Even if I don't know the first thing about being either one.

He stepped into the room, and both Kevin and April turned to look at him.

"Buddy," Shane said gently. "Can you give your mom and me a minute?"

Kevin looked between them, his face crumpling again. "Am I in trouble?"

"No." Shane kept his voice calm. "We just need to talk. Adult stuff."

Kevin nodded miserably and sat back on his bed, pulling his knees up again. Shane guided April back into the living room.

"He manipulated us," April said the moment they were out of earshot. Her hands were shaking. "He schemed and lied and—"

"April." Shane caught her hands. "Look at me."

She did, and he could see the panic in her eyes. The old fear rising up.

"Kevin didn't manipulate me into loving you," Shane said firmly. "I already loved you. I've loved you for half my life. He didn't create these feelings. He just... gave us excuses to finally get over our past and spend time together."

"But the lying—"

"Was an eight-year-old playing matchmaker. That's it. That's all it is."

"How do I know the difference?" April's voice broke. "How do I know he won't grow up to be like Vince? Lying and scheming and manipulating people to get what he wants?"

Shane pulled her close, wrapping his arms around her. She resisted for a moment, then collapsed against his chest.

"Because you're raising him," Shane said into her hair. "Because he has you as an example. Because when Kevin sees someone in trouble, his first instinct is to help—even when that someone is a kid who's been cruel to him. That's not manipulation. That's compassion."

April's fingers curled into his shirt. "What if I'm wrong? What if I'm missing the signs?"

"You're not wrong. And you're not alone in this anymore." Shane pulled back enough to look at her. "We'll figure it out together. You, me, and Kevin. As a family."

"A family," April repeated softly.

"Yeah. If you want that."

"I want that." She closed her eyes. "God, I want that so much it scares me."

"Me, too."

She opened her eyes and looked deeply into his. "You're scared?"

"Sweetness, I'm fucking terrified. I'm so scared that I'm going to fuck all this up." He stroked her cheek. "But I'm never gonna let fear stop me from being with you again. So let's be scared together."

They stood there for a long moment, holding each other. Then April straightened, wiping her face.

"I should go talk to him again."

"Want me to come?"

"Yeah." She nodded. "I do." Then she grinned. "You said it yourself—let's be scared together."

They walked back to Kevin's room hand in hand. Kevin was still on his bed, looking small and as scared as they were.

"Kevin," April said, sitting beside him again. Shane leaned against the doorframe. "I'm not mad about you wanting Shane and me to get together. But I need you to understand something. No more schemes. No more tricks. If you want something, you talk to us. Okay?"

"Okay." Kevin's voice was small. "I'm sorry."

"I know you are." April touched his cheek. "And I love you. Always. No matter what."

Kevin threw his arms around her neck. "I love you too, Mom."

When Kevin pulled back, he looked at Shane. "Are you guys like... together-together now? Like for real?"

Shane glanced at April, who nodded.

"Yeah, bud," Shane said. "For real."

Kevin's face lit up. "Cool." Then, tentatively: "Can I call you Dad? Or is that weird?"

Shane's throat went tight. He'd been a lot of things in his life—SWCC operator, bodyguard, son, brother, friend. But this? This was different.

"If you want to," he managed. "But no pressure. We can take it slow."

"I want to." Kevin looked at April. "Is that okay, Mom?"

April's eyes were shining. "Yeah, baby. That's okay."

Kevin smiled—the biggest smile since he'd spotted them from the bus. Then he launched himself at Shane, and Shane caught him and lifted him clean off the ground in a hug that felt like coming home.

Over Kevin's head, Shane met April's eyes. She was crying again, but smiling this time.

"Family," Shane mouthed.

April nodded, mouthing back, "Family."

Later, after Kevin had unpacked and taken a shower and eaten his weight in pizza, Shane found April standing in the kitchen, staring out the window at nothing.

"You okay?" he asked, sliding his arms around her waist from behind.

"I think so." She leaned back against him. "Today was... a lot."

"Yeah, it was."

"But we're good?"

"We're great, Sweetness."

April turned in his arms, studying his face. "You really meant it? About loving Kevin?"

"Every word."

"And about us being a family?"

"Every. Word," Shane repeated. He kissed her forehead, then her nose, then her mouth. "You're stuck with me now, April Taylor. Both of you."

"Good," April whispered against his lips. "Because I love you, too."

"I know." Shane kissed her again. "I know."

From the living room, Kevin called out, "Are you guys kissing? Because that's gross but also cool!"

They broke apart, laughing. Shane called back: "Mind your business, kid!"

"It's my house too! That makes it my business!"

April shook her head, grinning. "We've created a monster."

"Nah." Shane pulled her close again. "We've created a family."

And for the first time, Shane let himself believe—truly, fully believe—it was actually true.

TWENTY-TWO

THREE WEEKS LATER, SHANE STILL COULDN'T BELIEVE this was his life.

They practically lived together, taking turns staying at each other's houses. April's toothbrush in his bathroom. Her coffee mug on his counter. Kevin's bike by the door, Pete's and Benny's toys scattered across the living room floor. The kind of chaos he'd never imagined wanting—and now couldn't imagine living without.

They'd fallen into a rhythm. April working at Riversong, Shane on whatever job Watchdog assigned, Kevin shuttling between day camps and friends and the hundred small adventures kids got into when school was out and summer just starting. Dinners together most nights. Movie marathons and hikes on weekends.

The fear that it wouldn't last, that something would shatter this fragile happiness—Shane shoved it down every time it surfaced. April was safe. Kevin was thriving. They were together. He had everything he ever wanted. And it was all better than he could have imagined.

Life was perfect.

————

RIVERSONG WAS PACKED.

String lights crisscrossed overhead, turning the outdoor patio into something out of a fairy tale. Brianna Taylor—April's cousin and a rising star in the bluegrass world—had her fiddle out and was leading an impromptu jam session with a few local musicians. The music floated over the sound of the St. Vrain River flowing twenty feet below, mixing with laughter and conversation.

The party was officially to celebrate paying off the predatory loan, and the Taylors finally being free of Daniel Foti's shadow, but really it was about community. About family.

Shane stood near the railing, watching April move through the crowd. She was glowing—there was no other word for it. Relaxed in a way he'd never seen her before. Happy. Free.

"So." Elias appeared at his elbow, followed by the rest of Mountain Division. "You and April."

Shane didn't take his eyes off her. "Yeah."

"Took you long enough," Elias said, dropping into a chair at the outdoor table where they'd congregated.

"Shut up." But Shane was grinning.

They settled around the table—Shane, Gabe, Elias, Waylon, Bear, and Ben. Waylon pulled a flask from his jacket pocket and set it in the center of the table.

"Since Riversong doesn't have a liquor license," he said with a smirk.

Gabe grabbed it first, took a swig, and passed it to Shane. "You happy?"

Shane looked through the window at April, who was laughing with Hannah about something, her whole face lit up. "Yeah. Really happy."

The flask made its way around the table. Waylon took his turn and pointed it at Shane. "Good. Because if you screw this up, we're all required to kick your ass."

"Noted."

"You thinking long-term?" Ben asked, his voice quieter than usual.

Shane met his eyes—his best friend since they were kids, the one who'd seen him at his absolute worst, now seeing him at his best. "I'm thinking forever."

Silence fell over the table. Even the music seemed to fade for a moment.

Gabe leaned forward to hear Shane's answer. "You gonna propose?"

"When the time's right."

"The time's been right since high school, man," Elias said.

Shane's grin widened. "Yeah. Maybe it has."

"You got a ring yet?" Waylon asked. He winked at Ben.

"Not yet. You know anybody who's good at jewelry?"

Elias held up his left hand and showed off the wedding ring Ben had made for him. "Nope, not a clue."

The other guys all held up their hands, showing off their equally exquisite wedding rings while they chorused, "Nope." "No idea." "Haven't a clue."

"All of you suck," Ben said as he raised the flask to his lips—which, it so happened, he'd made for Waylon.

Bear clapped Shane on the shoulder, damn near causing it to bruise. "About damn time, brother."

They sat there for a while, passing the flask and talking shit the way they always did. Shane felt it settle into his bones—this rightness. These men were his brothers in every way that mattered. And now he had April and Kevin, too. A family he'd built himself.

The front door opened. Charlie King emerged from inside carrying an empty tray which she began filling with empty glasses and coffee mugs. She was out of her usual bodyguard uniform—no dark suit, no sunglasses—just jeans and a casual top with her hair down. Shane had known Charlie for years of course. Served with her in the Navy, worked with her on a dozen jobs at Watchdog. She'd always been one of the guys to him—she could tell dirty jokes and drink any one of her crewmates under the table. She'd also saved their damn lives on more than one mission. But seeing her like this, relaxed, almost unrecognizable, he understood why Ben kept sneaking glances her way.

Ben stood abruptly. "I'll help her."

Shane watched Ben intercept Charlie at the edge of the patio. Ben reached for the tray at the same moment Charlie adjusted her grip. Their hands touched. Even from across the patio, Shane saw the electricity arc between them.

They froze. Just for a second. Staring at each other.

"I've got it," Charlie said. Her voice was steady but her cheeks were flushed.

"I know. Just trying to help."

Charlie dropped her gaze, then looked at him through her lashes. "Thanks, Ben."

"Any t-t-time." Ben's old stutter—the one that only surfaced now when he was nervous or exhausted—slipped out.

He looked mortified. Instead of taking the tray, he turned quickly and walked back to the table. Charlie stood there for a moment, hurt flickering across her face before she carried the tray inside.

Ben sat down heavily and reached for the flask.

"You ever gonna ask her out?" Elias asked.

"Nope."

"That's healthy," Waylon said dryly.

"Shut up." Ben took a long drink and passed the flask along.

Shane caught Gabe's eye. They'd all seen it—the way Ben and Charlie circled each other, never quite connecting. It was painful to watch.

But before Shane could say anything, the sound of an expensive engine cut through the music. A sleek black Mercedes pulled into the parking lot, and Shane's entire body went rigid.

He knew that car.

"Oh shit," Waylon muttered.

Yvonne Foti stepped out of the driver's side, and for a moment she just stood there, clutching a bouquet of flowers, staring at the party like she wasn't sure she had the right to be here.

Then her gaze settled on Shane, and she started walking toward him.

"Would you look at the time?" Elias said as he stood.

Waylon shot up next to him. "Gettin' late."

"We should—" Gabe started.

"Go inside," Ben finished.

"What?" Bear asked, still sitting with his back to the parking lot. "What's—" Ben bumped him and jerked his head. Bear turned, took one look at Yvonne, and stood surprisingly quickly for such a huge guy.

"Gotta go check on Ellie and Star," he mumbled as he followed the others to the entrance. Shane watched his brothers disappear into Riversong, leaving Shane standing alone as his mother approached.

"Yeah, thanks, guys," Shane called after them. At least Waylon had left Shane his flask.

Yvonne stopped a few feet away, holding the flowers like a shield. "I'm sorry to crash the party. I just... I wanted you to know."

Shane kept his voice carefully neutral. "Know what?"

"I'm leaving your father. I filed for divorce."

Shane's chest loosened. "Good."

"I should have done it years ago." Yvonne's voice wavered. "Should have protected you."

"Mom—"

"Let me finish." Tears gathered in her eyes. "I was weak. I was scared. And I let him hurt you. I stood by and watched and did nothing, and I will never forgive myself for that."

She was crying openly now, mascara starting to run. "I don't expect forgiveness. I just wanted you to know I'm trying to be better."

Shane closed the distance between them and pulled her into a hug. She went stiff with surprise, then collapsed against him, crying softly into his shoulder.

"I forgive you," Shane said quietly. "I forgave you a long time ago."

"You shouldn't. I don't deserve—"

"You're my mom. You made mistakes. So did I. We're both trying to be better." He pulled back enough to smile at her. "And despite all my brothers chickening out and going inside when they saw you, we all have your back if you need us."

Yvonne let out a wet, broken laugh. "They ran pretty fast, didn't they?"

"Yeah, they did."

"Shane?"

He turned to find April standing in the doorway, her expression uncertain. Shane held out his hand, and she came to him immediately, sliding under his arm.

"April." Yvonne's voice broke again. "I'm so sorry. For everything Daniel said, everything he did—"

"You're not responsible for his choices," April said firmly.

"But I stood by—"

"And now you're not. That takes courage to stand up for yourself. To leave a violent man. I know that better than anyone."

Yvonne looked at them both, then for a long moment at the flowers she was still holding, gathering herself. "These are for the party. For Sonny and Miriam. To thank them for... for being kind to Shane when I couldn't be."

April took the flowers with a gentle smile. "They'll love them. Come inside. Have something to eat. Join the celebration."

"I don't want to intrude—"

"You're not intruding," April said, as her gaze slid to Shane. "You're family."

My God. This woman. This strong, kind, amazing woman.

Yvonne's eyes filled with fresh tears. "You two... you're good together."

Shane looked down at April, at the woman who'd held his heart since they were seventeen. "Yeah. We are."

"Be happy. Both of you." Yvonne wiped her face. "God knows you've earned it."

She stayed for another hour, sitting with Sonny and Miriam and apologizing for things that weren't her fault. But they were gracious, the way the Taylors always were, and by the time Yvonne left, she was genuinely smiling.

Shane watched her car disappear into the night, and April leaned against him.

"That was hard for her," April said.

"Yeah."

"But good. It was good."

"Yeah," Shane said again. "It was."

The party wound down slowly. Brianna packed up her fiddle. Guests drifted away in pairs and small groups, calling out thanks and goodbyes. Shane helped clean up, stacking chairs and carrying dishes inside while April and Hannah worked in the kitchen.

Finally, it was just the family left—Sonny and Miriam, Hannah, April, Shane, and Kevin, who'd spent the evening running wild with the other kids and was now passed out in a chair, Pete curled at his feet.

"I'll get him," Shane said.

He scooped Kevin up carefully. The kid didn't even stir, just made a sleepy sound and tucked his face against Shane's shoulder. Pete scrambled up, tail wagging, ready to follow.

They said their goodnights and headed to Shane's truck. Kevin went in the back seat, Pete on the floor. Shane drove toward April's house—it was closer—and April sat beside him, her hand resting on his thigh.

"Today was perfect," she said softly.

Shane thought about his mother, about the forgiveness that had felt impossible for so long. About his brothers and their terrible jokes and unwavering support. About Kevin calling him Dad and April falling asleep in his arms every night.

"Yeah," he agreed. "It was."

He pulled into April's driveway and cut the engine. Kevin

was still dead to the world, and Shane carried him inside, Pete trotting alongside. April unlocked the door and held it open, watching as Shane navigated the familiar path to Kevin's room.

He laid Kevin on the bed and pulled off his shoes, then covered him with a blanket. Pete jumped up and curled at Kevin's feet like always. For a moment, Shane just stood there, looking at this incredible kid who'd somehow become his.

April appeared in the doorway. "You okay?"

Shane turned to her, this woman who'd turned his entire world upside down and put it back together better than it was before.

"I thought life was perfect," he said. "I was wrong."

April's brow furrowed. "What do you mean?"

"My mom is leaving my dad. She's trying. You forgave her." Shane crossed the room and took April's hands. "You and me and Kevin and Pete and this messy, chaotic, beautiful life we're building. *Now* life is perfect."

April's smile was soft and a little sad. "Nothing's perfect, Shane."

"This is." He kissed her forehead, then her nose, then her mouth. "This is perfect."

She kissed him back, slow and sweet. "Yeah," she whispered. "I guess it is."

They stood there in Kevin's doorway, holding each other while their son slept and the dog snored and the night wrapped around them like a promise.

"But I can make it even more perfect," April added.

"Yeah? How?" Shane grinned, already knowing her answer before she started pulling him down the hallway toward their bedroom.

Perfect.

———

APRIL'S THIGHS trembled against his shoulders, her fingers buried in his hair as she gasped his name like it was the only word she remembered. Shane didn't let up. He knew what she liked now—how to circle his tongue just right, how to suck her clit gently and then harder until her breath hitched and her hips rolled up to meet his mouth.

"Shane," she moaned, the sound breaking apart as her orgasm crested. She fell apart on his tongue, shaking, her thighs tightening around his head like she never wanted to let him go. He grinned against her, greedy for every last tremor.

When she finally sagged back against the pillows, she let out a breathless laugh and covered her face with her forearm. "Oh my *God*, what was that?"

He crawled up over her, kissed the inside of her knee on the way, then the slope of her hip, the curve of her waist. "That was me," he murmured into her skin. "Showing off."

April let her arm drop and looked up at him, flushed and glowing, hair spread wild across the pillow. "You're terrible, you know that?"

"Only for you." He kissed her again, slow and deep, his fingers trailing over her ribs. "And you love it."

She reached between them and wrapped her hand around his cock, stroking just once—slow, deliberate, wicked. His breath caught.

"I want you," she whispered. "Now."

He reached over to the nightstand, tore open the foil packet, and rolled on the condom. His gaze never left hers. And God, that look in her eyes—that soft, hungry, completely-in-love look—nearly wrecked him.

He lined the head of his cock up with her, sweet, wet pussy and pressed against her without slipping inside.

"Is this what you want?"

"Shane, don't tease me."

He ran his cock up and down her lips until she gave him a soft moan.

"*Please*," she begged. "I need it."

When he pushed inside her, they both gasped. She was still warm and slick from coming, and he sank in deep, her body welcoming him like coming home. He held still for a beat, forehead pressed to hers, trying to hang onto the rapidly fraying thread of control he had left.

"I love you," he breathed.

April's gaze softened even more—somehow—and her arms wrapped tightly around his back. "I love you, too," she said, voice thick with need. "So much."

And that—*that*—was what undid him.

He started to move, slow and deep, every thrust matched by the curl of her hips. She moaned into his mouth, her fingers digging into his shoulders as their rhythm built. This wasn't frenzied, wasn't frantic. It was reverent. They both knew what they had and neither wanted to take a single second for granted.

Her body tightened around him, her breath catching on a whimper, and he felt her pulse around him as she came again. He wasn't far behind. The moment she whispered his name again—so full of trust—he let go, burying himself deep as he came with a low groan, her name broken on his lips.

They stayed tangled, bodies slick with sweat, hearts racing in sync.

Shane pressed a kiss to her temple, then another to her lips. "You're everything to me, Sweetness."

April blinked up at him, her smile soft and a little awed. "And you're everything to me, too."

He brushed her hair back and just stared for a moment. No fear, no hesitation. Just this—*them*—finally whole.

"Perfect," he said, like a promise.

She pulled the sheet over them both and tucked herself into his side. "Yeah," she murmured. "It really is."

TWENTY-THREE

THE SUNLIGHT WAS ALREADY SNEAKING AROUND THE edges of the curtains when April blinked awake. Her body was sore in the best way, stretched and satisfied, every muscle still humming from the night before. Shane's arm was heavy across her waist, his chest warm against her back. She smiled and tried to shift without waking him.

No such luck.

He grumbled something low and possessive and tightened his hold. "Nope. Not ready to give you up to the world yet."

She laughed softly so she wouldn't wake Kevin in the next room. "Too bad. I've got to drop a kid off at camp and get to work."

"Mmm. Can't someone else make the coffee today?"

"Nope."

He nuzzled the back of her neck, clearly trying to change her mind with kisses. "Can't Pete take Kevin?"

"You want our dog to drive the truck?"

"Only if he promises to stop for donuts."

She wriggled around to face him, biting her lip to keep

from laughing. His hair was a mess, his eyes still half-closed, and he looked so stupidly handsome she wanted to crawl right back under the covers.

Instead, she kissed him. Slow. Sweet. A little filthy. Which became a lot filthier as she made her way down his body to his cock. He was already half-hard and quickly stiffening.

He groaned. "That's not helping me let you go, April."

"Shh. You'll wake the kid." April slipped his cock into her mouth and ran her tongue around and around the tip until he was gripping the sheets. It only took a moment for him to come after she plunged his entire length into her mouth.

"You're...amazing."

"I know." She pushed the blankets off and sat up, reaching for the t-shirt he'd peeled off her the night before. He grabbed her hand and refused to let go. "Uh-uh. If you want more of that tonight, you'd better let me get on with my day."

He smacked her ass as she stood. "Then go, Sweetness. But you'd better keep that promise tonight."

She grinned over her shoulder. "I always do."

APRIL WALKED into Riversong mid-morning still wearing a smile she couldn't quite wipe off, no matter how hard she tried.

Not that she was trying too hard. Why not let the world know how happy she was?

She'd dropped Kevin at day camp half an hour ago, kissed the top of his head as he scrambled out with his backpack half-zipped. He hadn't even looked back, too busy chasing his new camp friends across the park.

Now, as she stepped into Riversong, the familiar scent of espresso and cinnamon met her like an old friend. She excused herself as she squeezed past a knot of customers— so many customers this morning! Riversong had been shared from here to Timbuktu all over social media since the day they announced the party a couple weeks ago—and made her way to the counter.

"Look who's glowing," Hannah said, one eyebrow lifted, her hair piled high on her head like a crown. "Someone had a very good night."

April rolled her eyes but couldn't fight the grin anymore. "Do you always clock the exact moment I've been thoroughly debauched?"

"I don't even need a clock. You're basically levitating."

April laughed and ducked behind the counter. She noticed Rochelle wasn't in yet today. A different woman sat in her usual window seat.

"Rochelle may have to fight for her spot today," she told Hannah.

"I was just thinking that. Crazy-busy. We should have had an after-hours party a long time ago."

"We'll make it a monthly thing," Sonny said as he set a custom-made Watermelon Sweet Tea on the pickup counter and shouted to one of their regulars, "Order up for lovely Lana!"

April grinned at Sonny's good mood.

The line was long—just out the door now—but no one seemed to mind. Sonny was working the espresso machine, moving like a man half his age as he poured shots and frothed milk with practiced ease. The espresso machine hissed and steamed, filling the space with that warm, rich scent that made so many people's mornings bearable.

April stood behind the register, greeting customers both old and new with easy smiles and quick jokes. The place buzzed with that Riversong kind of magic—Sonny's favorite old jazz station playing overhead, laughter, clapping from someone who'd just won a game of checkers in the corner, the owner of Do's and Donuts dropping off a dozen mixed flavors for the pastry cooler. She barely had time to take it in. The line kept moving. Regulars, tourists, a few college kids home for the summer. She passed change, scribbled names on cups, made small talk about the weather, thanked people for tips.

The next customer stepped up.

"Morning!" April said brightly, already reaching for a cup. She didn't recognize him at first—it had been almost ten years, and the time he spent in prison had not been kind. "What can I—"

Her voice cut out. Her fingers froze around the cup.

Because standing in front of her, calm as you please, was Vince Romano.

He'd aged. Badly. He was ten years older than April but looked her age when they met. Now he looked like he had twenty years on her. The smooth confidence he'd worn like expensive cologne was still there, but his face had gained forehead wrinkles, and crow's feet behind his dark glasses. Lines bracketed his mouth that hadn't been there before. His biggest pride—his hair—was still thick and dark, but heavily threaded with gray at the temples. His sense of style hadn't changed. He wore a meticulously pressed and fitted jacket over a smooth silk shirt, and of course his Rolex Deepsea watch, which he liked to falsely brag he won off of James Cameron in a private poker game.

Oh yes, April remembered that watch well, but not for the Cameron connection. It had left quite a bruise on her face when Vince backhanded her.

Run. Grab Kevin and run.

"Hey, looks like I found my jackpot," Vince said, and his voice was exactly as she remembered. Smooth as good whiskey going down. "Long time, baby. You're looking good."

April couldn't breathe. Couldn't move. The cup in her hand felt like it weighed a thousand pounds.

"April?" Hannah's voice came from somewhere far away. "You okay?"

Vince's smile widened. He pulled off his sunglasses with deliberate slowness and tucked them into his jacket pocket. His eyes, now those were the same. Dark and assessing and not quite as warm as his smile. "Surprised to see me?"

April found her voice. It came out cold and flat. "What are you doing here?"

"Getting coffee." He gestured at the menu board behind her. "This is a coffee shop, right?"

"You need to leave."

His expression shifted—just a flicker, like a mask slipping for half a second before sliding back into place. "Whoa, whoa, whoa, baby. I just want to talk, April. That's all."

She was aware of the line behind him. Of customers watching. Of Hannah frozen beside her, eyes wide. Of Sonny looking up from the espresso machine, his expression sharpening.

"There's nothing to talk about except for you leaving," April said quietly.

"April, baby, please." Vince's expression went soft and sad. "It took me so long to find you. I'm not mad, okay? I just want to talk. Can't we talk?" He looked around, caught the eye of the customer standing behind him and shrugged while laughing lightly, as if he'd only asked April the time.

"You heard my sister," Hannah said, her voice colder than April had ever heard it. "Get the hell out of our shop."

April felt her father suddenly at her side. His face was set in that expression April knew too well—the one that meant someone was about to get thrown out bodily if they didn't leave immediately.

"You must be Vince," Sonny said, his voice carrying authority. "You need to leave. Now."

Vince glanced at him, unimpressed. "And you are?"

"The owner. And I'm telling you to get out of my shop."

April put her hand on her father's arm. "Sonny, I'll take care of it."

Vince's eyes went wide. "Oh, you're Sonny Taylor. My apologies." He extended his hand. "I should have realized you're my fiancée's father. Good ta meet ya, sir." Sonny just stared at his hand.

April nearly died right there. Then her fury rose, blotting out everything except Vincent Romano.

"Your *fiancée*? How dare you call me that? It's been almost ten years, Vince. Are you delusional?"

Vince covered his heart. "Love has no expiration date, April."

April actually laughed. "Okay, yeah, okay. You *are* delulu." She wiped a tear of mirth from her eye. "Yeah, Vince, we can talk." She looked at the customer over his shoulder. "Sorry, sir, Hannah will be right with you." She pulled the tie on her apron and grabbed the neck strap.

"April, no," Hannah said, still glaring at Vince.

Sonny looked at her, then at Vince, then back at her. "You sure?"

"I'm sure. This won't take long." She set the apron on a low shelf under the counter and started to go past her father.

He didn't move immediately. Just stood there, a wall of protective father energy, before finally stepping back. But he watched ever move his daughter made.

April walked out from behind the counter. "Come on," she told Vince.

"Lead the way, baby. I'll take you out to the finest restaurant they got in this little pisshole town."

God, that was equal parts hilarious and fury-inducing. He'd just put her in the position of defending the hometown that hated her.

"Yeah, well, I grew up in this little pisshole and I love it." She was struck by the fact that it was true—somewhere along the way, she'd come to love her hometown.

Now's not the time for shocking revelations, April. One conversation with this clown—who seems more pathetic than scary now that we're face-to-face—and send him on his way.

"Sorry, baby."

She hated that he called her that. Hated it with a fury that made her hands shake. But she kept it together and headed toward an empty table in the back corner that hadn't been bussed yet—the one farthest from the other customers but still visible from the counter. "I'm not going anywhere with you."

"Whatever you want, baby. It's your call." Vince followed.

Cringe.

April sat with her back to the wall, the way Shane had taught her. Hannah worked the register and poured coffee with one eye on her sister. Same with Sonny, but with the phone to his ear. April imagined he was calling the police.

Vince took the chair across from her, still smiling that terrible smooth smile that fooled her so long ago.

"Let's get right to it. How did you find me?"

And how did Watchdog not know you were here?

Vince grinned and spread his arms as he looked around Riversong. "How does anyone find anything these days? This place was all over social media, celebrating something. Saw a picture, thought I saw the woman I loved," He stopped, lifted a finger, "*still* love, excuse me. And I had to come and make sure it was you."

Oh no. Oh shit. Shit.

How could she be so stupid? April wracked her brain, trying to think about which picture of Riversong and the family Hannah had posted. Was Kevin in it? April did her damndest to keep her son's face off the internet, so she didn't think so.

"You look so good," he said softly, his voice the embodiment of warm whiskey by the fire. "You don't look a day older than they last time I saw you. Colorado agrees with you." He reached for her hand and she snatched it away.

"Don't."

"Don't what, baby?"

"Don't touch me, don't call me baby, and do *not* act like this is a friendly reunion. Don't pretend you have any right to be here. So you found me, big deal. I'm not yours. You lost that chance a long time ago."

Vince leaned back in his chair, spreading his hands. "I did my time, April. Paid my debt to society. They even let me out early for good behavior and my parole officer helped me end my parole early. I'm a free man now, and I want to make amends."

"Amends."

"Yeah. For everything." His voice dropped, going soft

and earnest. "I was a different man then. Angry. Scared. Greedy. I made terrible choices, and I hurt you. I know that. And I'm sorry. But I did it all for you, ba—April. I wanted you to have the best of everything."

April stared at him. He sounded sincere. Looked sincere. And for just a second—just the briefest, most treacherous second—she wondered if in his sad little deluded mind, he meant it.

Then she remembered the feel of his watch connecting with her jaw. The sound her body made hitting the floor. The pain in her ribs when he kicked her, knowing he was aiming for her belly. Aiming for her unborn child. The fear of Vince finding her—and the fear of picking the wrong man again, she realized—that had lived in her bones for years. That had kept her from opening her heart back up to Shane the minute he walked into Riversong.

"You hit me," she said quietly.

Vince looked down as he rubbed his forehead. "I know. And I *hate* myself for it." He dropped his hand, leaned forward, and she regretted her seat against the back wall that gave her no room to retreat. "Prison changes a man, April. I had a lot of time to think. To get help. I went through anger management, group therapy, found God, all of it, just for you, out of regret for what I'd done. I'm telling you, I'm not that guy anymore. I've found peace."

"Yeah, right."

Vince leaned on the table, fixing her with sorrowful eyes. "I've changed, April. For your sake, yeah. But now I know why God really set me on the path to better myself." He smiled through suddenly teary eyes.

April's blood froze.

Oh no. Please no.

"I want to be a good father to our son."

April closed her eyes and clenched her jaw. Of course, he knew. How could he not?

"Kevin, right? That's what you named him? I like it. Kevin Romano's got a good ring to it."

April's eyes flew open. The protective fury that surged through her was so fierce it almost knocked her sideways. "You don't get to say his name. *Ever.* Especially attached to yours."

"I want us to be a family. It's only right a boy should know his father."

"You wanted me to get rid of Kevin. You told me to get an abortion the day I told you I was pregnant." She gripped the table, white-knuckled, tempted to flip it. "You hurt me trying to hurt the baby."

His eyes filled with tears again. "I've learned life is *sacred*, April. You can't know how deeply I regret my weak moments. But you gotta understand I was terrified. I didn't know how to be a father because my old man was a dirty bastard. I panicked, and I did things I didn't mean." He shook his head. "But I've spent years wondering if you had the baby. Thinking about the child I've never met, if you did. Was it a boy or a little girl? Did he look like me? Did she look like you? Were the two of you okay, or out there lost somewhere?" He wiped away tears April was sure had more in common with a crocodile than with any true sorrow. "When I got out and started looking for you, I was also looking for our child. Our little Kevin."

That did it. "You shouldn't have looked. You shouldn't be here. Now get out. Out of Riversong, out of Lyons, out of Colorado. Like the song says, we are never ever getting back together."

Vince's tears dried up like someone turned off a faucet. His eyes turned hard.

"He's my son, April. He should have a father and I have a right to know him."

"You have no rights. You gave those up when you told me to—" She cut herself off, aware of how her voice was rising. She took a breath and lowered it. "When you tried to get rid of him. And Kevin *does* have a father—more of a father than you could ever hope to be."

Vince was quiet for a moment. Then, "Yeah, I heard you're with someone. A Navy guy? Some kinda Special Forces?"

April's blood went cold. "How do you—"

"Told you, internet." He shrugged and grinned. "Is it serious?"

She thought of Shane. Of the way he looked at her like she was the answer to every question he'd ever had. Of Kevin calling him Dad. Of the life they were building together.

"Yes," she said. "It's serious."

"Can't be too serious." Vince's smile turned sharp. "He hasn't put a ring on it."

The words landed like a slap. April felt her face heat.

"That's none of your business."

"Sure it is. If my son is being raised by some guy—"

"By his *father* in the truest sense of the word."

Vince crossed his arms. "No, April. As much as you wanna deny it, I'm his actual father. And I want to be part of his life." Vince leaned back again, all casual confidence. "I'm not trying to cause trouble here. I just want a chance. To meet him. To be a *dad*."

"Never," she hissed, her voice pure, cold steel.

"You can't keep him from me forever."

"Watch me."

"He's my kid too, April."

"He's nothing to you. Your name isn't even on the birth certificate."

Vince's smile never wavered. "DNA test can fix that. Courts are pretty good about a father's rights these days."

"Not when he's been to prison. Not when he tried to induce an abortion. Not when he's in his forties and washing dishes for a living. I'm the co-owner of Riversong, which, just look around, is a very successful business, thank you very much. I've been providing for him all his life and that's not gonna change."

Vince sighed, like she was being unreasonable. "*You* look around, baby. This place—" He gestured at Riversong, at the walls covered in local art and Wren's landscape photos for sale, at the customers laughing over coffee. "Sure this is nice. Quaint. But it's not exactly the penthouse suite, is it?"

April's hands curled into fists under the table.

"You used to have class. Style," Vince continued. " Remember Vegas? Designer clothes, champagne, that Louis Vuitton Murakami Speedy Thirty purse you loved so much?"

She blinked in surprise. "I can't believe you actually paid enough attention let alone remembered my purse."

"Of course I did, April. That was your lucky purse you used to carry everywhere. I remember everything like it was yesterday. We had it good. So good. We hit the jackpot, you and me." His eyes raked over her, assessing and apparently finding her wanting, judging by his sneer. "Now you're what? Slinging shitty coffee in your parents' shop? Looking like you shop at a thrift store?"

The fury that rose in her was white-hot and righteous. "First of all, there is absolutely nothing wrong with shopping in a thrift store. But more important, I left because you were a criminal and an abuser."

He looked affronted. "I was never convicted of abuse. You never pressed charges."

"Because I was terrified of you."

"That's not how I remember it." His voice dropped, intimate and poisonous. "I remember you loving the lifestyle. The money. The attention. My *cock*," he sneered. "You weren't exactly complaining when I was paying for everything."

"I remember splitting the bills. Mostly I remember you hitting me."

"You remember wrong." He said it so smoothly, so confidently, that for a second she doubted herself. Then he softened. "But hey, I forgive you. For running. For taking my son. For hiding from me for all these years. I'm a changed man, April. I did my time. And now I want my family back."

"Never," April said. Her voice was shaking but firm. "Never happening."

Vince studied her for a long moment. Then the mask finally dropped completely. What was underneath chilled her to the bone.

"We'll see what a judge says. You can't keep a father from his son, April. I have rights. Parental rights. And I'm going to exercise them."

She pointed to the door. "Get out. *Now*."

"Oh, I'm going." He stood, pulling his sunglasses back out. "But I'll be seeing you soon. In court, if that's how you want to play it. Don't expect to win a jackpot there." He paused, looking down at her. "Do you even have that Speedy Thirty? Hope you didn't hock it to keep this shithole running."

She sat up as straight as she could. "As a matter of fact, I do, and fuck you, Riversong is not a shithole. Now. Get. Out."

Vince held up his hands in mock surrender. "I'm going. But think about what I said, April. I'm not the bad guy here. Just remember, I tried to play nice first and you fucked it up. I just want to know *my* son. Little Kevin *Romano*." He put on his sunglasses, turned to leave, then looked back over his shoulder. "See you soon, baby."

He walked out of Riversong like he just bought the place. Like he knew he'd just shattered April's entire world with twenty minutes of smooth lies and veiled threats.

April sat frozen at the table, her heart hammering so hard she thought it might crack her ribs.

Hannah and Sonny appeared at her elbow. "April? Baby girl, you okay?"

She looked up at her sister, then her dad, and whatever he saw in her face made him crouch down beside her chair.

"What'd he say to you?" Sonny asked, though his tone suggested he already knew.

"He knows about Kevin," April whispered. "He wants custody."

Sonny's expression went thunderous. "I should have thrown him out the second he walked in."

"You didn't know." April tried to stand, but her legs wouldn't cooperate. "I need to call Shane."

"Already did." Sonny pulled out his phone. "Called him the minute the two of you sat down. He should be here any—"

The door burst open hard enough to rattle the frame.

TWENTY-FOUR

SHANE CAME THROUGH IT LIKE A HURRICANE, HIS GAZE scanning the room until he found her. Behind him came the rest of Mountain Division—Gabe straight from the rec center, Elias and Waylon still in their EMT uniforms, Ben, and even Bear down off his mountain.

Shane crossed the distance to her. "Are you okay? Did he touch you?"

April shook her head. She still couldn't seem to make her voice work properly.

Shane cupped her face in his hands, tilting it up so she had to look at him. "April. Talk to me. What happened?"

"He—" She had to stop, swallow, try again. "He wants custody. He's going to sue for full custody."

"The hell he is."

"He said he has rights. That a judge will—"

"No." Shane's voice was flat and absolute. "He's not getting near Kevin. I promise you that."

"What if he knows where we live? It's easy enough to look up all that now that he's found me. He... He knew about *you*—" April's voice cracked. "He knows everything, Shane."

Shane pulled her into his arms, and she went willingly, pressing her face against his chest. His heart was pounding as hard as hers.

Over her head, She felt Shane looked at Sonny. "Where is he?"

"Left right before you got here. Silver rental car, headed east. I got the plate number."

"I'm texting Kyle," Gabe said. "We'll pull traffic cameras."

"What do we do?" April pulled back to look at Shane. "He said he's going to court. He said—"

"We get you a lawyer. We document everything. We fight this." Shane's jaw was set in that way that meant someone was about to have a very bad day. "But first, we need to get Kevin."

April's heart skipped. "Kevin. Oh God, What if he knows where Kevin goes to camp? Kevin—"

"He's safe. The camp is the other direction." Shane's hands were steady on her shoulders. "But we need to pick him up. Now."

She nodded, trying to pull herself together. "Okay. Okay, we go get Kevin."

"Waylon, Elias—you're with us." Shane looked at the rest of his brothers. "Gabe, Bear, Ben—find that rental car. I want to know where he's staying, who he's been talking to, everything."

"On it," Gabe said.

Shane looked back at April. "Ready?"

No. She wasn't ready. She would never be ready to tell her son that the man who'd wanted him dead before he was born was now demanding visitation rights.

But she nodded anyway. "Let's go get our son."

———————

THEY TOOK Shane's Watchdog SUV. Waylon and Elias followed in Waylon's truck, still in their EMT uniforms. April sat in the passenger seat, her hands twisted together in her lap.

"We should shield him from this," April said. "He doesn't need to know yet. We could just—"

"April." Shane's voice was gentle but firm. "We talked about this. Remember? We decided we weren't going to lie to Kevin. Not about the important stuff."

"I know. But—"

"It won't work anyway. Kid's too smart. He'll know something's wrong the second he sees you."

April looked at him. "Is that why you brought backup? So he'd know something was wrong?"

"I brought backup because if Vince knows where Kevin is, I'm not taking any chances." Shane's hands tightened on the steering wheel. "But yeah. Kevin's going to know. And we need to tell him the truth."

"What if he wants to meet him?" The words came out small and scared. "What if he thinks—"

"He won't."

"You don't know that."

Shane reached over and took her hand. "I know Kevin. And I know he loves you more than anything in the world. He's not going to choose some stranger over his mom."

"But Vince is his biological father—"

"And I'm his dad." Shane said it simply, like it was fact. "Kevin told me so himself. Biology doesn't change that."

April squeezed his hand, unable to speak past the lump

in her throat. That was almost exactly what her dad had told her.

They were both right.

They pulled up to the camp in time for their lunch break. Kevin was near the front, talking to one of his friends. April watched him look up when Shane's SUV pulled in, watched his face light up the way it always did when he saw them.

Then he saw Waylon and Elias getting out of the other vehicle, still in uniform, and his smile faltered.

April and Shane got out of the truck. Kevin ran over.

"What's wrong?" he asked immediately. "Is someone hurt? Is Grandpapa okay?"

"Everyone's fine," April said, crouching down to his level. "But we need to go. There's something we need to talk to you about."

Kevin's eyes went wide. "Am I in trouble?"

"No, baby. Not at all." April pulled him into a hug. "Come on. Let's get in the SUV."

They drove in silence. Kevin sat in the back, Pete out of his crate and curled beside him, and April could feel the weight of his worry pressing against her from behind.

Finally, Kevin asked the question April had been dreading.

"Does this have to do with my bio-dad?"

April turned in her seat to look at him. "How did you—"

"I figured it out, Mom." Kevin's voice was quiet. Small. "And...I may have eavesdropped on you guys again."

"Oh, Kevin." Though she had herself to blame, too. She thought back through the evenings when they thought Kevin was asleep and they discussed the ongoing surveillance, how Vince seemed to be less of a threat every day. Of course Kevin would try and listen in. She should have known better.

"But now you both look scared," Kevin went on. "And Uncle Waylon and Uncle Elias are following us." He swallowed hard. "Is he here? Did he come? Is he...a bad guy?"

Shane pulled over into a parking lot. Turned off the engine. He twisted around to face Kevin.

"Yeah, bud. He's here. In Lyons."

Kevin nodded slowly. "Does he want to see me?"

April's heart cracked clean in half. "Kevin—"

"It's okay, Mom." But Kevin's eyes were bright with unshed tears. "You told me he wasn't ready to be a dad when I was born. Maybe he's ready now?"

"Kevin." Shane's voice was steady and sure. "I need you to listen to me. Can you do that?"

Kevin nodded.

"Your biological father—Vince—he showed up at Riversong today. He told your mom he wants to meet you. But here's the thing, bud. He doesn't get to just walk into your life and demand things. He gave up that right before you were even born. I'm not saying you can't meet him if that's what you want. But right now, we need to keep you safe while we figure out what he really wants. Okay?"

Kevin looked between them. "Do you think he wants to hurt Mom?"

"I don't know," Shane said honestly.

"So he is a bad guy."

"We're still trying to figure that out. But if he is, I'm not going to let him near you or your mom. Neither are your uncles. You're safe. Your mom's safe. That's what matters."

Kevin was quiet for a long moment. Then he said, in a voice so small it barely qualified as a whisper, "I don't want to meet him. I don't need him. I have you."

Shane looked like he'd been punched in the chest. "Kev—"

"You're my dad. Not him, not even if he's a good guy. *You.*" Kevin's tears spilled over. "Is that okay?"

Shane unbuckled and climbed into the back seat, pulling Kevin into his arms. "Yeah, buddy. That's more than okay."

April climbed back too, wrapping both of them in her arms while Pete whined softly and licked Kevin's hand.

They sat there in Shane's truck in a random parking lot, holding each other while the world tried its best to break them apart.

———

SHANE DIDN'T TAKE CHANCES.

Within two hours of Vince's appearance at Riversong, April and Kevin were in one of the Watchdog safehouses—the former Sanders property on Watchdog's sprawling foothill compound east of Lyons. Walter Sanders had been Arden's neighbor, Ellie's uncle, who'd passed away after a long battle with dementia. Bear had fixed up the house beautifully—new security system, reinforced doors and windows, but keeping the warm touches that made it a home rather than a bunker.

April hated it anyway.

Not the house itself—it was lovely, actually. Comfortable furniture, a well-stocked kitchen, windows that looked out over acres of protected land. Kevin could run around outside, play with Benny who they'd brought to the safehouse to keep his spirits up.

But it still felt like prison. Like hiding. Like Vince was winning just by making them afraid.

"It's temporary," Shane kept saying. "Just until we find him."

But they couldn't find him.

Vince Romano had vanished like smoke. No credit card transactions. No hotel bookings. The silver rental car turned up abandoned in a grocery store parking lot in Longmont—wiped clean, no prints, no evidence. Traffic cameras showed him ditching it and walking away, but after that? Nothing.

Watchdog dug into his life with the kind of thoroughness that would have been illegal if they were law enforcement. Flint worked his contacts at every federal agency that owed him favors, calling in markers he'd been saving for years.

The results were beyond frustrating.

"I don't understand it," Flint admitted three days in. Sitting in the safehouse living room, he looked exhausted, bags under his eyes, his usual confidence replaced by something that looked almost like shame. "No paper trail. No digital footprint. It's like he knows exactly how to stay invisible."

"He's had help," Shane said. "Professional help."

"Has to be. The restaurant in Vegas is clean—just a normal kitchen job. No big deposits in his account. We still can't find him on any commercial flights, and now with the rental car abandoned..." Flint rubbed his face. "I'm sorry, Shane. I should have caught this earlier. Should have seen he was here."

"You were monitoring him and he'd kept to his routine. He checked in with his PO that morning."

"Which we now know was bullshit. PO's claiming Vince was there, but I'd bet my pension he was already in

Colorado by then. Someone got to that PO. Money or threats, doesn't matter—he lied."

"Keep looking."

"I am. We all are. But Shane..." Flint's voice dropped. "Whoever's backing Vince, they're good. Really good. And they've got resources we can't track."

April listened to all of this from the couch, Kevin visible through the window playing fetch with Benny and Pete in the yard. She felt like she was disappearing—erased from her own life. April didn't go to Riversong at all; Hannah and Sonny covered her shifts. The world kept turning without her.

Kevin was handling it better than she'd expected. Having Benny there helped—the dog slept in Kevin's room at night, and during the day Kevin could work with him, practice commands, run around the property. Arden gave them an open invitation to visit the ranch up the road to see the horses and alpacas. Charlie took Kevin on hikes through the woods within Watchdog's massive property. Their family and friends visited, bringing dinner and staying to eat and talk and just spend time with them. April was deeply grateful for everyone trying to bring her and Kevin a slice of normalcy.

But when Kevin was still, when he wasn't distracted, April could see the weight of it pressing down on him. The knowledge that somewhere out there, his biological father was planning something. Waiting. It brought her down, too.

Kevin asked twice when Vince was going to leave, when they could go home.

April didn't have an answer for that.

On the fifth day, Sonny showed up at her door in the middle of the day.

"Papa? What are you doing here, what's wrong?"

Sonny came in, his face grim. "A courier came in, said he tried your house first but you weren't there. I had to accept this. I'm so sorry."

He held out an envelope, return address—Family Court, Boulder County.

"It's okay, Papa. We can't stay here forever, waiting. I'm actually a little relieved the hammer finally fell."

Still, April's hands shook as she opened it.

Vince Romano v. April Taylor. Petition for Emergency Custody Hearing.

The words swam in front of her eyes. Vince had filed for an emergency hearing. He wanted a DNA test to establish paternity. He wanted joint custody. The right to walk into her house to see Kevin.

The hearing was scheduled for ten days from now.

"April?" Sonny's voice seemed to come from very far away.

She looked up at him, and her voice when she spoke was hollow. "He's actually doing it. He's suing for custody."

Sonny's face went hard. "We'll fight him. We'll get you the best lawyer in the state."

April looked down at the summons again. At Vince's name printed in cold, official letters.

"I'm not losing my son," she said quietly. The fear was still there, sharp and cutting, but underneath it was something harder. Something fierce.

"Damn right."

April grabbed her phone off the table. "I'm calling Arden. She told me she knows the best family lawyers in Boulder if it comes to that."

"Right. Her patients." Arden ran an animal therapy

program for kids with autism, PTSD, and physical disabilities.

Arden picked up. "April, hey. What do you need?"

"He did it. He filed for an emergency custody hearing and got it."

"Oh, shit. I'm so sorry. Let me text you a phone number. One of the parents just went through a custody hearing and she loved her lawyer."

"I'm worried I have to appear in person. I wonder if I can do a video from the safehouse?" April asked, though she already knew the answer.

"Probably not for emergency custody hearings," Arden sighed. "It depends on the judge. Some require physical presence. There, I just texted the contact info. Good luck. We all love you and Kevin. I can come down after my next appointment if you need company."

April teared up. Sonny put his arm around her and pulled her close. "We love you, too. Don't worry, my dad's here right now." She smiled up at him. "We'll see you later."

——————

SHANE'S HANDS curled into fists. "It's the one time you have to be exposed."

April stared at the summons lying on the table. She'd shown it to Shane the minute he came home from work. "Maybe we can do a video conference?"

"We'll see."

Over my dead body is he taking Kevin from me.

From us.

But to fight for Kevin, she'd have to leave the safehouse. She'd have to walk into that courthouse—the one place

Shane couldn't carry a weapon, the one place she'd be vulnerable.

And somehow, she knew Vince was counting on exactly that.

TWENTY-FIVE

Aᴘʀɪʟ's ʟᴀᴡʏᴇʀ ʜᴀᴅ ᴀɴ ᴏғғɪᴄᴇ ɪɴ Bᴏᴜʟᴅᴇʀ ᴛʜᴀᴛ felt more like a cozy living room than a legal firm. Soft gray walls, comfortable chairs in warm fabrics, plants on the windowsill catching afternoon light. A framed photo of Gabriela Vasquez with her family sat on the desk beside her diplomas—three kids and a golden retriever, all smiling. April had gotten the referral through Arden. Thanks to her therapeutic animal ranch for kids and vets with PTSD, Arden knew the best lawyers practicing family law in Boulder County. Gabriela was sharp-eyed and no-nonsense, and April liked her immediately—right up until she started talking.

"No video," Gabriela said, her hands folded on her desk. "You have to be there in person. I'm sorry."

"This shouldn't be happening at all," April said. "He's not on the birth certificate."

"He has biological rights. Without documented abuse—police reports, hospital records, restraining orders—it's your word against his."

April's stomach dropped. "But he hit me. Multiple

times. He tried to—" She couldn't finish the sentence. *Tried to hurt our baby. Tried to make me lose Kevin.*

Gabriela reached for April's hand. "I believe you." Gabriela's voice was gentle but firm. "But family court requires evidence. And Mr. Romano has served his time for his crimes. A judge may see him as rehabilitated."

"He's not rehabilitated. He's—"

"Dangerous. I know." Gabriela leaned forward. "Which is why we're going to fight this. But I need you to understand what we're up against and get ready to fight."

April nodded, her throat too tight to speak. Then she thought of Kevin and a calm resolve filled her.

Shane's hand found hers under the table. "We've got this."

She smiled fiercely. "We've got this."

————

APRIL BARELY SLEPT for the next week.

Every night with Shane's arm around her, she lay awake staring at the ceiling worrying about Kevin as he slept just down the hall. Every night, she imagined a judge ruling in Vince's favor. Imagined Kevin being forced to spend weekends with a man who'd wanted him dead. Imagined losing her son to the monster she'd run from, who only wanted Kevin to get back at her.

Kevin had asked twice if he'd have to see Vince.

The first time, April had been making dinner. Kevin was at the table playing with a fidget spinner, and the question came out of nowhere, small and scared.

"Do I have to see him? My bio-dad?"

April's hands stilled. She set down the knife she'd been using to chop tomatoes. "I don't know, baby. Maybe."

"I don't want to." Kevin's voice got smaller. "He's not my dad. Not my *real* one."

Tears in her eyes blurred the cutting board on the counter. April went to him, pulling him into her arms. "I know. We're going to fight this."

"But what if the judge makes me go with him?"

April held him tighter, her heart breaking. "That's not going to happen."

He was quiet for a moment, and in a soft voice, he said, "If we have to run, can we take Shane with us?"

"Oh, baby, we're not going to run. It won't come to that, I promise."

It was a promise she hoped she could keep.

The second time, Shane was there, too. They were all on the couch watching a movie, Pete sprawled across their feet, Benny curled up in Kevin's lap. Kevin had been quiet all evening, and then suddenly he was crying—big, silent tears rolling down his cheeks. Benny woke and tried to lick his face. Kevin gently set him on the floor.

"What if I have to go?" he whispered. "What if the judge says I have to live with him all the time and I never see you guys again?"

Shane pulled Kevin onto his lap, and April wrapped her arms around both of them.

"Listen to me, bud," Shane said, his voice steady and sure. "He's not going to win full custody. The judge won't let him take you from us. In the meantime, I'm not letting anything happen to either of you."

"But what if—"

"No what-ifs." Shane's hand was gentle on Kevin's head. "Your mom and I are going to fight for you. And we're going to win."

Kevin fell asleep between them that night, and they carried him to bed.

Later, in the bedroom after making love and safe in Shane's arms, April whispered into the darkness.

"What if we do lose him?"

She felt Shane's jaw set. "We won't." He kissed her temple. "If somehow the impossible happens and they grant Vince custody, I'll burn the world down to get our son back."

————

THE MORNING OF THE HEARING, April stood in front of her closet trying to figure out what a good mother was supposed to wear to fight for her child.

Professional. Put-together. Respectable.

She pulled out a navy-blue dress—conservative, knee-length, the kind of thing a PTA mom would wear. Added a cardigan. Took it back off. Stepped into heels, then flats, then back into lower heels. She picked up her grandmother's pearls. Her hands were shaking so badly she had trouble with the clasp.

Shane appeared behind her and fastened it without a word, then smoothed his hands down her arms. "You look perfect."

April stared at herself in the mirror. She didn't look perfect, she looked terrified. Like someone who was about to lose everything.

Her gaze drifted to the top shelf of the closet. To her Lucky Louis purse sitting exactly where she'd put it after Ellie's party. She'd pulled it out of storage to impress Claudia, or at least not appear completely impoverished, and look how that turned out. Not only was Claudia a new friend, but relations continued to thaw between April and Yvonne.

What'd you do, hock it to keep this shithole running?

"Fuck him," April said quietly.

Shane followed her gaze. Without a word, he walked over to the closet and pulled it down. She took it out of its dust bag and transferred her essentials—wallet, keys, phone, lip gloss—into the purse. It felt strange in her hands, like holding a piece of her past. A reminder of who she'd been when life was nothing but one gamble after another, when she thought love and security meant expensive things and penthouse views.

Now she knew better.

Now she knew the fierce love of a man who'd burn the world down for her and their son. She knew the innocent love of a boy who trusted her with his whole heart. A family who'd turned an old empty building into a coffee shop that added something beautiful to the community. Friends who stuck by her, surrounding her with love so strong she felt surrounded by a fortress wherever she went.

She looked at Shane. "I'm not ashamed of who I was or what I survived."

His smile was fierce and proud. "Damn right you're not."

"I'm ready."

Shane's fierce smile turned softer. "You need one more thing." He touched the old purse. "This tells Vince who you were. When you walk into that courtroom, I want you wearing something that will show him who I hope with all my heart you want to become."

April tilted her head. "What do you mean?"

"I mean this."

Shane reached into his jacket pocket and pulled out a little velvet box.

TWENTY-SIX

SHANE TRIED TO KEEP HIS HAND FROM TREMBLING. HE watched April's expression go from confused to wide-eyed, her lips parting, mouth opening, her gaze riveted on the velvet box—the most important possession he'd ever owned. He thought back to the beginning of its creation ten days ago.

———

THE EARLY-SUMMER HEAT had settled into Colorado like it meant to stay. Shane stepped out of his SUV and studied the big Victorian Ben had meticulously renovated. Bear usually got the credit for being the handyman—and he deserved it—but Ben? Ben was an artisan. Always had been, even when they were kids.

That's why Shane was here. He needed Ben's artistry.

He'd called ahead. Ben told him to come around back to the forge—said he'd be in the middle of something for the Renaissance Festival west of Castle Rock. Shane took the gravel path around the side of the house and through the garden As he got closer to the backyard, he heard it. The steady rhythm of hammer on metal. Not the wild clang of a novice, but measured, patient strikes—each one landing with precision, ringing like iron bells.

The river behind the property ran high with snowmelt, loud and fast and silver in the June light. Cottonwood fluff drifted through the yard like someone had opened a down pillow and shaken it out. The smithy windows were thrown open, the doors too—heat shimmered at the threshold. Working a forge in the summer was no joke. It was a test of endurance, precision, and brute strength in equal measure.

Shane stepped inside.

The scent hit him first: cedar, smoke, and hot metal. Coals glowed in the arched brick oven he'd made, kicking out waves of dry heat. The anvil sat in the center of the room like an altar, the floor swept but still stained with years of blood, sweat, and ash.

Ben stood with his back to the door, a mountain in motion.

He was shirtless, skin sheened with sweat, muscles working with every swing of the hammer. His dark hair was tied back with a leather cord at the nape, grown long for his summer run at the Ren Faire. He wore a black utility kilt, boots, and a leather apron folded down at the waist, revealing the full flex of his shoulders and back as he turned a glowing piece of steel with his tongs. He struck again.

Ben looked over his shoulder. "Heard you coming. You stomp like a guilty man."

Shane huffed. "I don't stomp. You just hear like a moose with PTSD."

Ben grinned. "I prefer hyper-vigilant artisan." He adjusted the steel on the anvil, gave it one more clean strike, then set the hammer aside. The piece went into the quench tank with a hiss, steam rising in a white cloud. Only then did he face Shane, sweat rolling down his chest in lazy trails, arms streaked with soot.

He nodded toward the house. "Got cold beers in the fridge. Go in. Help yourself. Give me a second to clean up."

Shane opened the screen door to a sunroom at the back of the house, built off the kitchen. Fans spun fast over outdoor chairs, tables, and a couch. He went inside, grabbed two beers from the fridge, and came back out. Ben had taken off his blacksmith's apron and put on a shirt. They sat down across from each other, a coffee table between them, and sipped their beers while Ben cooled off.

Finally Ben said, "So. Tell me why you're here." He rubbed the cold bottle along the back of his neck.

Shane exhaled slowly. "It's time. I want you to make our rings."

Ben didn't react big — he just blinked once, steady. "Okay," he said, like Shane had told him the forecast. "When do you want them?"

"Before the hearing in ten days. Vince is still missing. We're preparing for every eventuality, but—" He stopped, jaw clenching. "I want her to walk into that courtroom wearing my ring. I want Kevin to know he's not going to lose us. And I want that asshole to understand he's already lost." Shane waited for Ben to tell him no, he needed more time.

Ben nodded once. "Done, brother."

"Jesus. Thank you, Moose."

Ben picked up a sketchbook from the table and flipped it open then reached for a pencil. "Tell me when you knew."

Shane's laugh came quiet, almost embarrassed. "High school."

The corner of Ben's mouth quirked up. "Obviously. But when recently?"

Shane leaned back in the chair. "Eldorado Canyon. Mid-May, right before Kevin got outta school."

Ben's pencil scratched — faint, rhythmic. He didn't hurry him.

"I'd asked April the night before if she'd consider giving me a second chance. She said she'd give me her answer after the hike. It was a beautiful day. Kevin's curiosity was dialed up to eleven, asking questions every three steps." The memory tightened his chest. "We stopped for a picnic." He traced a lazy circle on the armrest with his fingertip. "A thunderstorm rolled in faster than we expected. We left ahead of it but it caught up to us. We took shelter at my house. Everything felt so right. The whole day, having them in my home, all of it."

"That's when?" Ben asked quietly.

"That's when." Shane cleared his throat. "She said yes to the second chance that night. And since then, I've done everything in my power to make damn sure she never regrets it."

Ben sketched for another minute, then his pencil slowed. He finished, set down the pencil and turned the page toward Shane.

"Dude, that's... Perfection."

Ben chuckled. He tapped the first ring sketch. Specifically, the grain rippling like river currents and canyon striations. Along the outer edge, topographic lines of Eldorado Canyon, rising and falling like breath.

"Damascus steel. Those lines will be made by the folds in the metal." His finger ran along the lines. "A river for Riversong. A gold interior band—light held safe inside strength."

Then he tapped the second drawing. "White gold. Thin inlay of Damascus." He looked up at Shane, then pointed to the outer surface. "Silhouette of Eldorado engraved here. Clouds and a lightning bolt for the storm you survived that day, and the one you'll survive now, understand?"

Shane nodded slowly, gazing at the drawing.

When placed side by side, the mountain lines of his ring would align with the river lines of hers, forming one continuous landscape. Home.

Together, two rings whose designs echoed and completed each other.

Shane didn't speak for a long moment. His hand came up, thumb pressing along the edge of the page like he could feel the metal under paper.

"That's it," he said. "That's us."

Ben nodded once. "She's going to cry."

Shane let out a breath that might have been a laugh. He scrubbed a hand over his jaw. "Yeah. So will I."

"Remember when we used to play in that canyon?" Ben asked.

Shane looked up with a grin. "Yeah, I do."

"Is that why you took her there?"

"One of the reasons," Shane said. "That place brought up some deep memories. Going back through it with her and Kevin... I could see all of us as kids. Playing soldier. Pretending we were invincible."

Ben huffed. "Funny how that all turned out, huh?"

"Yeah," Shane said. "Sure is."

He went quiet a moment, then added, "I'm still haunted by the day April left."

Ben nodded. "Yeah. I know you are, brother. Never should've happened."

"I'm thankful you stepped up—"

Ben waved him off.

"I wasn't," Shane admitted.

Ben scrubbed a hand across his face. "Your dad met me at the door. I was expecting you. He told me you'd changed your mind and shoved an envelope full of money into my hands. Told me to head to the bus station and give it to her."

"I had no idea, Ben. No idea you were walking into all that."

"I didn't know you were lying in a hospital bed," Ben said quietly. "Didn't know you'd been there since the night before. That that bastard put you there."

Shane grimaced. "He lied to them, you know. Told the staff I was having a psychotic break. He caught me trying to kill myself. Said he was trying to restrain me."

Ben didn't say anything, just listened to him.

"They believed him," Shane said bitterly. "He showed them the defensive wounds on his arms, claimed I'd attacked him. I was covered in bruises. Covered in my own defense wounds. They fucking believed *him*."

He looked down at the table. "I did fight back—unfortunately. I should've just taken the knocks, not given him anything to use against me."

Shane's jaw clenched. "So not only was I hospitalized for the beating, they put me on a seventy-two-hour psych hold. They drugged me. I spent two months in that mental wing."

His voice dropped. "Just long enough for her to disappear. Just long enough to break me. After that, I did whatever my father told me. Took me another couple years to snap out of it."

He looked up. "It was April. She was the one. I realized I couldn't live without her. I spent years trying to find her,

Ben. And when I found out she was back in Lyons—back home—that's when I got scared."

"Scared she'd turn you away?" Ben asked.

"Yeah."

"But she didn't."

Shane shook his head. "No. She didn't. She's a hell of a lot stronger than I've ever been. And she'll never give herself credit for that."

"Then give yourself credit," Ben said. "For being a good man today."

They both looked back down at the sketch. "I've got an aquamarine stone the exact shade of a Colorado summer sky. It'll go right there." He pointed at a spot on the river ring. "I'll have them done for you in a week, brother," Ben said.

"I can't thank you enough."

Ben shrugged, looking away. "It's my pleasure, man." Then, more quietly, he added, "Don't know if I'll ever make one for myself."

Shane gave him a look. "Man, you've gotta get over that, brother."

Ben huffed a dry laugh.

"Look, I've known Charlie forever," Shane continued. "I can—"

"She's an extraordinary woman," Ben interrupted. "Way above my pay grade."

"Yeah, yeah," Shane said, grinning. "I seem to recall Elias thought the same thing about Wren, too. Look how that turned out."

Ben chuckled. "There's a world of difference between Elias and me."

Shane laughed. "That's fair. Out of all of us, Elias was

the one who picked up the most women. That golden-boy thing—blonde hair, blue eyes, steady stream of jokes and compliments. No woman stood a chance."

Ben smirked. "The bastard."

"Meanwhile, you were steady. Confident. Hell, you've always been confident—just not when it comes to women."

Ben gave him a flat look. "Thanks."

Shane laughed, then sobered. "But like I was trying to say before, I know something about Charlie that you probably don't. Something she *loves* to do."

Ben froze and went deathly pale. "You guys never... you d-didn't—?"

"Hook up? Oh hell, no," Shane said, appalled. "King's one of the guys. Always has been. I love her like a brother."

Ben exhaled as the color returned to his face.

"No, this is something else. And believe me, you're gonna beat a path to her door, double-time." Shane's mouth curved as he leaned in and told Ben what he knew.

Ben's eyes narrowed. "You're serious? You're not messing with me?"

"Dead serious." Shane told him, watching the shift—Ben's posture straightened then relaxed. His expression softened. Eyes lit up. "There's your in, brother."

"You think so?"

"Dude. I know so." Shane gave him a look. "So get over yourself and ask her out."

Ben looked down at the sketch between them. Tapped the corner. "Yeah," he said quietly. "Yeah. Maybe I will."

———

SHANE TRIED to keep his hand from trembling. He watched April's expression shift—confused, then wide-eyed, her mouth parting, breath catching, gaze locked on the velvet box in his fingers.

"Is... is that—?" Her eyes snapped to his, blinking hard.

He dropped to one knee as she gasped.

He opened the box.

The aquamarine caught the light—sky-colored, set low into a white gold band etched with a river that shimmered like it was in motion.

Shane looked up into her eyes.

"There is no doubt in my mind that you could hold up the entire sky by yourself if you had to, April. But I'm here to tell you—you don't have to. Not because you can't, but because you shouldn't have to. Not all alone. Not as long as I'm back in your life. I'm not here to tell you that you're weak. I'm here to help you be strong."

Her breath hitched.

"I wanted you to walk into that courtroom today wearing something that makes it clear you're not alone," he said. "That Kevin has two parents who would go to war for him. That you have someone who's not just fighting beside you, but building a life with you, if you'll have me," he said, as he blinked back tears. "I love you. I've been in love with you since we were seventeen."

April nodded vigorously. "Me, too. I've loved you since we were seventeen, too. I could never forget you." She bit her lower lip as a sob escaped her.

"So, April Taylor. Will you do me the great honor of being my wife?"

Tears spilled down her cheeks, but her smile shone through them.

"Yes," she whispered. Then, louder, "Yes, Shane. Of course, yes. Yes!"

He slipped the ring onto her shaking hand.

She pulled him up into a kiss that said everything else didn't matter—because she had her whole damn sky now, and he was right there under it with her.

TWENTY-SEVEN

SHANE DROVE TO THE COURTHOUSE. APRIL SAT IN THE passenger seat, purse in her lap, fingers twisting the most beautiful ring in the world on her finger. Clouds gathered on the horizon as the forecaster on the radio promised rain throughout the day. April watched the landscape roll past the window without really seeing it.

"You okay?" Shane asked for the third time.

"No." April looked at him and smiled. "But I will be."

They pulled into the courthouse parking lot, and April's heart kicked into overdrive. This was it. This was where she either kept her son or lost him to the man who'd tried to destroy them both.

Shane cut the engine and turned to her. "Whatever happens in there, we're in this together. You, me, and Kevin. Nothing changes that."

April nodded, not trusting her voice.

They walked into the courthouse together, then through security and the metal detector—Shane had to leave his weapon in the SUV, and she could see how much he hated it. Then down the marble-floored hallway, their footsteps echoing.

Gabriela was waiting outside the courtroom with her briefcase and her game face on. She'd asked her parents and sister not to come—they were watching Kevin at Riversong because she'd wanted something normal for him today.

So she was shocked to see her family there—her Watchdog family.

April stopped short. Rochelle and Gabe. Wren and Elias. Waylon with Frankie and her baby bump. Ellie and Bear with Star in his arms, her tiny hand curled around one of his fingers. That sight alone was enough to make April cry a river to rival the St. Vrain. Gina and Lach. Arden and Kyle. Ben, who smiled when he saw her wearing the ring Shane told her he'd spent a week crafting just so she could wear it today.

Her throat went tight.

"What are you all doing here?" she managed to squeak out.

"Supporting you," Rochelle said simply. "What else?"

April's eyes filled with tears. Seeing her friends here, seeing the people who'd become her family—

"Thank you," she whispered. "Thank you."

And then her fortress of friends converged on her and she was literally surrounded by love. One hug after another, after another. A thousand words of encouragement. And from Mountain Division, whispered promises of protection, no matter what.

Then came the cheers when she held up her left hand. "I said yes!"

She hugged Ben a second time, kissed his cheek, and thanked him.

Shane's hand was warm on her back. "You ready?"

April looked at the courtroom doors. At Gabriela with her briefcase full of evidence that might not be enough. At her friends who'd shown up to bear witness.

"I am now."

———

VINCE ARRIVED ten minutes later with a lawyer who looked like he charged more per hour than Riversong made in a month.

Where is he getting the money for this?

As if to mock her, Vince was in a Louis Vuitton suit—charcoal gray, perfectly tailored. His hair was perfectly gelled and styled. His shoes were polished. He looked like a successful businessman, not a convicted felon fresh out of prison. He smiled when he saw her. That same smooth, confident smile that had fooled her once.

April felt sick.

Vince took out his phone. His thumbs tapped quickly. Who was he texting? His lawyer glanced at him and frowned, said something low that April couldn't hear. Vince pocketed the phone with a shrug.

Shane's hand tightened on April's shoulder.

"All rise. U.S. District Court for the Middle District of Boulder is now in session," the bailiff announced as Judge Patricia Preston entered the courtroom and took her seat behind the bench. She looked to be in her fifties, with steel-gray hair and reading glasses on a chain. April settled in to wait for their case to come up on the docket.

Eventually, the case was called. April and Gabriela approached the defendant's table. Vince and his lawyer took their places. Vince continued to put on his charming act, though he kept looking back at the public seating area until he spotted Shane.

Yeah, take a good look at my fiancé. If you try anything, his is the last face you'll ever see.

"We're here today regarding the petition of Vincent Romano for emergency custody hearing in the matter of—" The judge glanced at her docket. "Kevin Taylor, minor child, age eight."

Vince's lawyer stood. Marc Brennan, according to Gabriela.

"Your Honor, if I may address the court."

Judge Preston waved a hand. "Go ahead, Mr. Brennan."

"Thank you, Your Honor. My client, Mr. Romano, only recently discovered he had a son. For eight years, he was denied the fundamental right to know his own child. Ms. Taylor disappeared from their shared home in Las Vegas without a trace after learning of her pregnancy." He paused and grinned. "After living under a false identity for nearly a decade."

April's hands clenched in her lap. Gabriela put a steadying hand on her arm.

"We have to ask," Brennan continued, his voice dripping with false concern, "what else Ms. Taylor might be hiding. What crimes she may have committed during those missing years. What kind of environment she's providing for this child. A woman who would deprive a father of his son, who would go to such lengths to remain hidden—can we trust her judgment? Can we trust her fitness as a parent?"

"Your Honor—" Gabriela started to stand. "My client has been working at her family business in Colorado for close to nine years. That's been documented. While Mr. Romano was serving time in prison for various charges including—"

"Your Honor, I was not finished with my—"

Judge Preston held up a hand. "Ms. Vasquez, Mr. Brennan, I'll stop you both right there. This is an emergency custody hearing, not opening arguments for a trial." The judge's voice was sharp. "And you're making some very serious allegations without presenting any evidence to support them, Mr. Brennan. False identity? Crimes? Do you have proof, or are you just throwing mud?"

"Your Honor, the pattern of behavior suggests—"

"Suggests nothing without evidence." Judge Preston looked from Brennan to April to Gabriela. "I think we need to discuss this in chambers before we proceed. There are too many irregularities here, and I want to hear from both parties without the theatrics." She stood. "We'll start with the defense. Ms. Taylor, Ms. Vasquez, please join me."

April's heart was hammering. Gabriela squeezed her arm and whispered, "This is good. She's on our side."

Shane caught April's eye as she stood. His expression said he didn't like this—didn't like her being out of his sight, didn't like any of it. But he nodded.

April followed Gabriela and the bailiff through the door behind the judge's bench. The chambers beyond were exactly what she'd expected—floor-to-ceiling law books, a heavy desk, framed diplomas, and photos of what looked like Judge Preston's grandchildren.

Judge Preston gestured to the chairs in front of her desk. "Please, sit."

April sat. Her knee was bouncing. She forced it to stop.

"Ms. Taylor." The judge's voice was gentler now, away from the courtroom theatrics. "I've read the filings. I know Mr. Romano served time for fraud and financial crimes. I know he also wasn't listed on the birth certificate. What I want to hear from you is why. *Is* he the father, or should we stop right here?"

April took a breath. "He is, Your Honor, but only because he 'donated' his genetic material." April felt her cheeks flush. "He's not Kevin's dad and never will be. The day I told him I was pregnant, he told me to get rid of it. When I refused, he—" Her voice caught. "He hurt me. He hit me. Kicked me on the floor, hoping to cause a miscarriage. And I knew if I stayed, he'd keep hurting me. Hurt the baby."

"Did you report the abuse?"

"No, Your Honor."

"Why not?"

"I was terrified. He had connections. Money. By sheer luck, he was arrested, and I saw my chance. I just wanted to get away before—" April's hands twisted together. "Before he killed me and my baby."

Judge Preston was quiet for a moment, studying April's face. "And in the nine, almost ten years since, Mr. Romano never attempted to contact you? Never tried to find his child?"

"He was in prison for most of that time. And I don't think he cared. He didn't want Kevin then. I don't know why he wants him now, except maybe to get revenge on me."

The judge opened her mouth to respond when the fire alarm started blaring.

The sound was deafening—a piercing shriek that made April's ears ring. She stood, her heart racing for entirely different reasons now. Fire? Here?

Judge Preston stood, looking more annoyed than alarmed. "Are you kidding me? We just had a false alarm two days ago." She grabbed her purse off a brass coat rack.

"Ms. Taylor, Ms. Vasquez, we'll have to continue this in half an hour when they allow us back in. We'll use my private exit."

She led them to a door at the back of her chambers—one April hadn't even noticed. It opened onto a narrow corridor, concrete walls and fluorescent lights. Service access, probably for staff and emergencies. The alarm was shrieking louder in here, echoing in the concrete corridor.

"This way," Judge Preston said, leading them down the corridor. April could smell smoke now—acrid, bitter.

"Wait, do you smell that?"

Before anyone could answer, two firefighters rounded a corner ahead of them at full jog.

Guess it's not a drill.

"Your Honor?" The one in front shouted over the alarm. "Smoke reported on this level. We'll escort you to the nearest exit." And now April could see the smoke beginning to fill the hall.

"My goodness." Judge Preston coughed. "This is real?"

"Yes ma'am. Stay in single file, keep moving. We've got some smoke ahead but it'll clear. Fastest way out. Let's move."

They fell into line, the first firefighter in front, then Judge Preston, then Gabriela, then April. The second firefighter brought up the rear right behind April. The smoke grew thicker the farther they went. April could barely see Gabriela's back ahead of her. Her eyes were streaming. The alarm was still screaming, disorienting, making it impossible to think.

"Keep moving!" The firefighter behind her called over the noise. "Almost there!"

April took another step. Her foot caught something— she didn't even see what—and suddenly she was falling, her ankle twisting hard as she went down. Pain shot up her leg and she cried out.

"April?" Gabriela's voice came from somewhere ahead in the smoke.

"I'm okay!" April called back.

"Keep going with them, Don, I've got her!" the second firefighter shouted. He was already sliding his hands under her armpits, helping her stand. "You all right to walk, ma'am?"

April tested her weight on her ankle and winced. "Twisted it but I think I'm okay."

Through the smoke, April could just barely see the others disappearing. The firefighter gripped her arm firmly, steadying her.

"Thank you. I don't know what I tripped on—"

She felt a sharp sting in her neck. For a second, she didn't understand. Thought maybe a spider bit her, or—

Her legs buckled. The firefighter caught her before she hit the ground.

"Something's wrong," she slurred. The smoke. She needed to get out of the smoke knocking her out.

When the firefighter spoke again, his voice sounded different. Accented. Cold.

"Shh," he said. "Quiet." He picked her up and slung her over his shoulder, then headed in the opposite direction from the others.

April tried to scream. Tried to fight. But her body wouldn't cooperate.

Shane. I need Shane.

Kevin—

The world went black.

TWENTY-EIGHT

"I THINK WE NEED TO DISCUSS THIS IN CHAMBERS before we proceed. There are too many irregularities here, and I want to hear from both parties without the theatrics." Judge Preston stood. "We'll start with the defense. Ms. Taylor, Ms. Vasquez, please join me."

Shane watched April and Gabriela disappear into the judge's chambers as a pit formed in his stomach. They knew there was a possibility that April's false identity would come back and bite her on the ass and they hadn't been wrong. He could only guess what the judge wanted to know. He pinched the bridge of his nose.

Vince Romano was back to texting on his phone. Was he gloating to someone? Placing a bet? God knew and Shane didn't care. His own phone had buzzed not long after the bastard had come into the courtroom, then twice again, and Shane smiled. He hadn't bothered looking because he knew the texts were just meaningless memes from Charlie. What mattered was the pattern in which they'd come in. One text, a pause, then two sent quickly meant that she had seen Romano arrive and had successfully put a tracker on his vehicle.

He owed her big time. Then again, if Ben actually went through with asking her out after Shane's pep talk, that would make them even.

If Ben didn't, well, Shane knew what Charlie liked. He grinned.

His grin disappeared when Vince looked back at him. He wasn't looking so cocky now. Maybe he had placed a bet on his phone and lost. Or, maybe he thought the judge would side with April.

This might have worked in our favor after all.

Shane patted April's lucky purse beside him.

Minutes ticked by. Vince stood and stretched, said something to his lawyer, and turned. He got three steps away from the plaintiff's table when a siren tore through the courtroom, followed by an automated announcement telling people to make their way to the nearest exits.

Shane shot up out of his seat. "The fuck?" People started filing out of the courtroom, herded by the bailiff.

"Don't worry, folks. System's been acting up. Please do not push or shove. Please do not open umbrellas until you're outside."

Shane looked at the door leading to the judge's chambers. It stayed closed. He started walking toward it when the bailiff stopped him.

"Wrong way, sir." He pointed toward the back of the courtroom.

"My fiancée's in there with the judge," he shouted over the damn siren.

"They've got their own exit. She's probably already outside." He pointed again. "Now please exit the courtroom."

"Fuck." Shane grabbed April's purse and tried to make his way through the crowd to his brothers and friends way ahead of him. His head was on a swivel looking for Vince. He spotted him briefly, then the crowd swallowed him back up. Shane caught up to Ben who gently but effectively cut a path through the crowd like a cruise ship through the ocean. The siren blared in the halls outside the courtrooms where more people spilled out. Dammit, he didn't want April outside without him. He pulled out his phone and sent off a quick text to Charlie.

You outside?

She texted back almost immediately.

No, I went in and sat at the back.

Shit. He'd hoped to send King looking for April before the crowd outside got too big. He didn't want Vince or his lawyer fucking with her.

Gabriela's with her though. She won't let that shit fly.

The gray clouds from the morning had let loose with a steady downpour, which only made it that much harder to find anyone in the sea of people and umbrellas. Thank God for Ben, who had started a group text. He directed everyone to a spot under a cluster of maple trees across the street from the courthouse. The trees offered them some shelter from the rain, which was slowing at least.

April was on the text thread, but her phone was currently in her purse hanging off Shane's arm. When Shane regrouped with his friends, he told them, "Everybody keep an eye out for April and Gabriela. April left her purse behind so she's not getting texts. They took the exit out the judge's chambers. Find Romano, too. I don't want him fucking with them." At least if he decided to leave, they could track his car.

Shane listened as rumors spread through the crowd that it was a false alarm. That it was a bomb threat. That the entire basement was on fire. Aliens from DIA, someone joked. Shane was in no mood to laugh. Fifteen minutes had gone by and no April. Fire rigs and paramedics had shown up about the time he'd gotten out the door. Elias was texting, seeing if he knew any of the crew, and Waylon had gone to his truck to check the scanner.

Bear stood like a mighty redwood, Star sheltered from the weather in a baby harness on his massive chest and Ellie pressed up against his side. He had one arm around his wife and the other cradling his daughter. The sight made Shane's chest go tight. He should have been home with April and Kevin, not fucking around in this bullshit.

"Shane!"

Finally. Shane turned at the sound of Gabriela's voice.

Except Gabriela was alone. And she looked worried.

"Where's April?" Shane demanded.

"I don't know. We got separated in the smoke—"

"Smoke?" His heart lurched.

"In the hall behind the judge's chambers. I tried texting but she's not answering."

Shane held up April's purse. "Her phone's in here."

"Shit. She fell and twisted her ankle but there was a firefighter with her. I thought maybe he'd taken her to an ambulance to get checked out, but she wasn't there. I asked all the firefighters if they'd seen her but no joy, so I thought maybe she wasn't hurt and was just in the crowd with you."

"No." Shane fought back panic that threatened to blot out his senses. April didn't need that. He took a deep breath and fell back on his training and got himself under control. "Have you seen Romano? I don't want—"

"Vasquez!" Romano's lawyer was wading through the crowd toward them. "Don't suppose you've seen my client, have you?"

"No," Gabriela answered. "But if he's off harassing mine right now, he's going to have problems."

That started an argument whose ending Shane would never know because he was already heading for Charlie.

"Where's Romano's car?"

She didn't say a word, just turned and led him down the street.

"Still there." She pointed to an older Honda Accord sitting in front of a meter. Shane had expected a flashier car, but if Romano wanted to stay unnoticed, Accords blended into traffic better.

"Shit. Is he still here, or did he take off with her in a different car?"

"No idea." Charlie looked lost.

"Shane! Charlie!" Gina came running toward them.

Oh fuck. Gina running was never a good sign.

"I got Elissa to hack into the cameras around here. It took a minute but she got in. There was too much smoke in the hall behind the chambers, but she caught footage from a gas station across the street of a firefighter carrying April over his shoulder. She looked unconscious."

Shane's world collapsed. "Where?"

Gina held up her hand. "I'm sorry. They disappeared after that. But." Gina closed her eyes. "We have a positive ID on the guy's face."

"Romano?"

"No. Worse. Much, much worse."

The rain picked up. Shane's jaw clenched. "Who?"

"Not here." Gina's eyes swept the crowd—reporters, lawyers, civilians with phones out recording everything. "This is delicate. We can't involve the authorities."

"Gina—"

"We may even have to bribe Romano's lawyer later to keep him quiet, but first things first. We need to get back to Watchdog. ASAP. I need to absolutely make sure I'm correct about this. I texted everyone. I'll see you there." Then she was gone.

Shane wanted to grab her, shake the answer out of her. But he'd worked with Gina long enough to know when she was operating on instinct versus certainty. And right now, he needed her to be certain.

The rain picked up again—steady, cold, the kind that soaked through clothes in minutes. Shane barely felt it. He clutched April's purse against his chest as he ran for his truck, Charlie keeping pace beside him.

"Are you all right to drive?" she asked when he got to his truck.

"Yeah, King, just go."

Charlie didn't hesitate. She dashed toward her black Watchdog SUV.

———

A LINE of SUVs caravanned back to Watchdog. Shane's windshield wipers beat a frantic rhythm that matched his heartbeat. April was gone. Taken. By professionals who knew exactly what they were doing.

His phone rang. It was a call from a private number.

Shane answered on speaker. "Vince," he guessed.

"Hello, Shane." Vince's tone held all the smug confidence Shane expected.

Shane's hands tightened on the steering wheel. "Where is she?"

"Safe. For now. That all depends on you."

"If you hurt her—"

"I don't want to hurt her, Shane. I just want what's mine."

"Kevin's not yours. You *never* had that right—"

"Not the kid." Vince laughed. Shane noted a slight edge of hysteria in it. "Jesus, you really think I give a shit about some little bastard?"

"Then what do you—"

"I want her lucky purse."

Shane's brain stuttered. "What?"

"The Louis Vuitton Speedy Thirty. I know you've got it. Saw you pick it up in the courtroom before I could fucking get to it." Vince's voice dropped. "Do not damage it. Do not go through it. Just bring it to me unharmed, and you get the bitch back unharmed, do you understand?"

"What the fuck, man?" Shane's voice rose. "Her *purse?* What kind of sick, twisted game are you playing?"

"No game. No purse, no April. Simple as that. You don't want Kevin to lose his mother, do you?"

White-hot fury burned through Shane's chest. "Is this some sort of fucked-up revenge against a kid you never met? What the fuck?"

"Just bring the purse—undamaged—to Echo Ridge Ski Resort. Midnight tonight. There's an old maintenance barn there by the lifts. You know where I mean?"

"I know it."

"Good. Midnight. Not one minute before, either, or she dies."

"You know I'm not coming alone."

"Yeah, I'm not stupid. Doesn't matter. Just bring the

purse." Vince paused. "And Shane? If that purse is damaged in any way, she dies. Understood?"

The line went dead.

Shane stared at the phone, then at the purse on the passenger seat. What the hell was so important about a designer handbag that someone would kidnap April for it? Unless it had some sort of misprint or flaw that made it a priceless one-of-a-kind? Were they dealing with an international ring of thieves who specialized in luxury items?

This just doesn't make sense.

The guard waved the line of vehicles through the front gate. Shane's first instinct was to go to the safehouse, check on April's family, on his son. But he couldn't waste a moment as long as April was in danger. He knew the plan— the women would gather at the safehouse with Kevin, his grandparents, and Pete and Benny, away from whatever shitstorm was about to unfold. Arden would be the one to tell Kevin. If anyone could help Kevin process this, it was her. Shane was grateful for that, as he pushed away the guilt gnawing at him for not being there himself.

His SWCC training kicked in—that cold, professional distance that let him function when emotions would only get in the way. He had a mission now. Objective: retrieve April. Nothing else mattered.

Shane pulled into the parking lot in front of Watchdog's main building, rain hammering the windshield, headlights cutting through the downpour.

Ben appeared at his window. "You okay?"

"Vince called. Wants the purse in exchange for April."

Ben's eyes widened. "The purse?"

"Midnight. Echo Ridge Ski Resort." Shane grabbed the bag and climbed out. Otherwise none of this makes sense."

They made a run for the main building, rain soaking them both.

———

THE CONFERENCE ROOM was at capacity. Shane, Gina, Lach, Kyle, Charlie, Bear, Ben, Elias, Waylon, Flint, Gabe. Dogs settled at their humans' feet—Camo beside Kyle, Fleur at Gina's, Sam near Lach.

Everyone had taken seats around the table except Gina. She never sat during meetings. Just paced or stood, her body trying to keep up with her mind. Whenever someone asked if she wanted to take notes, she'd tap her temple and say, "Got it all up here."

The speaker at the center of the table crackled. "Reporting in," Elissa said. She was the head of Watchdog Security in Los Angeles and rumored to be one of the best hackers out there. Shane thought she always sounded like the quintessential California Girl. But today, her tone had weight to it.

Shane didn't waste another second. He told them about Romano's call.

"Shane?" Elissa said. "First of all, I'm so bummed this is happening to you. But we will get her back. Right, Spooky?"

Gina gave the speaker a fierce grin. Her golden eyes flashed. "Damn straight we will."

Flint's fingers flew across his laptop keyboard. The screen on the wall flickered to life, and Shane's worst nightmare appeared in black and white—a firefighter in full gear carrying April over his shoulder. She was limp, unconscious.

Not dead. Please not dead.

Shane felt his chest constrict. He forced himself to breathe.

"Unfortunately," Elissa continued, "this is the best image we could get. It was a well-coordinated and orchestrated group effort. They used strategically placed smoke bombs to fake a fire and cover their escape. I found Romano on a lobby cam." The image on the screen changed to an overhead shot of Romano in the main crowd flanked by a couple other guys wearing dark glasses and baseball caps. "All three disappeared, like, literally into smoke."

Shane's jaw clenched.

"But," Elissa added, "the good news is, Spooky ID'ed our fake fireman and I've since confirmed the identity."

Everyone looked at Gina. She slowed her pacing and took a deep breath. "Thanks, Lis. Then it's time to make the call." She glanced at Kyle, and something bitter flickered across her face. "This should interest you, Pup."

Kyle straightened. "Who is it?"

"The one who targeted you over this very land."

Understanding dawned on Kyle's face. "No shit. This is—"

"An old Capitoline ghost. We had an agreement, and I can guarantee he's not going to be very happy with his employees."

Gina pulled out a satellite phone. If Elissa had gotten her hands on it, Shane imagined its encryption was so heavy even the NSA would have trouble cracking it.

The room went silent. Even the dogs sensed the shift in energy.

The call connected. Gina switched it to speaker.

"Konstantin," she said. "It's Gina."

There was a long pause. "What a surprise. It's been long

time, Smith. What can I do for you?" The man's accented voice dripped with false warmth.

"We had a deal."

"Da. And I have kept to it."

"Your men kidnapped someone under my protection."

"What men?" Konstantin's tone shifted, going carefully neutral.

"Dimitri Volkov. Vince Romano. Three others. Right here in Lyons, Konstantin."

Ice crept into his voice. "I gave no such order."

"You're telling me they went rogue?"

"Yes."

Shane exchanged glances with Kyle. Whoever this Konstantin was, he'd just confirmed what Gina suspected— the kidnapping wasn't sanctioned. Which meant Dimitri and his crew were operating independently.

Which was either very good or very, very bad.

"What do they want in return for your friend?" Konstantin asked.

"They want her purse."

Silence. "Really? How much is purse worth?" He sounded vaguely amused.

Gina's eyes flashed. "Stop fucking with me, Konstantin. I know how to find you. I'll always know how to find you. Capitoline is gone. The Repair Shop is not."

"No? I hear different story these days."

"Vladimir Peskov."

Konstantin paused. "What about him?"

"It wasn't an accident."

A long, heavy pause followed. "Fine. It was for crypto payout."

Shane looked around the table at faces that looked as confused as he felt.

Crypto? What does that have to do with April? She never once mentioned any sort of crypto to him.

"What do you mean?" Gina asked, though her tone suggested she already knew.

"My men. They met Romano in prison. The man bragged all the time about his hidden fortune, said that when he got out, he would go after his jackpot. They told him about Dimitri, said he could help. One year after Romano's release, he comes to Dimitri. He needs help finding his woman who has crypto numbers memorized and promises nice big payout from his jackpot."

All eyes in the room went to Shane. He shook his head, dumbfounded.

Konstantin continued. "Dimitri brought the matter to my attention. I gave help—job, car, nice apartment. We found his woman, what, couple weeks ago? And persuaded his parole officer to fake Romano's check-ins. Romano went after her like she might be lovesick bird waiting for him. No such luck for Romano because she has fiancé now. He asked for more help and when I looked into fiancé, I saw my...mistake."

Konstantin's voice went flat. "I told my men, no more help for Romano. The woman was not to be touched, Gina."

"They didn't listen."

"Obviously."

Gina stopped pacing. "What does the purse have to do with it?"

"I don't know."

"Konstantin."

"This is truth. I do not know. She was supposed to have numbers memorized. Maybe yes, maybe no. Maybe code is in her purse instead."

Shane looked down at April's purse in his lap. Hidden

somewhere in this bag that April had carried everywhere in Vegas, that had sat on her top closet shelf gathering dust for years, was the string of numbers that would unlock some crypto. And she never had a clue.

How much crypto are they talking about?

Gina asked the question for him. "How much crypto are we talking, Konstantin?"

"Enough to make Dimitri think he can disappear from me."

"Can he?"

Dangerous quiet. "He can try."

"He can also fuck things up for you. Actually, he already has."

"Da."

Gina leaned against the table, her golden eyes hard. "We had been even, you and I. I can take care of your problem for you, Konstantin. But then you will owe me again after this."

"Understood." Pause. "Is different world now. Perhaps one day we will work together instead of against each other."

"I doubt it."

Konstantin's laugh was low, without humor. "Dasvidaniya, Gina Smith."

The line went dead.

Gina bent down to scratch Fleur behind the ears, using the dog to ground herself. When she straightened and looked at Shane, her expression was all business.

"Can I assume April never mentioned anything about a crypto fortune?"

"Yes, you can." He set the purse on the table. "He played her."

"Sure sounds like it to me," she agreed.

"Whelp," Elissa said, "his request not to go rummaging through her purse makes a whole hell of a lot more sense now."

Gina pushed off from the conference table. "We need to prepare for the exchange."

Kyle's jaw was set. "I don't care if this was an accident. He fucked with me and mine before. I don't trust him."

Gina glanced at Kyle. "Nor should you, Pup. Nor should any of us."

TWENTY-NINE

April gradually woke to the sound of falling rain.

She was sitting in a soft chair. A recliner? Her head throbbed like someone had taken a hammer to her skull. Her mouth was full of something thick. Cloth. Was she chewing on a blanket? She tasted copper and chemicals. Something was wrong with her hands—they were behind her back, circulation cut off enough to make her fingers tingle.

How did I fall asleep in a chair with a blanket in my mouth? What—

She tried to turn over to take the pressure off her arms and couldn't. Her torso was pressed against the chair, held in place. So were her legs.

Memory crashed back in fragments. The courthouse. Judge's chambers. Fire alarm. Smoke in the corridor. Tripping, her ankle twisting. A firefighter helping her up, his hands steady on her arms.

Thank you so much, I—

The sting in her neck.

Oh God.

April's eyes snapped fully open, adrenaline burning through the fog in her brain.

She was sitting in an oversized recliner, the kind that belonged in someone's man cave. She didn't have a blanket in her mouth—what was she thinking? It was a gag, the cloth cutting painfully into the corners of her mouth. She wasn't just lying on her hands—they were zip-tied behind her back. Her legs were bound to the chair with rope. Her torso was secured with more rope across her chest and belly.

She'd been kidnapped.

A wave of nausea passed over her. April forced herself to breathe slowly through her nose, fighting the panic that clawed up her throat—the fear of getting sick and choking on her own vomit. Panicking wouldn't help. Panicking would only make it worse.

She looked around, taking inventory.

Unfinished basement. She was in a corner where two concrete walls met—both outer walls, probably. One wall had a small window with a window well. The well was covered with a clear plastic cover, yellowed with age and streaked with mud, but she could see through it enough to make out gray daylight. Rain fell steadily, drumming against the plastic cover. Through the murky plastic, she could see the shapes of leaves and branches moving in the wind.

The only sound was the rain.

April listened hard, straining to hear voices, footsteps, traffic, anything that might tell her where she was. But there was nothing. Just rain.

She didn't scream. The house could be in the middle of nowhere for all she knew. And if she screamed, they'd know she was awake. Better to wait. Better to gather information first.

April replayed the abduction in her mind, trying to piece together details. The firefighter. His accent had been American at first—professional, calm, reassuring. *Can you walk?* But at the end, right before everything went black, his accent had changed. Russian. She was sure of it.

Is Vince behind this? Why would he do this to me? Oh my God, is Kevin safe?

She heard footsteps.

April's heart slammed against her ribs. Someone was coming closer. She heard the metallic sounds of a door being unlocked, somewhere behind her.

The door opened. Artificial light poured in.

April held perfectly still, watching the pale shadow of a man on the wall in front of her.

An overhead light turned on, bright and harsh, making her squint. A man walked around the recliner to stand in front of her. The same firefighter who'd "saved" her. Except he wasn't dressed like a firefighter anymore. All black—black pants, black shirt, black jacket.

How stereotypical, the detached part of her brain observed. *A kidnapper dressed all in black. I guess the TV shows got it right.*

He studied her for a moment, his expression unreadable. Then he smiled.

"You're awake already, April Taylor," he said, his Russian accent thick and unmistakable now. "Or is it April Meyer? I suppose you've gone back to Taylor, haven't you? Smart. Made it harder for Vince to find you."

April's blood ran cold. April Meyer. Her name in Vegas. The name she'd buried when she ran.

"I am going to remove your gag," the man continued, his tone conversational. "But before you waste any energy on screaming, let me tell you—no one is close enough to hear you. So why don't we do this the easy way? I remove the gag, you do not bite me, you do not scream, and you answer my questions. Do you understand?"

April nodded. She tried to say yes, but it came out muffled against the gag.

The man chuckled. "All right. The gag is coming off."

He reached forward and untied the cloth, then pulled it away from her mouth. April gasped, relief flooding through her even as her throat burned. She tried to speak and realized her mouth was bone dry. She coughed.

"Oh, of course." The man stepped back, disappearing from view. "You must be very thirsty. One moment. I'm a terrible host."

April heard plastic wrapping tearing, then the squeak of plastic moving against plastic. He returned with a water bottle, cap already removed.

"This should help," he said, his voice a mockery of politeness and hospitality. "I'm afraid I don't trust you enough to untie your hands, so I will give you the water."

He put the bottle to her lips.

The part of April that wanted to fight, to resist, to spit in his face—screamed at her to refuse. But the rational part, the part that wanted to get back to Kevin and Shane, told her to wait. To drink. To stay strong. To hold off for the right opportunity to escape, to fight, to kill if she had to.

She drank.

The water was cold, clean, the best she'd ever tasted. She nodded when she needed a breath, and he pulled the bottle back, then brought it to her lips again. It took a few minutes, but she drank the entire bottle. He crumpled it in his fist and tossed it into the corner.

"Now," he said, settling back on his heels. "I just got done speaking with Vince."

April's voice came out raspy. "What does he want?"

"He wants you to cooperate, of course. We all do." The man smiled. "This can go very easy for you, April. Of course you'll get a cut. Vince promised you that a long time ago, and we will honor it."

April stared at him, completely lost. "A cut? A cut of what? I don't know what you're talking about."

The man chuckled, shaking his head. "I see that we can't do this the easy way." He leaned forward, his eyes cold. "Listen. Vince made some bad choices. I am one of those bad choices. He came to me for help to find you after he got out of prison. He tried finding you on his own and no luck. He promised us a big, big cut. We gave him nice things. He said you ran away when he was arrested. I don't judge you for that. I don't blame you. I would too, if I knew what you knew."

"I told you. I don't know what you're talking about," April said again, her voice stronger now.

"Vince already gave up the password," the man said. "We persuaded him to. And he was ready to sell you out anyway, I have to say. He was begging for his life." His smile turned cruel. "He tried to convince us we should traffic you instead. Said we could make good money that way. He didn't care what happened to you."

Horror crawled up April's spine. Vince had tried to traffic her?

"So we have the password from him," the man continued. "And all we need from you are the seed numbers."

"The what?"

"The seed phrase. The recovery code that grants access to the crypto wallet." He said it slowly, like he was explaining something to a child. "Vince said you counted the cards when you played Blackjack in Vegas." He tapped his temple. "That takes a good memory, no?"

That wasn't really how card counting worked, but April wasn't about to school him.

"Vince has the password. You have the seed phrase memorized. Together, they unlock a very large fortune."

April's mind reeled. Crypto? Seed phrase? What the hell was he talking about?

"I'm still confused," she said, her voice shaking. "I swear, I don't know what you're talking about. I don't know anything like that."

"Oh, I think you do," the man said. "Otherwise, why would you run? Why disappear so completely that even Vince couldn't find you for ten years?"

"I ran because he beat the hell out of me!" April's voice rose. "I ran because if I didn't, he would have hurt our child. That's why I ran. Not because of some...some crypto scheme I don't even know about!"

"Oh yes, your child, little Kevin." The man's smile widened. "Such a sweet boy. Don't you want to go home to him? If you give us the code, you can. And as I said, we will even cut you in. I don't like to hurt women. I don't like to hurt mothers of sweet boys like Kevin. Just give us the numbers, and we will let you go. There is plenty for everyone. That's all you need to do."

April's chest tightened. He knew Kevin's name. He'd seen Kevin, or at least knew enough about him to—

"I'm telling you, I don't have it," April said desperately. "Vince is scamming you. There is no crypto. There is nothing. I don't know why he's doing this."

The man's expression hardened. "Then I'm afraid we're going to have to get a little rough with you, April, because I don't believe you. I don't believe you at all." He stood, looming over her. "You are a gambler. A card counter. A cheat, really. You lived that life. Vince said you were part of his operation before he went to jail."

"That's not true!" April pulled against the zip ties, panic flooding her system. "I had nothing to do with any of that!"

"Maybe that's part of the reason why you ran," the man said thoughtfully. "You didn't want to be caught. You were the one who had all the money. But Vince kept the password as a safeguard. Wise of him, I think."

"This is crazy." April's voice broke. "He's making all of this up. Please, please just let me go. I promise I won't turn you in. I won't tell anyone, I swear it. Please just let me go."

"No, April." The man's voice went cold. "I'm afraid this was your last chance, and now we're going to have to get a little—"

The door burst open behind her.

"Dimitri!" a man said, followed by rapid-fire Russian—angry or upset, April couldn't tell which. The man in front of her—Dimitri, she assumed—fired something back in Russian, sharp and commanding.

He looked at April. "I'll be back in a moment, dear."

The overhead light went off. She heard the door close. Then she was alone.

April immediately started working at the zip ties, twisting her wrists, trying to find any give in the plastic. Nothing. She tried to throw her weight forward, then back, hoping to loosen the ropes around her torso. But whoever had tied her up knew what they were doing. The recliner was heavy and didn't budge. Her legs were bound too tightly to attempt any of the zip tie tricks she'd seen on YouTube.

She was trapped.

She realized she was still wearing her engagement ring.

She ran her thumb over it again and again, feeling the contours, the smoothness of the blue-sky stone.

An eerie calm settled over her. Shane would find her. He had to. They had a whole life in front of them.

Minutes passed. Then an hour. Then forever.

April watched through the muddy window as the gray afternoon light slowly faded. The rain never stopped, steady and relentless. Finally the daylight was gone completely. A light came on outside—streetlight or yard light, she couldn't tell—casting shadows of dancing leaves across the plastic cover.

Night had fallen, and no one had come back.

April's arms had gone completely numb. Her twisted ankle throbbed. Her mouth was dry again, her throat aching. But worse than the physical discomfort was the fear. The not knowing.

Where was Shane? Was Kevin okay? Did he know she was missing yet? Had they told him? God, her poor baby. He'd be terrified.

Oh, God. And he'll blame himself for this.

She watched the rain fall, the shadows dancing in the light from outside, and her mind drifted to another rainy night. Running from the downpour into Shane's house for the first time. Kevin laughing, Pete shaking water everywhere. The cozy warmth of Shane's living room, the way Shane had looked at her like she was something precious.

The contrast nearly broke her.

If she died here—

No. Stop it. Don't think like that.

But the thought persisted. If she died here, Kevin would be okay. He'd have Sonny and Miriam and Hannah. He'd have Shane, who would petition to adopt him in a heartbeat, and no one would fight that. He'd have all of Watchdog, all those fierce, protective men who'd shown up to the courthouse just to support her. Kevin would grieve, of course. He'd mourn his mother. She knew no one could ever completely replace her, but he'd have her friends, the most amazing women in the world, stepping in to be the next best thing.

He would be okay. Ultimately, he would survive this if she died.

The realization was both devastating and oddly comforting as she listened to the soft, steady rain and stroked her engagement ring.

Except I have no intention of dying. And every intention of fighting.

Vince had gotten himself in way over his head with the Russian mob. And for whatever reason, he'd lied to these people about her. Told them she had access to some crypto fortune. Why would he do that? What did he possibly have to gain?

Unless he really believed it. Unless he'd convinced himself over the years that she'd stolen from him somehow.

Footsteps again.

April's head snapped up. The door opened. The overhead light came on, harsh and bright, making her squint. Dimitri walked back into her view, and this time he had the gag in one hand and another bandana in the other.

"What are you going to do to me?" April asked, hating the tremor in her voice.

"Oh, we're going for a ride." Dimitri's smile was back, but it didn't reach his eyes. "It looks like this is your lucky night, April Taylor. You will return to your son and your fiancé. But only if you cooperate."

April's heart leaped. Return to Kevin? To Shane? But she didn't trust this man for a second. For all she knew, he was going to blindfold her, drag her outside, and shoot her.

"I can use the needle on you again," Dimitri said, watching her face. "But I would prefer not to. Or you can walk. Which will it be?"

April swallowed hard. "I'll walk."

"Good choice."

"But I really, really have to pee."

Dimitri sighed. He moved behind her, and she felt him tying the bandana over her eyes. Not a gag this time—she was too nauseated for that, and maybe he knew it. The world went dark.

She heard the door open again. Another man entered—she could tell by the second set of footsteps. Two against one now. No hope of fighting.

She felt the ropes go slack around her legs, then her torso, as one of them untied them. "Up," Dimitri said. April's muscles screamed as she stood, her twisted ankle protesting.

Someone grabbed her arm and pulled her forward. Something cold and hard pressed against her back. A gun. "The bathroom is to your right. I will untie your hands so you may use them. This door will stay open, the blindfold will stay on. You will hurry. When you are done, I will tie your hands again. No funny business." Dimitri prodded her with the gun to emphasize his point.

April nodded and a moment later her hands were free. Completely numb, they were practically useless. She stumbled forward and found the toilet about three steps in. At least she was wearing a skirt and could preserve some of her modesty. She finished, flushed, and stumbled back out. Her hands tingled painfully as the circulation came back, just in time to be tied up again.

They started walking. The two men spoke in Russian,

their voices low and fast. April caught Vince's name once, then again. What were they saying about him?

They crossed the basement, April stumbling occasionally, her ankle throbbing, then up a set of stairs and through what felt like a couple of rooms. A door opened, and she felt the temperature drop. Two steps down. Everything sounded echoey now and she felt a cold breeze to her left.

Garage, she realized. They were in a garage.

And the door was open.

An engine started. A heavy door opened—a van door, by the sound of it.

Run.

She was halfway through thinking the word and her body was already in motion. She ran blindly toward the fresh, cool air, screaming. If they were in any sort of neighborhood, maybe someone would hear her before—

Strong hands grabbed her from behind and lifted her off her feet.

"Bad girl." Dimitri carried her kicking and screaming into the garage and threw her into the back of a cargo van. April hit the floor hard, her shoulder taking the impact. She heard the van doors slam, then a moment later, heard the men open other doors and get in. The van backed out of the garage before she even heard their door close.

There had to be at least three people—the driver, Dimitri, and the other guy who'd been with her in the basement. Maybe another guy sitting in the passenger seat, which would bring the total to four. Was Vince driving or was he riding shotgun?

"April."

April's heart stopped. The voice was right next to her.

"Vince?"

"Hey, baby." His voice was strained, terrified in a way she'd never heard before. "Looks like we're both screwed."

"What are you doing back here?" April twisted toward his voice. "What are you—"

"They're gonna kill both of us," Vince said, and he sounded like he was crying. "April, God, I didn't think—I didn't know they'd—"

The van lurched forward. Whoever was driving was going fast.

April's mind raced. Vince was in the back of the van with her. Which meant he wasn't in control. Which meant he'd gotten in *way* over his head with people who were now going to—

Going to what? Drive them somewhere remote and kill them both? Or was this the exchange? Were they taking her to Shane?

She had no idea. And tied up in the back of a van, blindfolded, with Vince sobbing beside her, April had never felt more helpless in her life.

The van sped on through the night, rain hammering the roof. April could hear the rhythmic thump of windshield wipers, the muffled voices of the men up front speaking Russian. It felt like they were gaining altitude—her ears always plugged when she went up into the mountains.

She couldn't take Vince's blubbering any longer.

"Can you at least take the blindfold off of me?" April asked.

"No way, baby. I'm not pissing them off any more than they already are." He sniffled. "Besides, my hands are tied and I've got a blindfold on, too."

"My God, Vince, who are these guys? What the hell did you do? Why did you tell them I had some sort of crypto code?"

She waited. And when she didn't think he'd ever answer, he said, "I guess it doesn't matter if I tell you now. Here's what happened." He took a shaky breath. "The money my crew and I made from counterfeiting the chips— I got this idea that we could put it all into crypto. Bought a bunch just a few days before I was arrested."

"Oh God, Vince, you didn't."

"Yeah. I put the seed code on a chip and I thought, just in case the police decide to raid our place, I'd hide it in something that belonged to you. Teeny tiny memory chip, not even as big as my fingernail. Easy to hide."

April's blood ran cold. "What are you saying?"

"You were clean. You had nothing to do with the operation. I told the cops that, you know. I kept you safe."

April snorted.

His voice took on a bitter edge. "I was thinking, once I got out, once I told you what I'd done and that the money was hidden, maybe we could make a deal. It's a lot of money, April. A huge jackpot. But when I got out, you were gone. You and all your favorite things. That was my mistake, putting it in something you loved."

Realization struck April like a physical blow. "That day at Riversong. When you were insulting me. You asked if I pawned my lucky purse."

"Yeah."

"It's in there, isn't it? It's been in my purse this whole time."

"Yup. It's in the lining."

"What? How did you—" April's voice rose. "Did you think I would just turn it over to you? Were you going to use Kevin as leverage against me? What was your plan, Vince?"

"Well." He gave her a pathetic little chuckle. "I figured I'd try and get us back together first. All I needed to do was get in your house, look around for the purse. Then I'd be gone out of your life. You would have never seen or heard from me again. You sure fucked that up, April."

"Oh my God. I can't believe you just said that."

"It's true. If you hadn't been such a bitch. If you hadn't fought me. If you hadn't run away to begin with—"

"Oh I am *not* taking the blame for this, you asshole!"

She quietly seethed as the van drove along, rain pummeling the top. April's rage burned white-hot, but beneath it was a terrible understanding. This had never been about Kevin. It had never been about custody or fatherhood or rights. It had only ever been about money.

"Why'd you tell them I had the seed code memorized?" April demanded. "Why?"

"Are you stupid? Because if I had, they would've found you without telling me and just broken into your house and stolen the purse themselves." Vince's voice was matter-of-fact. "You were my insurance, April. I told them I'd sweet talk you into working with us. But then once I realized I wasn't gonna get back in your panties, let alone in your house, I played the I-wanna-meet-my-son card. I'd get visitation rights or something, get into your house when I picked him up, excuse myself to take a piss, find the purse."

"Well that sure worked out great, didn't it?"

"Fuck you, April. You think I wanna be back here with you?" He exhaled. "Just for the record, grabbing you like this wasn't my idea, it was Dimitri's. Man's got zero patience. I don't know, maybe something happened with his boss. So I figured if he grabbed you today, once they had you and your purse, I'd give them some made-up password. And then—"

He stopped.

"And then what?" April asked, though she already knew.

Silence.

"It's true, isn't it?" Her voice shook. "You would have let them torture me to try and get the number out of me while you left with the purse."

More silence. Damning silence.

"You would have left me there to die," April whispered. "Tortured to death over something I didn't even know existed."

"Easy come, easy go, baby. You abandoned me first."

"Oh my God." April was shaking now, fury and horror warring in her chest. "If I weren't tied up I'd kill you right now. You idiot. You fucking asshole. You son of a bitch."

By now April was yelling, and she didn't care that the Russians up front were laughing at her. *Let them laugh.* Let them hear how pissed off she was.

The van took a hard right and April slammed into Vince, who, judging by the thud and the swearing, hit his head against the metal wall.

"Ha! Serves you right, you bastard."

"Fuck you. That fucking *hurt.*"

"So what's happening now?" April demanded. "What's going on? Where are we going?"

"Well." Vince sounded resigned. "Once I saw you were too stupid to bring your Lucky Louis with you into the judge's chambers, I tried to call off the plan, but it was too late. Alarm went off, your boyfriend grabbed the jackpot before I could get over to it. I tried to sneak away but they grabbed me, too. They knew they couldn't trust me by then. Or maybe they'd always planned to double-cross me. Who the hell knows. Doesn't matter—same thing happened. They drove us to this house on the outskirts of town, about five fucking minutes from the courthouse, can you believe that?"

Shit. How long had she been less than a mile from Shane?

Vince went on.

"They put you in one room and me in another. I knew they were trying to turn us against each other by lying. Yuri was questioning me, and he said that you had already given them the seed numbers. That you had betrayed me. Well, of course I knew he was bluffing. I knew you didn't have it. And I figured Dimitri was probably doing the same thing to you, telling you that I had given up the password."

"Yeah," April said bitterly. "That's exactly what happened. He told me you didn't care if they sold me into slavery. You said they could traffic me."

"Fucking liars." But Vince's voice held no real heat. "The minute they said you'd given up the seed number, I knew I was fucked. They'd torture you to death, and then they'd have no use for me. Hell, they might even figure out you didn't know it, think I was completely lying. So I told them the truth. I told Yuri that you didn't know anything. That it was in your purse and your fiancé had it. But that if they would arrange a trade, they'd get the purse. And then I'd send them the password twenty-four hours after they let me go."

April lowered her voice. "And they actually believed you would send them the correct password?"

"Looks like it, babe." He paused. "They made me call Shane. Gun to my head. Told me to tell him midnight at Echo Ridge, bring the purse undamaged, he'd get you back undamaged."

April's heart lurched. Echo Ridge was a little mom-and-pop ski lodge. The couple who built it died without a clear inheritance plan and it was still in probate years later. In the meantime, the building stood abandoned and derelict, with nothing else around for miles.

"Oh my God. I can't believe this is happening."

"Believe it." Vince's voice was hollow. "So, how much does that fiancé of yours love you? Is he gonna let you twist?"

"Never." April's voice was fierce despite her fear. "Shane would never, ever let me twist. He would raise a fortune just to ransom me because he knows what love is. And now I do too, with him."

April only prayed that Shane would stay safe. That he wouldn't die in the attempt to save her.

That somehow, they'd both make it through this alive.

THIRTY

SHANE'S HANDS WERE WHITE-KNUCKLED ON THE steering wheel as he drove through the storm toward Echo Ridge. Gina sat beside him, her phone glowing in the darkness, fingers flying across the screen as she coordinated the team.

The text with the location had come in an hour ago. Just one hour. Not enough time for proper recon, not enough time to set a perimeter the way Gina liked. But enough time to get there, get in position, and pray the storm covered their approach.

"Flint's got satellite imagery," Gina said, her voice calm despite the chaos. "Maintenance barn, upper lot. Single access road, service road behind. It's exposed."

"Still thinking it's a trap?" Shane said. "You think Konstantin's coming."

"I know he's coming. Dimitri went rogue. Konstantin doesn't forgive that." She looked out at the rain. "He'll send a cleanup crew, and he'll want the crypto. With Capitoline scattered, times are tough for oligarchs these days," she said as she smirked. "I know he's getting low on funds. Get down to your last billion, you start wondering how you can afford your caviar and the payments on your dozen mansions and pieds-a-terre."

She grew serious. "The question is, does Dimitri know it, too? Is he counting on letting Konstantin's men and Watchdog kill each other while he walks away with the purse?"

Shane reviewed the contingency plans they'd gone over earlier in the day. Let Konstantin think he's got the upper hand. Position our people where they can adapt fast. When his team shows up, we're ready.

Except...

"One hour isn't enough time—"

"One hour is what we've got." Gina's eyes were hard. "Bear, Ben, Elias, Waylon—they're Rangers. They can set up in the dark in a goddamn hurricane if they have to. Kyle and Lach are SEALs. Charlie's one of the best tactical operators I've ever seen. And you—" She looked at him. "You're a Swick. You know how to adapt under fire."

"We get April out first. Everything else is secondary."

"Agreed."

The barn loomed out of the rain like a ghost. Shane killed the headlights, coasted into the upper lot. Two other vehicles were already there—dark shapes in the storm.

Ben's voice came over the comm. "In position. North side."

"East perimeter set." Bear.

"South corner. Eyes on door." Charlie.

"Overwatch, ridge above." Pup. "Limited visibility but I've got enough."

One hour. They'd done it in one hour.

Shane looked at Gina. "Ready?"

"Let's go get your girl."

———

THE RAIN HITTING the barn's tin roof sounded like a barrage of bullets—unceasing fire from the sky. As Shane and Gina approached the barn, lightning flashed in white stabs that turned the world into a black-and-white photograph. He felt the storm pressing in—a pressure that scraped at his ribs and sharpened his focus to a razor's edge. The bulletproof vest under his rain jacket was a familiar second skin, heavy and reassuring. He'd never been so grateful for Gina's paranoia.

His earpiece crackled with quiet confirmations—his team acknowledging positions, ready to move on Gina's signal. Shane carried April's purse in his left hand, keeping his right free.

The big doors were wide open. They stepped inside the dimly-lit barn. It was quieter in there, but not by much.

Dimitri stood beside a card table with an electric lantern, a radio, and a laptop. One hand rested casually on the pistol at his hip. When Shane and Gina got within ten feet, he said, "Stop. That's close enough."

Against the wall behind him, two men in tactical gear flanked April and Vince.

Shane's eyes went straight to April. Her hands were bound behind her back. She looked small between the Russians, wet and exhausted, but her chin was held high. When her eyes found his, he saw fear but also determination.

Hang in there, sweetness. We're getting out of this.

Vince stood beside her, hands free but shaking. His eyes

darted between the purse in Shane's hand and the door behind them. He was sweating despite the chilly air.

Over the comm, Shane heard Gina breathe, "Three hostiles visible, west wall. Stay sharp. Over."

"No hostiles on the entrance road, over," Bear responded.

"Maintenance road clear, over," said Lion.

Dimitri's radio crackled—Russian, fast and low. He listened, then smiled.

"You brought friends," Dimitri called over the drumming rain. His English was good, his accent light but unmistakable. "Six, seven people maybe? Scattered around my barn." His smile widened. "It won't matter."

Shane's blood ran cold. Dimitri wanted them here.

Gina's whisper over the comm, deadly quiet. "You have company. Proceed as planned, over."

"You told me to bring the purse," Shane called back. "I brought insurance, too."

Dimitri laughed. "Smart. I would have done the same. Actually, I have." He gestured to the radio. Shane wondered how many of his men waited in the dark.

"Then let's do this," Shane said. "You get the purse. We get April."

"Not quite so simple." Dimitri gestured to the laptop. "Set the purse on the ground. Both of you take ten steps back, hands visible at all times."

Shane started to crouch, but Gina's hand on his arm stopped him.

"No," she said, her voice carrying across the barn. "We exchange April for the purse at the same time."

Dimitri's smile didn't waver. "I'm afraid we can't do that. You can blame Vince Romano for the complications."

Vince made a small, desperate sound.

"Here's how this works," Dimitri continued. "You set the purse down. Take ten steps back. Yuri will bring April forward to identify the purse—make sure you didn't bring a decoy. Once she confirms it's hers, we will verify the contents." He tapped the laptop. "Vince will provide the password. If everything checks out, you get April and walk out of here. Simple."

"What about me?" Vince's voice cracked. "What about my share?"

"If you lie again," Dimitri said matter-of-factly, "you are already dead. If you tell the truth and give the correct password, you go free."

"And my crypto?"

Shane almost laughed. Even now, Romano was putting money above everything else.

"Considering the trouble you've given us, you should get nothing." Dimitri's voice hardened. "But I'm a reasonable man. If you've been truthful about the amount, there is plenty to go around. I'll transfer your share into your wallet right after you give me the password."

Vince's shoulders relaxed visibly. "Yeah. Yeah, okay, Dimitri. That's fair."

The poor bastard actually believes him.

Shane didn't care what happened to Vince Romano. Once he had April free and clear, Dimitri and Vince could kill each other for all he gave a damn.

Shane started to lower the purse to the ground when another voice came over Dimitri's radio, sounding urgent. Dimitri frowned.

At the same time, Moose's surprised voice. "Anyone else hear that?"

"Shit." "Yeah." "Affirmative."

"Direction?" Moose.

"North by northwest." Lion.

That's when Shane heard it. His SWCC training screamed at him before his conscious brain caught up. A vibration that wasn't the storm.

"Spooky, I think we've got incoming, over," Pup said.

"I hear it." Her voice was ice. "Positions, now!"

Dimitri's face went pale. He drew his gun. "Helicopter," he breathed. "That mudak—he sent a fucking helicopter."

Shane watched as Dimitri and Gina locked eyes and an entire conversation passed between them. They'd both set up for hostiles along the roads. Both knew Konstantin would send enough firepower to kill everyone in this barn. Dimitri's crew. Watchdog. April. Vince. No witnesses. Their only hope was that he wanted the purse enough not to just firebomb the whole fucking barn from the air.

One second. That's all it took.

Gina gave a sharp nod.

Temporary truce.

The world exploded into chaos.

The helo was on them. Shane heard the helicopter come in fast and low, rotors churning the rain into horizontal sheets, and swoop over the barn. The roar drowned out everything—thunder, rain, voices. Wind and spray battered the barn's tin roof.

Shane spun around. The barn's roll-up door faced the clearing where the helicopter hovered, rotors screaming, twenty feet off the ground. The side door opened.

Men in black tactical gear jumped—fast-roping down through the rain. Five of them. Professional. Armed. Moving like they'd done this a thousand times.

"K-Team on site, five tangos, engaging!" Charlie's voice, sharp and controlled.

K-Team. Konstantin's cleanup crew.

Dimitri's weapon shifted—not toward Shane and Gina, but toward the door where Konstantin's men were advancing.

Shane was already moving. He dropped the purse, lunged for April just as gunfire erupted.

Outside, Dimitri's men were already firing on Konstantin's crew. Muzzle flashes lit up the clearing like strobe lights. One of Konstantin's men hit the ground, brought his weapon up, fired into the barn. Bullets punched through corrugated metal. The electric lantern exploded in a shower of glass.

Shane tackled April and rolled, his arms protecting her head. In a flash, his knife was out and her hands were free. His body shielded hers as they rushed toward the corner behind a workbench.

"Stay low." He pulled his Sig.

April nodded. She pressed into him, breathing fast but controlled as they watched the room.

Good girl. Stay with me.

Shane listened to the helicopter lift higher, hovering out of range of return fire. Smart pilot.

K-Team advanced into the barn.

Ben appeared at a side door, weapon up, laying down covering fire. Bear and Elias flanked the main entrance. One of Konstantin's men went down hard.

The storm had eased—rain still falling but the worst of it passed. Lightning flickered in the distance.

Shane heard tires on gravel at the same time his teammates still outside confirmed it over the comm.

K-Team reinforcements coming in.

Echo Ridge became a war zone.

Shane braced against the workbench, weapon up, keeping April pressed behind him. A Konstantin operative moved into his line of sight. Shane put two rounds center mass. The man's vest caught it, but the impact made him stumble.

Ben finished him with a headshot from the side door.

Dimitri and Gina moved like professionals—covering each other, coordinating fire. For a moment, they weren't enemies. They were soldiers in the same fight.

Then Shane saw Vince crawling across the floor toward the purse, low to the ground, thinking no one would notice in the chaos.

Dimitri saw him, too.

Raised his weapon.

"Vince, no!" April's voice, shocked.

Dimitri fired.

The shot took Vince in the head. He dropped, hand outstretched toward the purse, reaching for his jackpot even in death.

April made a sound—not quite a scream, more like all the air leaving her lungs at once.

"Don't look. Stay down."

The firefight intensified as new men who'd made it past the teams outside stormed the barn. The barn filled with smoke. Thunder rolled overhead, punctuating every exchange of gunfire like the sky itself was passing judgment.

Charlie appeared near their position, weapon up, controlled bursts toward the door. "Two down. Three new tangoes still engaging."

One of Konstantin's men tried to flank through the side entrance. Bear met him with a brutal takedown—hand-to-hand, fast and vicious. The Russian went down and didn't get up.

That left two standing.

They were retreating now, firing blind to cover their escape.

The helicopter descended, coming down fast to extract them.

Lion's voice over the comm. "I've got a clear shot on the pilot—"

"Stand down!" Gina's voice. "Let them go. They're done."

The two surviving Konstantin operatives reached the helicopter, hauled themselves inside. The bird lifted, rotors screaming, fighting the wind.

For a moment it looked like they'd make it.

Then the sky split open.

Lightning—not a fork but a column of white fire—slammed into the ridge. The bolt arced and caught the helicopter's tail rotor. Metal sheared. Sparks cascaded like a waterfall.

The helicopter spun, yawing sideways. The pilot fought for control—lost it.

The bird went down hard behind the tree line. A dull crump. Orange fire bloomed through the rain, brief and furious, then swallowed by darkness.

Silence.

Just the rain and the ringing in Shane's ears.

Shane scanned for threats. Bodies littered the barn floor —Konstantin's men, Dimitri's henchmen. And Vince, hand still reaching for the purse that had killed him.

Dimitri was slumped against the wall only a few feet away, blood spreading across his chest. One of Konstantin's men had gotten him in the firefight. He looked at Shane, managed a bloody smile.

"Told you," he rasped. "It wouldn't matter."

Then his eyes went dull and empty.

Shane pulled April to her feet and into his arms. She was shaking, silent tears streaming down her face.

"I've got you," Shane murmured. "You're safe now. It's over."

Shane held his breath until he heard every single teammate check in. When he checked in, he confirmed that April was safe.

"Hurry, people," Gina said. "We need to get the hell out of Dodge." The team was already moving around them and keeping up a steady stream of communication through the comms. Bear checking bodies, taking Dimitri's phone and laptop, and making sure the team left no trace of their presence. Charlie and Ben swept for additional threats inside while Gabe and Waylon covered the grounds outside. Gina and Lach speaking in low voices, comms off.

Kyle approached them. "How is she?"

"I'm okay," April answered. "Kevin?" Her voice was barely a whisper. "Is he—"

"Safe," Kyle said gently. "Everyone's with him. I contacted Arden and she's talking to him right now, telling him his mom and dad are safe and coming home soon."

His dad. Those two words and their truth warmed Shane's chest.

April nodded, sagging against Shane.

Gina crossed the barn, her face grim but satisfied. She picked up the purse from where Shane had dropped it, checked it over. Muddy. Scuffed. But intact.

"Time. Move out, team."

The team moved. Shane started guiding April toward the door.

"You're limping."

"Just my ankle. It's fine."

Before she'd finished speaking, he'd swept her up into

his arms and turned her head toward his chest, shielding her from the worst of what was left behind.

The rain had gentled to a steady drizzle. Lightning still flickered along the ridge, but the thunder was distant now, the storm moving east.

They made it to the SUV. April had started shivering somewhere on the way. Shane helped April into the passenger seat, buckled her in, and placed a gentle kiss on her forehead.

He climbed into the driver's seat, started the engine, turned the heat up high. April's teeth were chattering, her skin pale in the dashboard lights.

Shane reached over, took her hand. It was ice-cold. He laced his fingers through hers and held on.

"It's over," he said quietly. "You're safe. Kevin's safe. It's over."

April turned her head to look at him. Her eyes were full of grief and exhaustion and something fierce that might have been gratitude or love or both.

"Vince is dead."

"Yeah."

"He died reaching for that purse." Her voice broke. "After everything—that's how it ended."

Shane had no comfort to offer. Just the truth. "He made his choices."

April closed her eyes. A tear slipped down her cheek. "I just want to go home."

Shane pulled out of the parking lot, leaving the barn and the bodies and the wreckage behind them. In the rearview mirror, he could see the orange glow of the helicopter fire, already fading. The rain washing everything clean.

April was alive.

And that was the only thing that mattered.

April opened her eyes, looked down at their joined hands, and took a long, deep breath. "I love you."

"I love you too. So, so much, sweetness."

Shane drove through the night toward Watchdog, toward Kevin, toward whatever came next.

THIRTY-ONE

SHANE'S HAND WAS WARM AND STEADY IN APRIL'S AS they walked into the Watchdog safehouse. She'd insisted on walking—she didn't want to scare Kevin. April was still shaking—from shock, from cold, from everything—but his grip anchored her.

The door opened before they reached it.

Kevin burst through, Pete and Benny at his heels. "Mom! Dad!"

Dad.

April's knees nearly buckled. Shane caught her, held her steady as Kevin crashed into them both, wrapping his arms around their waists. They melted into a family hug.

"I knew Dad would save you, Mom," Kevin said, his voice muffled against Shane's jacket. "Dad and all my uncles can do anything."

April finally—finally—let herself cry for real. Happy tears. Relieved tears. The kind that came from surviving something that should have killed you.

Shane held them both, and April felt the hitching in his shoulders. He was crying, too.

The safehouse living room was full—Sonny and Miriam, Hannah, Arden, the whole Watchdog crew. But they stayed back, giving the three of them this moment.

April heard quiet movement. Her friends slipping out, giving them space. Wren squeezed her shoulder as she passed. Rochelle whispered, "Call me tomorrow." Stephanie just smiled, tears on her cheeks.

But Arden lingered.

She crouched beside April, her hand gentle on Kevin's back. "He's going to be just fine," she said softly. "And if you ever need to talk—about anything, anytime—I'm here."

April nodded, not trusting her voice.

Arden stood, but her eyes held April's for a moment longer. Understanding passed between them. Arden knew what it was like to survive trauma. To wonder if you'd ever feel normal again. And she knew what it took to help someone else get through it, too.

Thank you, April mouthed.

Arden smiled and left.

"LET'S HEAD INSIDE, BUD," Shane said. Kevin nodded. Shane helped April up.

Sonny, Miriam, and Hannah waited in the living room, tears in their eyes. April watched as Sonny approached Shane. The older man paused, then pulled Shane into a bear hug.

"Thank you, son," Sonny said, his voice rough with emotion.

Shane's face crumpled. April knew what this meant to him—receiving the love of a good father figure for the first time in his life. Being called *son* by a man like Sonny Taylor.

Miriam was beside April then, wrapping her in soft arms and the scent of vanilla. "Oh, baby girl. You're safe now. You're safe."

Hannah was crying—happy tears streaming down her face as she joined the hug.

Sonny pulled away from Shane, turned to April. His hand came up to cover his heart, a hummingbird fluttering, the sign language they'd created together when she was little. *I love you. I'm so glad you're home.*

April's vision blurred. Sonny opened his arms and she went to him, burying her face in his shoulder like she was six years old again.

"Papa."

"My brave girl," he whispered. "My brave, brave girl."

They stood like that—family, whole and safe—while the rain finally stopped outside and the world slowly righted itself.

———

TWO DAYS LATER, April woke in Shane's arms.

They were at her house—finally safe to return. The bed was familiar, the room hers, but everything felt different. Better. Like coming home after a long journey.

Shane's chest rose and fell beneath her cheek, steady and warm. She felt his hand stroke her hair.

"How'd you sleep?" His voice was rough with morning.

"Good, actually." April tilted her head to look at him. "I keep waiting for the nightmares, but they don't come."

"That's good."

"I'm not sad about Vince." The words came out small. "Does that make me a bad person?"

Shane's hand cupped her face. "No, sweetness."

"He died reaching for money. After everything—that's how he chose to end." April closed her eyes. "I feel sorry for him. But I'm not sad over him."

"You don't have to be."

They lay there in the quiet, listening to sounds from the kitchen. Cabinets opening. The clink of dishes.

Shane smiled. "Think we should check on him?"

"Probably." April grinned. "He's been okay though, right? Talking to Aunt Arden every day?"

"Every day. She's good with him." Shane kissed her forehead. "You planning to talk to her too?"

"Yeah. Soon." April sat up, stretched. "But first—coffee. And whatever disaster Kevin's creating out there."

They dressed quickly, then padded down the hallway in bare feet.

The kitchen smelled like cinnamon and sugar. Kevin stood at the counter, a plate of cinnamon toast in front of him, rainbow sprinkles scattered across the surface like confetti.

"Morning!" Kevin beamed. "I made you breakfast!"

April's heart swelled. "So I see."

Benny sat at Kevin's feet, a suspicious sprinkle clinging to the corner of his mouth. Pete had the brains to look guilty as he licked his chops.

"Did the dogs help?" Shane asked, fighting a smile.

"Maybe a little," Kevin admitted.

They ate cinnamon toast with rainbow sprinkles while morning light streamed through the windows, and April thought: *This. This is what I was fighting for.*

———

THE WATCHDOG CONFERENCE room smelled like coffee and leather and the fresh flowers in a vase on a side table. April sat between Shane and Kyle. Lach sat across from her. Gina stood as usual. There were almost as many dogs in the room as there were humans—Sam, Fleur, Camo, and Pete. Kevin was up front with Miss Jodie, working on a puzzle.

"The authorities attributed Echo Ridge to warring gangs," Gina said, her voice calm and professional. "Russian mob elements fighting over territory. Vince knew Yuri from prison and was in the wrong place at the wrong time."

"What about Vince's lawyer?" April asked. "And Gabriela? She saw me leave with—"

"Handled," Gina said. "Vince's lawyer was compensated to maintain client confidentiality. He won't talk about his former client's activities or whereabouts that day."

"And Gabriela was told that on the day of the hearing, an ambulance took you to the hospital," Kyle added. "You'd twisted your ankle and hit your head. They wanted to check for concussion."

"You had a minor one," Shane said, squeezing her hand. "You couldn't call us from the clinic because I had your phone. Then you were resting so I got back to her for you and explained everything. You're perfectly fine now."

April blinked. "She believed that?"

"She had no reason not to," Gina said. "The courthouse was evacuated. There was confusion. An ambulance was there for the smoke inhalation cases. The story fits."

"But will authorities track it back to us?" April's voice rose slightly. "What if—"

"They won't." Gina's golden eyes were steady. "And if somehow they did, it would be fixed immediately."

April wasn't sure she wanted to know what *fixed imme-diately* meant in Gina's world.

"Now," Gina said, pulling out a familiar object from her bag. "Let's talk about this."

April's Lucky Louis. Battered now, from the shootout, but still recognizably hers.

Gina opened her hand. On her palm lay a tiny memory card, no bigger than a fingernail.

"Unbelievable," April whispered. "Something that small caused all of this."

"We found it in the lining," Gina said. "But we need the password." She dropped the chip into April's palm. "Any idea what Vince might have used?"

April stared at the tiny chip. This was it. This was what Vince had killed for. What he'd nearly gotten her killed for.

"I could try a few things," she said. "How many attempts do I get before it locks?"

"The encryption allows unlimited attempts," Gina said. "But every wrong guess adds exponential processing time. After three or four failures, we're looking at hours between tries."

"No pressure," April muttered.

Shane squeezed her hand. "Take your time."

Gina set up a laptop, inserted the chip into a reader. A prompt appeared on screen, cursor blinking.

ENTER PASSWORD

April's hands shook. "This is the biggest bet I've ever placed."

"Would it be your birthday?" Shane asked.

April laughed despite herself. "Oh hell no. Vince was way too self-absorbed. It would be his birthday. He used his birthdate as the code for our home safe. Vince was not a complicated guy. He liked himself. He liked money. He liked fine things."

She waited until her hands stopped shaking, then typed:

PROSECCO0815

INCORRECT PASSWORD

April groaned.

"It's okay, sweetness," Shane said. "Try again."

"What if..."

She tried again:

VUITTON0815

INCORRECT PASSWORD

April dropped her chin, closed her eyes.

"It's okay," Gina said gently. "You can try again later if—"

"Wait." April looked up. "It's stupidly obvious. Vince loved winning more than anything."

She typed:

VUITTONJACKPOT0815

The screen flickered. Lines of code scrolled past. Then:

ACCESS GRANTED

"We're in!" She turned and hugged Shane. "So...now what do I do?"

Gina leaned in. "Elissa walked me through this once. Let's see....there it is, the code. Now, for the wallet."

April was too nervous to pay attention to what Gina was typing, until she saw:

WALLET BALANCE: 2,847.3 BTC

Below it, in smaller text: **USD EQUIVALENT: $47,382,916.00**

April stared at the screen. Read it again. For the first time in her life, a number didn't make any sense to her. It just couldn't be.

Shane had to catch her before she slid out of her chair.

"Whoa, hey. I've got you." His arms were solid around her. "Breathe, April. Just breathe."

"Forty-seven million dollars," April whispered. "After taxes—do I have to pay taxes?—that's still—"

"A lot of money," Gina finished. She was smiling. Actually smiling. "Yeah. That's a lot of money."

April looked at the laptop screen again. The numbers didn't change.

Then she looked at the ruined purse in Gina's hands.

"It was my lucky purse," April said, and something between a laugh and a sob escaped her throat. "It'll cost a fortune to repair."

Shane pulled her closer. "We'll get it repaired. Or buy you ten new ones."

April touched the damaged leather. "Oh. Yeah. I guess I can now."

She could fix a lot of things. Like a certain espresso machine.

"We'll have to make this legitimate with a believable story," Gina said. "But don't worry, I have a plan."

———

THE CONSIGNMENT STORE was one of the fancier ones in Vail. April browsed the racks, running her fingers over silk scarves and designer jackets.

She'd been there half an hour when the bell over the door chimed.

A woman walked in—sixty-something, elegant, wearing a Hermès scarf and oversized sunglasses, a leather tote bag on her arm. Her silver hair was cut in a sharp bob, and she carried herself with the quiet confidence of old money. She approached the counter.

"I'd like to consign these, please. My late sister's belongings. She had such good taste, but I simply can't keep everything."

"Oh, well, let's see," the owner said.

April drifted closer, watching as the woman laid out a diamond ring, a Coach wallet, and—

April's breath caught.

Her Louis Vuitton Speedy Thirty purse. Obviously damaged, but still beautiful in its own way. April actually took offense when the shop owner picked up the purse, examined it, then turned her nose up.

"Louis Vuitton. Authentic, but in rough shape. We don't sell damaged goods here."

"Oh my God," April breathed. "Is that the Speedy Thirty?"

The shopkeeper looked at her, surprised. "It is."

"I'll take it," April blurted.

"My dear, it's in terrible shape. I can show you a pristine Versace that came in—"

"Are you kidding?" April picked up Lucky Louis and caressed the leather. "A purse like this has a history. It's probably been through so much that it never asked for, but here it is. It's lovely."

The silver-haired woman, smiled slightly. "You have good taste, dear. It was one of my favorites, too."

April looked at the shopkeeper. "How much?"

"Oh, I wouldn't take money for that. I have a reputation to keep up." She waved her off.

"I can tell." She turned back to the woman in sunglasses. April's hands were shaking as she reached for her wallet. "Ma'am, can I buy it directly from you? I'll give you—whatever you're asking. Please."

"Goodness, take it, take it. Just knowing it's going to

someone who loves it as much as my sister obviously did is enough for me."

The store owner named a price for the ring and wallet.

"You know, I think I'll keep them after all. My sentimentality is getting the best of me today." She picked up the ring and the wallet and put them back in her tote bag. She gave April one last enigmatic smile, and left.

April clutched the purse to her chest, marveling at her luck.

Only later, safe in her car, did she burst into laughter.

Gina's disguise had been perfect. Even knowing it was her, April had barely recognized her. Nettie—Gina's master makeup artist friend—was apparently worth every penny.

The story was set. April had found a battered Louis Vuitton at a consignment shop. Inside the lining, hidden away, was a chip containing crypto. The find of a lifetime. She'd tried to track down the woman who donated it, but no one could find her.

If reporters came sniffing—and they would—the shop owner would tell that story. The woman in the Hermès scarf would remain a mystery.

April Taylor had gotten very, very lucky.

———

THE NEW ESPRESSO machine gleamed like a spaceship in the morning light, all chrome and brass. April stood behind the counter at Riversong, admiring it, and thought about the journey that had brought her here.

The old machine sat in the corner like a retired war horse—polished, honored, but no longer in service. Sonny hadn't been able to let it go, but he'd agreed to retire it.

Maybe they'd move it to the Boulder location when that opened.

It was a rare lull, and April welcomed it.

"When are Wren and Rochelle supposed to be here?" Hannah called from where she was wiping down tables. "And Stephanie? I need help planning this wedding, and Steph has some ideas that sound either brilliant or completely insane."

April laughed. "Yeah, that's about right. Knowing Stephanie, her ideas are probably both. They'll be here around three, should be soon."

"Perfect." Hannah grinned. "I'm so glad you asked me to be your maid of honor."

"Well of course, because you are my sister and I love you and you're going to look absolutely gorgeous in that dress you already picked out, *and* you're planning the most amazing wedding."

"Mom! Dad's here!" Kevin called from the back office, followed by Benny's excited barking and Pete's deeper woof.

April smiled. Hearing Kevin call Shane *Dad* still gave her a thrill every single time.

Shane came through the door with sawdust in his hair and a grin on his face. He'd been helping Ben and Bear with renovations—new kitchen, updated bathrooms, and plans to rebuild the front porch.

"How's it going?" April asked, already pulling a shot for his regular—an Americano.

"Good. Ben says another two weeks and the house will be perfect." Shane leaned across the counter to kiss her. "Then we need to decide—your place or mine?"

"*Our* place," April corrected. "Whichever one we choose."

"Our place." Shane's smile was soft. "I like the sound of that."

"Me, too."

"When I came in, Kevin was FaceTiming with another day camp friend who already goes to his new school," Shane said.

April smiled. "That's the fifth one."

Shane got a funny smile on his face. "That'll make six of them total."

April knew exactly what he meant. "Six is a perfect number for a group of friends."

"It sure is."

Kevin had been nervous about switching schools, but when she'd shown him the private academy's program—the science labs, the art studio, the climbing wall—he'd lit up. And now he'd have five friends from day camp to show him around.

"He's a good kid, our son," Shane said.

April's chest warmed. "The best kid." She slid the Americano across the counter. "On the house."

"You keep doing that, you'll go broke."

"Oh no, whatever will I do then?" April laughed.

Shane took a sip, watching her. "How are you doing? Really?"

April knew what he was asking. Echo Ridge. Vince. The money.

"I'm good," she said. And meant it. "Better than good. Yvonne came by this morning."

Shane's eyebrows rose. "Yeah?"

"Yeah." April wiped down the counter. "She apologized again." April met his eyes. "She's trying. Really trying. And Kevin—he's starting to warm up to her. She brought him a book about horses and he actually hugged her goodbye."

"That's good." Shane laced his fingers through hers across the counter. "You're giving her a chance. That's all she can ask for."

"She's Kevin's grandmother. And she's trying." April squeezed his hand. "That counts for something."

"You're a good person, April Taylor."

"I don't know about that." But she squeezed his hand. "I'm trying."

The bell over the door chimed. Wren walked in, took one look at the new espresso machine, and let out a low whistle.

"Damn, April. That is one sexy piece of equipment."

April laughed. "Right? It practically makes the coffee for me."

"Must be nice, being loaded." But Wren was grinning, no real envy in it. Just the good-natured ribbing of a friend who was genuinely happy for her. "Am I the first one here? I want to talk wedding photos."

Hannah came around the counter. "Yup, just you and me for now." She turned to April and snapped her fingers in the air several times. "Oh garçon, our usuals please, and make it snappy."

"Garçon means boy," April clapped back. "Having so much money is weird," April admitted. "Like, really weird. I keep waiting for someone to tell me it was all a mistake."

"It's not a mistake." Shane's thumb traced circles on her palm. "You earned it. In the worst possible way, but you earned it."

Maybe. April still wasn't sure about that. But she was learning to accept it. The money. The life. The safety.

The love.

She started making two Dubai Chocolate Mocha Lattes, their new specialty, for Hannah and Wren. Kevin bounded out from the back with Benny at his heels, Pete following at a more sedate pace. "Dad!"

April caught Hannah elbowing Wren as they both looked at Shane's expression. Could a man look more blissed out?

"Yes, son?"

Another elbow to the ribs. They were loving this.

"Can we go to the ranch? Aunt Arden said I could help with the new horse!"

"Sure, bud." Shane ruffled Kevin's hair. "Your mom okay with that?"

"Are you kidding?" April smiled. "Go. Have fun. Just pick up dinner on the way home."

"Teriyaki wings, extra ranch?" Shane winked.

"You know it."

Kevin grinned and disappeared back into the office to grab his jacket.

April finished making the coffee drinks on autopilot, muscle memory taking over while her mind drifted.

She'd been tied up in a basement, terrified for her life. Now she was here. Safe. Loved. Renovating a house and figuring out a new school, and a future that stretched out bright and possible.

"Hey," Shane said softly. "Where'd you go?"

April blinked, and came back to the present. "Just thinking."

"About?"

"About how lucky I am." She looked at him—really looked at him. The man who'd protected her in a gunfight. Who'd carried her in the rain while she shook with shock. Who'd driven her home and stayed, and kept staying, and would keep staying for as long as she'd have him.

"Lucky," Shane repeated, his mouth quirking. "That's one word for it."

"It's the right word." April came around the counter, wrapped her arms around him, and pressed her face against his chest. He smelled like sawdust and coffee and home.

Shane held her, steady and solid and real. "I love you," he murmured into her hair.

"I love you, too."

The espresso machine hissed. Benny barked at something outside. Hannah chatted with Wren at a table in the corner. Kevin laughed in the back room, bright and unafraid.

Normal. Beautiful. All theirs.

April had spent ten years running from Las Vegas. Ten years afraid. Ten years thinking luck was something you found at a poker table, something you could only hope for but never control.

She'd been wrong.

Luck wasn't in the cards. It wasn't in a purse or a crypto wallet or any amount of money.

Luck was this. Standing in a coffee shop she helped build with her loving parents and sister. Her sister and friends helping her plan her wedding. The man she loved holding her while her son laughed in the next room. The future spread out before them, wide and bright and full of possibilities.

April Taylor was the luckiest woman alive.

And this time, she wasn't running away from it.

THIRTY-TWO

BEN "MOOSE" MASSEY

BEN WALKED into the Watchdog reception area and found Jodie at the front desk.

"Hey, Ben! What brings you here?" she asked with a bright smile.

"Just here to take Shane out to lunch. I owe him."

"Oh, if you're going out for burgers, bring me back some fries?" She batted her eyes at him.

Ben felt himself start to blush. It didn't matter what woman it was. Didn't matter if she was serious or kidding. Didn't matter how long he'd known her. He lacked the confidence his brothers had around women.

"Sure," Ben said. "I'd be happy to."

"Great! I think Shane's in his office. If not, he's out with Alex and the dogs. Go on back."

Ben nodded. "Thanks, Jodie."

He started down the hall. The offices could be a bit of a warren, and he wasn't exactly sure where Shane's office was, but he'd find him. If not, he could ask. The place was full of people he knew. Most of them friends. Some just acquaintances.

And one very special lady.

Charlie King.

Just thinking her name did something wonderful to his belly. And, he had to admit, a place just south of his belly.

Charlie wasn't just the most beautiful woman he'd ever seen—though she absolutely was that, with her intense eyes that could pin a man at fifty yards and that smile that made his knees weak on the rare occasions she aimed it his way. But it was more than that. She was *talented*. Brilliant, really. She could clear a room faster than most of his Ranger buddies and moved with a lethal grace that was somehow both terrifying and mesmerizing to watch.

She was someone he'd want at his back in a gunfight without hesitation. Hell, she'd *just* had his back in a gunfight at Echo Ridge Ski Lodge.

When bullets were flying and the world had gone to hell, Charlie had been steady as a rock, professional and deadly and absolutely fearless. Watching her intelligent face as she took in the plan Gina laid out. Seeing her in action during the firefight—grace and power and bravery. She had to be the bravest woman he'd ever met—

A sudden, unexpected sound stopped him.

Wait—is that Charlie...screaming?

Ben took off at a run down the hall. Where was she? What was going on? Something had to be seriously wrong. He'd never heard her scream.

He turned the corner.

And there she was, standing in the middle of a cubicle maze.

Charlie was a tall woman—just over six feet, he guessed.

But for some reason, he could see all the way down to her waist over a cubicle wall.

Wait. Charlie's not that tall, he thought. *What's going on?*

She was in profile, looking down at something below her, with a look of absolute terror on her face.

"Charlie!"

Her head whipped around in his direction. "Ben! Oh—ah—um—"

He ran to her. She was standing on an office chair. Well, that explained the extra height.

"What's going on?"

"It's—it's—" She pointed.

Ben looked. On her desk was a day planner, a laptop, some sticky notes, and a pen caddy. She was pointing at the pen caddy.

"You're afraid of pens?"

"No! No, no. Look closer. Look on *that* one." Her hand shook as she leaned forward and pointed.

Ben bent down and looked closer. A tiny jumping spider—fuzzy and as adorable as a kitten—sat on top of a pencil eraser, staring at him.

He grinned. "Hey, little guy." He looked up at Charlie. "Congratulations, you've got yourself a pet jumping spider. Technically it's a *Phidippus audax*, better known as the Bold Jumping Spider. And wow, he's got yellow spots instead of the usual white—"

"Ben."

"Yeah?"

"Please?"

Ben was absolutely confused. She looked terrified. Was she messing with him? This was the same woman he'd watched take down two Russian oligarch henchmen with brutal efficiency.

But judging by her expression and the fact that she was standing precariously on an office chair, he was pretty sure she was serious.

"You're telling me the warrior princess is afraid of an adorable, fuzzy little jumping spider?"

Charlie reared back. "What did you just call me?"

Oh God, I really overstepped. The words had just flowed out of him without thinking.

"Um. Warrior princess. Emphasis on warrior," he added quickly.

Charlie blinked. Several times.

"I mean, you're a bodyguard. Former SWCC. That makes you more warrior than princess, right?" He tried a smile.

Something flashed across her face, too quick for him to catch. Disappointment, maybe?

"Please don't tell anybody I was afraid of a spider," she said quietly.

"No, of course not."

"I'm just lucky everybody's off to lunch." She looked around. "I'd never live it down."

"Cross my heart, I won't tell anyone."

"Thank you." She smiled sheepishly. "And do you think maybe you could—take him with you? Or something?"

"Yeah, sure. I—" Ben looked back down at the pen caddy. "Hang on, where'd he go?"

Charlie had been stepping down from her chair. She immediately stopped and jumped back up. "What do you mean? You can't find him?" She looked around wildly. "Oh my God, he could be anywhere." She looked up at the ceiling above her head as if the spider would materialize there and drop into her hair.

"Charlie, he wouldn't have gotten that far that quick."

"But you said he's a *jumping* spider! Couldn't he have, I don't know, jumped up onto the ceiling?"

Ben chuckled. "Well, they do jump pretty far, but not *that* far." He peered into the pen caddy again. He didn't want to rummage around in it just in case the little guy had gone to the bottom. He'd feel terrible if he squished him by moving the wrong pen at the wrong time.

"Maybe you could take the whole caddy?" Charlie suggested. "I don't know."

"I could," Ben started, "except I'm a little afraid of crushing the guy if he's down at the bottom."

"Oh. Right. I mean, I don't want him *dead*. I just don't want him crawling on me." She shivered.

"Hmm. All right, I'll just be very careful with it then."

He picked the caddy up gingerly, carefully, so that not a single pen or pencil moved. There had to be at least twenty-five shoved in there, and he noticed they were all different colors.

"Once I de-spider your caddy, I can bring it back to you."

"Oh, thank you! That would be great."

She stepped down from the chair. They were almost eye to eye. God, she was beautiful.

And they were standing so close.

And no one was shooting at them.

She took a step toward him.

But then her gaze fell back onto the caddy in his hand and she stepped back. Her cheeks turned pink.

Absolutely adorable.

"You promise?" she asked. "Promise you won't tell anybody I'm afraid of spiders?"

"I promise-promise. And don't worry—it's one of the

most common phobias. You're hardly alone. My guess is that half the guys who work here have arachnophobia, they just aren't brave enough to admit it. Which puts you ahead of them."

Shit, should I have said that?

"Well, I need to get going," he added quickly. "Shane and I are going to lunch and—oh, I'm late—and, uh, caddy, and I'll clean it up for you and—okay, bye."

Ben took off back through the maze of cubicles toward the kennels.

Smooth. Real smooth, Moose.

But as he carefully carried the pen caddy away, searching for one tiny fuzzy spider among twenty-five colorful pens, he couldn't stop smiling.

Charlie King was afraid of spiders.

And just now, she'd let him be her knight in shining armor, even if it was just for a jumping spider no bigger than his thumbnail.

He'd take it.

READ BEN and Charlie's story in Avalanche on the Mountain: Watchdog Mountain Division, Book 6.

AFTERWORD

First, thanks for reading!

Between long Covid and some minor surgery (everything's fine, promise!) I lost most of last year and part of this one being unwell, and the other part of this year recovering. So, I appreciate you for sticking with me. Knock on April's Lucky Louis purse, I seem to be coming out of the woods now, and I anticipate writing much faster next year.

I've wanted to write April and Kevin's story ever since Kevin's first appearance in Protecting Brianna. Badger had just come into the coffee shop to meet Brianna's family for the first time. Kevin, who was much younger then, comes tearing out of the back of the shop, runs right up to Badger and asks him, "Do you fart when you poop?"

Little kids, man.

April was of course mortified. And tired. And funny as hell, especially when teasing her dad, Sonny, who is one of my all-time favorite side characters. I knew I wanted to write more about these three. I wanted April to have someone special. That was a few books ago, and it took me a while to figure out who she belonged with. Figured it would be someone in the Watchdog Protectors series, someone I hadn't met yet.

I was half right and half wrong.

I don't want to give away too many spoilers, but let's just say that at one point, I thought Watchdog might have a mole working for Capitoline. I didn't know who it was, but I strongly suspected one of the bodyguards, a side character who was acting a little suspicious and had a secret he was keeping from everyone, including me.

It was Shane.

There's a saying in the author world which means you sometimes have to get rid of a scene or chapter or character that you really love but that just doesn't fit in the book—kill your darlings.

Never kill your darlings. Put them in an orphanage because they will often grow up to have a book of their own.

Shane was a darling.

I got to a scene in Protecting Sylvie when Kyle was convinced Shane was a mole. Trust me when I tell you, Shane was thiiiissss close to getting his brains blown out for being a traitor and a spy.

"Tell me!" Kyle (and I) demanded. "What are you hiding?"

And so, gun to his head, he told us.

Turns out, he was hiding the ENTIRE Mountain Division series.

And I had almost knocked him off. Killed my darling.

Somehow, he connected himself to this guy named Bear who would not get out of my head. And there were others—still nameless, not much more than sexy shadows in the dark, but Shane swore up and down that they were the good guys—just maybe colored outside of the lines of the law.

Heck yeah, we like that.

And who do you think took one look at April and said, *She's the one?*

Yup.

And April took one look back and said:

"Nope."

"Nope?" I asked.

"Uh-uh."

"But he's so—"

"He's really not."

"What about—"

"No way."

"Okay. Fine," I said. "I'll find you someone else. Someone in Protectors. But you *will* be making appearances in Mountain Division."

"Sure, no problem. More customers that way. But I will not be tricked into falling for Mr. Full-of-Himself Shane Foti."

"Oh. Oh, I see." I grinned and backed away.

"What?"

"Nothing. Carry on."

"*What?*" she demanded.

"Can I get a latte with—"

"No! Not until you tell me why you're smiling like that."

"It's just that, well...I'm thinking...enemies to lovers."

"NO!"

And she kicked me out of Riversong—and her head—for a long time.

But Shane was *insistent.* April was his.

The problem was, he was just as secretive about their relationship as he was about Mountain Division.

Wouldn't tell me a thing about their past, just that they had one. Didn't tell any of his friends, either, so I couldn't pump them for information. And Ben, who did actually know? He was faithful to Shane and wouldn't talk.

Their book got closer and closer and I still had no idea.

Finally...FINALLY...April opened up.

And boy oh boy was she *mad*.

"I am not the bad guy here. And this is why."

She told me about the bus stop. About how she sat there feeling alone and sick to her stomach and betrayed.

Boy was I mad, sitting right there next to her in that station, waiting on that cocky son of a gun to show, knowing he wasn't going to.

But Ben did.

And I can't WAIT for you to see what he and Charlie have in store. All I'll say is that their pairing also took me by surprise and changed the entire trajectory of the series.

Again, thanks for reading! You mean the world to me.

xoxo

Olivia

October, 2025

ACKNOWLEDGMENTS

As always, first and foremost, you Lovelies!

Trinity for always being there even when I'm not. That's a true friend. Love you!

Lover of purses, Caitlyn O'Leary for being my good friend and guardian angel and laughing at my weird jokes and eccentricities. See you in Vegas, baby!

Riley Edwards for making me laugh for three solid hours on the phone at least once a month. Tiki, my Tiki!

My talented, super-nice and very attractive mastermind group—Jamie Davis, Kat Healy, Danielle Pays, and Scott Walker. You guys get me through.

Michelle! Ma belle! (She hates that but I get to do it because it's my acknowledgements and I've known her since we were fifteen, so there!)

Owen, who is probably reading this very line as he formats the book. Thank you! Sorry for being me! Let's go to Bud's in Sedalia for cheeseburgers when you get done, sound good?

FOLLOW OLIVIA

Follow me to catch my latest releases at:

Newsletter:
https://oliviamichaelsromance.com/

Amazon:
https://www.amazon.com/author/oliviamichaelsromance

BookBub:
https://www.bookbub.com/authors/olivia-michaels

Facebook:
https://www.facebook.com/oliviamichaelsauthor

Instagram:
https://www.instagram.com/oliviamichaelsromance/

Want more? Come be one of Olivia's Lovelies on Facebook. I can always use another ARC reader or two...

https://www.facebook.com/groups/
639545290309740/

ALSO BY OLIVIA MICHAELS

Watchdog Security Series

More Than Love

More Than Family

More Than Puppy Love: A Christmas Novella

More Than Paradise

More Than Thrills

More Than Words Can Say

More Than Beauty

More Than Rumors

More Than Secrets

Watchdog Security Series Box Set, Books 1-3

Watchdog Security Series Box Set, Books 4-6

Watchdog Security Series Box Set, Books 7-9

Watchdog Protectors

In Susan Stoker's Special Forces Operation Alpha

Protecting Harper

Protecting Brianna

Protecting Sylvie

Watchdog Mountain Division

Bear On The Mountain

Timberwolf On The Mountain

Lion on the Mountain

Blizzard on the Mountain

Thunder on the Mountain

Avalanche on the Mountain

Free Mountain Division Short Story

Tell it to the Bees – A Bear and Ellie Short Story

ABOUT THE AUTHOR

Olivia Michaels is a life-long reader, dog-lover, gardener, and a certified beachaholic. When she's not throwing a Frisbee for her fur-baby, harvesting tomatoes, or writing, you can find her playing in the surf, kayaking, or kicking back on the sand and cracking open a romantic beach read.